The Cure

The Cure

Book 1

Bryan Evans

Bryan Evans Books

To Heather,
who listens to my endless ideas with love and
enthusiasm.

The two lights moved in sync, like tiny moons attached with wire, drifting effortlessly in the night sky. Below, the desert, illuminated by the lights of cars and filled with teenagers blowing off steam. The last hurrah of summer. Unaware of the luminous orbs above.

This night is one that will live forever in the minds of the pleasure-seeking adolescents. The same night that will soon be just another story on television. More online clickbait for those wanting snippets of breaking news to chop up the monotony of daily life.

A green flash accompanied by panicked screams. The two hardly noticeable lights retreating into the stars. And now, the object. Hurtling toward the desert like a yellow-tailed dragon.

Vehicles scatter like ants, flinging dirt into the air. The pandemonium of terror-fueled escape. Windows crack under the intense pressure of the object as it breaks the sound barrier. All engines die with the fireball overhead. Earth-shattering silence for a millisecond... then impact. A wall of sand erupts from ground zero. It moves with motive, rushing over every trace of matter in its path. Screams are muffled as it overtakes the hapless adolescents. The shockwave finishes off the cracked windows...then silence.

Moonlight reflects off the dirty mist that now fills the air, making it appear more early morning than night. The sand soon settles over the safe, dumbstruck flock of teens.

In less than two hours the site will be infested with personnel. Skilled individuals with a similar purpose: containment and retrieval. The object of the crash will be quickly moved and studied in a laboratory. A simple fist-sized rock, covered in red dots, encased in a glass ball of ice no bigger than a softball.

In several days, the personnel will move out and the story will spread. But the world will continue on as it always has. The same, yet forever changed. The product of a single event in the long history of Earth.

2

Angela

Three years later...

"Come on, you're going to be late if you don't get a move on!" Angela yelled up the stairs to her teenage son. "I don't need another call from the principal, lecturing me on how important it is you get to school on time." She looked in the large round mirror hanging on the wall by the stairs and tightened her long, dark ponytail. Stepping back, she examined her whole outfit, straightening her white t-shirt and admiring her favorite faded jeans.

"I know, Mom. I'm coming," said the teen as he stumbled down the stairs. He slipped a baggy black shirt over his head and went straight for the refrigerator.

"I made some eggs and bacon if you want some."

"Oh, thanks," he said, turning and grabbing some bacon with his bare hands. "Wait a second." He moved closer to her face and squinted like something was on her. "I think I see a new wrinkle."

Angela rolled her eyes and swatted at him. He dodged her strike and stood there with a cheesy grin.

"Just kidding. I had to do it. You only turn 35 once."

"34!" she exclaimed, playfully swinging at him again.

"I know," he said laughing. "I left a present for you on your bed. Happy birthday!" He gave her a quick hug and then shoved bacon into his mouth.

"Thanks, Michael." She caught a whiff of something and sniffed the air. "Is that the same shirt you wore yesterday? Gross! Here," she said, picking a random shirt out of a clothes basket on the couch. "Take this."

"Nice. I just couldn't find anything clean," he said, pulling off the dirty shirt and putting on the clean one.

"I told you last night they were right here to fold." Annoyed, she took the dirty shirt from him and tossed it down the hall toward the laundry room. "By the way, I'm meeting with a newer company that makes candy without dyes. They want us to carry their products in the store. They can only meet in the evening, so I'll probably be home a little late."

"No problem. I'll hang out at the skatepark 'til close to dark, but then it's cake and ice cream for the birthday girl!" he said, grabbing his backpack and heading out the front door.

"Can't wait! Love you!" Angela yelled at the closing door.

A few seconds later, it opened back up. He jogged over to her and quickly gave her a kiss on the cheek. "Love you, Mom."

After Michael left, Angela sat down at the kitchen island to finish her morning coffee and watch some news on her laptop. There was a morning show she usually streamed each day during the week. The hosts were a married couple and seemed well-informed on whatever they reported on. It was some of the only news that Angela felt didn't pick sides. They just asked questions, sought out answers, and left judgment up to the viewers.

"I'm Rebecca Holth," the reporter started. "My co-host David Holth will be joining us live in a bit from the demonstrations outside of the Capitol Building here in Austin. Welcome to Top News

Today. I'm joined this morning by Dr. Miguel Perez and Dr. Jacob Frixell. They are the creators of the wonder treatment NALGAL, which has now been produced and administered to most of the globe. The drug is administered up the nose as a mist in two separate doses."

She turned to the two men, "Doctors, by now we are all very familiar with your drug. It is required for adults in over forty countries, and although it isn't yet required in the United States, the president has said that she wants it readily available for every US citizen over the age of nineteen. It seems to be a cure for just about every illness and disease and has saved millions of lives. People have named it *The Cure*. However, so many are still against taking it. Some are going so far as to have rallies that oppose it. Dr. Perez, why do you think so many are in opposition to it?"

The camera zoomed in on Dr. Perez's tired face as he sat up in his chair, straightened his glasses, and spoke. "First of all, thank you, Mrs. Holth, for having us on your program. I do want to clear up though, that NALGAL is not a drug. It is an all natural treatment manufactured purely from a very specific type of cultured algae."

"An algae from a meteorite, correct?" Rebecca asked.

"Yes," Dr. Perez continued. "The spores from that algae are then extracted and delivered to a patient through inhalation, making its way into the bloodstream and aiding the patient in combating all manner of viruses, bacteria, and diseases. As to why so many are against it, is beyond me—"

"Doctor, you've been quoted as saying that you believe children and teens shouldn't take this treatment. Stating that their bodies might not react the same as an adult to this treatment. Could you expand on this for our viewers?"

"It... It is a bit complicated in that—" Dr. Frixell tapped Dr. Perez'z arm as if to stop him from talking.

Rebecca didn't hesitate to continue. "Well, doctor, what do you say to those who think not enough research has been done about the long-term effects of the The Cure? Some have speculated that we could be on the verge of a huge population explosion due to the near eradication of major diseases. Others wonder if children born to women who have received the treatment may have serious side-effects in the future."

"We have worked for three long years developing this treatment. Thanks to the many congressmen and women, along with senators who have gotten behind our research, we have gotten a natural and safe product to the masses without the use of large pharmaceutical companies. That alone is a hurdle that is virtually unheard of. I don't—"

Dr. Frixell interrupted him and shifted forward in his chair like someone about to go on a verbal attack. He spoke aggressively toward Rebecca.

"This treatment has been cleared and backed by multiple nations under the most strict regulations. It is saving lives. Anyone who is against it is just crazy. There has—"

Rebecca jumped back into the conversation quickly.

"Some of our viewers may have a slightly different outlook. Dr. Frixell, I don't think it's crazy—"

"Well, look at the facts," Dr. Frixell said, interrupting again. "There has never been a single negative side-effect from this treatment. Not one! Literally millions have received The Cure, and nothing even resembling a negative side-effect has come up. That has never happened in the history of medicine! This treatment saves lives. Period! If people can't see that, they deserve to end up like the so-called 'New Gaians' from the Chicago riot."

"Alright," Rebecca said, obviously a bit shaken from Dr. Frixell's aggressive outburst. "We're going to take a short break, and when we come back, we'll continue our talk with the doctors. And up later, the five-year endeavor to build an international system of wireless power and communication is complete. The Lightning Pillars are set to become operational across the globe this week, bringing with it unprecedented progress. We'll discuss what this could mean for our communities."

An ad popped up in the stream, and Angela closed her laptop. "Shithead," she said, standing up and putting her mug and plate from breakfast in the sink.

She couldn't help but feel upset about the doctor's remarks. The New Gaians were an innocent group of people that named their organization after the Earth goddess, Gaia. They believed that humans should depend on the Earth for health and generally opposed the NALGAL treatments, since they were not 'of this world' where human bodies had evolved. She was heartbroken when she learned that twenty-seven New Gaians had died in a standoff with authorities when an unknown person threw firecrackers into their peaceful protest, causing law enforcement to open fire with live rounds.

How dare he verbally attack those poor souls who had lost their lives!

She realized her hands were clenched in fists and took a deep breath.

Come on, Angela. Don't allow yourself to be angry at him. Karma takes notes," she thought to herself.

She put the leftover eggs and bacon in a dish and stuck it in the fridge. Grabbing her purse, she headed out the door and started the short walk to her store. The walk would make her feel better, just like it always did.

3 |

Sean

The sound of the motorcycle's engine cut through the country air, reverberating off the trees and bouncing off the asphalt. Living in Texas, there are not a lot of days with refreshing temperatures, so an eighty-one degree autumn morning, like today, was perfect for a drive. Since he had the morning off work, Sean had time to enjoy his ride. Opening the visor of his helmet, he felt the cool air brush his face and go down the front of his t-shirt. He was alone on the long, winding stretch of road. For the moment, it was his road. Sean slowly leaned side to side, his bike drifting effortlessly to the left lane and back into the right.

His large, brown eyes caught sight of a dark green car on the side of the road ahead. A beautiful young woman in her twenties stood behind the vehicle, waving him down as he approached. Her smooth, mocha skin was accentuated by the light jeans and yellow crop top that hugged her body in all the right places. Sean had to take an extra breath as he slowed down and pulled up into the grass behind the car. Anyone passing could see what the issue was. The trunk was open, and a spare tire sat on the ground, leaning against the car. A young boy was nearby, playing in the tall grass and using a stick as a pretend sword.

Turning off his bike, the twenty-six year old stepped off and removed his helmet, making a point of checking his hair in the side mirror. The young woman noticed and rolled her eyes, but a small smile appeared on her face.

"What seems to be the problem, ma'am?" Sean said in a fake, overly thick country accent. "You're much too pretty to be out here all by your lonesome. There could be crazy people out in these parts."

"Oh, really?" she said, her smile lifting on one side. "What will I ever do without a big, strong man to keep me safe? I guess you would protect me, right?" she continued sarcastically.

"Well, I suppose it would be my duty," he answered back, walking up to her, still using his ridiculous accent. "I would, however, require one thing from you."

"And what's that?" the woman asked, getting closer to him, her face now less than three inches from his.

"A kiss," he replied, moving so that their lips were almost touching.

Her hand shot up between them, and she placed it on his lips. She leaned over his shoulder and whispered in his ear.

"What would my boyfriend say?"

"Uh, I think he'd be totally okay with it, ma'am," Sean said, reaching his arms around her.

Her arms embraced him back, and they shared a soft, sweet kiss in the warm sunlight. The kiss was cut short by the young boy playing in the grass.

"Gross! Bleck!" he said, shielding his eyes from the couple.

"Oh, come on, Jayden," Sean said, turning to face the eight-year-old boy and dropping the accent. "Let us have some fun. You'll understand one day."

Jayden stuck his tongue out at Sean, made a disgusted face, and went back to swinging his stick in the grass. Sean turned to the woman.

"Hey, babe. I missed you so much. How was your first conference? How was New Orleans?"

"It was boring!" Jayden answered for her, not even looking up at Sean. "The hotel was old, and the WIFI didn't work sometimes. And Kristen made me go to some old graveyard. I should have stayed with you. We could have tried out the new fishing pole."

"I missed you, too," Kristen said, waving off Jayden and giving Sean another hug, pecking him on the cheek. "The conference went great, but I'm happy to be back. I'll tell you all about it later."

Sean looked at the rear passenger tire. "So, you said one of the lug nuts was stuck?"

Kristen walked back toward the car and pointed. "Yeah, one of them. I tried and tried, but can't seem to get it loose."

Sean walked over to the car and picked up the tire iron. "Stand back, ma'am, while this, uh, big, strong man gets this thing off for you."

"My hero," she said in another sarcastic tone.

Sean worked on it for a minute before stepping back and shaking his head. "So I think I can get it off, but since it's a little too tight, the lug bolt will probably snap off. The other bolts will hold on the spare, but it'll have to be replaced if it breaks."

"Just do it, I guess. We can't go anywhere with this flat," she answered.

He put the tire iron on the lug and put a foot on it. Holding onto the car, he hopped up and put his weight on it several times. Sure enough, the bolt snapped off, still attached to the lug nut.

"I'm off tomorrow morning too, so I can take it into Tony's and get it fixed," he said, inspecting the broken bolt in his hand. "Just drive it to my house, and you can borrow my truck."

Kristen rolled him the spare tire, and he put it on. After he had lowered the car back down and placed the flat tire and jack in the trunk, he called out to Jayden.

"Hey, bud! I brought my extra helmet if you want to ride back with me."

Jayden threw his stick into the ditch and ran toward the motorcycle.

"You're okay to drive it back to my place, babe. Just keep it under fifty. I don't trust spares."

Kristen peeked around Sean at Jayden, who was busy unstrapping the extra helmet from the side of the bike. She walked up to Sean, grabbed him by the collar of his shirt, and pulled him in close.

"What do you say Jayden and I come over tonight after work and stay the night? Jayden can sleep in the guestroom, now that you moved your old bed in there. And we can..." She pulled him closer and stopped again with her lips almost touching his before continuing. "Test out the new mattress you bought." She pushed him away without kissing him, leaving Sean standing with a big, dumb smirk on his face.

"I'll bring home some pizza," he said. "And some wine?"

"Come on, Sean!" yelled Jayden, who was now sitting on the motorcycle, wearing the helmet.

"I'm coming, man!" Sean hollered back to him and then turned back to Kristen. "And as for you, my love, I don't have to be in the office until 2 pm. I can't wait to hear about the conference and how your presentation went."

Kristen turned and walked back to her car, making sure to move her hips in a seductive way. Getting in, she turned and spoke before closing the door. "I have something exciting to tell you. Well... I hope you think it's exciting." Her eyes glowed like two bright stars in the morning sunlight. "Later, though. Oh, and I don't want to ever be away from you for that long again."

After she shut the door, Sean put his hand over the pocket of his jacket and squeezed a small box. "Me either," he whispered. "Me either."

"It is time," said a man in a dark blue business suit. He wore a red tie with a stark white, pressed shirt. His skin was so pale; his veins were visible throughout his hands and face. He was completely bald and devoid of eyebrows or any hint of facial hair. The dim light in the room cast shadows from three figures—the man in the suit, a cloaked figure sitting in a chair nearby, and a middle-aged woman in front of a large oval computer screen filled with a map of the world.

"Activate the pillars and initiate the linking sequence," the man in the suit said, walking toward the screen.

Without speaking, the woman began working on the computer. The click clacking sound of computer keys filled the quiet room.

"You have done well," said the cloaked figure. His breathing was labored, and his voice scratchy and snake-like. Standing up, he walked toward the man in the suit. His steps were just as haggard as his breaths. A frail hand reached out from under his cloak with a small object in it. The object lit up as he placed it near his face and breathed slowly.

The screen in front of them cast a glow on their faces as lines slowly moved outward from a single location. The lines stretched toward dots that littered the map.

"Pillars activated," the woman said, continuing to work. "Approximately twelve hours until initial connection is finalized. Eighteen hours until full power and linking sequence complete."

"Good," said the man in the suit, folding his arms and looking satisfied. "It has begun. Let me know as soon as it is complete so we may begin the next stage."

Angela

"Another black out!" complained Angela, wandering into the kitchen. "Third one this week." She reached into a drawer and pulled out a small blue flashlight. The blackouts were said to be a byproduct of the Lightning Pillars being tested. They usually only lasted an hour or so but seemed to be becoming more frequent as of late. Now that it was autumn, it wasn't as big of a deal. During the summer it had been brutal though. Any time the electricity had come back on, trying to cool down her house and especially her store cool had been borderline impossible.

The Lightning Pillars were built in sets of three usually right outside of major cities. They were tall, slender, black towers that each came to a point at the top, the typical obelisk-style shape. It had been a worldwide undertaking, but with all of them completed, they were set to bring wireless power and instant communication without the use of potentially harmful signals. Though many, Angela included, weren't so sure about those claims.

Michael tossed his phone on the couch beside him. "Internet's down too," he said, standing up and stretching. "Do we have anything for breakfast?"

"Yeah, I made some toast before the power went out. It should be easy on your stomach," she said, pointing to a plate on the counter with several pieces of toast stacked up. "How are you feeling today?"

"I feel great. I think I just had too much cake last night." He grabbed a piece of toast and shoved half of it in his mouth. "Yuh don nee a worry," he continued, breadcrumbs escaping from his lips.

Angela rolled her eyes. "Promise me that you'll go to the school nurse if you start feeling bad, okay?"

"You got it. Though, it would be a shame to miss Chemistry," he said sarcastically.

"Ha ha. Speaking of Chemistry, did you ask your teacher what you could do to bring your grade up?"

Michael pretended not to hear and shoved another piece of toast in his mouth.

"Michael?"

"I forgot," he finally answered. "Besides, we had a substitute yesterday. I'll ask today."

"You better! You have one more week before grades come out."

He quickly grabbed his backpack. "Don't worry, Mom. I'll take care of it," he said, pausing. "Um, how about some lunch money?"

"What happened to the money I gave you at the beginning of the week?"

"Well, I bought some snacks at the gas station after school. Can I just get a couple more dollars?"

"Of course," she said, digging in her purse and handing him some one dollar bills. "But...I'll be taking it out of your paycheck from the store."

"Ah...fine," he reluctantly agreed, taking the money and sticking it in his pocket.

"Just a reminder, it's Thursday, so I'll see you at the store after school."

Michael looked at the date on his watch. "But, Mom. I told Nick that I'd meet him at the park. There's a new ramp tha—"

"Michael." She gave him the look she often used to let him know that she meant business and no debate would be had. "You made a commitment that you would help me every Thursday."

Michael stared at his mom, the annoyance on his face very apparent. The look didn't affect her at all, though. Angela knew that as an almost seventeen-year-old, he needed that time with his friends. But she also knew she didn't have much time left with him. She needed to make sure he still knew to follow through with what he promised. Plus, he wanted spending money of his own. What better way to help him, help herself, and get to spend time with him than to have him work at the store with her?

"I'll be there," he said, changing his expression to look more conquered than annoyed.

"Remember to head straight over right after school."

"Got it," he said, giving her a hug and heading for the door. "Love you, Mom."

"Love you," she said as the door shut behind him. She sat down at the kitchen table and drank her coffee in partial darkness. Out of the kitchen window, she saw one of the neighbors from across the street. He was outside, looking up into the sky and waving something around. She got up to get a better look at what he was doing.

He had some sort of meter in his hand and was trying to measure different parts of his yard.

"What are you up to, Donald?" she thought to herself.

Donald was the neighborhood weirdo, or better described as the friendly neighborhood conspiracy theorist. He wasn't rude but always acted like he thought everyone was out to get him and mainly kept to himself in his home.

Fetching her things and getting ready to leave, the electricity snapped back on. "Perfect timing," she mumbled, heading straight for the AC thermostat to reset it. As soon as her hand pulled back, *click*, the power went off again. "Whatever."

The walk to work took Angela through a partially wooded park and was usually one of the calmest fifteen minutes of her day. Besides the occasional senior out for a morning walk or a deer feeding near the path, she was typically by herself on a short, rocky trail. The trail gave her a few minutes of peace and quiet. But today's peace was short-lived. A large dead bird sat at the head of the path.

It wasn't that uncommon to see a dead creature here. She was, after all, in an area with nature and animals. What was uncommon about today was that a few feet away lay another dead bird. And a little farther up, two more. She didn't see any signs of injury, though she didn't want to handle the birds or get too close. Worried that it could be a disease of some sort, she made a wide arc around the poor birds and continued on her way. As she neared the end of the path, the sound of a siren in the distance destroyed any calm she had left.

Hope everyone's okay, she thought to herself as she made her way to the street that ran toward her shop.

Coming around the corner, the high-pitched sound of a frantic woman wailing shook her to the core. She scanned the street and saw a man holding the screaming woman. Next to them, a car had obviously crashed into another vehicle. Angela jogged toward them to see if they needed any help and assumed the approaching siren was for them. The man held the inconsolable woman from going near the car.

"Is there anything I can do?" Angela asked as she made it to the couple.

The man turned toward Angela, fear in his eyes. He shook his head in a way that looked more like a warning than an answer. Blood covered the wailing woman's forehead while the man holding her appeared to have no scratches at all. Angela assumed he probably wasn't in the vehicle.

Another bystander jogged to the scene from farther up the street. He walked toward the driver's side door and started to open it. From behind the car, Angela could see the silhouette of a man hunched over the steering wheel.

The bystander stepped back a few steps. "Oh my god!"

A voice in her head told her not to, but Angela took a step toward the car. If there was something she could do for the driver, she would. Walking to the passenger side, she peered inside. Shock and dread slammed into her from the sight of this poor man. His head was turned toward her, his eyes and mouth wide open. His eyes had a haze to them, like a dark mist had settled in. They were visibly bloodshot but with black instead of red lines spider-webbing from the irises. The veins in his face, neck, and arms were visible and dark. As if the blood in his body had turned completely black. She stepped back, breathless, her chest heavy.

The ambulance pulled up beside them and two young men jumped out. The bystander pointed them toward the driver, unable to speak himself. Angela couldn't make out what the paramedics were saying, but they seemed to have no idea what was happening with the poor driver either. They spoke in frantic, hushed tones. The hysterical woman was now on the ground with the man squatting nearby, still trying to comfort her. Her crying was at a volume much more bearable.

A police car pulled up, and an officer stepped out. Seeing Angela first, he addressed her. "Are you okay, ma'am? Is this your vehicle?"

"No...yes. I mean, yes, I'm okay, and no, it's not my car. I–I think it's hers," she replied, pointing at the woman. "She's bleeding."

"Did you witness the accident?"

"No."

"Are you a family member or friend?"

"No," answered Angela, feeling a bit more comfortable now that the police were here.

"I don't think there's anything you can do here now. We'll take care of this, ma'am. You should probably go." The officer went to tend to the woman.

Angela began to back away slowly. She agreed with the officer. She wished she could help, but the driver was obviously dead, and the woman was in good hands now. Completely shaken, she turned and headed toward her store. At least there she could put her mind into work and try to keep the image of that man out of her head. The horrendous image of his dead face, staring at her through cloudy eyes.

Her store was just a couple blocks away now. Taking deep breaths and trying to focus on something else, she managed to calm herself a great deal by the time she made it to the parking lot. Once inside, she would give herself a few minutes before opening up.

"Great," she mumbled when the store was in sight. There was a lady already standing out front, waiting to be let in. The look of impatience was apparent on her face. She noticed Angela as she approached. "Oh, do you work here?" she asked in a tone that made Angela feel as though she was getting buttered up.

"I do. I actually own this shop. Can I help you with something? I'm afraid we don't open for another thirty min—"

"Yes, I was hoping to get something for my husband. He wasn't feeling well this morning, and I need to be at work soon. Would you be willing to let me in before you open so I can get him something?"

She would normally be annoyed, but after witnessing the scene from minutes earlier, she was feeling extra compassionate. Besides, her store had taken a noticeable hit since The Cure had come out.

Her main products for years had been natural products that promoted health. With not as many people worried about their health, she had seen a sizable drop in customers. She had her regulars that came in each week, but new customers were few and far between nowadays.

"Sure," she answered the lady. "I'm happy to help you out."

"Thank you," the lady said, her tone changing now that she had gotten what she wanted.

Angela opened the door, and the lady rushed in after her, bumping into her and not apologizing. She rolled her eyes at the woman, the compassionate feeling slowly fading away. She started her opening procedure of turning on all the lights and getting ready for the day. Angela's hands were shaking a bit as she quickly put her phone behind the counter. She didn't like looking at her phone while working. She had worked hard to start her own business and as a woman, didn't want to let anyone think she was lazy. She constantly saw workers checking their phones at other stores and couldn't help judging them.

After a few minutes, the woman came to Angela looking annoyed. "Do you have any of the NAGAL at-home treatments?" she asked impatiently.

Angela cringed inside. The at-home treatments had just barely been approved for sale. They were a pill form of the NAGAL treatments. They were for those who wanted a more gradual dose of the medicine over a longer period of time, or if they wanted a quick fix when they felt they might be getting a bit sick for some reason. She didn't carry them in her store and had received some criticism because of it on multiple occasions.

"I'm afraid not, ma'am. I do have plenty of other products that may help your husband. Maybe you can tell me how he's feel—"

"What?" the woman almost yelled. "How can you claim to sell natural products and not have the at-home treatments?"

"Well, I'm afraid the at-home treatments have just come out and with very conflicting data—"

"Oh, you're one of those New Gaian weirdos. Bunch of freaks. If it's natural, safe, and works, who cares if it came here on an asteroid, comet, or whatever?"

Angela tried to not get defensive. Most who didn't actively support The Cure were lumped in with the New Gaian movement, which she was not a part of. She really just wanted this lady out of her store. "I'm so sorry that we don't carry it ma'am. I believe Phil's Pharmacy on the corner carries some."

The woman looked at Angela in disgust. A delivery man walked in the front door as she continued to berate Angela. "I bet you haven't even taken the treatment yourself, huh?"

Angela cringed again. She wasn't against the treatments but had decided not to have her or her son take them as it hadn't been out long. She wanted to know the possible long-term side effects before she would take or endorse them. She believed in the natural products she'd been using for years on both her and her son.

"I don't think that's any of your business."

The lady was speechless for a moment, her mouth open as if stuck in a gasp. She quickly turned and headed for the door, stopping in the doorway to yell one more time before leaving. "I hope you like bad reviews!"

The delivery man stepped between Angela and the door as it closed. "Don't worry about her. It seems most people just want something to be mad at these days."

"Yeah, sorry. It's been a day."

"We've all been there. She's not worth giving another thought to."

Angela closed her eyes, took a deep breath, and nodded. Her hands were shaking again, but this time out of anger.

"Well, anyway, I have a couple boxes for you. Where would you like 'em?"

Angela scanned the room for a spot out of the way. She knew the boxes were new items for her store, and they didn't have shelf space yet. "You can put them over here," she said, directing him to a spot on the floor near some vitamins.

"You got it. I'll be right back."

Angela went back to her daily tasks of organizing and cleaning the shop while the delivery man went back out to his truck to retrieve the packages. Seeing a spot on the outside of the front window, she grabbed a cloth to clean it. Birds would sometimes fly into the glass and leave smudge marks. She walked outside and looked at the smeary mark. It was almost too high to reach, but if she jumped, she thought she could reach it. Her first jump smeared the spot and made it more of a small streak. "Figures," she mumbled. She would have to go back inside and grab her spray.

Suddenly, she heard a moan and turned around in time to see the delivery guy fall to his stomach on the pavement. He was conscious and trying to get up as she made it to his side.

"Are you okay? What happened?"

"I'm fine," he said, slowly coming to his feet. "Just overdid it a little, I guess. No big deal."

"Are you sure? Come on in and sit down." They went inside, and Angela pulled up a folding chair from behind the front desk for him to sit on.

"Thank you. I..." he paused as though he didn't want to share what had happened. After a moment, he continued. "I was recently diagnosed with an auto-immune disease. I can't even pronounce the damn thing, but the doc said I need to take the NAGAL treatments.

I'm supposed to get my second dose tomorrow. She said it may take some time to start to repair my body. Last night, I got this dizzy spell. I had another one at around 4 am this morning, but it only lasted a minute. I brushed it off as just a side effect or a flare-up of my auto-immune disease."

Angela pulled a glass water bottle out of a small fridge behind the counter and handed it to him. "You should go see your doctor right away. Do you need me to call anyone?"

"No, no. I got it, thanks. The warehouse isn't too far away. I think you're right, though. I'll drop off the truck and go get checked out."

"Are you sure it's safe to drive?" Angela asked, sounding just like a mother. "You could leave the truck and I could drive you." She couldn't do anything for the driver earlier, but at least she could help this delivery man.

"I'll be fine, thanks." He took a long drink from the water bottle and stood up. He steadied himself using the counter and stayed in that position until he was ready to move. "Yeah, I'm good to go. Let me get those boxes for you."

"No, no, let me get them," Angela pleaded.

"I can handle them, ma'am. Besides, company policy says you can't get in the truck anyway."

Angela stood watching by the window as he walked back to his truck. He really did seem okay now, but Angela couldn't help but worry. He emerged with three large boxes on a dolly. She held open the door for him, and he wheeled the boxes to their spot.

"Sign here, please," he said, handing her a tablet. "Thank you for helping me, and don't worry. I'm going straight back to the warehouse and then to the doctor."

"Please take care."

He nodded and gave her a wave goodbye as he left. Angela walked back to the counter and noticed he had left his bottle of water. Picking it up, she saw something and moved the bottle closer to her face to get a better look. Just above the bottom of the glass bottle was a dark, phlegmy substance. It reminded her of when she would spit out the remnants of charcoal toothpaste in the sink. She thought maybe it was chewing tobacco though she hadn't noticed him chewing anything. "Weird," she said, grossed out.

6

Sean

Sean sat on the back patio and stared out over his property as he took the last sip of his coffee. It wasn't much to look at, but it was his. The grass was green and healthy all the way to his fence line. Almost exactly at the line where the barbed wire fence crossed, the grass was dry, brownish, and full of weeds. That side of the fence was his neighbor's land.

The cows would sometimes stick their head through the barbed wire to get a taste of his grass. Even with the constant chickens that also wandered onto his property, Sean and his neighbors got along really well. He had no need to be upset over the animals. He just enjoyed keeping a good lawn that he could go out and enjoy. His house sat on two acres and with woods on both sides. The front was open to an almost private street. Across the street, his other neighbor's front porch was visible from his. They were a nice couple who raised some livestock and sold plants and trees in their spare time.

As he sat enjoying the view, a pair of hands reached from behind Sean and covered his eyes. He reached up, grabbed the person attached to the hands, and pulled her into his lap.

"I don't want to leave you yet, but I gotta go," she said, smiling and looking deep into his eyes. "Jayden's gonna be late for school again if we don't get a move on."

Sean ran his fingers slowly over the smooth, dark skin of her face. "Am I going to see you tonight?" he asked, pulling her in closer.

"I might have to stay late for a meeting at the university, but I'll give you a call when I get off."

"Is that a yes?"

"We'll see," she said, pushing him away playfully.

Jayden popped up next to them with a biscuit in his hand. "Thanks for breakfast, Sean," he said, crumbs speckling his face and shirt.

"No problem, man." He brushed the crumbs from Jayden's chest. "Gotta look good for the ladies, right?"

Jayden rolled his eyes and pulled away, wiping his own shirt to get any remaining crumbs off. "Oh, I made this for you, Sean." He held up a neon pink paracord bracelet. "I saw a video online on how to make it and did it at the hotel. There's nineteen feet of 550 cord there. 550 means it'll hold five hundred and fifty pounds!" He handed it to Sean with a proud look on his face.

Neon pink was not a color Sean liked, but he recognized the work and care Jayden must have put into it. "Wow, man! Thanks so much. I'll put it on right now."

"Okay, we need to get rolling," Kristen said, standing up.

"My truck should have just about a full tank. I'll take your car in to get the flat fixed." Sean walked her and Jayden out to his truck in the front yard.

Kristen got in the driver's seat and leaned out to give Sean a kiss.

"What was the exciting news you wanted to tell me?" he asked. He had asked her once last night, but she seemed too nervous to tell him, and he didn't want to make her uncomfortable. She was not someone who enjoyed being pushed. She would tell him in her own time. He just thought maybe if she had a chance to slip it to him on the way out, it would be easier for her.

"Tonight, Sean."

"Okay, love. Call me when you get to work so I know you made it safely?"

"Of course."

"See you later, Sean!" yelled Jayden from the passenger seat, already fiddling with the radio.

"Later, bud. Be good at school today. Remember what we talked about if that punk, Liam, messes with you again."

"What exactly did you two talk about doing?" Kristen asked quickly, her eyes squinting in suspicion.

"Nothing much. Just guy stuff," Sean replied.

"Guy stuff, huh?"

"Yeah, guy stuff," Jayden chimed in.

Kristen rolled her eyes and looked at the clock in the truck. "We really have to go. I love you."

"I love you too." Sean let his hand hold on to hers for as long as he could while the truck started moving. He waved and watched the truck throw up dust and disappear down the road when a shout made him turn.

"Hey, Sean!" his neighbor, Rob, yelled from his own property across the street. "If you have any time this weekend, I could really use a hand for a couple minutes with my gate. It wouldn't take long. That wind a couple days back broke one of the hinges, and it's been tough keeping the goats in. Plus I've been itching to show you my new side-by-side!"

"What's tomorrow, Saturday? I'll probably have some time tomorrow morning if that works," Sean yelled back to Rob.

"That works great! Thanks! See ya in the morning!"

Sean waved goodbye and checked the spare tire that was on Kristen's car. It didn't look like it had lost any air, but it was definitely low. Before going in to get ready for the day, he started his garage air compressor so it could pressurize while he took a shower.

His morning routine usually involved listening to loud music as he showered. It helped wake him up and get him ready for the day. At one point, he thought he heard his phone ringing, but after listening for a second, he dismissed it and finished getting ready. It wasn't until he was fully dressed that he walked into the kitchen where his phone lay on the table.

"Holy crap!" There were nine missed calls from his work. Rather than search for a voicemail, he called them straight back.

"Hello, Sean?" a woman's voice asked. There was a noticeable crack in her voice as if she'd been crying.

"Yeah, it's me. What's going on, Jill?"

"It's Mr. Randall... H-he died this morning."

Sean sat down in a chair, speechless. Mr. Randall was the managing partner and one of the most loved of the firm Sean worked at. Sean looked up to him because he was a great lawyer but also had integrity and compassion as a human being. Something that didn't usually, in Sean's opinion, go along with the job. As a man who was healthy and had recently celebrated his fifty-first birthday, his sudden death was a great shock. Sean managed to pull himself together to get a few words. "That's awful. Do you know what happened?"

"No, but there are federal agents here wanting all his files. They said it's for a case they were working on with him. They need you to come down and pull all the files."

Sean knew exactly which case she was talking about. It involved many elderly individuals that had been taken advantage of by a fake business. Hundreds of thousands of dollars had been stolen.

"Me? What about Maxwell?"

"We haven't been able to get ahold of him," she strained through sobs.

"Ok, tell them I will be there soon. I'm on my wa—" He looked at the phone. The call had dropped, not unusual for his house out here in the country. He ran outside, put some air in the spare tire, and set off for the office. Several miles down the road, he saw three cars pulled over near the ditch. The one in the front had all its doors open. The other two had several people standing around as if they were waiting for something.

Probably a fender bender, he thought.

There was nothing he could do with all those people already there. He needed to let Kristen know that he was going into the office in case she couldn't reach him. He really hated to use the phone and drive. He never texted while driving, but Jayden had recently shown him how to use speech-to-text so he didn't have to take his eyes off the road. His phone was already synced with Kristen's car. He debated on if he should wait until he got to the office, especially since he wanted to focus more while driving on a spare, but he decided to go for it.

"Text 'my love, Kristen'," he began.

"Alright, texting 'my love, Kristen'," the phone's voice chimed. "What would you like to say?"

"I'm sorry, but I have a work emergency. I don't know how long it will take. I will text you if I get a break. I love you. Send."

"Sending..." There was a pause. "No service, message cannot be sent now."

"Figures." This part of the road often had no service.

His mind wandered to Mr. Randall's poor wife as he drove. She would come to the office weekly to eat lunch with her husband. They had no children, but his desk was full of pictures of them and their travels together. They always seemed so in love. Sean, a hopeless romantic, had only been with Kristen for a year and a half, and he couldn't imagine what it would feel like to lose her.

Sean heard the siren before he saw the actual fire truck. At first, it sounded far away, but suddenly, it came around the curve in the road going in the opposite direction. It was partly in his lane since it was taking the corner so fast. He got over as much as he could, but with no shoulder to the road, his front passenger tire went into the grass, causing him to swerve off the road. Without losing complete control, he brought the car to an abrupt stop with all four tires in the grass. His adrenaline was pumping when he got out to see if there was any damage to the spare or car. No, all looked good. He made a mental note to make an appointment with the fire station and discuss it with them. Just last year, he represented a husband that had lost his wife and child to an accident involving an ambulance driver who jumped the curb while driving quickly. Right now, he didn't have the time to worry about it.

The car had barely gotten back on the road when he heard more sirens in the distance. A police car, followed by a sheriff this time. Then an ambulance close behind. If it was for the cars that were pulled over aways back, it seemed like a lot more vehicles than necessary. He hadn't even seen any damage, and no one appeared panicked or injured. He tried to put it out of his mind and just focus on getting to the office safely.

It was normally at least a thirty minute drive to his office, but the traffic was a little lighter than normal today. Sean chalked it up to it being after rush hour. When he pulled up, there was a black car he had never seen sitting outside. He parked and took a deep breath. "Here we go."

Inside, the receptionist, Jill, was in tears. Several other employees were gathered around her desk, watching something on her computer and trying to console her with obvious grief on their faces as well.

"Hey everyone," he said, swallowing his own emotions. "I'm sorry to hear the news of Mr. Randall. I'm going to see what the authorities need help with, and when I'm done, I'm here to talk with anyone who wants to."

No one acknowledged him except Jill. She pointed toward Mr. Randall's office, her other hand wiping her eyes and face. The door was open and the lights were on. She tried to mutter something, but the words couldn't get past the sobs.

One of the other employees spoke up. "The agents are in there."

"Thanks. Has anyone reached Maxwell yet?"

Jill shook her head.

"Okay," he said, taking another deep breath and heading to the office.

There were two federal agents standing around talking as Sean entered the room. The older one was clean shaven and had a look of sympathy on his face as he made eye contact with Sean. Agent Morgan was his name. He'd had multiple meetings with Mr. Randall over the last year, and Sean had talked with him several times in passing. He didn't recognize the younger agent who wore clothes that seemed a bit large and had a worried look on his face.

"Hi, Sean. This is Agent Canterbury," started Agent Morgan. "First of all, I'd like to say, I'm sorry for your loss. Mr. Randall was a great man. His dedication to justice and his integrity were was the main reasons we started working with him—"

Agent Canterbury's phone started ringing. He excused himself and stepped out of the room.

Agent Morgan continued. "I'm sorry to bring you in under these circumstances and with everything going on, but we need your hel—"

Agent Canterbury came aggressively back into the room, looking even more worried than before.

"We need to go right now!" he blurted out to Agent Morgan.

"Wha—"

"It's getting even worse. Reports say the death toll is probably over a hundred thousand. All agents are being called in. We have to go now!"

Death toll? What are they talking about? Sean felt completely lost. "What's going on?"

It was Agent Canterbury's turn to look confused. "Have you not seen the news?"

"The news... what? No. What's happened?" Sean said, trying desperately to understand.

"Reports have been coming in all morning of sudden deaths," Agent Morgan said calmly.

"What are you talking about?" asked Sean, feeling anxiety start to rise in his chest.

"We really don't know much more than that, Sean. I'm sorry," Agent Morgan said, directing Agent Canterbury toward the door. "We need to go."

The agents left in a hurry with Sean standing in the doorway. He peered out at his colleagues still standing around Jill's computer, realizing that they were probably watching the news. He quickly walked up behind them. He was right.

"What's happening?" he asked the group.

The only answer that came was a finger pointing at the computer screen. They all appeared to be in a state of shock. He moved where he could get a good look at the screen and hear the reporter.

"... authorities are at a loss as to what is causing so many unexplained deaths," spoke the reporter. "Reports are coming in from almost every country now. We are getting unconfirmed reports that

Australia's Prime Minister may also be in the numbers of those who have died. With riots happening seemingly everywhere, we're all left to wonder, what's next? The president is set to speak any moment now directly from the White House where we hope to get some answers."

The news feed changed to the Oval Office. The president walked in and sat at the desk. Her hair was disheveled, her blazer open, her tie hanging loosely away from her neck. After a few moments, she looked out at the cameras with a sullen, worried expression and took a long, deep breath before addressing the nation.

"My fellow Americans, as you are aware, many of our citizens are succumbing to something unknown. Experts are working tirelessly to find the cause of what is going on...but I'm afraid we just don't know yet. We are not the only country suffering from this mysterious killer. At this time, we do not believe it is an attack by anyone on our people. That being said, we don't have any more information on this condition that has claimed the lives of so many people...We just don't know."

The president looked down at her desk and then straight into the camera with a serious face.

"We advise you to please not panic. Riots are breaking out all over the country. Looting is taking place in major cities and small towns alike. We must band together in a time like this and not resort to such behavior. Effective immediately, I am enacting an emergency state of martial law for all fifty states. The National Guard, along with other branches of the military, is being dispatched to all major cities. Please—"

Secret Service agents interrupted, rushed her off camera, and the feed went to a waiting screen.

"Oh, God!" Jill shrieked and continued her sobbing.

Everyone in the office started to panic and talk over each other. Sean was quiet as he tried to process the situation. Though he really felt like he had no clue about what was going on. Continuing to subdue his own feelings, he yelled over the noise of the office panic.

"Hey! Here's what we're going to do. You are all going to go home right away to your families. Just go. Don't worry about anything else. And be safe. It's all going to be okay."

No one stopped to say anything else. Everyone immediately began grabbing their things and heading for the door.

Sean grabbed his phone and tried to call Kristen. After a few seconds of the line not working, he looked at the phone. No service. "Shit!" Standing alone in the building, he picked up the landline on Jill's desk. There was no dial tone. Fear gripped him, squeezing his chest tight. He had to get to her right now. Giving up on calling, he grabbed his keys and ran for the car. She would either be at work or at her home in the city by now.

7

Sean

Sean was trying to stifle panic as he drove to Kristen's house. He was usually a calm, laid back individual, able to keep his cool in most situations. It's one of the reasons he felt like he was a good lawyer. But after checking at the university where Kristen worked, his anxiety was ramping up. There hadn't been a soul to be found in any of the buildings. The traffic was even lighter than earlier, at least in the direction he was going. Very few cars were on the road, and even those weren't a problem since no one was driving slowly. The occasional police car or fire truck would pass, usually in a hurry and going the other way. Kristen and Jayden lived in a large subdivision several miles from the university.

The quiet neighborhood streets felt odd. No one was out. No movement besides him and his car. As he turned onto Kristen's street, a minivan parked in a neighbor's driveway laid on its horn. He passed slowly as several kids and a frantic mother fled the house and loaded into the vehicle. The father was already behind the wheel. The frightened energy in the air made him even more anxious. He accelerated down the winding street, keeping an active eye out for children that could be outside.

He didn't see the cat until he was almost on top of it. It darted out from under a car to cross the road. Its long black body crouched low as it slithered. Sean slammed the brakes and swerved. His wheels screeched, and the car skidded at a diagonal. The back driver's tire slammed into the curb, jerking the car back straight. He got out quickly to check the vehicle. The tire seemed fine, but the rim had obvious damage. It was drivable. He glanced back to see if he had hit the cat. He spotted it under a truck and watched it slink off and disappear into a storm drain with a bird in its mouth. "Nine lives, huh?" He jumped back into the car and got moving toward Kristen's house again.

As he neared her house, he saw his truck wasn't in her driveway. He got out to check the house anyway. Even if Kristen hadn't made it home, maybe Jayden had made it back from school. The schools would have had to shut down and take the kids home. "Jayden, it's Sean!" he yelled, banging on the door and trying to look through the front window. Kristen had taken the house key off her car's key ring when she took Sean's truck. With no answer, he ran around back. Kristen kept a spare key under the lid of the grill. He let himself in the back door and started going through the house, hoping that Jayden and maybe even Kristen were there somewhere. "Kristen! Jayden! Are you home?"

Seeing that no one was home, he searched for any signs. Maybe there was a note or message for him, but he found nothing. His next best thought was that Kristen would try and get to his house. He grabbed a piece of paper from Kristen's office and made a quick note in case she came back.

"Kristen, if you make it here, please stay. Lock the doors and stay safe. I've gone back to my house in case you went there. I will be back as soon as I can. Love, Sean."

He raced back outside, locked up, and went back to the car. The spare tire still looked good, and since it was all he had, there was no choice but to drive on it. The car's clock read 2:04 pm.

The freeway out of town wasn't abandoned like the roads he had taken to the university and Kristen's house. It was congested, with cars driving in multiple lanes and the shoulder. As he finally approached his exit, everything stopped. Drivers were honking furiously. People stood on top of their cars to see what was going on. Sean got out and walked toward the grass for a better look. A ways up, there appeared to be a wreck. It blocked the entire road. But instead of the vehicles moving out of the way, the drivers were fighting. Bystanders watched on as the fight took place. Sean didn't want to get involved, but just like everyone else, he was stuck in the jam.

Jogging to the scene, he waved his arms and shouted to get their attention. The two men that were fighting were now on the ground wrestling, and neither seemed to be winning. As Sean got closer, a large gentleman came up beside him.

"If you can grab the one in blue, I'll grab the other one," he said.

"Got it," Sean replied, and the two men moved in on the fight.

Another man heard their plan and joined in. They carefully approached the wrestling men. The large gentleman grabbed one fighter and pulled him to his feet, holding him in a chokehold from behind. Sean and the other bystander grabbed the one in blue and pulled him back, pinning him to the ground. It took both Sean and the other man to hold him down.

"Okay!" yelled Sean. "We aren't solving anything, and fighting's not helping right now. If your car works, please get back in and drive. We all have people we need to get home to. No police are coming. You need to get off the road and go on your way."

"Fine!" yelled the man that Sean held down.

"Okay!" the other gurgled from his chokehold.

The large man gave Sean a nod and slowly released his chokehold on the man. The man rubbed his neck and coughed. Sean let go of the man he held and slowly stood up. The man in blue got up and wiped blood off a cut on his face. Both men stared at each other, anger still fuming from their eyes. Sean and the other two helpers watched as the men began to walk back to their cars. Suddenly the man in blue lunged at the other man. Before Sean could even take a step toward them, the sound of a gunshot made everyone stop. Sean dropped beside a car and looked around. A woman in business attire stood with a gun pointing in the air.

"Get back in your cars and go!" she yelled with authority. Sean stayed by the car he was crouched behind and watched. The man in blue was already getting back in his car and the other wasn't far behind. Tires squealed as both the wrecked cars and others nearby peeled out and went down the ramp toward the feeder road. Sean stood up just in time to not get hit by the car he was near. He jogged to the shoulder to let other cars pass and began making his way back to his vehicle. The men that had helped him out were already getting back to theirs as well. Within thirty seconds, it was as if no accident or fight had occurred.

Sean moved like he were in an arcade game to get back to his car, dodging and waiting until he made it past the mad dash of vehicles trying to leave town. Once back inside the car, he started it and exited the freeway with most everyone else. He took some back roads to avoid the flow of traffic, and it was smooth sailing back to his house. Mental prayers and pleadings occupied his thoughts until he pulled up, quickly being replaced by panic since his truck wasn't there. He slammed on his brakes and the car skidded to a stop in the grass of his front yard. He raced inside.

In the time he had been away, the living room had been decorated like a small birthday party. Blue and green streamers danced across the room, and blue balloons lay scattered all around the floor. It caught him off guard, but he didn't stop to pay it much attention. Checking the house, there was no sign of Kristen or Jayden. He stopped in the kitchen and checked his phone. No signal. Out of the corner of his eye, he saw a note on the counter. He picked it up and read it.

"Sean, I wanted to surprise you with a little birthday celebration with just you and me since I missed your birthday when I was out of town. I just saw the news and can't get service on my phone to call you. Jayden was supposed to stay with a friend after school. I'm going to pick him up and go to my house. The news said the roads are getting packed and to stay home, so we'll stay there tonight. If you get this note, please stay here and don't go back out. You can come in the morning when it's safer. Promise me that you won't go back out! We will be okay. I love you. Kristen."

The note eased his panic a bit, but he still wanted to go out and get to her. Early on in their relationship, they had both agreed that if they used the words 'promise me,' they would honor the request. She didn't use the phrase often, but when she did, he knew she meant it. He glanced at his watch. It was a quarter after 4 pm. He couldn't think of anything besides Kristen and Jayden. The rest of the world didn't matter. Waiting here would kill him.

Not being able to do anything else, he decided to check on the tire. Any sense of control was better than no control. The car had started pulling to one side the last mile or two. He walked up to the side of the car and sighed. The good news was that the tire wasn't completely flat. But it had definitely lost a good amount of air. He went and grabbed a can of *Fix-a-Flat* from the garage. After using the whole can, he got his compressor out and started airing it back up. He watched it intensely for any bulges in the sidewall, hoping that it would hold air. All good. Once it was up to pressure, he checked and listened for any leaks. Again, everything seemed okay. Leaving the compressor outside in case he needed it later, he went back toward the house. Two dead birds lay on the ground under a tree in his front yard. He stopped to look at them for a second and then turned away and went back inside.

Sean walked in the living room and sat on the couch, feeling completely useless. Looking around at the decorations that Kristen had put in the room, he chuckled out loud. She wasn't the kind of person who had a sharp eye for decorating. It looked as though a ten-year-old boy had gone crazy with tape, streamers, and balloons. No, she wasn't a decorator, but she was super intelligent and a hard worker. Her mother had died in childbirth with Jayden when Kristen was a sophomore in high school. When she was a senior, her dad had fallen off some scaffolding at his job and broken his neck. He spent two days in a coma before passing away. The then eighteen-year-old Kristen immediately got a job and started taking care of Jayden, who was still a toddler at the time. The company that her father had worked for set up accounts for both Kristen and Jayden to go to college, so she did. She continued to work and take care of Jayden the whole time. After receiving her bachelor's degree, she got a job as a medical researcher at the university where she now worked. She continued studying and now held a master's degree. Sean had met her over a year ago while doing some pro bono legal work for the university.

He looked around again, unsure of what to do. After a moment, he turned on the TV. Maybe he could find some news, he thought. The TV tried to load but popped up with the phrase, *no network connection, try again?* He went to the modem and checked it. It was powered on but had no internet.

"Where is that radio?" he said out loud to himself. He checked several cabinets and closets with no luck. *Maybe the garage?* He went through several boxes before finding it with the camping equipment. Surprisingly, the batteries still worked. He went slowly to find any channel that was on the air, but just like everything else, nothing seemed to work. "Dammit," he said, tossing the radio back in the box. Having absolutely no communication with her or anyone else was one of the most unnerving experiences of his life.

He paced back and forth. Some intense primal feeling of panic was bubbling up inside of him. He checked his watch. It was 5:23pm. He couldn't stand it anymore. Her wishes of him staying home and not coming to her were to keep him safe. But his only desire was to keep her safe, and he couldn't do that from here. He ran back inside, got the keys, and raced to the car. He gave the tire a quick glance before jumping in and getting on the road. He was used to driving carefully on the dirt road that he lived on. There were woods on either side, and the road stretched for several miles before joining a paved street. Deer and other animals frequented the area, so keeping your eyes peeled was good practice. He sped down the road faster than normal but with his eyes wide, watching for any movement. He was almost to the paved street. His attention hyper-focused outside of the car for anything that could jump out. The sound of the tire blowing out snapped his attention back to the vehicle. The back end of the car started sliding to the left. He turned the steering wheel to straighten up, but the car kept sliding and went off into the ditch. Sean tightened up and braced for impact as the car spun and the driver's side slammed into a tree.

8

Angela

Angela stared out the window of her lonely shop. It had been several hours since the delivery man had gone, and no one had come in since. She hadn't thought much of it as it was normally slow this time of day, and she had been clearing out space for new products. But she wasn't used to having nobody come in at all. Glancing at her watch, it was just past 1:30 in the afternoon. An uneasy feeling rose inside her as she watched the street that ran in front of the shop. There were nearly no cars on the road. She walked out of her shop and glanced in the window of the business next door; a small auto parts store. She couldn't see anyone, and the lights weren't on. Angela and the store owner didn't get along all that well as he was constantly complaining about her clients parking in his spaces. There were two spaces allotted to her and two for him. She debated in her mind whether or not she should knock to see if he was in.

Naw, that old man'll just find something else to gripe about.

She went back inside her shop to find her phone. Maybe there was something going on that she didn't remember about. The town was always having little celebrations and events. She tried to bring up her calendar, but it wouldn't load. Realizing that her phone wasn't connected to WIFI, she went to the router, unplugged it, and plugged it back in.

That should fix it.

The router would take several minutes to boot back up, so she put her phone in her pocket and walked around, straightening some items on the shelves. The sound of a siren and a loud voice over a speaker grabbed her attention. Jogging to the window, she peered out and caught sight of the police car. It was the only vehicle on the road. She stuck her head outside to hear better. She couldn't make out exactly what the officer was saying over the speaker, as the sound was bouncing weirdly off the brick wall by her head. But she did catch some small pieces that confused her.

"... inside your homes...until further notice..."

The car slowed down and made a u-turn. Angela went out to meet the officer as he pulled up in front of the building, staying on the street. He rolled down his window to speak to her. He was a larger man with a belly that almost touched the steering wheel.

"Ma'am, you need to go home." His stern voice sounded patronizing.

"What? Why?" she asked in a sassy tone, refusing to be talked down to.

He looked at her with a puzzled expression as if he couldn't believe that she wouldn't just blindly follow his instructions.

"Because of everything that's been happening, ma'am. There is a mandatory curfew in effect."

"What's going on?" she asked, her anxiety increasing.

Again, the officer looked at her as if she should know exactly what he was talking about.

"Uh, um, people are dying, ma'am," he said, changing to an apologetic tone. "Nobody knows why. One minute they're okay, and the next, they're...not."

Angela stood, processing what she was hearing. It sounded made up and unbelievable. Like a low budget movie nobody would watch. Her mind scanned all that had happened today. The dead man in the car accident, the delivery man almost passing out, the lack of customers, the fact that there were no cars or people anywhere to be found in the streets, even the random dead birds scattered in the woods.

The cop continued, though his voice was mostly muffled in Angela's ears.

"Ma'am, there's a curfew in effect, and you need to go home. If you have any family nearby... Well, I pray they're okay and waiting for you there."

"What...I don't—"

"I'm afraid that's all I know, ma'am. Please just go to your home and stay there until this is all over. Good luck, and God be with you." He slowly pulled away, leaving Angela standing in the street alone. The police siren returned and faded down the road, the sound of the speaker vibrating off the buildings around her.

Shocked and unable to comprehend what she had just heard, Angela's mind went to a bad place. A place usually reserved for moms sitting in the dark of night, thinking of the future of their children. "Michael!" She turned to go toward her house, not even bothering to lock up her shop. Tears welled in her eyes before her feet had even taken three steps. Checking her phone on the move, it had no service. No way to contact her son.

Is he home? Is he okay? Why hadn't he come to the shop?

The worst scenarios played through her head as she began to run. She jumped curbs and darted through yards. Adrenaline carried her the whole way home. Sweating and out of breath, she made for the front door. Hoping it was unlocked, she grabbed the knob and twisted it aggressively. Not even a jiggle. In her hysteria, she had forgotten to grab her keys from the shop. She slammed on the door with her fist. "Michael! Michael! Are you home? Michael!"

She ran around the house to the kitchen window that rested above the sink. Because it was a higher window and most people couldn't fit through it, it was the only window she ever left unlocked. The screen was bent and barely holding on, a product of Michael's own constant forgetting of keys. Angela ripped it off, throwing it behind her. Standing on her toes, she pushed the window up to open it. The nearby garbage bin acted as a makeshift ladder. Climbing on top, she began to pull herself through the tiny window. Her shoulders barely fit through, and after a few seconds of struggling, she was able to get the upper half of her body through. With one hand on the sink below her and one on the window frame, she pushed herself through. She fell arms first to the floor as the trash bin tumbled over outside. Pain was the last thing on her mind as she continued yelling for her son.

"Michael!" She ran up the stairs toward his room, slipping on the next to last step and slamming her shin. Hobbling to his room, ignoring the pain, she burst through his door and panic-scanned for him. No Michael. She immediately searched for his skateboard, turning over dirty clothes and the sheets that lay on the ground. She couldn't find it anywhere. Her anxiety steadily increased until she noticed his backpack sitting on the floor at the foot of his bed.

He's been home! But where did he go?

A slamming noise from downstairs made her freeze. Michael? She hurried downstairs screaming his name, her voice cracking.

"Michael? Michael?"

"Hi, Mom." Michael's voice hit her ears like a baseball bat. A welcome hit.

A powerful wave of solace overwhelmed her, and she fell on him, squeezing him tightly as he walked in from the living room. Unable to hold back, she bawled, her grip only getting tighter.

"Are you okay, Mom?" he asked, awkwardly holding his mother up.

After a moment, she let go and stepped back, wiping the tears and snot from her face with the sleeve of her shirt. "I'm fine. I was worried about you! Where did you go?!"

"The school let us go early due to all the crazy stuff going on. The phones aren't working. They made us all take the bus home, but since you weren't here, I went to the shop to find you."

Angela let out a single chuckle through her tears, trying not to start bawling again. He was safe, and they were together.

"I'm just so happy you're okay," she said, latching hold of him again for a few more seconds.

"Do you know what's going on, Mom? Have you seen the news?"

"No, all I've heard was that some people have died, and we're under a curfew now."

"People are dying everywhere. Nobody knows why. Ms. Ramander had the radio on while we were stuck in class." Michael seemed excited and nervous as he talked about it. A gift of egocentric youth: No one to be worried about.

"What's going on?" Angela asked under her breath, struggling to make sense of the situation. She had no idea what was happening out in the world. She felt terrible that so many people were suffering, but they weren't her responsibility, Michael was. "You said the radio was working?"

"It was, but it went out while we were listening to it. Ms. Ramander was crying, and none of the stations were working."

The electricity went off and on again as they stood talking. Since they were probably going to be stuck inside for a while with no contact to the outside world, Angela wanted them to take their minds off everything else. They were together, and that was all that mattered.

"Why don't we sit down and play a board game? Since there's nothing else to do, you know?" she asked, hopeful that he would. It was how she used to distract him as a kid when something bad had happened. Like when their twelve-year-old dog, Harley, had died. She also knew it would distract her own mind, and she needed it.

"Sure, Mom," he said in a knowing tone, evident that he understood what she was doing. "I'll go get some from upstairs."

"I'll clear the kitchen table." She watched as her teen went upstairs, thinking of all the years she had protected him and kept him safe. He was growing into a good human, but how much longer could she keep him out of harm's way?

He came back down with an armful of games, and they spent the next few hours playing and talking in the kitchen. Despite everything, Angela was grateful to have this rare opportunity to be with her son in this way.

They stopped to have some dinner, and Angela sat on the couch to rest her heavy eyes while Michael began to wash the dishes. She had taught him well.

The excitement and physical activities of the day were catching up with her. Before she knew it, she was asleep.

She woke up to an eerie lack of sound. No AC running, no cars in the distance, and no crickets chirping outside. It was starting to get dark outside, and the electricity was out. She assumed it was close to 6:30pm. Michael must have put a blanket over her and gone to bed early. She crept up the stairs and down the short hall to his room. With no air conditioning, the stagnant air was already heating up. She opened his window carefully and checked on him in the low light. Sound asleep. Since he'd become a teen, he could sleep anywhere and through anything. It felt like it had been so long since she had gone in his room and watched him sleep. She stood watching him for a few minutes before going to bed herself. Within seconds, she was out again.

9

Sean

"Shit," Sean muttered, scanning his body for injuries. Besides tightness in his neck, he didn't feel like anything was really hurt. The car had spun a full two hundred and seventy degrees before slamming into the tree, driver's side first. The driver's door was pinned, making it impossible to open. He crawled across to the passenger side and pulled himself out. The car didn't fare as well as him. The side was smashed in, and the spare tire was in shreds. He looked back down the road toward his home. With the sun going down and all the trees lining the road, it was already getting dark.

The motorcycle! I can charge the battery and take that to get to Kristen.

The battery had been having trouble holding a charge lately, and he hadn't gotten around to getting a new one.

"Better get walking," he said to himself.

He walked slowly at first, still trying to make sure his body was okay. He had heard too many stories of people getting in an accident and not realizing how hurt they were due to adrenaline and shock. A cold sensation dripped down his left arm. A cut on his elbow. In the low light, there wasn't much he could do for it until he got home. After a minute, he sped up to a power walk.

A truck coming up the road from behind gave him a short honk, followed by a familiar voice. "Hey, Sean, you need a lift, or you just out for a stroll during a world crisis?" It was his neighbor, Rob. He pulled up beside Sean and was sticking his head out the window with a big grin on his face.

"Man, am I glad to see you, Rob," Sean said with a relieved sigh, hopping into the passenger side.

As they started driving, Rob began the conversation. "It might be none of my business, but what's got you out here during all this?"

"Kristen's at home in the city. I can't get ahold of her, and I'm just trying to make it there."

"Sorry, son, but I don't think you're gonna make it into the city. The National Guard has it shut down tight. Nobody in, nobody out."

"Ugh!" Sean grunted in frustration. "I can't—I just..."

"I know. I was just there myself trying to get to my sister and her kids. 'Fraid there's no way through."

Sean felt even more useless. How could he just sit and do nothing? The truck drifted across the road toward the ditch. "Rob! Rob! Ditch!"

"Whoa!" he said, straightening up the vehicle. "Sorry 'bout that. I've been having dizzy spells off and on all day. I'm good now."

Sean watched Rob's face. The color had drained from his cheeks. He could swear he saw Rob's eyes change for a second. Like a cloud had drifted across them. He shook off the thought as they pulled up to Sean's house and he got out. "Thanks for the lift, Rob. I appreciate it."

"Ah, no big deal. Say, Sean, why don't you come on over for some dinner. Since I planned on bringing my sister's crew back, my wife made enough for more than just us."

"I don't—" he started but quickly changed his mind. Stacey was a good cook, and maybe some company would distract his mind from spiraling. At least while his motorcycle's battery was charging. "Sure, thanks."

"Great! I'll have Stacey swing by to let you know when it's ready." Rob turned around in the grass and headed toward his house while Sean went straight to his bike.

He usually put it on a trickle charger the night before he planned on riding it. Hopefully if he hooked it up now, it would be ready to go after dinner. He kept his bike behind the house under a cover by the back door. He plugged the charger into the extension cord that he always had run by it. After getting the charger hooked to the battery, he went inside to check out his elbow.

It wasn't bad. Probably could use a stitch or two, but a couple butterfly bandages and some athletic tape would hold quite nicely.

Unable to wait, he went out back to check on his bike to see if it would start. No luck yet. "Come on old girl. I just need you to get me there."

"Sean, sweetie," Stacey's voice came from the front yard.

"Good evening," he said, wiping some of the grime from his hands on his jeans.

"Dinner's ready. Would you still like to join us?"

"Yes, ma'am. That'd be great."

Rob was already sitting at the dining table with a beer in one hand and a piece of garlic toast in the other when they came in. A large bowl of spaghetti noodles sat next to a crock pot full of meatballs in sauce.

"Stacey, are these your famous venison meatballs?" Sean asked.

She often brought food over for Sean. She said she hated seeing a bachelor not have a 'proper home cooked meal'.

"They sure are. We went bow hunting last weekend."

Rob took this chance to brag on his wife. "Yeah, he wouldn't turn for me, but Stace was able to drop him right where he stood! Did ya know Stace used to do competitive archery? She's the best."

Sean faked a shocked and impressed face. "Impressive!"

Stacey looked at Sean and smiled. She knew he'd been told about her archery days on at least a dozen occasions.

They dished out their food and began to eat. While they talked and ate, Sean kept checking in on Rob. He would sometimes look like he was close to passing out. Sean's mind kept thinking of all the people who had passed away that day, and he was worried for his old friend.

"Uh, Rob. You still having those dizzy spells?"

Rob glanced at Stacey. He must have been keeping it from her.

"Dizzy spells, Robert?"

"Well I..." he began. His face went pale, and he fell sideways out of his chair.

"Rob!" Sean yelled, running to his side.

"I'll be fine," Rob said, trying to pick himself off the floor. "I think I need to get a little rest. Do you think you could help me to the couch?"

Sean assisted him to the living room while Stacey got a pillow and blanket. When they had him set up, Stacey returned to the kitchen.

Sean didn't want to overstay his welcome. Rob obviously needed rest. Besides, the battery could be charged enough by now. "Rob, I'm going to go, but you take care of yourself, ya hear?"

"Sorry to cut dinner short."

"No worries. Just feel better, friend."

Stacey came in with some old whipped cream containers. "Take these, Sean. I'll take care of this old guy."

"Thank you, Stacey."

Stacey walked him outside to the front porch. "I started to feel he was all in the clear. After he beat the cancer last year, he seemed to be returning to his old self." She wiped a tear before it could fall. "Then when his doctor gave him those treatments, his energy and strength all came back so fast. But now...with all this—"

"He's going to be just fine, Stacey," Sean reassured her. "That man is too strong and too stubborn to be taken down. You just take care of him. I'm going to try a head into town tonight, but hopefully I'll be back sometime tomorrow with Kristen and Jayden. Then I'll be right across the road if you need anything."

"Going into the city tonight? Oh, please be careful, Sean. All the crazies are out."

"I'll be okay."

She nodded, and Sean returned home. It was dark out, and the clouds were visible in the sky due to the bright moon. A waxing gibbous. Kristen was really into moon phases and the energy each would bring. It was interesting to learn, but for some reason, even the moon made him feel useless right now.

The bike didn't start again when he tried. Going inside, he paced around the house cleaning and organizing. Doing anything to pass the time and keep his mind busy. Constantly checking on his motorcycle. He didn't know what time it was when he finally sat on the couch to rest for a few minutes.

A blood curdling scream yanked him from a deep sleep. It was morning. Small beams of light were visible through the blinds on the windows. He sat up and listened to make sure it wasn't just part of his dream. This time, the scream was louder and more panicked. Running to the door, he ripped it open and ran toward the road.

His eyes streaked across the fields and trees, looking for the origin of the sound until he saw the source. Rob and Stacey's front yard.

Rob was dragging Stacey by the arm through the dirt toward their truck. Sean's confusion caused him to pause for a moment. This wasn't like Rob. He was always such a kind person and often called Stacey his queen. He was the last person who would become physically abusive.

Running toward his neighbors, Sean yelled in an aggressive tone, "Hey! Let her go, Rob! What the hell are you doing?"

Rob didn't seem to notice Sean. His eyes never moved from the truck. Stacey was kicking and flailing, but it didn't seem to slow him down. Sean got to Rob just as he shoved Stacey in the back seat and closed the door of the truck.

"What's gotten into you, Rob?" Sean yelled, putting his hand on the driver's door to stop him from getting in too.

Rob's eyes met Sean's, and it made Sean step back. His eyes were glazed and cloudy. Like a gray dark mist had settled inside. His facial expression was blank. Rob grabbed Sean by his shoulder. His fingers dug deep into Sean's skin. Sean immediately hit Rob's wrist, releasing his grip.

"Rob! Stop!"

Sean didn't enjoy hurting others. He had taken up boxing in college but only participated in several bouts before quitting and then used it only for a good workout. But one thing he always felt called to do was stand up for those who couldn't help themselves.

He grabbed Rob and threw him to the ground. Turning back to the truck, Stacey was getting out the opposite side. Rob's arms suddenly wrapped around Sean. They were both about equal in size, but for some reason, today Rob's strength was far superior. Without even a moment to struggle, Sean was tossed across the yard like a rag doll, rolling when he hit the ground. Jumping up, Sean charged and swung. His punch landed squarely on Rob's cheekbone. Like a scene out of *The Terminator*, Rob barely flinched, though his cheek was now bleeding. Again, Sean stepped back. The blood that oozed from the wound was more maroon than red. Rob reached to grab him again, but Sean blocked his arms down and landed a left hook to the jaw. This time, Rob stumbled back toward the truck. Before he could regain his balance, Sean slammed him into the truck with a powerful shove. Rob's lower back hit the truck bed step by the rear tire, and he fell to the ground in pain.

Stacey stood on the opposite side of the vehicle in shock, screaming.

Sean called out to her, "Get to my house, Stacey!"

"What's wrong with him?!" she screamed.

"Just get to my house!"

Leaving Rob on the ground, they both ran to Sean's place. Once inside, Sean grabbed his cell phone and handed it to Stacey. "Call the cops!" He went to the front window and looked outside. Rob was trying to stand up.

"No service," Stacey said in tears. She began to sob and yell. "What's wrong with him? His eyes! Is he okay? Oh, his eyes!"

She was inconsolable, and they didn't have time for her to calm down. Something was terribly wrong with Rob, and he was insanely strong. Sean put his hands on her shoulders and looked into her eyes. "Listen, we have to go. Come on!"

The keys to Sean's motorcycle were by the front door on a hook. He grabbed them and made another look out the front door window. He couldn't see Rob.

"We have to take my bike. Go out the back. It's on the side of the house by the garage. Go!" he yelled to Stacey.

Rob's hand came through the front door's window with enough force to throw glass onto Sean. The bloody hand fumbled for the deadbolt. The oddly dark blood smearing across the door and frame.

"Go!" Sean and Stacey ran out the back door and around the house to his bike. Throwing the trickle charge off, he slammed the seat back into position. Stacey was still crying and panicking, but he managed to get her on the back seat.

"Come on. Start."

The first crank wasn't enough to start the engine. He pushed the choke down and gave it another go. This time it started. The engine's RPM's ramped up, the sound cutting through the tense air like a knife.

With no time to let the engine warm up, Sean put it in first gear and peeled out. Gravel and dust kicked up behind them as they took off. He glanced back at Rob who somehow was gaining on them with incredible speed. Sean gave it more gas and went through the shallow grassy ditch to the road. Rob slowly disappeared from view as they literally left him in the dust. Sean watched in his rearview mirror, half expecting Rob to burst through the cloud of dirt. They flew down the road, their houses fading from view.

10

Angela

Sunlight streamed through Angela's window, waking her up. Her mind replayed the day before. Feeling uneasy, she got up and went to Michael's room. His door was closed. She didn't want to wake him if he was still sleeping, so she put her ear to the door to listen. She couldn't hear anything besides the low hum of the air conditioning, which, if the temperature was any indication, hadn't been on long.

She quietly crept down the stairs to make some coffee. The time on the coffee maker was blinking since the power had been out. Filling the pot with water, a piece of paper on the counter caught her eye. It was one of the scorecards from a *Yahtzee* last night. She filled the coffee maker and picked up the card to throw it away. On her way to the trash, she rubbed the sleep from her eyes and stretched, looking out the kitchen window. Nothing moved outside. It reminded her of a painting. The trees were still, and the world was silent. Not even a blade of grass seemed to budge. She must have slept in, as it appeared to be mid-day outside.

The gurgle and hiss of the coffee maker broke her stare. She stepped to the trash can and dropped the card in. Handwriting on the back hinted that it was a note. She quickly pulled it from the can and read carefully, praying it wasn't what she thought it might be.

> *"Mom, I'm going to the park to board. I told Nick I'd meet him there this morning. Be back by lunch. Love you. Michael."*

"Shit, Michael! What the hell are you thinking?" she yelled. How dare he leave with all that was going on? "When I get ahold of you..." she mumbled, trying to slow down and catch her breath. Familiar tears welled up as she ran to get dressed. She threw on the first thing she could find, a pair of jeans and a black t-shirt. Some old tennis shoes were sitting by the front door, so she put those on and left the house for the skate park.

Angela was a jumble of anxiety and anger. Her fists stayed clenched, and she mumbled as she ran all the way to the skate park several blocks from her home. Something that always seemed to help her calm down was having a complete conversation by herself. It felt as though she could get all her feelings out without saying something she'd regret to the person she was mad at. To anyone else, she would have looked deranged. That was if there had been anyone else around. The streets were devoid of movement. No running cars, no humans, no sounds. It was a ghost town. Vehicles sat abandoned in the middle of the streets, as if people just stopped and walked away. The scene only added to her anxiety.

At the skate park, there was no sign of Michael or his friend at all. Not allowing her voice to crack, she began to yell for them at the top of her lungs, becoming more frantic with each yell.

"Michael! Michael! Nicholas!" Her heart raced as she searched the area. The only building in the park held the public restroom. Bursting into the men's room, she searched each stall with no luck. She couldn't cry. Her determination to find her son won out over any other emotion she could possibly feel. She ran all the way home to see if he had come back, but he wasn't there either.

Michael's best friend, Nick, lived with his grandparents in a small duplex close to the compact downtown area of the city. People referred to the downtown area as 'The Square' since it was built in a large square around the historical courthouse. Angela made her way toward The Square as fast as she could, her heart beating wildly as she ran.

The sound of whimpering made her stop and listen. She surveyed the area, her gaze stopping on a car with the back door wide open. Approaching slowly, she made her way to the driver's side. A woman inside lay sideways across both front seats. Her eyes were open and staring directly into Angela's as she came to the window. Her moans were a mixture of pain and sadness, her breaths labored.

"Are you okay?" Angela asked, cautiously pulling the door more open.

The woman tried to sit up but couldn't. Angela leaned in and got her first good look at the woman. Mascara streamed down her face from tears. Her skin was pale, like all the blood had been drained out of it, but the veins all over her body were black and protruding. It reminded her of the man from the car accident the day before.

"Th-they took her," she cried out, her voice both panicked and hoarse.

"Took who? What can I do to hel—"

The woman suddenly began to scream at Angela. "The people took her, my little girl!"

"It's gonna be okay. We'll find your daughter. Did you see which way they went?" she asked, standing up and scanning around for a little girl.

"In a car. Find her, please!" the woman yelled, reeling in pain.

"Stay here. I'm going to come back for you." She left the woman in the car and ran toward The Square. The screams of the woman continued as she ran. She was still primarily looking for her son, but as a mother, she needed to help try and find this little girl as well.

Rounding the corner into the old downtown plaza, she saw a group of five people walking away from her. She jogged toward them and called out.

"Excuse me, can you help me? I'm looking for someone! It's my son, he's—" She stopped in her tracks at about twenty feet away. As the group turned around, almost in unison, their appearance shocked her. The emotionless expressions on their faces were made worse with how their eyes looked. Even at this distance, they were noticeably opaque and glassy. Angela started to walk backward away from the group. All at once, as if their brains were connected, they started to come toward her. Scared, she took off running in the other direction, not looking back to see if they were chasing her, though she knew they were. Their footsteps beat on the pavement like the hooves of horses, gaining and gaining. She turned down an alley and then down a side street to escape.

She had barely taken four steps down the street when two men popped out of a door. They grabbed her aggressively and yanked her inside the doorway with them, all three falling to the floor.

"Get the hell off me!" she yelled, thrashing at the arms that held her.

"Ssshhh, you're safe!" one of the men whispered loudly.

Realizing that the grip was just holding her there and not taking her anywhere, she gave in and froze long enough to hear the footsteps of her chasers fading into the distance.

As the arms let go of her, Angela jerked away and stood up. She was in a dark room with a few streaks of light peeking through some windows on one side. As her eyes began to adjust to the darkness,

Angela realized that she was in the local smoke shop. The front windows were heavily tinted, and there was cardboard taped over most of them to completely block anyone from seeing in. One large, burly looking man walked to the windows and was spying out through a crack in the cardboard nervously. In one hand, he held a pistol with a grip so tight his knuckles were white. He had on a worn, dark t-shirt, jeans, and a black and white trucker style cap. His beard was jet black with white hairs throughout and long enough to partially cover up what Angela could only guess was a rock band logo on his shirt.

"What is going on?" she asked as she rubbed her arm where she had been grabbed. She looked down at her knee. In the low light, she could see a small circle of blood on her jeans where it must have slammed on the ground when she was pulled inside.

"Sorry, miss," a skinny, nerdy guy crouching next to her said. "We didn't mean to hurt you. We just didn't want to see you get taken, too."

"Get taken? What are you talking about? Who are you?"

The large, burly gentleman spoke up. "My name's William, but you can call me Bill. That's Shane over there. People around here are acting strange. It started this morning. Groups of people looking like zombies. They've been grabbing normal folk and taking them away."

"I've been telling people for years that the zombie apocalypse was coming," Shane blurted out.

Angela glanced at the gun in Bill's hand. She was trapped in a room with two men apparently out of touch with reality. She began moving toward the door. Was it better to be in a room with two crazy guys or to be chased by an unnatural mob?

"Well, thank you for your help, but I have to get back out and find my son," Angela said.

"You want to go out there?" Shane exclaimed.

"I have to," she said, still wary of the company she was in.

"Suit yourself, miss, but don't lead those guys anywhere near here!" he said, throwing his hands up.

"I'll help you, ma'am," Bill said calmly.

"No, that's okay. I'm sure I'll be fine," she lied. She kind of wanted some help, or at least some company. But she was nervous about this guy. He seemed genuine, but he could just be a crazy stranger with a gun. And due to his physical shape, he might slow her down.

"I can't in good conscience let you go out all by yourself."

"But you'll leave me here by myself?" squeaked Shane.

"You're more than welcome to come along," Bill said, sounding annoyed with him.

"No way! I'm not getting eaten or turned into a zombie!"

Angela knew she could really use the help, and Bill was her only option as the world seemed so empty. "Well I guess we should get going then," she said, troubled that she wasn't out already looking for Michael.

Shane huffed. "Not with my gun, you're not!"

Bill walked toward the counter where the nerdy man stood. He placed the gun on the counter next to him, glaring with disapproval. Then he turned and walked toward the side door he'd pulled Angela through. He peeked out of the crack one more time. "It looks all clear. Let's go." He slowly opened the door and stuck his head out.

Angela was right behind him. As soon as they were out, Shane shut the door from the inside. They heard a quick fumble and the clank of the metal lock.

"No turning back now. He won't open that thing for anybody. I had to push him out of the way to help you when we saw you through the window. Where do we start? Do you have a car?"

"No car, but I think we should go to the police station. The chief of police is a friend, and maybe he's there. He can help. Maybe he's seen my son or best case scenario, picked him up and took him there to be safe."

Bill had a sympathetic look on his face.

"It's a couple blocks this way," she said, not paying any attention to the look. She knew it was a long shot, but it was her only hope.

Please, please, please, God. Let him be there.

She walked fast, Bill tagging along behind.

11

"Stage One is complete," said the woman sitting at the large computer. "All drones are moving to their terminals."

The man in the cloak leaned forward in his chair and said in his snake-like voice, "Good, and the young vessels?"

"Being assembled," she said, continuing to work.

"What about those who have not gone through the modification, Arub?" the man in the suit asked the cloaked man.

Arub answered without removing his eyes from the screen. "Young Lugal, everything is completely under control. You need not worry yourself over such inconsequentials. You have a duty to complete. I believe it is time you begin Stage Two."

"But what will—"

"It is under control," Arub repeated. "I will let you know if there is a concern."

"Yes, Arub, thank you for your counsel," Lugal said, annoyed. He turned back to the woman on the computer. "Begin Stage Two. Let me know as soon as all nuclear facilities have been occupied."

"Stage Two initiated."

12

Sean

Sean didn't stop until they made it to the nearest gas station, about ten miles from his house. It was void of activity. He parked the motorcycle beside the building, out of view of any passing car. Rob's included. He hoped if Rob chased them, he wouldn't see the bike and suspect they were there. Stacey was still crying but had calmed down to just a few tears and sniffles. The pair walked to the front and peered into the window. No one was there, and the lights were off. The front door was unlocked, so they let themselves in. The windows offered the only light in the building.

"Hello!" Sean yelled. "Anybody here? AJ? AJ, you here?" Even with everything being shut down, he assumed AJ, the store owner, would still be there.

AJ, was a middle-aged gentleman who loved interacting with all his customers. It was so strange just being in the building without AJ greeting him. Sean almost felt like he was trespassing in someone's home.

Sean glanced at Stacey. It was clear she was still in shock from what had happened with Rob.

"Why don't you sit down and rest," he suggested, walking behind the counter and pulling out the chair AJ usually sat in.

"No," she whimpered. "I just need to go to the restroom and put some water on my face." She walked slowly with her head hung in sadness.

"Okay, take your time. I'll try and get on the phone." He picked up the landline phone by the register. The line was completely dead. *Dammit. Maybe there's another phone or something in the back.*

He walked toward the back room and pushed the swinging door. It ran into something and wouldn't open. He pulled the door this time and gasped. Lying on the floor behind the door was AJ. "AJ! AJ!" He crouched down and checked on him. There was no pulse, and his body wasn't warm to the touch. Something was secreting from his mouth. At first, Sean thought it was blood, but it was thick and black, almost tarry.

Stacey's scream made him jump. She had come up behind him and seen AJ. He quickly closed the door, blocking AJ from her view.

"I know, I know," he said, trying to calm her down. "It's okay." The words sounded hollow coming from his mouth. None of this was okay. None of this would be okay.

"What's going on?" she managed to get out through choked sobs, backing away from the doorway and AJ. "First my Rob acts like that, and now AJ is dead!"

Sean wrapped her in a hug. "I don't know what's going on. It's gonna be okay, Stacey. We'll figure this whole thing out and get Rob some help..."

"Help?! Did you see his eyes? It was like he was sick and something had taken over him! Like his soul wasn't there anymore!" Stacey yelled and started pacing up and down the aisle in a frenzy. "And what about AJ?! Can you help him?"

Sean looked away from Stacey, racking his brain for something. Anything. Anything that could make sense of what was going on. Something he could at least say to help.

"I'm sorry, Sean," Stacey whispered, stopping her panicked march. "I feel like I'm going crazy and the whole world is falling apart. I-I just don't know what to do." She sat on the floor and cried. Her arms were wrapped around her legs and her face rested on her knees like an upset child.

Sean was usually good at knowing what to say, but right now, he had nothing. For one of the first times in his life, he couldn't think of anything. He just stood there for what felt like an eternity.

Stacey got up after a few minutes. "I'm sorry, Sean. I haven't even thanked you for helping me out. I'm lucky you were there."

"Don't worry about it. I'm sure Ro—" He stopped, not wanting to bring up Rob again. "I wish I knew what was going on."

He glanced at a blanket for sale on the shelf near them. The least he could do was cover poor AJ up. He opened the package and unfolded the blanket. On it was a giant picture of a wolf. "I'll be right back. Why don't—"

"AJ was my friend too. Let me help you."

Sean nodded, and they laid the blanket over AJ's body together. "Rest well, my friend," he whispered. He wiped a tear from his eye with his sleeve and looked down at the watch Kristen had given him for Christmas last year. It was almost 9 am. His brain snapped back to Kristen and Jayden. "I think we should push forward and head into the city."

"If the city's even still there. I think I saw smoke in the distance. And no phones are working. Where are we going to go?"

Sean stood up and walked to the window. Sure enough, there was black smoke visible above the tree line in the direction of the city. "I need to get to Kristen and Jayden. And sitting here isn't helping, so

I think it's our best bet. AJ usually parks his truck out back. It's old, but it'll get us into town. Grab some water, food, and maybe a first aid kit." He walked back to the back room and stood over AJ's body. "Sorry, old buddy. I'm gonna need to borrow your keys." He took a deep breath, squatted down, and carefully moved the blanket so that he could reach AJ's pockets. The body was starting to become rigid, rigor mortis setting in. He found the keys on the first try and quickly replaced the blanket.

The truck was worn, and the inside smelled of cigarettes. As Sean got in the driver's seat, his mind wouldn't stop racing.

What's going on? How come there's nobody at all on the roadways? Even with the lockdown, surely we'd see at least one car. All the phones are down, AJ is dead, and Rob attacked his own wife. There's no explanation.

As they drove toward the city, neither spoke for a few miles. Still no other cars were on the road. They were alone. The smoke seemed to be coming from one area. As they were getting closer, Sean realized exactly where it was coming from. The military base was just outside city limits. Stacey must have been thinking the same thing.

"It's gotta be the Army Training Base," she said. "Please go check. My nephew was stationed there. I think he's on leave, b-but I don't remember."

He nodded. "Okay, but let's keep our eyes peeled. I don't have a good feeling."

Dark black smoke billowed out of a truck that was upside down in the ditch just inside the gates. The gates were smashed open, but from the inside. Like someone was trying to escape from the base. Several bodies lay on the pavement. Stacey's watery eyes darted back and forth, looking for her nephew in the carnage. Though the smoke made it hard to breathe, Sean drove slowly through the area, scanning the wreckage and bodies for any signs of life. From the blood on the pavement, it seemed as though the truck that was upside down in the ditch had run over at least some of the poor souls strewn on the ground. The tire marks showed it had been traveling away from the base.

They pulled up alongside the first building they came to. The whole base seemed abandoned. No movement or signs of life beyond them. Sean stopped the truck and turned off the engine.

"I remember now, he's not here. My nephew. His wife just had a baby. Let's go," Stacey said, sounding almost panicked again.

Sean looked at her with sympathy in his eyes.

You're getting out, aren't you?" Stacey asked in a quiet voice.

"I just want to check things out. I'll see if anyone needs help and be right back." As he reached for the door handle, his eyes caught sight of a large ratchet in the floorboard by Stacey's feet. He bent down and picked up the large, heavy tool. "Just in case." Walking to the door of the building, he heard the lock of the truck door behind him. He didn't blame her for locking it. He didn't want to be out here either. There was an eerie heaviness, like someone was increasing the pressure of the air around them, and he couldn't shake the feeling of being watched.

The door was unlocked, so he walked right in. No lights on. He found the switch and flipped it, bracing himself for a sight similar to what he saw at AJ's gas station. The electricity at least worked, but no one was there. He was in a barracks. The bunks looked as though everyone had left in a hurry. The sheets were untucked and pillows were scattered on the floor. As he walked farther, he saw what he had expected—another body. The body of a young man in his prime.

Jesus Christ. It's even getting the young, healthy ones.

Reluctantly, he bent down to get a closer look. There were dark lines running down his neck as though something black had run through his veins. The same black substance that had come out of AJ's mouth, Sean presumed.

"What the—" Sean said, jumping back. Had he just moved? Was that a breath? He lay the ratchet on the floor and checked for a pulse. "Hello, can you hear me, sir?" The man's skin was still warm but felt oddly hard to the touch, like pressing a finger into a stress ball filled with corn syrup.

The young man let out a moan in agony, rolled over, and looked up at Sean. His eyes were not cloudy like Rob's; they were black. Completely black. As if the substance that darkened his veins had flooded the entirety of his eyes.

"I'm gonna get you some help," Sean said. "It's gonna be okay." He grabbed a blanket from the bunk next to him and put it on the young man. He didn't know how he was going to get him back to the truck. He obviously was in no condition to walk.

"Get... out," the man said through labored breaths.

"Don't worry. I've got you. You're going to be just fine."

"Hurry... before they... come back."

"Before who comes back?

The young man arched his back in pain and let out a deep breath. His eyes stayed open, but he didn't breathe back in. The black substance bubbled and oozed out of the corners of his mouth and eyes.

"Stay with me, man—"

Suddenly, the sound of Stacey screaming came from outside.

He ran for the door, burst into the sunlight, and ran for the truck. There were two men flanking the vehicle. They both glanced at Sean with a look that made him almost stop in his tracks. The same look Rob had. A dark, cold, slightly dazed look. "Hey! Leave her alone! Get away from that truck!"

One of the men turned and started toward Sean. The other started pulling on the door handle. Sean's adrenaline kicked in. Time to fight. As he approached his would-be attacker, Sean didn't give him a chance to prepare for anything. He started swinging, landing multiple punches to the man's face, ear, and jaw. Continuing because his attacker was still standing and seemingly uninjured, he dropped another strike to the body out of reflex, thinking that the man would be trying to protect his head. However, the attacker remained unruffled and simply grabbed Sean by the shoulders. The grip was intense. It felt as though the bones in his upper arm may snap at any moment.

Just then, Sean heard glass shatter and Stacey scream again. Sean glanced toward her and saw that the man by the truck must have broken the window with his bare hands. They were covered with the dark, maroon blood, and he was trying to reach into the truck to unlock the door from the inside. Stacey kicked wildly at his hands. It was an older truck, and his wet, bloody hands didn't seem to be able to grip the small door lock knob to pull it up.

Sean reared back his arm and struck his attacker in the throat as hard as he could. It didn't do much, but the man's grip did loosen enough for him to break free. With a quick set of punches to the face, he once again dropped low and hit the attacker in his right kidney area. The man suddenly fell to the ground, reeling in pain.

Sean ran toward the truck and punched the other man in the back of the head. He then threw his arm around the man's neck and started choking him while dragging him back. Severe pain caught him by surprise as something smashed into the side of his head. He fell to the ground, his arms becoming heavy. As he did his best to try and stay conscious, a loud bang rang out.

A gunshot? Was I shot? No, I didn't feel anything.

One of the men fell to the concrete in front of him, dead. Deep burgundy colored blood seeped from a wound on his head. *BANG!* Another shot.

Still fighting to not lose consciousness, he saw an older man holding a rifle jog up beside the truck and speak to Stacey. He couldn't make out what he was saying as the impact to the side of his head left a ringing in his left ear. He felt hands grabbing under his armpits and trying to pull him to his feet.

"Can you move?" said the older man, his voice muffled.

"Yeah," mumbled Sean.

"Then move, son!" he said as he half carried, half dragged Sean toward a black jeep. Stacey was already in the passenger seat and turned back to help pull Sean into the back. Sean blacked out as the vehicle raced away from the base.

13

Angela

"One more block," Angela said, peeking around the corner of a building. She and Bill stood on a sidewalk, just outside the main downtown area known as, The Square. The courthouse sat in the middle of The Square. Perfectly straight streets surrounded the courthouse with buildings and businesses making up the perimeter; the police station was one of them. It was almost exactly straight across from where she now stood, barely blocked from sight by the courthouse. It felt miles away, yet touchable at the same time. A small group of three men and one woman were standing about a hundred feet to the right of the front door of the station. They walked in perfect unison, as if they were military personnel on a mission. Angela had a feeling she should steer clear of them. She was sure she could outrun the group and make it into the police station as long as she ran around the left side of the courthouse.

"We're going to have to make a run for it. Let's go!" she said, preparing for a sprint.

Before she could step out from behind the cover of the building, Bill quickly grabbed her arm and pulled her back. "Hold up, ma'am!

How do we even know if there's anyone in there who can help? For all we know, it could be a building full of these zombies!"

Angela yanked her arm loose from Bill's grip, partly annoyed that Bill was slowing her down from finding her son and partly annoyed that he was probably right. Her annoyance was almost canceled out by the comfort that he was there with her. Almost. "We don't, but it's my only chance to find my son," she said without hiding her attitude.

"Let's see if there's another route that doesn't involve running. I'm not sure you could keep up," he said jokingly, trying to ease the tension a bit.

There was no other route, and Angela knew it. She used to take Michael here every weekend to skateboard when he was younger. The police chief was an avid skateboarder and invited kids on the weekends to the area to board, mostly to keep them out of trouble.

"This is it, Will."

"Bill."

"Sorry, Bill. There's no other way."

"Then how about a distraction?" he suggested.

Angela looked at him puzzled. Her brain imagined the large man doing jumping jacks to draw attention, his beard bouncing up and down with each jump.

He must have noticed her confusion because he quickly added, "Not me. I'm not about to be the bait. I saw some bricks aways back. I was on a champion softball team years ago. I bet I can throw one through a window to the left over there, and when or if they go that way, we can get to the station."

Angela had no other option. It was worth a shot. "Okay, but hurry if you can."

Bill turned and walked quickly back in the direction they had just come from. Angela looked around the corner again and this time could only see the three men standing there. It made her a little uneasy that the woman was no longer in view. She was currently alone, standing on a sidewalk, and could no longer see one of the people she could only describe as "zombie" like. The hair stood up on her neck as she heard strange noises coming from the direction Bill had gone.

Shit! He must have gotten caught!

Frantically looking around for any place to hide, a small dumpster beside the building near her caught her attention. She would have to cross a point where she could easily be seen for a split second to make it. She had no other plan and was running out of time. If someone came up behind her, she'd be caught. If she went for the dumpster, she might be seen by the group. Checking if the coast was clear, she saw her chance and ran for it.

She didn't turn to look at the group to see if they saw her until she had squatted behind the dumpster. It seemed that they didn't, but she was second guessing her decision to hide there as she now felt pinned in place. The smell of garbage wafted into her nose. Next to her right hand, a disgusting gooey yellow liquid dripped from a hole in the dumpster and splashed on her arm. Her stomach churned. She swallowed. No time for vomit.

Spying slightly around the dumpster to look down the sidewalk where Bill had gone, she could see fairly well. Bill was now jogging back and looking around as if trying to find her.

Great! I let fear put me behind this shitty dumpster when I could have just stayed. Now I'm stuck.

As she tried to get his attention as subtly as she could, two guys stepped around a corner from another building behind him. They weren't from the group that was in the main part of The Square. It took them a second to notice Bill. He was at least fifty steps away from them, but they both turned toward him and continued their walk.

Angela had no idea what to do. Should she continue trying to get Bill's attention, risking that she too would be seen? Or should she do nothing and hope that Bill turned around in time? Partially under the dumpster was a small piece of wood that looked to have once been a part of a pallet. She grabbed it and wiggled it free. Just as she leaned around the dumpster and was ready to throw it at Bill to get his attention, their eyes met. She signaled for him to look behind him. Bill turned and noticed the guys walking in his direction.

Angela stayed where she was and continued to watch Bill. He moved away from the men and started speed walking. He burst onto the main street of The Square and turned left, toward the group that was walking together near the businesses and police station.

After he was in clear view of the three men in The Square, he let out a large yell, "Hey everybody!" He then continued to walk. He turned left again down the next sidewalk, purposely leading them away from the police station. They followed, walking slowly at first and then running as Bill moved away from The Square.

Angela couldn't believe what she was seeing. Bill was obviously sacrificing himself so she could get to the police station safely. She had just met the man, and they didn't even know if getting to the police station would help. Gratitude brought a lump to her throat. It felt like she'd swallowed a full-sized toad. Fighting back the tears that she could feel coming, she stayed crouched behind the dumpster until the entire group of three men plus the additional two had disappeared down the sidewalk.

She scanned around for the woman. She was nowhere in sight. It's now or never.

She ran. Across the street, over the grass of the courthouse, and to the front door of the police station. She pulled it open slowly and quietly went in. The station was dark. Not a soul in sight. Scared to be too loud and attract attention from anyone who would be less than eager to help, she crept around the building, pushing open each door and checking each room. No one, not a soul.

Despair began to set in, and she fell to her knees crying. She had hoped that, at the very least, Tony, the police chief, would be in. That she would have some help in finding her son. That someone would have an answer as to where he could be. And this had been the only other place she could imagine Michael going.

Get up and keep searching, dammit! Crying's not helping anything right now. He's out there. You just have to keep going!

She stood up and wiped the tears and snot from her face. Tony wasn't here, but she'd seen his car parked out front. Maybe his keys would be in his office. His personal vehicle was a sapphire blue muscle car that he always kept looking immaculate. He was always saying how it was built for power and speed. Angela went to his office and closed the door behind her. She began ripping open his desk drawers and rifling through his things, throwing useless objects and papers to the floor. Unable to find the keys, she looked frantically around the room. On a hook by the door was a denim jacket. Instinctively, she ran to it. When she got to the jacket, she reached into the pocket and felt the sharp edge of keys in her hand. "Yes!" she said with a sigh of relief.

A noise made the hair on the back of her neck stand up. The sound of the front door closing. She ran behind the desk knocking down the desk chair as she did. The loud clunk of the metal chair hitting the tile floor echoed through the otherwise quiet room. She ducked behind the desk, waiting for someone to walk through the office door any second. Very slowly, she positioned the keys in her hand so they poked out of her fist like a spike, careful not to let them produce any sound. The outline of a large man became visible behind the glass of the office door. She ducked farther behind the desk, hoping the man would continue past the office. But had he heard the chair fall? What other reason did he have going in there? The doorknob turned slowly and opened. She could only see the man's boots from below the desk. Her heart was beating fast. She prepared herself to fight and run, every inch of her ready to pounce. Her muscles tensed and her jaw tightened as the man took another step in the room.

"Angela? Are you in here?" said a familiar voice. It was Bill!

"Yes," she said, with a sigh of relief. "But I didn't find the chief or Michael. There's no one else here."

"Well I suggest we get outta here pretty quickly then. I think I lost those guys, but they might come looking."

"Right, let's go!" She stood up and shook the keys.

He nodded, his face very pleased. They jogged to the front door. Peering out, Angela could make out several figures walking in the direction of the police station.

"I think we can make it to that car if we run," she said pointing. "The blue one."

"Looks nice, but does it come in red?" Bill said with a half-smile, knowing it probably wasn't the time for jokes.

Angela gave him no time for any more comments. "Ready?" She pushed open the door hard and yelled, "Now!"

They went into a full run. The car was parallel parked just off the street, less than twenty feet from the door. She glanced to see if the figures coming up the street had seen her. They obviously had as they went from a walk to a jog.

Angela yanked open the door, jumped in, and put the key in the ignition. Bill was getting in as she noticed that the car was a manual.

"Shit!" she yelled, looking down at the floorboard toward the pedals.

"Can you drive stick?" Bill asked.

"Yeah, I just haven't for a while." Truth be told, she hadn't driven ANY car in years. Once she had opened her shop, she and her son hadn't needed one. Everything was within a short walking distance.

She pushed on the clutch and started the car. The people running up the street were getting closer, their speed frighteningly fast. There was no car behind them and they were too close to the car in front to pull out forward. With a little work, she put it in reverse and hit the gas. It stalled. "Come on, Angela!" she yelled at herself as she gave it another try. Pushing the gas hard, she sped in reverse and turned the wheel quickly. The back end ran up on the curb jarring them and putting the back end on the sidewalk. The people were almost to them. Angela put it in first and gunned it. The engine roared as the RPMs shot up before she fully released the clutch. The tires squealed, trying to catch traction. The people running toward them turned to cut them off, but Angela didn't care. As the car lurched forward, she rammed the first one with the front corner of the bumper, throwing him several feet to the side. The second dove onto the hood and held on. She slammed the break as hard as she could like she'd seen in so many of the action movies her son loved. The man slid off the hood and rolled. She hit the gas hard again before he could stand up. Angela felt the bump as the passenger front tire rolled over one of the man's legs.

The rest of the people chasing them never caught up as they sped off down the road. After a minute of driving, Bill got up the courage for comments, trying to break the tension. "So...remind me not to piss you off."

Angela didn't respond and kept her eyes on the road. She was on a mission.

"Where we going?" Bill asked, realizing that no amount of humor was going to ease the situation.

"My house," said Angela, finally. "My best chance now for finding my son is to go back there." It was hard for her to focus on anything. She just wanted her son back, and she had for sure just maimed a man in a gruesome way. She tried to rationalize that it had been a necessary thing, though thoughts that it may have been more anger than necessity lingered in the back of her mind. After another minute of silence, Angela looked over at Bill.

"Thank you, Bill. F-for what you did back there. You barely know me, yet you put your own—"

"Don't mention it," interrupted Bill.

"But I—"

"Don't mention it at all. I did what I had to do, just like you."

The clock in the car read 4:44. It was silent for the rest of the five-minute drive. They pulled up to her house and got out. The front door was still open. She had left in such a panic that she hadn't closed it. Running in, she went straight for her son's room again, yelling his name. The electricity was on. She came back down the stairs disappointed and walked to the couch to sit down, racking her brain for anywhere to look for him. The lump in her throat returned, and she tried to swallow it back.

Bill slowly walked past her and looked out the front door with a puzzled face. "Do you hear someone talking?" he asked.

Angela ran to the door and listened intently, hoping it was Michael and his friend. After a moment, she knew exactly where it was coming from. "C'mon!" she said, running across the street toward a neighbor's house.

14

Sean

"So what the hell are you two doing around the base? You got a death wish or something?" the old man asked Sean, as he drove his off-road vehicle away from the base. The smoke wasn't visible in the distance past the trees. The old man was short and stocky with a head full of gray hair and a braided goatee beard that extended three inches past the collar of his t-shirt. He had a gruff appearance but was well-groomed. Even the fingernails of his hands were well kept.

Sean was checking the lumps forming on his head. Besides some scratches on his arms, he didn't seem to be bleeding, but he could feel a headache coming on.

Stacey spoke up. "I had a nephew that was stationed there. We went to look for him. Then Sean wanted to check and see if anyone needed any help."

"Help? Ha! The whole damn world's gone mad. Not a lot any-one can do to help as far as I see it. Best thing to do is look out for yourself."

Sean spoke up, "Is that what you were doing at the base? Looking out for yourself?"

"Shoot, I saw you two lunatics driving toward the base and thought you were gonna steal all the rations for yourselves. Had to do something. A man's gotta eat ya know," the old man said with a wink. "The name's Rusty, but most people call me Sarge," he said, reaching his arm to the back seat to shake hands with Sean.

"Sean."

"Stacey."

"Pleased to me ya. Wish it was on better terms, but gotta admit it's good to see two actual humans who made it." Sarge turned down a dirt road that led off toward the woods.

"Humans?" asked Sean, puzzled at the expression.

"Yeah, everyone seems to be acting like machines! No expressions, strong as hell, and they don't seem to feel any pain. Doesn't sound like any human to me."

Stacey interrupted, pointing at the road, "Where are you taking us?"

"I have a cabin out here. No humans ... or machines for miles. It's just up the trail here. Ol' Dawn," he tapped the dashboard of his vehicle, "will get us there in a jiffy. We'll be safe there for a bit."

Stacey looked back at Sean, obviously worried that this stranger was taking them into the woods to his cabin.

Sean mouthed, "It's okay," trying to ease her mind. He didn't know how much he trusted Sarge either, but he had saved them, and a short rest and some ice wouldn't hurt.

"Here we are!" said Sarge as they pulled through a patch of trees and into a clearing. In front of them was a small log cabin. It looked old but well kept. What appeared to be a garage was behind it, a little more set back into the woods. The garage was larger than the cabin itself.

They pulled up near the cabin and parked. As they all got out, Sean could see an old army vehicle through the open door of the garage. He glanced at his watch. 10:15am. The air was warm with a slight breeze that made the large trees that surrounded the property sway slowly back and forth. Leaves rustled; Sean shivered.

"Come on in. Make yourself at home," Sarge said, opening the cabin door and walking in.

Sean and Stacey followed close behind. The inside was clean and well kept. Sean thought to himself that, in another life, this would make a good *Airbnb*. A remote cabin, secluded from the rat-race of life. The only thing wrong with it was the smell. It smelled of cigars and wood. There were boards with hinges on the windows that locked into place. Sarge went around lifting each board and letting in light.

"Thank you so much, sir, for everything. We don't want to overstay our welcome. Just give us a few minutes to rest, and we'll be on our way," said Sean.

"None of that 'sir' crap. I got enough of that back in the Marines. And stay as long as you need. I got more than enough space to share. Y'all want some grub?"

"Yes, please!" Stacey blurted out.

Sean nodded. Sarge walked toward an old refrigerator and grabbed a container from the top shelf. Then he got out two plates and scooped out cold beans from the container. He handed one to each of them. "I'm afraid you'll have to share a spoon. I only have one. I don't get much company 'round here."

"Thank you so much," Stacey said.

Sean and Stacey sat on an old, worn futon. Sean struggled to keep his eyes open. Sleep seemed to want to drag him down against his will. He closed his eyes for a moment, allowing himself to lean back against the futon.

Sean woke up to the slam of the front door. His eyes flashed open.

"How long have I been out?" he asked Sarge, who must have just come in from outside.

"A couple hours. You needed your beauty rest after that scuffle you were in."

"A couple hours," Sean said to himself. He glanced at his watch again. It was a quarter after four. He tried not to panic. Getting to Kristen soon was important, and he'd just slept for about six hours.

His head was throbbing but feeling much better. "You've already done so much for us, so I hate to ask, but do you happen to have another vehicle we can borrow to get into the city?"

"Why, I'm going in this evening. Gotta find some rations. I can take you there."

It wasn't the answer Sean was hoping for. "I really need to get there sooner rather than later. My girlfriend and her young brother live in the city, and I haven't been able to get ahold of them."

"Say no more! I got ya covered! I was going to wait until near dark, but I guess there's no time like the present! Let me load some stuff up, and we can leave in a bit."

Sean felt a huge temporary relief, but with every passing minute, he felt more and more anxiety about how Kristen was doing. Sarge seemed like a good guy, and his experience from the military would probably help out as they went into the city.

Out of the corner of his eye, he caught a glimpse of Stacey. She had tears gathering in her eyes. Sarge didn't notice as he walked past her and went out the front door.

"How you holding up, Stacey?" Sean asked in a sympathetic voice. She didn't respond at first, so Sean moved closer to her and the futon. He put his arm around her as she started to sob.

She spoke between breaths. "What's—going to happen—to Rob? I don't know where he's at. Or if he's okay. I don't know if he'll ever be okay again."

Sean didn't know what to say. Being at a loss for words seemed to be happening more frequently. As a lawyer, he relied on thinking fast and coming up with solutions, but what could he do? This was a terrible situation with no sign of cause or resolution. The two just sat there for several minutes in silence.

Sarge's gruff voice broke the silence as he came back in. "Y'all ready? I'm all loaded up!"

Stacey wiped her eyes as they both stood up.

"I've got some jerky for the road," said Sarge, holding up a very used plastic storage bag with beef jerky in it.

Stacey rode in the back seat while Sean was in the front with Sarge. Instead of going back the direction they came in, Sarge turned his vehicle toward a trail behind the cabin. "Short cut," he said with a wink.

15

Sean

The drive into the city took only twenty minutes. Sarge talked pretty much the whole time. Mostly comments about how he believed people had been taken over by machines and how he thought the government must be responsible. Sean tried to listen, but his thoughts weren't focused on what was going on but on how he was going to get to Kristen and Jayden. It was getting later into the afternoon now, and every passing second felt like eternity.

Sarge went silent for a few moments, just a long enough pause to break Sean's thoughts and get his attention. Then, as if he had come to a sudden realization, he said, "I think I may have an idea what's going on 'round here. Back in the Marines, there were rumors the higher ups had been working with secret psychic technology for years."

"Oh yeah?" said Stacey, more than a hint of doubt in her voice.

"Yes, ma'am! All the classified shit they keep hidden from civilians. It makes sense. They have to be controlling these people somehow, though 'til now, I never really took much stock in that stuff myself."

Sean and Stacey exchanged glances of disbelief but didn't say anything.

"Heck, I even heard the psychic stuff stretched into different countries' governments," he continued. "Who knows? It's the only thing that makes a lick of sense. Some sort of mind control technology or something."

Sean didn't say it out loud, but with all the weird stuff that had been happening, he had to admit that anything could be a possibility. All these people seemed to be possessed by something. The looks in their eyes, the superhuman strength. Nothing really made sense.

Seeing their turn coming up, he pointed it out. "Turn right up here," Sean said. "It's just two blocks down the street."

Sean didn't wait for the jeep to fully stop as they neared the house. He jumped out and hit the ground running. There was no truck in the driveway.

Please be home! Please be here! Oh God, please be here!

He got to the front door and knocked eagerly. Impatient for an answer, he ran through the gate on the side to the back yard and unlocked the back door.

"Kristen? Kristen, it's me! Are you home? Jayden?" He frantically searched each room. Adrenaline pumping through his veins as he ran desperately through the empty house. Defeated, he made it back to the kitchen. Stacey and Sarge were walking in the back door. Stacey's eyes showed her sympathy, a reaction from Sean's disappointed face.

"I'm sorry, Sean," she said in a comforting voice.

"I don't know... What—" Sean started but quickly stopped. He thought he had heard something outside. A tiny, familiar whisper in the wind. "Shhh! Listen." He walked out the back door and stood still, listening.

"Sean," said a small voice.

Sean scanned the entire yard looking for the source of the voice. "Jayden! Where are you?"

"Up here."

Sean's eyes stopped on the large oak tree near the back fence line. Clinging to a large branch and peeking out from behind it was the young boy. He slid down as Sean ran to him. Jayden latched onto Sean's waist like a magnet to a fridge.

"Where's Kristen?" Sean asked.

Jayden looked down at his feet, a sad expression on his face. "Someone was running down the street yelling. She went to go help him. He looked real sick. She came back and told me to stay here while she took him to get help. She said to wait for her here and play on my tablet. And I did. A while after she drove away, some guys came to the door, but I didn't answer, just like you taught me. I peeked out the window and their eyes looked funny. So I hid until they left. Then I climbed the tree. She didn't come back. Should I have gone to find her?"

"No, buddy. You did great. Did Kristen happen to say where she was going?"

"No, she just said she was helping the sick man."

Sean was silent for a few seconds, trying to think.

If she needed to help someone who was sick, where would she go? Not the hospital. Probably the university.

She was studying for her doctorate in medicine and had plenty of supplies there. Jayden stayed close to Sean, eyeing the two adults standing near the house. Sean noticed his discomfort.

"These are some friends of mine," Sean said. "This is Sarge, and you remember Stacey, right? She's my neighbor, the one that made those homemade donuts for us a couple weekends ago."

"Hi," Jayden said, being a bit more shy than usual. He continued to stand behind Sean, peeking out at the other adults.

"Pleased to meet you," said Sarge as he touched the tip of his old cap. "How old are you?"

Jayden glanced up at Sean as if to ask if it was alright that he talk to this stranger. Sean gave him a small nod.

"Almost nine," Jayden replied, looking down at the grass.

"Hi, Jayden," Stacey said with a calming, motherly tone. "Why don't you grab some clothes and pack anything you want to take with us? I think we'll be leaving soon to go find your sister." She looked at Sean who gave her a nod.

With a small pat of approval from Sean, the young boy shuffled off into the house, watching Sean the whole way in.

"I'm going to help him out," Stacey said, following him in.

Sarge looked at Sean. "I'm sorry about your girl, son. How do you want to play this from here?"

"We need to go to the university. She's most likely there."

"Odd place to go, but in that case, I think I'm gonna grab a bag from ol' Dawn and take some supplies for us from here if that's alright."

"Grab whatever you need."

As Sarge walked away, Sean went inside and stood in the kitchen. After a minute, Sarge returned with an old duffle bag.

"Beautiful house. Plenty of room for a young boy to grow up into a man," Sarge said, breaking the silence. "Is this your house too, or is it just the little man and your girl?"

"I don't live here, just them. Their dad passed away a few years back. Kristen's been raising him ever since."

"Every young boy needs a man to look up to. With a guy like you in his life, I think he's got a good one. He seems to be comfortable with you too."

"He's a good kid. Hard working, stubborn as hell, and mostly respectful. Pretty much all you can want from a kid," Sean said, looking at the floor. He thought for a tough and rough guy, Sarge was surprisingly comforting to talk to.

Jayden came running up with a small backpack, Stacey right behind.

"Where are we going, Sean? Do you think Kristen's okay? Will we find her?" he asked.

Sean put his hand on Jayden's shoulders and squatted down to look into his big brown eyes. "I think she's just fine. We're going to the university to check there for her." Sean glanced up at Stacey.

Her eyes started to look glassy, and she sniffed back any tears.

"Why don't you go wait in the living room with Stacey. I'm going to help Sarge grab some things, and I'll be there in a minute. Then we can go."

After Jayden and Stacey were out of the room, Sarge turned back from grabbing food out of the pantry. "If you don't mind me asking, are you and his sister serious?"

Sean reached into his pocket and pulled something out. "Yeah. I've been carrying this thing in my pocket for weeks. Waiting for the right time to pop the question." He showed Sarge a silver ring with a blue stone in the middle.

Sarge looked at Sean sympathetically. "We better make sure that can still happen. I'll go wait outside. Take your time, son." He picked up the now full duffle bag and walked out, leaving Sean standing in the kitchen alone.

He looked around the vacant room. He knew Kristen was okay. She had to be. He could feel it. But looking around the energy-less room, it weirdly felt as though this would be the last time he would ever be here. Though he had hope, he felt that when he left, it would be like losing a piece of Kristen somehow. He took a couple of deep breaths and shook back the tears starting to form.

She's alright. She's the strongest woman I've ever met. She's gotta be okay.

Just in case she made it back home, he wanted to leave a note. He found the note he had left her earlier and flipped it over to write:

"Kristen, Jayden is with me. We are going out to look for you. If you get this, please stay here and be careful. You two are the only things that matter in my life. Know that I will keep Jayden safe no matter what. I love you with all of my soul. Love, Sean."

He took one final look around and went to the living room to get Stacey and Jayden. "I think we're ready," he said, helping Jayden with his backpack. They walked outside to find Sarge already in the vehicle waiting to begin the drive to the university.

"Let's go," Sean said. "I'll lead you there."

16

Angela

Angela hadn't even thought of her neighbor Donald during all this. Who better to help in a crazy situation like this than the crazy man who was constantly preparing for the 'end of days'? He lived a couple of houses away on the other side of the street.

Angela ran straight up to his garage door, Bill following slowly behind. She could hear talk coming from a speaker inside the garage. Probably a radio. Without thinking, she slammed her fist several times against the aluminum door. Immediate regret washed over her. What if he was zombified too?

Screw it. It's too late now. Might as well see if he's home.

"Donald, it's Angela from across the street. Are you in there?" she yelled, holding her breath and listening.

The talking suddenly went silent, but there was no answer. Maybe he was contemplating if she was trustworthy or not. No time to wait. She left Bill standing there and impatiently ran to the front door. She was about to slam her fist on it as well when it ripped open. Out poked a rifle, aimed directly at Angela's chest.

"Woah, woah, woah!" she exclaimed. "It's just me! It's just me!"

Donald stood in the doorway eyeing Angela's face. He was a shorter, skinny man with a pale complexion. The hair he had left was jet black, and his beard was sparse and patchy on his cheeks. Squinting at her, his face softened, and he looked around as if to see if they were being watched.

"Get in here, quick," he said. He raised his gun again, but this time at Bill, who was walking up behind Angela.

"He's with me," Angela said quickly.

Donald lowered his weapon, squinted at Bill, and motioned with his head for him to come in too. He quickly closed the door after they were in and locked three separate locks from the inside.

"Donald, this is Bill. Bill, Donald," Angela introduced them in a hurry.

"Sit down, sit down. It's good to see other real people," Donald said with a half-smile.

"Real people?" Angela said, hoping he knew what was going on.

"Yeah, since all this started, everybody's been taken over like some robots. I don't know how they did it. The water, a signal in the phones, or maybe some kind of microchips or nanobots in the food."

Bill rolled his eyes. Angela saw him and motioned for him to stop.

"Okay," he mouthed at her.

"Y'all want some water?" asked Donald.

"Sure," said Angela quickly.

Donald walked to the kitchen, and Angela quickly moved right next to Bill. "I know this guy seems nuts, but he has a ham radio in the garage. I've seen it before, and that must be where the noise was coming from. It's the only way we have to communicate with the outside world since everything else is down. We have to play along. Maybe he knows what's going on."

"Okay, I get it. I'll play along," Bill said, putting his hands up like he surrendered to the situation.

Donald came back into the room and handed them both glasses with water.

"Caught and filtered that water myself. Can't trust that city water with all those chemicals and who knows what else in it."

Angela nodded and took a sip. Bill eyeballed his and slowly set it down on the living room coffee table.

"Donald, do you know what's going on out there?" Angela asked.

His eyes lit up like she'd told him he just won the lottery. "Oh yeah! I've been on the radio non-stop since shit hit the fan. Pardon my language. Come on!" He got up and led them to his garage. It was well lit but humid and smelled of body odor and mildew. Donald sat down at a chair in front of a large radio hooked to even larger speakers. "I came and listened some more just before you got here to see if there was anything new. I'm about to pack this up and get out of here. I'm licensed to operate this radio, so you know they have my location."

"They?" Bill asked in a semi-sarcastic voice.

Donald didn't catch the question. He turned the radio on. Angela could hear chatter from several people speaking back and forth. Her eyes rested on a notepad full of writing. She couldn't read much because the penmanship was so poor.

"So when this all started," Donald finally continued, "and the cell towers and lines went down, I got straight in here and got on the horn. We have people all over the area. Here's what we know. There are groups of these different robot people doing different things. Some are building stuff, some are taking apart machines, and some are capturing us humans and taking them somewhere. There's even talk of them grabbing kids."

"Kids? Do you know where they're taking them?" asked Angela, more worried yet hopeful that she could have new information.

"Well I don't know for sure. Some type of gathering place. These radios can't reach but a few miles, but I heard from the relay that the closest one to us is probably 'bout a hundred miles east of here. In some hospital off the interstate."

"A hospital?"

"Yeah. I don't know what they're doing there, but it can't be good. They say that they only see robots leave the hospital. No humans."

"And they're taking kids there too?"

"Sorry, couldn't tell you. Just know they're taking people there."

Angela's thoughts went to a dark place. If anyone laid a hand on her son, they were going to pay. "Okay...uh, thank you, Donald!" Angela said, turning to leave. "Let's go, Bill."

"Hold on now, you ain't thinking of going to that hospital are you? You'd have to be out of your mind!" Donald said, standing up. "From what I hear, that place is crawling with those robot people."

"I don't care. My son might be there."

"Oh. Well I don't mean to sound unsympathetic, but from what I can tell, everyone who gets caught is either dead or stuck in one of those gathering places where no human comes out. So your son ..."

Angela held up a hand. She didn't even want him to finish the thought. "My son is okay. He has to be. Or I'll kill every last one of those zombies." Her body tensed and her heart began to race. She was left with a shaky and slightly dizzy feeling. Her fists were clenched as she continued to think of what she'd do if someone hurt Michael.

"Ha! I knew I liked you," Donald said with a big smile. "But if you're taking on those robots, you better take some stuff for protection. I'll be right back." He ran back into the house excitedly.

"Angela, do you really think we can get into a building full of these zombie people and search for your son?" asked Bill, deep concern in his voice.

"I'm going to try. You don't have to come, but I do..." her voice trailed off, then turning to look Bill in the eyes, she asked, "Do you have any kids?"

"Just one. All grown up. Moved to Germany to go to school last year."

"And what would you do for your kid?"

Bill looked at her with a half-smile. "I get it, Angela. I'm with you. I don't like it, but I'm with you. Let's go get your son back."

"Thank you, Bill."

Donald came back holding a large black duffle bag. "I can't give you all my guns, but I can spare a few and some ammo. Let me walk you through how to use them." He sat down the bag and pulled out three pistols and a large box full of different ammunition types divided in sections. He gave them both a quick tutorial of how to load and shoot the weapons and placed the guns and ammo back in the bag. "Be careful out there," he said, "and good luck. I hope you find your son. He was always kind to me...even when others weren't."

"Thanks, Donald."

Bill picked up the bag, and he and Angela left. The clicks of Donald securing three bolts to lock himself in sounded so final. If Bill hadn't been standing next to her, it would have felt alienating to Angela. Like she was all alone. But she wasn't all alone. She had Bill. She didn't know him very well, but her trust in him was growing. In a time of so much distress, he was her anchor to humanity.

As they were walking back toward her house, they heard several trucks coming up the street.

"Hurry! Get inside!" Angela yelled, bolting toward her front door. Bill barely made it in as two trucks pulled up in front of

Angela's house and stopped. The hair on the back of her neck stood up as she braced and listened. The doors of the trucks slammed shut. Then, nothing. Not a sound.

17

Sean

The university was just several miles away. Cars dotted the shoulders of the streets, but no other drivers could be seen.

"Does it almost seem as though the roads have been cleared?" asked Stacey from the back seat.

"I was just thinkin' the same thing," said Sarge, looking through squinted eyes as they drove. "Looks like all the cars have been pushed outta the way."

The sun was starting to dip behind the buildings as night approached, the shadows from the buildings slowly devouring the road ahead.

"Turn right up here and go through the parking lot," Sean suddenly said excitedly. "It's that building in the back." His own voice raised his mild, nagging headache from a three to a five, and he felt at times as though he had trouble focusing. But as they neared the building, his mind cleared, making it as sharp as ever. "Stop! Look!" he blurted out, pointing at a small group of people walking away from them between two buildings. After what had gone down at the military base and with Stacey's husband, Rob, Sean was suspicious of everyone who wasn't currently with him.

Sarge must have been on the same page because he slowed down quickly and parked in the closest spot he could find. "I don't think they saw us," he said, shutting off the engine. "Looks like we'll have to walk from here."

As more and more daylight disappeared behind the buildings, the street lights in the parking lots started to come on. The four sat in silence for a minute, watching for any movement, then Sarge spoke up.

"The parking lot is sparse, but the shadows from these lights and cars can give us some cover to get in. Now I don't have any clue who or what's in the building or where to even start looking for somebody. So Sean, that part's up to you." Sarge made a motion with his head toward Stacey and Jayden in the back seat. "I think it's best if the young man stays here and looks after Miss Stacey." He winked at Jayden.

"No, Sean! I want to stay with you!" Jayden's panicky voice squeaked.

Sean stared at Jayden. In the soft light, he could see Jayden's eyes glistening. And though he didn't want to let him out of his sight, he knew there was no other way. "No, Jayden, you'll be safer in the car with Stacey. Don't worry, we'll be back. I NEED you to stay here. Promise me."

Jayden crossed his arms and slammed himself back in the seat. "Fine!" he yelled looking out the window.

"Jayden. Promise me."

Jayden looked down, back at Sean, and then whispered, "Okay. I promise."

"Thanks, Jayden," Sean said softly then held out a fist. "Trust?"

"Trust." He gave Sean a hard fist bump, still angry about having to stay behind.

"Do you know how to use this?" Sarge asked Stacey, drawing a pistol from under the seat.

Stacey took the pistol and gave Sarge a nod. "I've put more marks in an X than anyone you've probably ever met," she said with a hint of playful disdain. "Sir," she added with a smile.

A large smile spread across Sarge's gruff face. "Well, ma'am, I'll leave you to it. Here's the keys," Sarge said, handing Stacey the keys to Ol' Dawn. "Treat 'er well."

"We'll stay right here," Stacey said, turning to face Sean. She looked deep into his eyes before continuing. "I'll keep Jayden safe until you get back."

She had never had kids of her own, but Sean knew her well. She would treat Jayden like he was her own offspring. A surrogate mother hen. It gave him a small amount of confidence that Jayden was safe for now.

After one long look around, Sarge and Sean quietly opened their doors and stepped out. Staying low, they carefully pushed the doors shut with a barely audible click and met at the back of the vehicle

"Stay down and stick to the shadows. We'll have to be each other's eyes," whispered Sarge.

Sean nodded. Crouching, they went one at a time from car to car through the parking lot toward the building, giving each other waves forward as one would watch for the other. They met together at the last vehicle near the entrance to the building Kristen worked in. Sarge held up a fist for Sean not to move and pointed toward the front door. As Sean froze, he saw a man exit the building and start walking toward the next building on the right. Sean could recognize him even with the increasing lack of daylight. It was someone that Kristen worked with. David or Daniel or something. He never liked the guy. His creepy vibe had made Kristen uncomfortable on more than one occasion. But Sean was happy to see him. It gave him a hope that he would find Kristen here. Though he didn't want to think what they might have done to her if they caught her.

The two men stayed beside the car, not moving, just watching the man as he entered the next building.

"So what's next?" whispered Sarge. "Do we bust in the front door guns blazing or find a way in unnoticed?"

Sarge was of course kidding about the 'guns blazing' part, or at least Sean thought he was. Sean thought for a few seconds before speaking. "Kristen leaves the second window from the left in her department's office partially unlocked in case she needs to come in on the weekends."

Kristen was always trying to get extra research hours in. Besides Jayden, medical research was her passion. Her main purpose and meaning in life. Most rooms inside required a badge swipe to get in, but access to the building was restricted to all on the weekends. So she'd rigged the window so only she could get in whenever she wanted.

Sean pointed to the left side of the building. Sarge pulled a pistol from a holster hidden in his waistband. With a nod of his head, he motioned for Sean to lead the way. The two had another look around and charged in behind the tall bushes that ran alongside the building. They made their way around and to the second window.

Sean suddenly felt dizzy, sat down, leaned against the wall, and closed his eyes.

"You good, son?" Sarge asked.

"Yeah, just some concussion symptoms from earlier, I guess. I'll be fine." He shook it off and stood up, immediately fiddling with a thin metal wire at the bottom corner of the window. "So Sarge, tell me the truth. Are you enjoying yourself right now?" The older man seemed more alive than before, his green eyes alight with the fire of youth.

Sarge smiled. "Just like old times for me. I'd be lying if I said it didn't feel good to be on a mission right now. But what are you doing? Is it locked?"

"No, Kristen rigged it to not just open. She didn't want people to be able to break in easily. This wire needs to be untwisted, and then it should pop open. I've only seen her do it a couple times, so it might take me a second." Continuing to fool with it for a minute, the wire slipped out into Sean's hand. "Got it!" Sean carefully lifted the window, hoping the screech it made wouldn't alert anyone. The lights were on in the room, but no one was there. "C'mon," he said, crawling through the open window.

Sarge followed, and though he was much older, he moved like a twenty-year-old, effortlessly sliding through the window frame. The room was mostly open. It was originally set up as a lobby of sorts, but had been used by Kristen and several of her co-workers as a makeshift office for several years now. The university had plans to redesign it and turn it into multiple rooms in the future, but so far no construction had begun. It had open doorways on two sides. The main entrance to the building and the stairs to the second floor were to the right, through a doorway in the next room over. Through the doorway to the left, there was a hallway that led to classrooms and more offices. There were four desks lining one wall and some old benches bolted to the floor in the middle of the room. Cream colored filing cabinets lined much of the wall with the window.

Sean and Sarge made their way to a desk on the other side of the room. Kristen's desk. Sarge kept a lookout as Sean searched the desk. He wanted to find anything that would let him know that Kristen was there.

Come on, anything, please. Just let me know she's okay.

His eyes stopped on the small picture frame on the corner. He picked it up and stared at it. It was a picture of Kristen, Jayden, and himself when they had gone camping last October, almost a year ago now. He couldn't help but think that life would never be the same again. What he wouldn't give to just have Kristen back safe in his arms. He looked up and saw Sarge staring at him with that same soft sympathetic look from before. It snapped him out of his pitiful stupor, and he continued searching the desk.

"Someone's coming," whispered Sarge, slinking behind the desk next to Sean.

Sean positioned himself as low as he could. With the desks being so close together, no one would be able to see him unless they walked behind the desk by the wall. As he crouched down and watched, Sean was able to see the legs of someone enter the room and walk right past the desk, heading in the direction of the hallway. Their footsteps were light and quiet.

Instead of watching the legs go by, something across the room grabbed his attention like a slap to the face. On the floor next to some benches in the middle of the large room was a small green backpack. He smiled. It was the bag he had bought for Kristen so she would have a place to put her phone and keys and stop losing them.

She's here!

As soon as the person walking disappeared through the doorway, Sean jumped up and ran to it, not even checking for any other visitors. Unzipping the bag and rooting around, he pulled out her phone. Fishing around more, he brought it back to the desk and dumped out the contents.

"No keys," he whispered, "but she's definitely been here."

"What's next?" asked Sarge, looking around in a paranoid manner, his eyes less youthful than before. They now darted back and forth, watching both entrances to the room like two prison spotlights trying to find an escapee. "Don't want to be pushy, but we're kinda out in the open right now."

Sean hadn't even been paying attention. He had been so excited about the prospect of Kristen being near that he had completely forgotten they didn't want to be seen.

"I guess we'll have to look around. All the offices and classrooms are here on the first floor. The labs are up on the second. I'll check up there if you want to look around down here." He picked up Kristen's picture. "This is her. We can meet back here."

After looking at the picture, Sarge glanced up at Sean and put a strong hand on his shoulder. "Now that looks like a good family. No matter what happens, son, just remember that the good memories are what life's all about. Hold 'em close and don't let 'em go. Life's bound to change, but you've always got the memories. No one can take those away." Then he gave Sean a nod and started off down the hallways toward the classrooms. He held his pistol in front of his stomach, elbows bent, pointing it outward.

Sean partly wished he had a weapon, though he didn't really want to have to hurt anyone. He took a deep breath and turned the opposite direction toward the stairs to the second floor.

18

Angela

Angela looked at Bill, who was slowly inching toward the blinds to look outside at the two trucks. A million things ran through her brain. She wasn't scared for herself. She was scared of what might happen to her son if something happened to her. If she got captured, she might never be able to find him. If she was killed, no one would come for him.

No. I'm going to survive. No matter what, these S-O-Bs aren't taking me. I'll make it to you Michael, I promise.

Then she remembered the duffle bag from Donald. Bill had dropped the bag the second he made it inside the door. She unzipped it and grabbed the first weapon she could find. She didn't keep any guns in her house, but one of her ex-boyfriends had taken her to the gun range multiple times. She could shoot well. Very well. Never in a million years did she think that one day she would be holding a gun and thinking about using it on another human. To Hell with anyone who got in her way. She was getting her son back by any means necessary.

Bill was staring out of the blinds through a small gap he made using his fingers. Angela walked up to the window next to him and peeked out the same way. There were multiple men that had come out of the two vehicles, but it was not her house they seemed interested in. It was Donald's.

"Should we warn him?" asked Bill quietly.

"I'm sure he knows. And how can we do that without letting them know we're here? There are so many of them."

"Yeah, I count eight, and I guess you're right. But we have to do something."

They heard a loud knocking come from across the street, and they both looked outside. Most of the men were standing in front of Donald's house. One of them was at the front door looking like a salesman politely waiting for someone to come open it. Another one was walking toward a window on the side. They obviously knew someone was home. Like Angela, it was probably from the radio sounds coming from the garage. The group looked intent on entering.

Bill and Angela both jumped when a loud bang rang through the air. The man near the window fell, dead before his body hit the grass. Another shot rang out, and the man by the front door went down. The rest of the men seemed unintimidated and moved toward the house. Some went at the front, and the others split and went around the sides.

More shots, more bodies. Then a loud pop came from Angela's TV as a stray bullet must have gone through the front wall of her house where it hung.

"Get down!" yelled Bill, grabbing Angela and pulling her to the floor with him. They army crawled toward the kitchen so that there was at least another wall between them and any other stray bullets. Sitting with their backs against her kitchen island, they listened for any indication of how the battle outside was going. Silence. No more shots fired.

"Do you think he got all of them?" asked Bill, breathing heavily like he'd run a mile to get to the kitchen.

"Or...they got him," Angela quietly replied.

Still crawling, they made their way to the blinds of the living room window and looked out again. There were several men on the ground. The two that Angela had seen go down and three more that had tried to go around the side of the house. There was no movement whatsoever, but she dared not move her eyes from Donald's house. The shadow of someone inside walked past his front window and moved in the direction of the front door.

Come on, Donald. Tell me your crazy ass made it.

She didn't blink. The door knob twisted and out stepped Donald. Angela let out a yip of relief followed by a gasp of worry. He was holding the left side of his head and didn't look to be in good shape. Bill ran to the front door and was about to rip it open when Angela yelled.

"Wait! They're still there!"

Bill looked like there was an internal battle going on inside him. An invisible hand keeping his own hand on the doorknob and Angela's voice, a lasso holding him back. He let go of the knob and came back to the window with Angela. Donald was stumbling toward his truck parked in the grass on the right side of the house while two men came up the left side.

"We have to help him!" Bill went for the door again.

"No. Bill, wait! Please!" Angela's desperate shriek held him in place. She wanted to help Donald as much as Bill, but how could she without putting herself at risk, therefore putting Michael at risk? "I have to get to my son, please!"

"Get back, you son of a bitch!" Donald screamed from across the street. "You motherfuckers ain't taking me nowhere!"

Angela looked back outside in time to see one of the men raise an object and point it at Donald. It wasn't a gun. She really had no idea what it was. It was small, black, and kind of reminded her of a taser or a fat remote control. There was no flash, no loud bang, only the sound similar to the ringing your ears hear when an old TV turns on after it has been off for some time. Donald's body went limp as a mist of red sprayed from his back, and he dropped to the ground. Angela couldn't tell if she screamed. If she had, maybe it didn't escape her mouth. She felt sick. She wanted to shout, fight, run, throw up, and cry all at the same time. She wanted to run outside, guns in both hands, firing like a cartoon cowboy in all directions.

Bill said nothing as they both watched. His face showed regret. No tears but anger and remorse mixed into a grimace beneath his long shaggy beard.

One of the men turned and walked back toward the truck they had come in and got inside. The other two went inside the house. The driver then pulled the truck into the driveway in front of the garage door of Donald's house. After a minute, someone opened the garage door from inside. They then proceeded to remove random equipment from the house. Including Donald's ham radio.

"He was right," Bill whispered. "They did know he had the radio, and they came for it. But why?"

When they had packed up all they wanted, they left all five of their dead comrades behind and drove off back toward where they had come from. Neither Angela nor Bill spoke for several minutes. They both just stood where they were. Angela could see Donald's lifeless body lying on the grass near his truck. She kept watching, barely breathing, conscious of his death but hoping for his chest to rise, desperate for a sign of life. Some indication that what she had just witnessed hadn't happened.

After a few more minutes, Bill spoke quietly and calmly. "Stay here, Angela. I'm going over there." He carefully took the gun from Angela's hand and left.

Angela continued to watch as Bill cautiously made his way over to Donald's body. He stopped next to Donald and squatted near his head, pulling off his cap and putting it over his heart, his head bowed in reverence. Angela couldn't stand to watch anymore. She felt nauseated and feverish. Her heart pushed into her throat, and she sank to the floor, sobbing.

Bill returned through the front door some time later. Without a word, he walked over and sat down beside her. He put his arm around her shoulders as if to offer a hug. She fell into his large arms and wept louder, her sobs drowning out the extreme silence that was now an ever-present reminder of the loneliness that they were facing.

He awkwardly held her for a few minutes until she sat up and spoke. "We could have ... I could have helped him. Why didn't I just do something? Now he's dead because of me!"

Bill's face showed a powerful sympathy. The look alone made her feel a comfort otherwise impossible in the situation. Staring into her eyes, he spoke with a gentle voice.

"Angela, let me tell you about my father. He was a great man. Kind, honest, and hardworking. He worked as a mechanic for most of his life, and though we didn't have much in the way of money, he still would go out of his way to help those around him in whatever way he could. He loved me, my sister, and my mother with a fierceness that no one could put into words. One day, he and I had a big argument over him lending money to one of my lazy uncles. You see, I wanted a pair of new jeans instead of the ones I always had to get at the secondhand store. I didn't understand why we didn't have money for new jeans, but we had enough to just give it away. I ended up telling him that he didn't really love me. You know, teenager stuff. Anyway, after a while, my mother came and sat on the corner of my bed and said this: 'William, your father is the kind of man who would sacrifice just about anything to help someone out. He would kick down the door of a stranger and risk his very life to pull them out of a fire. But...I also know he would let the whole world and everyone in it burn if it meant saving us.' And I know that she was right. He would help everyone out if he could. But if it came down to them or us...he would always choose us."

He paused for a moment and looked directly into Angela's eyes, a hint of a smile bringing several wrinkles next to his eyes. "And you, Angela, had to make a choice. You had to decide if you would risk losing your son to save someone else or if you would sacrifice another for the chance to save your son. I personally think you have no blame. Loving your son above everyone else is what being a great mom is all about. In this life, we do what we have to for those we love."

Angela nodded, wiped her eyes, and softly whispered, "Thank you." Her gratitude for Bill increased the longer he was around. This man was much like his father. Kind and willing to help a stranger like her do the impossible.

Bill gave a small nod of his own and leaned back against the wall, resting his clumsy arm on the end table next to him. The lamp on it wobbled and nearly tipped over. He grabbed it just in time to keep it from falling. "Whoops."

Angela slowly stood up, continuing to wipe her eyes. She glanced out the window. It was late afternoon. It would be dark soon. Bill must have moved Donald's body, as it was no longer on the grass where he had fallen.

"It's getting late. There's no sense in getting on the road now. I think a car going down the road with lights on will stick out like a sore thumb. Are you hungry?"

Bill looked down, grabbed his belly with both hands, gave it a little shake, and said, "I'm a big guy. I'm always hungry."

"Good, the electricity is on, and I've got some leftovers in the fridge that need eaten. If we stay in the kitchen, no one should see any lights if they drive by. Then I can make up the couch for you to sleep on. I'd like to leave as soon as we can for this hospital gathering place first thing in the morning."

19

Sean

Sean's heart was beating out of control. He could feel it in his ears. The fast rhythmic thump of anticipation, mixed with fear and cautiousness. His headache was only noticeable when he focused on it, but his current mission occupied all of his thoughts. His eyes searched back and forth for any sign of movement. His ears listened for voices or footsteps other than his.

As he approached the stairs, he leaned forward and looked up. No one seemed to be on the stairs coming down. He suddenly wished that he had taken the service stairs instead of the large main stairs in the lobby, but he was here now. Holding the rail, he silently started up toward the second floor.

The main stairs emptied into the hallway for the labs. With lab rooms both to the left and right of the stairs, he had to choose one direction to start. He peeked around the corner into the hallway carefully. No one seemed to be around. Kristen typically worked in the labs to the right, so that would be the way he went first. Continuingly checking both in front and behind him, he made his way to the first window that looked into one of the labs. Squatting low so as to not stick his head noticeably in the normal line of sight of anyone who may be in the room, he started at the bottom corner with one eye and slowly moved until he could see through the window with both eyes.

There were people working on some sort of small handheld machines. It looked like they were assembling TV remotes. He couldn't tell how many, but he guessed at least twenty workers. He recognized one as a colleague of Kristen's, but the rest he had never seen before. Frantically scanning, he saw no trace of Kristen, so he ducked below the windows and crawled toward the next lab.

As he made it to the next lab's window, he copied the same procedure from before. This lab had less people than the other, and they seemed to all be working on something in the middle. It looked like a small, black, egg-shaped pod with a seat inside not large enough for an adult. Still no Kristen.

There was one more lab on this side of the hall to check before trying the other side. It too had at least twenty workers that were feeding shiny metal bars into machines. The other side of the machine was producing shiny flat plates, like small mirrors or something. His scan for Kristen was short as there were only men working in this lab. Then he saw someone moving for the door that was just three feet to his right. They were pushing a rolling cart that had many of the shiny plates stacked on top. His choices were to stand up and make a run all the way back down the hall toward the stairs he had come up, or hope that the janitor's closet at the end of this side was open and that he could make it there fast enough not to be seen. The janitor's closet was less than ten feet away, and it looked as though the door was somewhat cracked open. The door opened inward into the room, so he should be able to just push it and enter.

He ducked his head and charged toward the closet. The door didn't budge. Something seemed to be jamming it from the other side. He put down his shoulder and hit the door. It moved but just a few inches. The man would be coming out of the lab any second, so he had to get in the closet now. He hit the door again, and whatever was jamming the door gave out. The clatter of falling items in the closet echoed as he rushed into the tiny, dark room. It sounded like someone had dropped a box full of marbles. Sean was sure someone would have heard it. He quickly pushed the door almost closed just as the man with the cart came out.

Through the crack on the hinge side of the door, he peered out and watched the man walk down the hallway toward the elevator on the other side of the hall. Sean took a moment to compose himself. Looking around with just the light from the cracked door to see, he found a broken piece of an old mop handle that was a perfect size for a weapon if he needed it. He picked it up and slowly opened the door.

Now he had to make it past all three of these labs and to the other part of the hallway, which had two more rooms to check. It felt as though it was his last chance to find Kristen. Staying low, he made his way down the long hall. It seemed even longer than before. Like some old scary movie where the hallway continues to lengthen as the character makes his way toward the end.

Finally, Sean made it to the window of one of the other labs. He caught the smell of something being cooked. He didn't know what it was, but it was an odor that made him sick to his stomach. Like plastic mixed with sauerkraut. He tried to peek in the window, but the room was dark. Squinting, he cupped his hands on the glass next to his head to block the light in the hallway and tried to make out anything in the room. There was definite movement in the lab, and it looked like they were taking white liquid from a large stock pot and packaging it into five-gallon beverage coolers. No Kristen, though, so he had only one more lab to check.

He crawled to the last room and peered in. It was a larger lab with multiple tables scattered throughout as workspaces. Three teams seemed to be putting together different pieces of gear. He could make out what looked like a large thick box lined with some kind of reflective material from one team. Another team appeared to be making a platform with a handle that reminded Sean of a utility cart without wheels. The third team was taking apart all kinds of equipment and bringing it to the other two teams.

His heart broke as he scanned for Kristen with no luck.

Where are you, love? Where do I go from here?

He tried to remind himself to think positive. But how could he? All he could feel right now was sadness and anger. There was a lack of hope. He didn't know where to even start looking for Kristen. The more he thought about it, the angrier he became. His breath felt hot, like the rage building inside of him was physically superheated.

"Just make it back to Jayden," he whispered to himself, trying to calm down his mind and breathing. As he started to crawl back toward the staircase in the middle of the hallway, a shadow crossed his path. He looked up in time to see a man standing at the top of the stairs looking down at him on the floor. Probably ten feet away, the man was average height and had a medium build, not unlike Sean himself.

The man looked puzzled, as if he was trying to understand the reason that Sean was on the floor. Sean stood up and looked the man straight in the eyes. His eyes were just like Rob's and the men who'd attacked him on the Army base. It was a similar trait that all these possessed, robot-like people seemed to share.

Those same damn cloudy eyes!

Although he knew he should probably run, he couldn't control it. Sean's fury bubbled out. He lunged at the man with the broken broomstick.

Sean hit the man's face with such force that the broken stick broke in two. The man hit the floor, rolled over, and immediately tried standing up as though he hadn't just caught a blunt object to the head. Sean was ready, though. He kicked the man in the face as he was trying to stand. The man again hit the floor, and this time, Sean jumped on him, pinned him to the ground, and started choking him, holding the small chunk of stick like a rolling pin to the throat. After only a second or two, the man threw Sean completely off and into the wall. Sean's adrenaline was too strong and his rage too high to be phased by the impact. He stood up, charged at the man again, and tackled him down the staircase.

Sean was on top as they made the first contact with a stair. The man's back took the most force as they hit and rolled down to the first landing. The top of Sean's shoulder slammed into the last step, and pain shot down his arm. Not paying any attention to the injury, he rolled to his stomach to push himself up and saw that the man was holding his own lower back. He was obviously in a great deal of pain.

Sean suddenly remembered both the fight on the base and the fight with Rob. He jumped up, ran over to the man, and kicked him in the kidney area. The man reeled in pain and was visibly unable to breathe. Sean made a run for it down the rest of the stairs as fast as his feet could carry him. Half tripping and half running, he made it down the stairs and was immediately grabbed by a man. He was just about to start swinging when the familiar voice of Sarge spoke up.

"Sean! Come on!"

They made a run for the front door and blew through it, not worried about being seen, just trying to make it back to their ride as fast as possible. Footsteps beat down behind them as they ran. The vehicle's lights flashed as the sound of the doors unlocking faintly resonated through the air. Ripping open the doors, they jumped in, and Sarge took off. He drove over the concrete blocks of the parking spaces to escape the possessed men and women in pursuit.

"They're catching up!" yelled Stacey.

Punching it as fast as he could, Sarge sped off down the street. Their pursuers faded in the darkness as Ol' Dawn carried them got farther and farther away. A moment later, Sarge slowed down, switched off his lights, and turned into a parking garage several blocks from the university.

"What are you doing?" asked Sean. "They might catch up to us!"

"Nah, I think we lost 'em," replied Sarge, still out of breath from running. "Let me sit a little, and I'll tell you why we need to go back."

"Go back? Did you see her?" Sean blurted out, wanting to grab Sarge by the shirt for an answer.

Jayden, who had stayed buried in Stacey's lap, quickly sat up eager to listen.

"Fraid not, but I did see something else. There are some semi's in the back that they're loading up. Don't know what they're haulin', but I reckon that if we can find out where they're going, it might help lead us to your girl."

"But with it being this dark out, they'll see our lights," Stacey said from the back seat.

"Yeah, I know. I have an idea, but don't think y'all are going to like it," Sarge said, looking back at Stacey and Jayden. "We need to get on one of the trucks. And by we, I mean you, Sean."

Sean glanced back at Jayden.

"Don't worry, I'll keep 'em safe," Sarge continued. "I'm sure I'll be the most help if you know these two are safe. I'll take 'em back to the cabin so you can find us when you need to."

"Sean," whimpered Jayden. "I want to be with you."

"I know, buddy," Sean said, putting his hand on Jayden's head, "but it won't be safe, and Stacey and Sarge will take care of you until I get back. And I promise I will be back. I'm going to find your sister."

Jayden looked down. Though tears were starting up, a somewhat accepting expression was on his face. Sean patted him on the shoulder.

"Alright, Sarge. Take me to the semi's."

20

Sean

Sarge drove slowly down a back road toward the university with no lights on. There were a few streetlights, but it wasn't a super well-lit street.

"Park here," Sean said, pointing at the back of a small business that was one street away from the university. They pulled up to the building and stopped.

"The loading dock is 'round back," said Sarge. "It looks like the trucks are being loaded one by one. I didn't see any of 'em drive off yet, so if you can get in one that's already been loaded, you should be good. Just don't be freaked out by how they load those trucks. It ain't natural. Here take this." Sarge handed Sean the pistol he must have gotten back from Stacey.

"Sean," Stacey said, placing her hand on Sean's shoulder, "you're going to find her. Jayden will be safe and cared for until you make it back." She wiped a tear away before it could drip down her nose.

"Thank you for being there for Jayden and me. I know he's in good hands." Sean opened the door and stepped out. Jayden flew out of the back and latched onto Sean's neck.

"Jayden, you be strong. I'll be back, don't worry. I'm going to find Kristen, and when I get back, we'll all be together again."

"Trust?" Jayden said, his voice cracking.

Sean couldn't see any tears in the darkness, but the side of his face and neck felt wet from Jayden's face.

"Trust," Sean softly replied.

Jayden squeezed Sean even tighter. Then, letting go, he got back in the vehicle. Sean started toward the university, trying not to look back. As he jogged, he couldn't help but feel guilty. He was leaving Jayden with two people he barely knew. And no matter what he told himself, he still felt like he should have been there for Kristen to keep her safe.

Coming up to the building, he stayed in the dark shadows and crept around the side. What he saw when he first peeked at the big rigs in the loading dock, made him stop dead in his tracks.

What the hell?

They were loading large wooden containers into the trailers of the trucks. But the equipment they were using to move the containers were levitating! They looked like normal flat carts, like the ones people use at lumber yards, but with an extra thick base and no wheels. Sean stared at the carts, squinting into the darkness, just trying to make sense of it. He didn't have the time to try and understand how they were working, no matter how crazy it looked. Getting to the truck was the priority, so he chose to ignore it and move on.

The very front semi seemed to already have been loaded. The back door was closed, and the ramp was up. He would have to get onto one of the other two. He watched for a moment to see when to make his move. Someone came out of the back door of the building and stood there, not saying anything. The individuals loading the trucks stopped as if he had just yelled something to them. They looked at the man, simultaneously left their carts that were still loaded with wooden containers, and went back into the building.

Now or never, Sean!

He made one look around and stood up to run. A gunshot echoed off the buildings around him. He drew his own gun just in case, though the sound seemed not to be close to him.

Was it Sarge? Oh, god! Jayden!

He turned and ran as fast as he could back to where he had left them, his brain racing a thousand miles per hour. As he ran down the street, he saw the Ol' Dawn one block away. It was wrecked, stuck partially in the wall of a barber shop. The driver's side front wheel was bent at an angle that would make it impossible to drive. The body of a man lay nearby. Sean squeezed the gun tightly in his hand, his heart hurting the inside of his chest.

He didn't recognize the man. The streetlight reflected in a pool of dark blood on the pavement around the body. A large wound on his neck was the obvious cause of death. Running past the body, Sean made it to the vehicle and ripped open a door. It was empty. There was normal, red blood on the driver's seat and door. The supplies they had taken from Kristen's house were now spilled across the back floorboard.

He hectically scanned the area for any sign of his group, feeling lost and helpless.

Why did I leave Jayden? He is my responsibility. I should have stayed with him.

"Sean!" came Jayden's voice from somewhere nearby.

Sean's heart jumped, a combination of fear and relief battling in his chest.

"Jayden!" Sean's voice squeaked in tearful desperation.

Across the street, Jayden dropped from one of the trees that lined the street. He ran to Sean, and they met on the road. Sean fell to his knees and wrapped his arms around the young boy.

"I'm so sorry, Sean! I just had to go to the bathroom. I-I didn't know they were there—"

"Whoa, whoa, buddy. Calm down. You're okay, you're okay," Sean said, frantically searching Jayden for any injuries.

"Yeah, I'm okay. But they took Miss Stacey and Sarge," Jayden said, tears welling in his eyes.

Sean's eyes jerked wildly around the dark area. They were too out in the open. "Let's get out of the road, and you can tell me what happened."

They made their way down the street. Sean checked the doors of multiple businesses in a frenzy until finally finding a loan office with the door unlocked. They went in and ducked behind the front counter. The only thing illuminating the dark room was the light from the streetlamp coming through the front windows.

"Alright, bud, tell me what happened," he said, trying to slow his breathing and have a calm, soothing voice for Jayden.

Jayden's voice was anything but calm. He spoke fast. "We-we were leaving, and I really had to go to the bathroom. Sarge said tha-tha-that he would pull over and let me go on the side of the road. He stood near to keep me safe. When we got back in, someone broke the window and grabbed Sarge. Then he crashed the car on purpose. And then he told us t-to run. And we did. Bu-but they grabbed Miss Stacey. I got away and hid in a tree—"

"It's okay, Jayden. It wasn't your fault," Sean said, putting his hand on Jayden's shoulder to calm him. "Did you see which direction they took them?"

Jayden shook his head, wiping the tears glimmering in the soft glow of the pale light.

"Well, I've got you now. We're gonna be just fine, bud." He hugged Jayden tight to him. He felt awful that Sarge and Stacey were missing but incredibly thankful that Jayden was safe.

"Sean?" asked Jayden.

"Yeah?"

"Please don't leave. I want to stay with you. I want to help find Kristen. Don't leave me."

Sean looked down at the young boy. He knew it would be dangerous but everywhere was dangerous at this point. He couldn't leave him alone. No one else would be able to keep the child safe as much as him. He would give up his life to protect Jayden.

"Alright, man. Deal."

"Trust?" Jayden choked out.

"Trust," Sean replied, squeezing him tighter. "I'm sure Sarge and Stacey will be alright wherever they are," he lied. "But right now, we need to find Kristen, okay?"

Jayden nodded.

Beside the front counter, Sean could make out a stack of canvas-colored cloth bags with the loan office's logo on them. Sean grabbed one as there was a small refrigerator near the front door that housed bottles of water, and they would definitely need some. Grabbing several for both of them, they stopped at the door. Sean opened it carefully and looked around. No sign of anyone. "Let's go."

Sean's first thought was to try and get some of the supplies from Sarge's wrecked vehicle, but as he checked the street it was on, he changed his mind. There were several men walking nearby. They were looking for something. Probably Jayden. Water would have to be enough for now. Sean couldn't afford to let the trucks leave without him and Jayden being on one of them. It was their only lead on where Kristen might be. He took Jayden and they made their way back toward the university and the trucks. When they got there, the trucks were still open, but there was no sign of any people.

"Okay, buddy. We're going to make a run for it. We're going to jump on that truck there and find a space to hide. Got it?"

Jayden nodded.

"Ready? Go!" When he and Jayden made it to the ramp, the gun slipped out of his waistband onto the concrete and slid beneath the trailer beside them. As he turned to try and retrieve it, a man came out of the building.

Screw it!

Leaving it behind, they climbed over wooden containers and found a spot they could sit and not be seen.

The doors to the back of the trailer shut less than a minute later, making it impossible to see anything. The sound of the latch locking the door was sickening to Sean. It felt like being trapped in a coffin, ready to be buried alive. They were stuck in a storage container going God knows where. They sat silent in the dark trailer and waited. The truck was still for so long that Jayden fell asleep on Sean's leg. Sean couldn't help but feel tired himself. He looked down at his watch. The face was smashed, probably from the fight with the man at the university. He didn't know what time it was, just that it was definitely late. His brain was screaming at him to stay awake, but his body was powering down.

The next thing he knew, he was jolted awake by the sound of the truck starting up. He tried listening for voices outside of the trailer but couldn't hear any, especially over the noise of the engine. The truck made a small lurch forward, and then they were off.

21

Angela

Angela was awoken by a dog barking in the distance. It had to be that little mutt from a couple doors down. That stupid thing was one of the ugliest dogs inside and out. Its face looked smashed in, the hair on its back was half missing, it constantly barked at everything, but the main reason that she hated it so much was that it would snap at anyone besides its owner. It would yap every morning at 6:30 am like clockwork, and although Angela despised the dog, today it was her morning wakeup call.

She rolled over to look at the clock. It was blinking 12:00 am, letting her know the power must have gone off and on during the night. At least she had gotten some sleep, though the night was one of the worst in her life. She didn't think she'd ever pass out. Her brain wouldn't shut down, and every five minutes had seemed like an hour.

Bill was still asleep in the living room, and she tried not to wake him as she put on a pot of coffee in the dark. Angela didn't want to turn on any lights. It was still dark outside and could draw attention to the house. She immediately went to work packing food and water for the road. The garage was where she kept all of their camping equipment and coolers. A wheeled cooler would be the best way to transport and store all the food they would need.

She searched all around. "Where is that damn red one?" Pulling boxes and equipment off the shelves, she finally found it in the back. "Oh!" she exclaimed as she opened it up. It had rancid food still in it. She must have forgotten to clean it out from their last camping trip. She quickly closed the lid and gagged. "Nope!" The odor lingered in the air as she started searching for anything else that may be large enough to transport food easily. In the corner of the shelf was a collapsible wagon. It might be able to fit in the trunk of the car they had commandeered yesterday. As she grabbed it, the electricity suddenly went out. "Great fucking timing," she muttered, stumbling toward the door to the house, feeling around in the pitch black room. The stress of not knowing where her son was at, was now morphing into short-tempered anger. It wasn't like her to be so easily frustrated, but the anger kept her from crying.

Dragging the wagon behind her, she made her way back into the kitchen. Bill walked in sleepily.

"Mornin'." He leaned against the counter, still trying to wake up.

"Good morning. I made some coffee if you want some. At least it brewed before the power went out."

"Thanks," he said through a yawn.

"I'm putting together some supplies and food for the drive. I'd like to leave soon to find the hospital they're gathering people in."

Bill nodded as he sipped his coffee. "You pack, and I'll load it up!"

"Bill?" Angela said in a very serious voice. "Why are you so willing to help a complete stranger like me?" It was something she'd thought of a lot during the night. She was all for good will, but it seemed overly kind. It made her a bit suspicious of his intent. "I just don't understand—"

"Angela," he interrupted. "You are a mother looking for her son. You could and probably would be completely okay without me here. But there's something inside me, especially since you're a mom, that just doesn't feel right about letting you go alone when I have the ability to try and help. Inherited trait, I guess. Maybe it's in my DNA."

"Well, thank you, Bill." She honestly didn't know if she could have gotten this far without his calm energy. She was spending so much of her own energy on not freaking out. Having him there was like having a personal guru to keep her on the right track.

They finished their coffee and got to work packing and loading. They worked fast and had everything in the car within fifteen minutes. Angela checked her phone. Though she had charged it overnight, with no service for so long, the time wouldn't even update. It just read, "searching for signal" on the screen.

"We can take turns, but who's gonna drive first?" asked Bill.

"I will," Angela said as she sat inside and tossed her phone in the center console. She was eager to leave and just wanted to feel as much control as she could.

There wasn't much conversation for the first half hour of the trip. Anytime Bill said something, Angela would answer with short one-word remarks. She wasn't in the mood for chit chat, and he eventually took the hint. There were no other drivers on the road. Any cars on the interstate seemed to have been moved to the side like something had come through and pushed them out of the way.

After a while, Bill said something that made Angela's heart drop. "Uh...I think we might be needing some gas in a minute."

She looked down at the near empty fuel gauge. She'd been so preoccupied in getting to and finding the hospital that she had zoned out everything else.

"I just saw a sign for a gas station at the next exit," Bill said, pointing at the exit they were coming up to.

She had been going almost ninety and barely had time to slow for the exit.

"Wonder if they take credit cards?" Bill joked. As with the whole trip so far, the joke fell on unimpressed ears.

They pulled up to the abandoned gas station, and Angela got out to pump while Bill went in to see what he could find.

"Dammit!" cried Angela, kicking the pump. Just like her house, the power was off here as well.

What are we going to do now? We're probably only halfway to where Donald said the hospital would be.

All the fear-based thoughts that she had tried so hard to keep at bay swam into her head.

Is this a wild goose chase? Is the information Donald gave us about the people-gathering hospital even right? What if I never see Michael again? Am I stuck in the middle of God knows where with no way to make it to where I think my son may be?

She kicked the pump again. Then she turned and kicked a trash can with a yell that turned more into a scream.

Bill came jogging outside, looking worried. "What's wrong? Are you alright?"

Angela nodded. "I'm fine, but it looks like we might be stuck. The power's out here too, so the pumps won't work."

Bill looking around as if he had an idea. "I'll be right back." He turned and went back inside the store.

Angela looked across the lot to some cars parked on the other side of the street. Maybe, she thought, someone left their keys in the car. She walked over and started checking the cars, one by one, with no luck. A dark gray electric vehicle made her jump back. In the passenger seat was the body of a young woman. Her head was slumped sideways, leaning on the window. A dark fluid was spurted across the window like it'd been coughed from her mouth as she died. Angela shuddered and covered her mouth. She wouldn't chance getting close. If there was anything that looked contagious, it was that.

"Angela!" Bill yelled from back at the station.

She turned and saw him carrying multiple gas cans and a rolled-up water hose. She knew exactly what he was thinking now.

Siphon the gas from other cars! Why didn't I think of that?

He walked over and set all the supplies down. "My dad taught me how to siphon gas. But the trick is to find an older auto. I worked with cars for a few years. Most cars after the early 1990s have something that will stop you from getting to the gas easily. There's one!" He pointed to an old pickup truck. "I'll fill up the cans, and you can fill up the car," he said with a smile.

Angela smiled too. For a moment, she felt hope again, the dead woman from the car nearby now only in the back of her mind.

They worked together, Bill filling a can, and Angela taking it to the car and bringing it back. They did this several times until it seemed that Bill couldn't get any more gas from the truck. The last can barely had anything in it. The smell of gasoline was heavy in the air.

"That's all I can get. We'll have to see if we can find another old car somewhere on the way."

"Should we try one of these other ones?"

"I tried that one for a second while you were walking back. No luck. I'll put the rest of this in the car if you want to go into the store and see if you can find some rope or string. Then we can tie the cans to the top of the car somehow. Don't want to be breathing in all these fumes."

Angela nodded and started back toward the station.

"And some chips, too, please! Any kind!" Bill yelled.

Inside the station, she found a small hardware section that had some tie-down straps. They would work great for the gas cans. Grabbing several packs, she went to find some chips for Bill.

Picking up a couple bags, she paused for a moment looking around at the store. This store had been somebody's job, their business, maybe even their dream. And now what? It was just a building sitting by itself on the side of the road. Full of products that no one was going to buy. She felt so removed from everything and everybody. It all felt like the old reality never really existed. Like life until now had all been a dream or just some TV show she'd watched about another type of existence.

A yell from outside got her attention. Running to the window, she looked out into the parking lot. To her horror, Bill was surrounded by a man and woman, his hands in the air. They were both pointing guns at his chest and having what looked like a heated argument.

The guns that Donald had given them were still in the car. They were no good to her now. She quickly started looking around the store for anything to use as a weapon. She grabbed a small pocket knife that was next to the cash register. It was a fixed blade with a handle shaped like a blue mermaid's tail. She'd have to be close, but it was the only thing she could find at the moment.

Back at the window, she saw they were leading Bill toward the store. She dropped to the floor so as not to be seen and clambered down an aisle. She could hear Bill talking loudly, probably trying to alert Angela so she would be prepared for their uninvited guests.

"You can have whatever you want. Just leave me out of it!" Bill yelled as he entered the store.

"Shut up and get inside," said the man, pushing Bill through the doorway. "Keep an eye on him, and I'll grab some things," the man said to the woman. He picked up a basket by the register and started grabbing items while going up and down the aisles.

Bill continued talking loudly to distract them both from seeing or hearing Angela.

"If he won't shut up, just shoot him!" yelled the man without looking up from the shelves. "We just need food and his car anyway."

Bill put his hands up higher and stopped talking. Angela kept her distance from the man and tried to make sure she wouldn't be on the same aisle as him. She moved back to the last aisle. There was nowhere else to go. She readied the knife in her hand, preparing to attack as he came around the corner. Her ears were ringing, and she could feel his presence like something heavy was pressing on her body.

He stopped just short of rounding the corner, pausing at the end cap. He set the basket on the ground next to his feet and laid his gun on the top of the items in his basket. He picked up something with both hands to look at it more closely.

Crouched down, less than three feet away, Angela saw this as her chance to grab the weapon. She inched closer, hoping that he wouldn't notice her until after she had the gun. Holding her breath, she reached her hand slowly toward the basket. As her hand latched onto the gun, his hand dropped on hers. Without thinking, she jammed the knife into his arm.

He let out a yell and pulled back in pain, the knife still protruding from his forearm. She had the gun! Standing up and backing away, she pointed it at his chest.

"What's wrong?" the lady shouted from the front of the store.

The man said nothing but put his hands up, his face a grimace of agony. Blood dripped from the knife in his arm. Angela didn't know what to do next.

What do you do after you stab someone?

"Move," she said finally, keeping her distance and motioning for him to walk to the front. When they rounded the corner and were visible to the lady and Bill, the woman grabbed Bill and held him in front of her.

"Drop it or I'll shoot him," said the woman.

"No, you drop it," replied Angela, struggling not to have a shaky voice.

Bill locked eyes with Angela and took a deep breath. He nodded at her as if to communicate something. She had no idea what he was doing. She was more focused on the woman with the gun; the one that could end his life in a second. Bill suddenly swung around and pushed the woman back, knocking her toward the window. Jumping after her, he reached out and grabbed her arm. A deafening shot rang through the store as they wrestled for a couple of seconds. Angela's heart slammed against her chest. Help or don't help? Join the fight or continue to hold the other man at gunpoint? Both she and the man watched the fight, trying to see who would get the weapon and if they were okay.

"Don't move," she managed to muster the strength to say to the man.

Bill stepped back, holding the gun in his left hand and pointing it at the woman.

Angela could feel her breath release, though she hadn't been aware she'd been holding it.

"Wait!" the man pleaded. "Please don't hurt her. We just need food and supplies. We wanted your car and thought you were going to take all the food. Keep the guns. Just let her go. Please." His brazen persona from before, was now reduced to that of a desperate man.

"You have twenty seconds to grab some stuff and get out of here," Bill said in a strained, gruff voice.

"Thank you... Thank you," replied the man, going to the woman and helping her off the ground.

Bill and Angela kept the guns pointed at them until they had taken some things and left. They watched them walk through the parking lot and down the street.

"Are you okay?" asked Bill.

"Yeah, just hopped up on adrenaline, I think. What about you?"

"I'm not sure." He turned toward her, holding his upper right leg in the middle of his quadriceps. Blood soaked his jeans under his hand.

Angela

"Stay still! I'm trying to stop the bleeding, and I can't if you keep moving," Angela said as Bill shifted uncomfortably in a chair they found in the back room of the convenience store.

"Are you sure you know how to take care of this?" asked Bill, wincing in pain.

"My kid is a skateboarder. I've never fixed up a bullet wound, but I've been in enough emergency rooms and seen enough stitches that I think I can at least help. I don't think the bullet is still in there. It looks like it went out the side." She grabbed Bill's hand and put it on the rags she had been holding on his leg. "You're gonna need to press hard and hold it in both places right there. I'm going to find a sewing kit and get this all sewn up."

"What? You didn't say anything about needles," Bill said in a slightly higher pitch than usual.

Angela rolled her eyes. "I'll get you a lollipop after." Searching the shelves of the store, she quickly found a small sewing kit, some more rags, some water bottles, and some superglue.

"What's all that for?" asked Bill as she made it back to him with all the supplies.

"We have to clean the wound with water first. Then try to dry it off. Then stitch it up. Then glue it together because these threads are made for clothes and not skin."

"Oh, no alcohol?" Bill asked, obviously trying to delay the inevitable pain he knew was coming.

"No, a doctor told me that alcohol damages the tissue and slows the healing process…"

"No, I meant to drink," he interrupted.

She rolled her eyes again and opened a water bottle. She took her time taking care of his wound. The bleeding was slow but constant. His continual twitches and whimpers made the work harder. When she was finished, she found some gauze and bandaged his leg. All in all, it had taken her just over twenty minutes to fix him up.

"Thanks. Am I good as new, doc?" Bill joked, still holding his breath from the pain. He looked like he'd lost some of his vitality; his face was paler than normal.

"You're welcome, and it's the least I can do with all that you've done for me," she said with a smile. "Do you think you can walk?"

"Let's see." Bill pushed himself out of his chair and came to a stand.

Angela could see the veins in his neck from him straining. She caught him under the arm and helped steady him.

"Let's get you to the car, and I'll get some extra supplies." They slowly made their way out the door and to the car. After helping him in, she went back inside. She filled some bags up with water and some other things she thought they might need before heading back outside.

Bill had his eyes closed and seemed to be resting. She didn't say anything to him as she started up the car and got back on the road. Best to let him rest if he could.

Angela felt as if time were moving slowly as she drove. Thirty more minutes of driving felt like hours. Her mind wouldn't stop focusing on Michael. And now with Bill hurt, would she have to get into the hospital alone?

The car's clock read 9:05 am when she finally saw the first sign for the hospital. It was barely visible under something spray-painted over the words. This had to be the hospital Donald had said they were gathering people at. She needed it to be.

Please! Please be it! Please be there!

She took the exit marked for the hospital and followed the signs. Bill must have noticed the turn because he was now awake and looking out the front window.

"That must be it," he said, pointing at a large building partially obscured behind a park with trees and playground equipment scattered throughout. "Wait! Stop!" he blurted out.

Angela hit the brakes, and they came to a jerky stop next to the park. "What is it?" she asked frantically.

He pointed to a large eighteen-wheeler pulling onto the road to the hospital. They watched in silence as the truck came to a stop. Only the front was visible between some trees.

"I'm gonna get out and try to get a good look. I'll be right back," she said, opening the door and stepping out.

"Be careful, Angie," Bill said as the door was shutting behind her.

She walked through the park to get a closer look and see what was going on. She found a large tree that she could peek out around and see the whole parking lot of the hospital. Some red graffiti was painted on the wall next to the front doors of the hospital. The red paint was really accentuated against the drab cream colored building. The doors of the semi opened. The driver and several more people got out of the cab and walked to the back. As they opened the back door of the trailer, Angela could see partially in. Bodies lined the floor. They looked very neatly placed, like they had been carefully laid down.

Are they alive? If you hurt my—

Several more people emerged from the front doors of the hospital, rolling stretchers toward the truck. They started loading bodies one by one and then took them into the hospital through the front door. More people came out and more stretchers.

Suddenly, one of the bodies jumped up and made a run across the parking lot. Two of the people who had been loading bodies let go of their stretchers and took off after him. The speed at which they ran was inhuman. It looked fake, like a video playing at a faster rate. They quickly caught him and held him tight as he thrashed about. A woman walked up to the group as they brought him back. She held an object to his chest, and his body went limp. Angela couldn't be sure from the distance she was at, but it looked similar to the device that had killed Donald. The limp man was then placed on a stretcher and wheeled into the building.

Angela jogged back toward the car where Bill waited. She felt sad for the people on stretchers. At least they were alive. She felt worried at the ease of which these robots, or zombies, or whatever they were, were able to take down so many people. But most of all, she was pissed at the thought of her son possibly being treated that way.

"So what did you see?" asked Bill anxiously as Angela got into the driver's seat.

She sat for a moment, trying to calm herself down enough to make sense of the situation and think of a plan. "I think they somehow put people to sleep and bring them here. There were so many people, Bill. I just don't know how to get in. The people working...th-they're not human. They're stronger and faster than anyone I've ever seen."

Bill nodded. "I know exactly what you mean."

Angela racked her brain for what to do next. She knew it would be tough, but sitting in the car wasn't going to get her son back. She needed an idea. She needed...a distraction.

"Bill, do you think you can drive?"

"I bet I can manage," he said, tapping his leg. "You need me to cause a fuss?"

"Exactly! I'll get as close as I can, and I need you to make a big enough distraction to allow me to get in."

She helped him into the driver seat and grabbed a pistol from the duffle bag in the back seat. As she started out toward the hospital, Bill called to her.

"Hey, be careful and good luck! Remember, you're a mom, so you can do anything."

She nodded to him and mouthed "thank you" so her voice wouldn't crack. She couldn't help but feel a sudden deep appreciation for Bill. He could be just about anywhere else right now, but he was there, helping a woman he had just met. Risking his life for a stranger. Taking bullets to the leg and not giving up on her. She wiped a tear as she jogged back through the park.

The main entrance would be too hard to get in without being seen. There was another door near the right side of the building that she thought would be a better bet. Creeping up and crouching down behind a small truck near the side door, she could still see Bill in the car through the trees. There was nobody left in the parking lot. All the bodies must have been moved inside. Her pulse quickened, and her muscles tensed as she waved at Bill to start.

The car jerked and moved slowly at first. So slowly that Angela thought something might be wrong. But as he turned the corner into the parking lot, he gunned it and started squealing the tires. Thick white smoke billowed out into the afternoon air. He cut donuts in the parking lot for nearly thirty seconds before anyone emerged from the main entrance. The individual was immediately followed by a large multitude of others flooding through the doors. Bill changed his trajectory and proceeded to move toward the parking lot exit.

When it seemed all eyes were on the runaway car, Angela made a break for the side entrance. Her heart sank as she pulled on the handle, but the door wouldn't budge.

"Dammit!" She had no choice. The main entrance it was. Staying close to the building, she ran as fast as her legs would go, determined to get in. She didn't want to even look in the direction of the mob of people in the lot. She ran straight to the front door and slipped inside as soon as the doors opened automatically.

23

Sean

Sean wasn't sure how long he'd slept, but it seemed to be all his body needed. Jayden had passed out again during the ride and didn't seem to mind the constant jolts of the bumpy roads they were driving on. Through cracks in the pull-down trailer door, he could see a bit of light outside. It had to be morning now. With plenty of time to think in the back of a semi, Sean was debating if his choice to bring Jayden with him was a good one. Should he have accepted that Kristen, along with most of the world as far as he knew, was lost to this situation and that his responsibility was now to look after and protect Jayden?

It doesn't matter now; we're stuck in this truck. At least until it stops. Wherever the hell it's going.

It didn't seem to be stopping for anything. It must have been plowing through stop signs and red lights. Weird how stuff like that didn't matter anymore. The law that he had spent much of his adult life learning and navigating no longer applied to anyone. It was a free-for-all. An every-man-for-himself world.

After a while, Sean decided to try and find out what was in the wooden containers. It would at least switch the focus of his mind off Kristen and Jayden. He may not be able to see well, but he could feel around and try to figure out. It was like the game Jayden liked to play where someone would place something in a box, and everyone else took turns trying to decide what it was just by closing their eyes and putting their hands in to touch it.

The wooden containers were in stacks that came up to his chin. Reaching over the edge of one and into the container, he pulled out an object that reminded him of a large electric razor. He had no clue besides that. Turning it over in his hands, a red symbol illuminated on what seemed like the handle. He didn't know what it meant. The symbol looked like something someone would have a tattoo of. Like a tribal tattoo or a fancy symbol from another language. No matter what it was, at least the light was bright enough for him to see his other hand a foot away.

Squeezing his body around to another box, he used the red light to peer inside. It was full of the large five-gallon beverage coolers. He cracked the lid of one and immediately regretted it. The odor wafted up to his nose. It was the same plastic-sauerkraut odor he'd smelled when he'd seen them filling coolers up at the university. Closing the lid, he stepped back, trying not to vomit.

The light suddenly went out on the device he had in his hand. He turned it over and over in his hands, but no light would come back on.

The semi braked suddenly. It knocked Sean off his feet, and he stumbled toward the front truck, slamming him into another stack of containers. Some of the top ones tipped sideways, wedging an entire row of containers from right to left in the trailer. "Shit," he whispered. Jayden was on the other side. Putting the impromptu flashlight in his pocket, he tried to climb over the toppled containers. Flimsy wood crushed under his weight and he fell to the floor.

"Sean?" Jayden's voice asked in the darkness.

"Yeah, man, I'm here. You alright?"

"Uh huh."

"These containers are stuck. Do you think you could climb over them to me, man?"

"Yeah."

"There should be a bag next to you with water bottles. Can you grab it?"

"It-it's stuck under something. I can't pull it out."

"That's okay, bud. Just follow my voice and climb over to me."

"Okay," the young boy replied. There was the sound of crunching as some cargo was obviously getting stepped on by Jayden.

Sean reached out his arms in the direction of where he thought Jayden would be. "Got ya," he said, pulling him down from the top of a crate.

"Where are we going, Sean?"

"I really don't know. We've been driving for a while now, but there's no way of seeing out."

The lighted symbol appeared near Sean's foot. He could see Jayden's body crouched down, holding one of the same objects Sean had. It must have fallen out when the containers shifted.

"What's this?"

Before Sean could answer, the symbol turned from red to blue.

"Wait, how'd you do that?" Sean asked, bending down to be next to Jayden.

"I just swiped my finger across it. Look." As he moved his finger across the symbol, it turned green and then back to red.

"I guess all I need is a kid to figure out technology."

The contraption shot out a flash of red light that went past his chest and struck the right wall of the trailer.

"Whoa!" Sean exclaimed. "What did you do?"

The spot that the beam struck was now a hole about the size of a computer mouse with edges that glowed red hot.

"Sorry, Sean. I didn't mean to!" Jayden said as if scared he was in trouble.

"It's okay, buddy. Just hand it to me slowly." With the dangerous object now in Sean's hands, he looked up at the hole in the wall and had an idea.

"Do you think you can explain how you just did that?"

"Um, yeah. I just held my thumb on the middle of that picture until it went off."

Sean held it in his hand, cautiously pointing it in a safe direction. His dad used to watch Star Trek in the evenings, and now it reminded him of the phasers they would use as weapons.

"Jayden, come over here," he said, pulling the boy behind him. He took a breath, readied his thumb to rest on the symbol, and turned his head in case this didn't work to plan. The phaser shot a beam that struck the wall at Sean's chest level. The hole was slightly smaller than the one before but worked perfectly as a way to see outside.

"Cool!" Jayden said, getting closer to the hole.

"Wait, man. It looks hot." He put the phaser in his other pocket. This could be useful, and two were better than one.

"What do you think the other colors do?" asked Jayden.

"I don't know, but we're not gonna figure it out here trapped inside a large metal box."

Jayden moved to the hole, peering outside.

"What do you see, bud?"

"Nothing, just the road. It looks like we're near some woods."

"Let me take a look."

Jayden stepped out of the way so Sean could see out of the hole. Jayden was right. They were traveling on a road that ran parallel to some woods. The sun was just coming up above the trees, casting large shadows across the road. The truck made another sudden slow down and started turning left. Since the hole was on the right side of the trailer, it took a few seconds for him to see where they had turned. They passed through a fenced area, and there was a large facility in the distance. They would be at their destination soon.

"Jayden, we have to hide," he said suddenly. There were several rows of containers that would have to be removed ahead of them. If they stayed low, they would be out of sight and may be able to sneak out during the unloading process. Or at least he hoped they would.

As the truck came to a stop, Sean held his breath. He did everything he could to listen for movement outside. The doors in the back were unlocked and slowly opened. The low morning sun flooded the trailer with light, making Sean squint.

He held onto Jayden but wasn't sure which one of them was shaking. In one hand, he squeezed the phaser device, ready to use it at a moment's notice. Through narrowed eyes, he watched through a small crevice between the wooden containers. A large ramp was placed on the back of the trailer. There seemed to be two unloaders with two separate hovering handcarts. As soon as he saw one of them get to the bottom of the ramp, he started counting in his head. He needed to know about how long they had between loads. He made it to about ninety when the first unloader made it back into view.

He waited one more round to see if the time was similar. This time he counted to ninety-two.

"Jayden," he whispered, "I'm not sure where we're going to go, but we are going to have to get out of this thing quickly and quietly."

Jayden squeezed the arm Sean had wrapped around him to let him know he understood.

"Ready? Go!" They stood up, clambered over some of the containers, and went for the doorway. As his eyes tried to adjust to the bright light, Sean looked around frantically, hoping for any chance of a hiding spot. He realized suddenly that they were in an empty parking lot and close to the front door of the facility. He made a quick decision to get to the ground and hide in the shadows under the semi and trailer.

He and Jayden hid behind the back left tires of the trailer. They were on all fours, but ready to run if necessary. Footsteps approached and stopped right next to the tires. Peeking between them, Sean could see the legs of someone standing less than three feet away and obviously facing the truck. He squeezed Jayden even tighter as the man started to crouch. Sean slowly raised the phaser, thumb ready. The man reached his hand toward the tire where they hid.

24

Angela

Her eyes scanned every inch of the hospital lobby in a second. Noting that not a soul was visible, she continued down the first hall she came to. She squeezed the pistol tight in her hand as she peeked in the window of room after room, praying that no one saw her but ready to take out anyone who might try to stop her. The hospital definitely had electricity as the halls were well-lit, but in the hallway she had chosen, all the individual rooms were dark and empty. She neared the end of the hallway and veered left down another. A man appeared at the other end of the hall, looking in the opposite direction. She quickly ducked inside the first door she came to so she wouldn't be seen.

It was dark and hard to see. There were machines making odd pulsating noises and a computer screen that had English mixed with weird blue symbols scrolling across it from right to left. She fumbled for a light switch and finally found one. Flipping it on, she jumped back. Hooked up to the machines were several people. Tubes ran everywhere between them and the machines, and the tubes seemed to be carrying blood. Angela felt suddenly sick, closed her eyes, and turned her head away from the scene.

What are they doing here? Is Michael hooked up to a machine like this?

Opening her eyes slowly, trying to muster the stomach to see more of what was going on, she noticed a small, black square box in the corner of the room near the door. It was making a low buzzing sound. She couldn't take her eyes off it as it gave off what looked like vibrations in water. Except there was no water. She could see vibrations moving out of it in the air. The vibrations moved toward the people on the machines, seemingly dissipating once they were a foot away from the machine.

Walking toward the small box and extending her hand slowly, she pushed her fingertips slowly through the vibration waves. They bounced off her skin, rippling away and disappearing. She began feeling sick to her stomach from the vibrations, like she was on a boat bouncing around in the sea. The sound of footsteps just outside the door took the nausea away in an instant. She bumped the box as she pushed her body against the wall so if anyone looked through the window, they wouldn't see her.

The light! Why did I turn on the light? They'll know something's up for sure.

She held her breath as the steps subsided down the hallway. A tone from the computer screen made her jump. The symbols flashed quickly across the screen. It reminded Angela of a computer trying to load a program from the old computer operating systems from when she was a kid in school. The tone went off again, and her eyes were drawn toward the tubes. The blood was starting to turn a dark, almost black, color. Visions of all the deaths she'd seen over the last couple of days flashed through her head. The dark veins and black substances expelled from people's mouths. She needed to get out of this room right now. Suddenly, not knowing was better than knowing what they were doing to these people.

She went for the door but caught a glimpse of the box out of the side of her eye. She must have knocked it sideways when she bumped into it. It was pointing toward the wall instead of the people. She stopped to fix it so no one would know that anyone had been there. It was heavy, so she placed the gun on the floor, and using two hands, turned the box back toward the people on the machines. The blood in the tubes immediately started turning red again, the computer tones stopped, and the symbols on the computer screen slowed. Angela tried to reason what was going on. If the machine made the blood look normal again, was it somehow stopping whatever it was that made people die and their blood turn black? Maybe they were using this hospital to turn people zombie-like. It would make sense that normal people weren't coming out if they were being changed into zombies.

Suddenly, the door opened, almost hitting Angela in the side. A woman stood in the doorway and looked directly at her, puzzled as to why she might be there. Her eyes had that same hazy look that all the zombie-humans seemed to have. Angela reached for the gun on the floor. The woman jumped at Angela, and they both crashed down. The woman's body immediately went limp on top of Angela. Angela wiggled free and stood up, grabbing the gun and pointing it toward the now unconscious woman.

She lay on the floor on her side, her hair covering her face. Wary of her, Angela carefully rolled her to her back and then stepped away, thinking that it couldn't be that easy to stop her. Her eyes were closed. If she hadn't been on the floor of a hospital, she would have almost looked peaceful. That's when Angela realized that the woman was lying right in front of the box, directly in the path of the vibration waves.

Angela bent down to get a closer look when the woman awoke. Her eyes no longer appeared cloudy as they had just a moment ago. The woman looked confused and frightened.

"W-what's going on?" she asked in a shaky voice. "Where am I?"

"It's okay," Angela said, trying to reassure her, now fairly confident that the box was stopping the zombie-like behavior. "But I think you need to stay here—"

The woman suddenly grabbed her side and lower back like someone had just stabbed her with a knife. Panicked screams erupted from her mouth. Angela wanted to help, but at this moment, her son was her first priority. She knew the woman's yells would draw attention and get her caught, so she made a run for it, out the door and down the hall. The woman's screams faded the further she got. Making it to a staircase, she fled up to the second floor.

Oddly there was still no one in the halls, but she could hear people in some of the rooms. It sounded like they were speaking English. She needed to get out of the open. Peering into one of the door windows, she saw at least twenty people jammed into the small room. They were up and talking to each other. A gentleman near the door saw Angela looking in and jumped back. She couldn't hear what he said, but the men in the room pushed forward and pulled the women back. It looked as though they were preparing to protect them from Angela.

One man stepped forward and walked to the door. He had on a worn-out gray cap. While he stared at her, she could tell that his eyes were clear and not cloudy.

He has to be a regular human! Could Michael be in there?

He must have deduced she also was normal because the whole room seemed relieved as he turned and spoke to them. Coming close to the door, he bent down and spoke through the small vent slats below the window.

"You're not one of them, are you?"

"No," she replied, shaking her head.

"Thank God! So the door is jammed from the outside somehow. Do you think you can get it open?"

Angela looked all around the door frame, trying not to panic. She was out in the open but desperate to now get into this room. These were normal humans. Humans that might know where her son was.

Nothing seemed to be wedging or bolting the door closed, but there was a small, black, circular device that was stuck on the door near the hinge side. It looked like a small hockey puck. She pulled on it, but it wouldn't budge. On the front of the disk, a blue circle appeared with a symbol similar to the ones from the computer screens. Holding her finger on top of the symbol, the circle turned light green and went back to blue when she removed her finger. The smart thermostat in her friend's house would do something similar when touched. She tried turning it like she would the thermostat, but nothing happened. She held the symbol and moved her finger in a circle this time. The green circle was vanishing as her finger went around. When she made it all the way back to where she started, there was a small click, and the disk slipped off into her hand. Reaching for the handle, she pushed open the door and ran in. A man immediately closed it behind her and watched out of the small window.

"You did it," said the man as sighs of relief went throughout the room.

Questions came from multiple people gathered around her.

"Who are you?"

"How did you get here?"

"Is there anyone else?"

"Is it over?"

"Everyone give her some space," the man in the cap commanded. He seemed to be the unofficial leader of the room.

She continually scanned the room for her son. "I'm looking for my son. His name is Michael," she blurted out, reaching into her pocket and yanking out a small photo she brought from home. "This is him. Have you seen him?" Hopelessly flashing it to as many people as would look at it, she was met with head shakes and pitied glances.

"I'm afraid not," the man said. "But there is a computer on the third floor that John said can find out exactly where someone is. They seem to have a list of everyone ... from everywhere."

"Who's John, and where is this computer?" she blurted out.

"He was a guy, not much unlike yourself, who wasn't captured and snuck in without getting caught. He saw a lot of what they do here."

"Where is he?" she asked impatiently

The man looked down at the floor. The crowd parted a bit, leaving her a clear shot of a corpse in the corner covered by a jacket.

"He didn't make it. He fought hard when they finally caught him, but there were too many of them. He told us about the computer just before he died. I can take you to where he said the computer was, but I need to know how you opened up the door."

Angela didn't know if she could trust the man. Something about him seemed off, but she had no other choice. If he could get her closer to her son, she would help. She flipped open her hand that was holding the small disk.

"These things seem to lock the door somehow. When you touch the middle, it lights up. Then run your finger in a circle and it unlocks. At least that's what happened when I did it."

"Thanks so much," he said with a look of relief. "Guys, you heard her. Are you ready for this?"

"What's going on? What are you doing?" she asked as some of the men made a push for the door.

"We're getting everyone out, now!"

"What about getting me to the computer?" she said angrily, partially regretting going against her intuition.

"I'll take you, just stay close to me," he said in an eerily calm voice. "Guys, let's go!"

The men in the front pulled open the door and rushed out. Everyone in the room made a giant push for the doorway, shoving people around in a panic. Angela fought for the door through the crowd. Busting into the hallway, she looked all around for the man she was supposed to follow. She saw him running the opposite way of everyone else. She ran after him, pushing past those running in the opposite direction. Some of the men were opening up the other rooms and getting people out. The previously empty hallway was now alive with the action of a crowded music festival, impromptu mosh pit included. People pushed, hit, kicked, and ran toward the exits.

With so many people in the hallway, she ducked her head and battled forward. Finally making it out of the crowd to the end of the hall where she had last seen the man, she spotted him hiding beside a vending machine. She caught up to him and crouched beside him.

"Shhhh," he whispered, pointing toward another large set of main stairs at the end of the hallway.

This hospital had to be old. Angela had never seen one with so many stairs and so few elevators. She ducked more beside the machine as people emerged on the stairs from the floor above. They stayed out of sight as the people ran past them toward the group of people trying to escape.

The man turned and looked at Angela. "I'm sorry, lady. I'm not getting turned into one of those things. Not for you, not for anyone.

The computer really is on the third floor, but you're on your own."
Then he pushed past her and ran to a service elevator just beside
the stairs.

So much for help. Looks like you're on your own again, Angela.

She stood up, faced the stairs, and reached for her gun. She'd
tucked it into her waistband when she'd opened the door for those
people. It was gone. It must have fallen out in the crowd.

Completely on your own, girl.

25

Sean

Sean slowly lowered the phaser as the person near the tires picked up an object that must have fallen off one of the shipments.

He doesn't see us!

He released the tight squeeze he had on Jayden's arm. Both he and Jayden watched as the two people continued to come back and forth, collecting containers and bringing them inside. Sean scanned the area. The semi was facing the front of the building which Sean thought was an odd direction to face if you were unloading the cargo from the back of the trailer. On the right side of the building, there were several large A/C condenser units within his eyeshot. Though only about half way back on the side of the building, it was a fairly long distance for a man and a young boy to travel while trying to avoid being seen. But it looked like their best bet.

The unloaders had to be at the containers that had fallen over during the drive. The sound of objects moving around above them and the amount of time it was starting to take for anyone to come out of the trailer, gave him the idea to use it as an opportunity to move.

He tapped Jayden on the arm and motioned for him to follow him. They crawled slowly underneath the semi in the direction of the building until they reached a part that was too low to easily move around. Coming out from underneath the semi, they stayed low, using the main part of the truck as a shield between them and those entering and exiting the building. When they reached the front of the truck, Sean pointed the units out to Jayden. Looking around one more time, he motioned with his fingers. One...two...three. They ran without looking back, not stopping until they ducked behind one of the large, square AC units.

"What are we going to do now?" asked Jayden, still panting from the run.

"We're too out in the open if anyone comes this way. We need to check out this building. Maybe we can get inside somehow," he replied, even more out of breath than Jayden. "I don't know if Kristen is here, but we have to check."

Still on the side, but toward the back of the building, there was a metal door with no window. Crouching as they moved, they made their way to it carefully. Sean put his ear against the door and listened. He couldn't hear any movement inside. Slowly twisting the doorknob, he let out a sigh. "Crap, it's locked."

"Crap!" repeated Jayden.

"Language, man."

Jayden shrugged and pointed to the left, back near the AC condensers where they'd hid. "How about that window?" Looking to where Jayden's finger pointed, Sean could see a small window that was partially open.

"I don't think I'm small enough to fit through that thing."

"But if I can get in there, maybe I can open this door from the inside!"

Sean was impressed with Jayden's problem-solving skills in a time like this, but he couldn't allow the young boy to go off on his own. "No way, man! You are not going in alone. What if you get cau—"

"I want to help! She's my sister!" Jayden interrupted, his voice cracking. "Let me help. I can do this. For Kristen."

In the mid-morning light, Sean could see a tear glisten on Jayden's nose. He wiped the tear with his thumb and grabbed Jayden, hugging him tight. "I know, bud. I know. Okay, let's go take a look first. If it looks clear, you can do it." He wasn't happy about letting Jayden try, but he could see it was important to Jayden. If it was all clear, it would get them inside. If it wasn't clear, they were stuck outside without another plan.

They snuck to the window, making sure to stay low enough to not be seen. Sean struggled to see inside as the bottom of the window was at his eye level if he stood on the tips of his toes. There was a desk directly below the window that he could just make out. It would make a great landing pad for entry. The room was dark as this tiny window was the only source of external light except for the screensaver of a laptop on a table on the far wall. He tried to see as far to the right as possible and make sure that the metal door nearby was accessible from that room. It was too hard to tell for sure, but it looked like it probably was.

This is a shitty plan. I shouldn't let him do this. But I guess it's the only plan we have.

"Okay, bud. You're clear, but listen to me. You stay quiet and see if you can open the door. If you can't get to it from here, you come right back. Do you hear me? Right back."

Jayden nodded but looked nervous.

"I believe in you, bud. Oh, and if anything goes wrong, hide and stay hidden. I will come and get you," Sean added.

Sean gave Jayden a boost to the window. Even with Jayden's small frame, it was a tight fit. He managed to squeeze in and make it onto the desk with a very small thud.

The dark room was a large contrast from the ever brighter daylight outside. Sean tried to keep an eye on Jayden, but his eyes wouldn't adjust to the low light. Jayden slowly climbed off the table, glanced back at Sean, and walked to the right until he was lost from Sean's view in the dark. Seconds felt like minutes to Sean.

Come on, buddy! You can do it!

He realized that he was bouncing in nervousness and tried to stop. Suddenly, a light flipped on and shone from a partially open doorway in the left of the room. Sean's eyes watched anxiously back and forth, looking for Jayden on the right and watching the lit doorway of the adjoining room on the left. No movement came from either side.

What's taking so long? Just come back! Forget the door.

The movement of shadows appeared in the doorway on the left. Sean prepared himself. If someone came into the room Jayden was in, he would yell to get their attention or maybe fire the phaser through the window. After that, he had no clue what he'd do, but at least he could draw attention away from Jayden. The shadows became darker as someone moved toward the door. Then the silhouette of a man was clearly visible in the light of the open door. He didn't enter the room Jayden was in but just stood there for a moment. The man then closed the door, making the room dark once again.

"Sean," came a whisper from Jayden. "Over here." Jayden's head was sticking out of the now opened door on the right.

Sean's shoulders dropped from relief, and he ran to the door.

"Way to go, man!" he whispered, trying to play it cool and giving Jayden a fist bump. "I knew you could do it. Now let's see what's going on in there." Sean entered the building behind Jayden then closed the door quietly. This part of the room was even darker since it was away from the window. Sean had to wait until his eyes adjusted. As they did, he realized that they were in an office with multiple workstations. It smelled of mildew, dust, and public restroom. Along with the odor, the heat and humidity of the room made it slightly hard to breathe.

From where they stood, he could see the light coming in from under the door of the adjoining room that he now contained at least one person. Holding Jayden by the hand, he led him to a desk and had him hide under it. He then crept over to the door and put an eye to the floor to see into the room. The feet of three people stood around a table in the middle of the room. He couldn't see what they were doing, but they must have all been working on whatever was on the table. He thought he heard a low groan, like someone in pain, but he didn't hear it again. This way was a no-go. They'd have to find another way to get further into the facility. Slowly, they hunted for another door. Still unable to see very clearly, he walked the entire perimeter of the room. The only other door in the office was a restroom that smelled as though it hadn't been cleaned in a while.

Dammit. How are we going to get in?

The sound of a door shutting got his attention. It seemed to have come from the other room. He walked back to the door and peeked underneath. The light was still on, but there were no more people in the room. Just the table in the middle.

He took a deep breath and carefully turned the doorknob. The knob was loose on the door but turned easily. Ready for a loud creak, Sean pushed the door open just a crack and looked inside.

On the table lay a man. A beast of a man. His tall, chiseled body lay perfectly still. He wore only pants and didn't move. The veins under his skin were raised as if about to burst. They were highly visible under his dark, ebony skin. He was breathing but barely. His chest went up and down with each quick, shallow breath. His eyes were shut, and his face made him look like he was asleep. Straps on his wrists and ankles held him down, though if he were awake he looked to have the strength to rip through his restraints.

Pushing the door open more, Sean stepped in cautiously. There were two other doors that led out of this room. He went back and retrieved Jayden, taking him by the hand and making him walk behind just in case the man on the table were to wake. As he walked past the unconscious man, he noticed strange marks on the man's stomach. Multiple scars in straight lines started under his belly button and stretched across his side toward his lower back. It looked like he had been cut open, put back together, and then the wounds somehow burned closed. Sean tried not to let Jayden see the poor man.

They had to move on, but which door should they take? Sean started with the door on the left. As he had done before, he slowly turned the knob and pushed it open just enough to peer out. It was a brightly lit, large, warehouse-type space filled with those same pod-looking machines he had seen being built in the university. There had to be hundreds or even thousands of the pods. Way too many people to count walked around pushing equipment and monitoring the pods. There was no way he and Jayden could get out there without being seen. Closing that door slowly, he made his way to the door on the right. He reached for the knob and squeezed it. Jayden tapped on his shoulder quickly.

"What is it?" Sean whispered. He turned, catching a look of terror on Jayden's face. The hair on the back of Sean's neck stood up.

Jayden was looking in the direction of the large man on the table. Sean quickly pulled Jayden behind him and stood facing the table, readying himself to fight if necessary. The man was lying still, but his eyes were open and transfixed on the two in the room with him. His face showed that he was in pain but also confused.

He spoke with a hoarse, labored voice. "You guys are either brave, stupid, or both."

Sean could see that the man's eyes were partially cloudy but not to the extent of the others. Still wary of the man, Sean spoke to him in a quiet voice. "Are you okay?" Sean was shocked with his own question. There was no rational reason to trust the man, but for some reason he had a feeling he should help.

The man squirmed and pulled at the restraints. "Never better," he said sarcastically, then coughed. "Can you unstrap me and help me sit up, please?"

"How do I know I can trust you?"

"Do I look like I'm in any condition to attack you? Little man could probably take me out if I tried."

"Stand over there in the corner, Jayden," Sean said, pointing to the spot furthest from the table. Hesitantly, Sean unhooked the Velcro straps on the man's wrists, leaving his ankles strapped as a precaution. He helped the man come to a seated position but kept Jayden behind him. He quickly stepped back and stood with Jayden.

"Thanks. I'm Marcus, by the way."

"Sean," he replied.

"Well, Sean," he continued through labored breaths. "Have you figured out just what in the hell is going on?"

Sean shook his head. The man strained with each movement before speaking again, sweat starting to bead on his forehead. "Huh, I guess I'm just about one of the only beings you'll meet that have the answers then. Let me catch my breath for a second, and I'll answer all your questions. Someone needs to know before I go."

Sean didn't know what to think. Unlike the others, Marcus was actually talking but had somewhat clouded eyes. He didn't look to be healthy enough to attack but had been strapped down to the table for some reason. Was he dangerous to Jayden? Or was he dangerous to the robot-people? Did he truly know what was going on? Sean felt desperate to know what was happening but wary enough to hold the phaser by his side pointed at Marcus. If he really had the answers, it could only help them in their search for Kristen. He moved and locked the doors to the room. He didn't want any surprises.

When Sean had finished, Marcus continued. "I think the whole thing can be shut down, but I can't do it. Oh, and don't worry about those guys coming back any time soon. They'll be gone for hours."

26

Angela

As she neared the top of the stairs on the third floor, Angela could see that the main area was empty of people. The screams and panic happening downstairs echoed through the hallways. She used this opportunity to look in as many rooms as she could. Most were dark, possibly holding more humans with blood running through tubes. Then she came upon one with the light on. Seeing no one in the room, she entered.

It was probably a doctor or nurse's lounge at some point. Futons sat against the wall on the left, small lockers ran along the wall beside the door, and coffee makers and tables were on the wall to the right. There was a large setup of equipment, including computer monitors, in the back of the room. Three monitors positioned around a chair scrolled names in English accompanied with weird symbols. The info scrolled too fast for Angela to read.

The screen on the far right had a text cursor blinking in the corner. She sat down in the chair and picked up the keyboard. After hitting 'Enter', the screen cleared and sat empty. It almost reminded her of a search bar.

This has to be it! Hold on, Michael. I'm coming!

She quickly typed in 'Michael'. A list immediately popped up on the middle screen with too many 'Michaels' to count. She added 'Morales' to the end. Again, a list immediately popped up, but this time, it had only eleven entries.

The names all read, "Morales, M." Since there was no mouse, she tried using the tab button to somehow highlight a name, but no cursor or movement happened. There were symbols next to each name. They kind of looked like the ancient language of Sanskrit, just like some of the natural products in her store, but she had no idea what they meant. They were very similar to the symbols on the puck-lock from earlier.

She stopped for a second, suddenly remembering the spray-painted hospital sign on the road and the red graffiti on the wall by the main entrance to this building. She hadn't paid much attention before, but now that she thought about it, it did seem like the paintings were similar to these symbols.

Maybe it's some way to mark locations! It could lead me to Michael!

Worried that someone could burst into the room at any moment, she looked around for papers, pencils, or even a printer but didn't see one in the room. Racking her brain, she searched for anything. Her eyes landed on the lockers.

She wildly opened them up, one by one. She found mostly clothes, wallets, and other random articles. "Bingo!" she said with a smile. She pulled out a mobile phone and held down the power button. The light came on, and it began to start up. As it powered on, she carefully watched out the window of the door to check for any visitors. She hoped that the phone didn't have a security lock. Maybe the phone belonged to a nurse or doctor with kids. She used to keep her own phone unlocked for Michael when he was younger.

It came in handy as an easy babysitter when she needed a moment to herself.

"Yes!" she said as the homescreen pulled up without a lock. The battery was at eighty-seven percent. She ran to the computer screen and took a picture of the names and symbols. Suddenly she heard footsteps coming fast down the hall. One of the futons in the corner had enough space for her to hide behind. Trying not to knock over the lamp wedged behind the futon, she crouched down as low as she could.

The door opened and closed slowly. The footsteps sounded like they were coming closer. Angela held her breath and silently reached for the gun in her waistband. Her fear intensified as she remembered that she lost it in the panicked crowd. The futon made a small squeaking sound as the person seemed to bump into it.

She wasn't a fighter by any means, but she was sure she could at least fight her way out of the room. Trying to get at least a glance at the person before she attacked, she peeked up over the back of the futon. There was a young woman staring at her, less than two feet away.

The young woman squealed, jumped back, and fell. Angela jumped over and was about to kick the downed girl in the face when she noticed something. The young woman's eyes were completely clear, and she was obviously very afraid of Angela.

"Are you human?" Angela asked in an anxious voice, still ready to kick her and escape. The question sounded weird coming from her mouth. What would've been a ridiculous question just a couple days ago, now felt paramount. The girl looked confused for a second and slowly nodded her head.

"Y-yes," she replied, still cowering in fear.

Angela reached out her hand. "We need to get out of here. Do you know a way out besides the front door?"

Taking Angela's hand, the young woman came to a stand and nodded again, still slightly cowering from Angela. "Yes, my girlfriend works here. I-I came to find her, and they grabbed me and put me in a room. I lost my keys, but my girlfriend's keys might be in here. Her car is in the lot on the side. When I saw her car, I was hopeful I'd find her in here somewhere. She usually keeps her keys in her jacket."

"Well let's find them and let's get out of here."

The woman opened one of the lockers and pulled out some clothes. "I don't see her jacket or keys," she said, turning to Angela. "Wait! There!" She ran to one of the futons and dug through a green hoodie. "Here they are!" She pulled out the keys.

The two went to the door and peered out to make sure the coast was clear. Angela motioned for the young woman to lead the way. They went down the hall and toward the emergency exit. Blocking the exit door were multiple large crates. They tried for a moment to make any of them budge, but it was pointless.

"There's another entrance to the emergency exit on the second floor," whispered the woman, her voice shaking. "Follow me."

They stopped at the top of the main stairs leading to the second floor. Angela listened intently but heard no footsteps. As they reached the bottom of the steps, they saw several bodies littering the floor. They lay motionless, obvious prisoners who hadn't made it out. Streaks of blood dripped down one of the walls, and marks where bloody bodies had been dragged were apparent on the floor. It made Angela's stomach feel sick. Besides older family members, she had never really witnessed death until yesterday, and now it was becoming a common occurrence.

"This way," the woman whispered, pointing to the exit just to their left.

As the young woman made it to the door, Angela noticed something beside one of the bodies. It was her gun!

"Just a second," she said as she ran toward the gun. When she was ten feet away, motion across the hall stopped her in her tracks, causing her to almost slip. Multiple people came around the corner toward her. They stopped for a moment and stared at her. The gun was nearly halfway between them and her, and she knew she couldn't beat them to it. Turning and running, she yelled at the young woman.

"Go!" The alarm immediately went off as the emergency door swung open and the two women fled through it. Angela had never gone down stairs this fast in her life. Her feet moved like a football player doing agility ladders. Her body felt light, as if she were falling down the stairs.

They reached the ground floor and burst through the door outside. The parking lot was just about empty on this side of the building. There were several cars scattered in parking spots, but Angela's attention was drawn to the body of a man on the pavement. As they ran past it, she recognized him. It was the body of the man who had tried to leave her behind. He had gotten his wish. He didn't get turned into one of those things. By the look of his damaged body, her guess was that he had jumped from a high floor to avoid getting caught.

They were maybe twenty feet from the building as the doors behind them slammed open. Looking over her shoulder, she saw their pursuers gaining on them. They weren't going to make it to the car before getting overrun. Bracing for a fight, Angela continued to run with all her might. The footsteps behind them felt like they were on top of her.

The squeal of car tires hammered in her ears. She looked to her right and saw Bill. The car drove right past her and slammed into a small group of the pursuers. His car swerved right and left before crashing into a parked vehicle.

Angela yelled to the woman, "Go, get out of here!" Then she turned and ran toward her friend in his wrecked vehicle. Another small group got to the car before Angela could even get close. They ripped Bill from the vehicle and tried to hold him down. Though he was wounded, he fought hard against them. Knocking one person to the ground, he managed to make it to his feet. Angela came up with a plan as she ran. She knew exactly where the guns in the car were. If she could get to them, they could fight them off together.

Bill wrapped his strong arms around as many of his attackers as his large body could reach. He tried to hold them there. Bill's eyes locked onto Angela's, and he gave her a head shake as if to say, *'Stay away. Don't come.'* Angela stopped in her tracks as the same sound that she had heard with Donald reverberated through the air. Her scream was muffled to her own ears as she fell to her knees. Bill's lifeless body slumped forward and fell to the pavement, taking some of the attackers to the ground with him. Unable to move on her own, Angela was pulled to her feet by the young lady and quickly led back toward her car.

Hurried footsteps came down the hallway. A short man came in and stood in the doorway looking at Lugal.

"What is it?" Lugal asked.

The man in the doorway paused and then spoke. "An alarm was initiated at one of the modification facilities. Approximately thirty-two have escaped and fourteen terminated."

"I see," Lugal said, looking down at the floor. "Very unfortunate. Send five sentries to the location."

"I would suggest, Lugal, that you should also send sentries to any nearby facilities," said Arub sitting in a chair by the wall.

"What facilities are nearby?" Lugal asked the man still standing in the doorway.

"There is an excavation zone seventy-two marks away."

"After the sentries scan the modification facility, have them also scan the excavation zone."

The man left the room and went back down the hall. Lugal turned to Arub.

"What of the nuclear facilities? Are they nearly shut down?"

"It is a process. It will be completed in due time. I will monitor them so you may concentrate on more pressing matters."

"That is good. And thank you, Arub, for your suggestions. Your presence here has been most helpful."

"It is my duty to help guide you in your leadership, Lugal," Arub replied, bowing his head.

28

Sean

Sean decided, like it or not, he had to trust Marcus. And even if Marcus proved to be untrustworthy, he was in such bad shape that Sean knew he could take him. He unstrapped Marcus's feet and gave him a moment to find a more comfortable position to rest in. Marcus took shallow breaths and began speaking.

"I'm not sure where to start. There's so much, and we don't have that much time." Unable to find a completely comfortable position to be in, Marcus shifted and moved frequently. "Well, so as you can see, I'm not quite taken over and not quite okay either. I have complete control over my thoughts and body, but I'm getting signals from them. Signals in my mind."

"Signals? Them? Who are they?" inquired Sean, confused still. "What are you talking about?"

"I'm getting information blasted into my mind from time to time. I don't really have a name for their kind. Some of what comes through is hard to translate anyway. Best I can tell is that they're what we would think of as aliens."

Sean was now sure this guy had to be crazy. He was hearing voices from aliens. But as Sean thought about it for a moment, though a bit skeptical that aliens were to blame, nothing else really made much sense with all the weird and unexplainable things he'd seen. At least this guy seemed to have some kind of idea what was going on. Or he seemed to really believe he did, anyway.

Marcus continued, "They have taken over humanity by using genetically altered algae. The same algae that they sent here, and we all took as a miracle cure."

"Wait, *they* sent it here?" Sean asked.

Kristen had done quite a bit of studying on 'The Cure,' who developed it, and how it was developed. Sean knew all about the algae. Marcus might be crazy, but he was starting to make more sense.

"Yeah, they orchestrated the whole damn thing. For some, it wouldn't bond correctly, and it killed them. Their body rejected it and their blood became thick and tarry quickly. For the rest, it bonded with our DNA and was activated to control and give information. They call anyone taken over *'drones.'* Their eyes get that scary cloudy look, and they're no longer in control of their choices, actions, or lives. They're essentially slaves, workers under control of the aliens. The Lightning Pillars activated a link between the aliens and the bonded DNA. The signal can only reach so far. That's why all the pillars needed to be complete before they started them up."

Now Sean felt almost fully on board with this idea. It all explained why the so-called drones seemed to all understand exactly what to do in places like the university. And with the algae from a perfectly encased meteorite from space and the towers just recently being finished, it all made sense. Never in his life did Sean think that he would be listening to someone talk about an alien takeover and believe the story.

"It's a little foggy to me, and I'm no scientist," Marcus said. "But I can hear what the guys who have been experimenting on me are thinking. I'm one of the ones whose DNA both accepts and rejects the bond. The Cure is in a constant pull between trying to kill me and trying to turn me into a drone. So I'm stuck in a kind of limbo of sorts. They're working on me to learn why. I'm like some damn lab rat to them." He glanced at Jayden, "Sorry for cursing in front of the boy."

"It's okay," Sean said quickly, mainly worried about getting more information. "So, you can read their minds? Do you know why the aliens are here and what they're trying to do?" He was desperately trying to make sense of what Marcus was saying. If he could understand what they were doing and why they were doing it, maybe he could put a stop to it and find Kristen.

"I'm not sure. I don't think I have all the information since my body rejects so much. Information gets broadcast into my mind, but only sometimes. Like I'm getting a strong signal, then nothing. The Lighting Pillars that control the signals can communicate to the drones, instantly and all at once. The drones can't communicate back, though there's no need to. The aliens have control of everything now. All I can gather is that different people are assigned different tasks according to their brain and body adaptations. Some build, some mine, and some capture others...including children." He stopped and glanced at Jayden with a sympathetic look before continuing.

Sean stepped in front to block him from Marcus's view. Marcus noticed the protective move, but didn't seem phased or offended.

"Anyone that they find that is not a drone is captured and... converted. The drones are all expendable. One is not more important than another in completing a task. They all just have different duties to do. It's like their minds and bodies are coded for one task."

The sudden thought of Kristen being captured and turned into a drone, made Sean sick. Stomach acid rose in his throat. His only goal now was to see if he could put an end to the whole thing.

He cleared his throat. "You said we can stop them, right?" he asked hurriedly. "How do we do that?"

"So apparently there is some sort of main control base here in the U.S. You can think of it like a central communication hub. It communicates to the Lightning Towers that bounce the signals all across Earth to keep the bonded DNA active."

"So let me make sure I understand. This main communication hub sends a signal to the Lightning Towers which in turn keeps a bond active with The Cure and human DNA?"

"Yes."

"Can we just destroy any of the Lightning Pillars to stop the signal?"

"Afraid knocking out local one's won't work. Their signals overlap, so you'd have to knock them all out. Plus they'll just send more drones to fix 'em."

"So we need to get to the communication hub, right? If we can stop the main signal, will everyone be released from their control?" asked Sean hopefully.

"Since I'm in and out, both physically and with getting and not getting the signal, it's a little fuzzy in my head. But I think so."

"Well where is it?" Sean asked. "This main hub?"

"That, I'm afraid, I don't know, either," Marcus replied, shifting again in discomfort. A bead of sweat from his eyebrow finally collected enough to drip down and flick his eyelash on the way by. He twitched, wiped his entire face with one hand, and continued. "All I know is a symbol that represents the building for the hub. Find me something to draw on, and I'll write it down for you."

Draw a symbol? What the hell? Are we playing Pictionary?

Annoyed and excited at the first bit of hope for stopping this whole mess, Sean looked around for something. Bringing Jayden with him, he went back through the door into the adjoining office.

He brought a notebook and pen back to Marcus. Marcus began writing. Sean watched him intently as he drew. It was a very well-done drawing of a symbol that looked similar to the one on the phaser.

"I used to be an artist, you know," Marcus said, his eyes seeming to reminisce in the memory of a life long past. "Had to give it up to make money. Worked as a technician on the Lightning Pillars. It's ironic, isn't it? We helped to build the damn things that are now being used to turn us into mindless drones."

Sean took the finished drawing from Marcus. "Okay, so how do we find this place?" He asked, studying the picture like an idea would jump off the page and give him a direction to start his search.

Marcus seemed to focus for a moment. He looked like he was reading something in his head.

Maybe he can tap into the main signal that's coming in if he thinks really hard. Hopefully it's one way, like he said. We can't afford for someone to know what we're trying to do.

Marcus took a long, wheezing inhale. "There is an excavation site not too far from here to the south. They're mining there for the specific metal they use in all their technology. I'm not sure, but if you can get there, you may be able to find one of the devices they use for information. They have one at most of their locations. To me, it kinda looks like a tablet. You know, like you'd play games or watch videos on. You should be able to use it like a map. If you can find that symbol on the device, it should lead you to the main communication hub."

"Is there not one of the devices here then?" Sean asked. If they had them at most of their locations, why not here?

"There is, but this place has a lot of drones. And strong ones too—physically. They move the vessel pods around." He glanced at Jayden again.

The look gave Sean a very uneasy feeling.

Marcus continued, "Those dark egg-shaped pods, they're..." His voice trailed off. His face looked sad, as though he may cry at any moment. "Well, we just wouldn't have a chance to get the device and get out with all these drones."

Sean had to agree that one man, one child, and a guy who could barely sit up had no chance with all the people he'd seen in that warehouse.

"Okay, so let's go get one of these tablet devices and find out where we need to go."

"One problem though," Marcus said ominously, "I don't exactly know how the device works. You may not be able to use it. You see, the drones communicate not with vocal words but with their minds, and only when close to each other. Like a weak Bluetooth signal or something. I'm not sure if the device is the same. It might be controlled by the mind."

Telepathic communication? That explains how they seem to work together. But mind-controlled devices? What's next, portals to another dimension to get there?

"Then that means you're going to have to come along," said Sean. "You said you get the signals, right? Then maybe you can operate the thing."

"I don't know if I can. In their experiments on me, they've cut me open and closed me back up a couple times now. And according to them, they think my body is going to lose the battle with the bond, if you know what I mean."

"So you'll become one of them?" asked Sean, stepping closer to Jayden.

"No." Marcus looked away as if to avoid eye contact. "I won't make it."

"Oh," Sean whispered, unintentionally looking at the floor as if he'd just been told someone died. "Well let's get you out of here, and maybe we can fix things before that happens."

Marcus just nodded, though Sean could tell by his expression that it wouldn't be the case. He helped get Marcus to his feet. Marcus couldn't stand up straight, even with Sean's help, so he had to lean slightly forward and sideways while leaning heavily on Sean. After standing for a moment, he tried to move.

"Good, let's go. You can do it," Sean encouraged.

Marcus barely moved a foot to take a step and almost fell. Sean caught him and helped him sit back on the table.

"I-I can't make it," he said, gasping for air from straining so hard.

"Hold on," Sean said, having an idea. "I'll be right back!" He ran into the office and came back a few seconds later rolling a wheeled office chair. "We can't just leave you here."

Jayden held the chair still as Sean struggled to lift and help Marcus onto it. The armrests allowed Marcus to lean sideways in a more comfortable position. They pushed the chair back into the office. Going out the door they came in would probably be best, but he still needed to do one more thing before they left.

"Y'all stay here. I have to check for Kristen."

"Oh, so that's why you came here. You're looking for a woman," said Marcus with as much of a smirk as he could muster. "Should have said something. I can help you there, too. First, there are no females here in this building. Their brains are viewed as more capable for different tasks and function at a higher rate. Sorry to end the battle of the sexes there. Women win the brains category," he laughed, coughing up and spitting out a dark phlegm on the carpet. "Second, the device that I told you about has a list of everyone either caught or being controlled. They use it to request more help when it's needed. The device has everyone's location—if they've been made into a drone."

Once again Sean felt sick. Once again he was in a place where Kristen was not. Though he hoped she hadn't been captured and turned into a drone, his only solace was that there was a possibility that he could find exactly where she was.

He squatted down and looked Jayden in the eyes. "Kristen is going to be okay, bud. We're going to shut this whole thing down. You with me, man?"

Jayden nodded, trying to look brave though concern hung on his tiny face.

"Well," Sean said standing up. "Let's get the hell out of here then." Sean wheeled Marcus toward the door.

"What's our plan once we're outside?" asked Marcus.

"We'll figure it out," replied Sean. The coast seemed clear as they came into the morning sunlight. No movement whatsoever. "Be right back. y'all stay here."

"Wouldn't dream of running off on you," Marcus said, flinching in pain as he chuckled at his own joke.

Sean went toward the back of the building to see if anything was behind it. Looking around the corner, he was met by a large chain link fence. The fenced area was full of old loading equipment and storage containers. No vehicles that he could drive besides a forklift. He made his way back to Marcus and Jayden. The semi they had come on was still in the parking lot in the front. He couldn't see anyone in it from where he was at. He wanted to check it out before taking them all to it.

He slowly approached the truck, every sense aware of all around him. He went to the passenger side and stepped up to look through the window. The windows were tinted well, but he could see enough inside to notice that the front driver and passenger seat were empty.

Squinting and looking as hard as he could, he was able to make out that the keys were still hanging from the ignition. He then crept to the back to find that the overhead door was shut for the trailer.

This is it! We have a ride!

He went back for Jayden and Marcus. They had to take it slow as the wheels of the chair were louder on the pavement the faster they went. There was still no movement from anyone else. They went to the passenger side because the truck blocked them from view of the building there.

"Jayden, squat down right there near the front and keep an eye out for us. Tell me if you see anybody coming," Sean whispered.

Jayden gave Sean a thumbs up and ducked down by the front of the truck to watch the building. Getting Marcus up and into the truck proved to be quite the ordeal. Marcus was pure muscle and even sitting in the chair was almost as tall as Sean. But after what felt like forever and lots of straining and sweat, Marcus was in the passenger seat. He immediately closed his eyes and seemed to pass out. Sean put the seat belt on him and signaled for Jayden to jump in. Jayden hopped up and stood between the two seats.

"There should be a back seat or bed behind the curtain, buddy," Sean told him, pointing to the curtain that ran the width of the cab behind the front seats. "You can jump back there."

Jayden gave him a worried look. "I want to be next to you," he said, his timid voice almost a whisper.

Sean just nodded. Arguing about seat belts while Jayden was this scared wasn't worth it. He motioned for him to have a seat on the floor between the two front seats.

Starting the truck would be loud, and Sean knew he probably wouldn't have much time to get moving before someone from inside the building came out to investigate.

"Do you know how to drive one of these things?" Marcus asked with his eyes still shut.

"Yeah, lucky for us my grandpa owned a sand and gravel business. I would help drive loads for him to earn extra money in college, so I got good at driving big trucks." Taking a deep breath, Sean started the engine and watched the door of the building. There'd be no time to let the engine warm up, so he put it in gear and started turning the truck around to exit the parking lot. No one ever came out of the building as he watched the door disappear in the distance.

Breathing a sigh of relief, he settled in and checked the sun. It was morning, so the sun was still in the east. Now he had his bearings and knew which way south was.

29

Angela

The trees on the side of the road seemed to fly past. The road noise was blocked out by the deafening silence in the car as the young woman drove. Angela stared out the window at the blur of the white line on the asphalt. She wanted to cry for Bill but couldn't. She felt as though hope was lost. Everyone around her was dying or dead. The only thing she had left now was a picture on a phone of symbols she couldn't read.

The car slowed, and they exited the freeway. They pulled up to a fast-food restaurant and stopped in the parking lot. The young woman driving the car broke the silence.

"I'm sorry about your friend," she said in a soft, tender voice.

Angela continued staring out the window.

Pausing for a moment, the woman continued, "Without him, we wouldn't have made it. He must have been a great guy."

Angela turned and looked at her. "He was," she said, feeling a lump rise in her throat. She had only known him a short while, but she felt as though her best friend had just died. But mourning now wouldn't help her find her son. She would have plenty of time for grief later, when her son was home safe. Swallowing hard, she mustered up the ability to continue. "I'm Angela, by the way."

"Jess," replied the young woman.

"Thank you for pulling me out back there." She paused for a moment, wondering if she should be courteous and ask about the woman's girlfriend. That's what Bill would have done, and normally, that's what she would do. But she couldn't help her right now; she needed to find Michael. "I-I'm looking for my son. His name is Michael."

"What does he look like?"

Angela pulled out the picture and showed her.

"Sorry, I haven't seen him," Jess said, a look of pity on her face.

"You don't happen to know what any of this means, do you?" Angela asked, showing Jess the picture of names and symbols on the phone.

Jess looked at the picture for a moment. "I'm sorry. I don't know what that means, either, but I did see markings like that on the front of the hospital."

"Yeah. I think they might be locations."

"I bet you'll be able to find him then," Jess replied. Her voice sounded somehow both hopeful yet doubtful.

"But how do I even go about finding any of them? Do I just drive around checking out every building in the world until I find one with a symbol?"

Jess's hopeful expression died out. They sat in silence for a moment before Angela spoke again.

"Sorry, I just don't know what to do. But I have to do something... You don't happen to have access to another vehicle, do you?"

"I actually might be able to help you out with that," Jess said, perking back up. "My stepdad lives nearby. He has an old car that still runs. We're just a few minutes away."

Angela breathed a sigh of relief. "Thanks so much." A small amount of hope sat in the corner of Angela's thoughts as they drove down some back roads. She didn't know how she was going to find any of the locations, but at least she would have a ride, even if it was an old one. They turned into a very expensive-looking neighborhood with high rod-iron fences and long driveways. They pulled up to a large two-story house with a detached garage.

"I'll go get the keys," Jess said, running into the house. Angela stood by the car for a couple minutes before Jess returned. She ran to the garage and went in a door on the side. A few seconds later, one of the garage doors raised.

Angela realized what Jess had meant about an 'old' car. It was a pristine classic car with a matte black finish. Someone had definitely put some work into keeping it looking like new.

"I don't know what it is, besides that it's old and it works," Jess said. "My stepdad loves this thing like it's one of his children. I've only seen him drive it a handful of times, but he starts it up and works on it every weekend." She gave Angela the keys with a smile. "Wait here, and I'll get you some things to take with you."

"You don't—"

Jess had already ran back to the house. She emerged with several grocery bags in hand. "It's just a few things you might need. There's some water and some fruit cups," she said, handing Angela the bags.

"Thanks!" Angela said, giving Jess a hug. It would have normally felt awkward to hug someone she just met, especially for Angela, a non-hugger. But it seemed right at that moment.

"You're welcome, but thank you. I wish there was something more I could do for you," replied Jess. "To get back to the interstate, just head down this road and turn left when you get to the stop sign. That road connects straight to it."

"Will you be fine here by yourself? What are you going to do?"

"I'll be okay here. Even though her car was there, I didn't find my girlfriend at the hospital. I think I'll gather some more food and water from here and go look for her."

"I-I'm sorry, I—"

"I'll be fine!" Jess interrupted, almost shooing Angela toward the car. "Just let me help you. Now go, find your son. And good luck!"

Angela got in the car and started it up. It smelled like leather and cleaner. The engine was loud and echoed off the garage walls. "Good luck to you and thank you!" Angela yelled, trying to be louder than the engine.

Jess stood back and waved as Angela drove down the driveway and toward the highway. The road was long, curvy, and lined by thick woods. She made it to a gas station next to the interstate and stopped.

Well, Angela, which way should I go? Left or right?

The familiar feeling of hopelessness started to creep back into her mind. She didn't recall seeing any sign of life on the way to the hospital, so she assumed she probably needed to keep heading east.

She was about to pull out of the parking lot when she saw a large dump truck drive past on the highway. "Got it!" She had to follow that truck. She let off the clutch too fast in her excitement and stalled. "Come on!" she yelled, restarting the car. The tires squealed as she sped off in pursuit of the truck.

She followed from a large distance, making sure to keep the truck just in sight. The whole time, she was stressed about the car. Would it break down? There was no gas gauge. Would she run out of gas soon and lose the truck? After an hour in pursuit of the truck, she started to get worried. The truck was still going, and they were in the middle of nowhere. Nothing but open fields and random patches of trees on either side of the road.

Finally, the truck veered off down an exit. Relieved, Angela felt her shoulders drop. Her hands loosened around the steering wheel she had been gripping so hard that her right pinky had gone to sleep. The truck turned down a dirt road that led through a field and over a hill. Angela slowed down but followed as the truck disappeared from view in a cloud of dust over the other side. She almost came to a stop to allow the dust to settle as she approached the hill. At the top, she could see some sort of huge mining site in the distance. There was plenty of movement at the site from people working on the large mounds scattered around.

There was no way that her loud car wouldn't be noticed coming down the dirt road. She saw a patch of trees up ahead on the left side of the road, just on the other side of the ditch. She carefully drove through the ditch and parked beside the trees, using them as cover. No one would be able to see her car from the road or the mining site. Only an old, beaten up shack was partially visible through the trees. Getting out and walking back toward the dirt road, she noticed a large sign up ahead.

The sign read, "Excavation Site, Restricted Area, No Trespassing, Property of US Army, All violators will be prosecuted." But what had been painted over it is what caught her eye. She whipped out the phone and pulled up the picture. Scanning it carefully, she suddenly had a burst of energy and excitement. The very first symbol on the list matched the symbol on the sign. Trying not to get her hopes up, she started to jog. She went through the ditch on the right and cut through the field toward the mining area.

30

Sean

It had been over eight years since Sean had driven this large of a vehicle. His tenseness driving the semi started in his toes and radiated to the top of his head, though there were no other cars on the road. He looked over at Marcus, who appeared to have passed out again already. They had only been on the road for a minute or so.

He reached over to put his hand on Marcus's chest and check for breathing. He really wished he could help Marcus, though selfishly he knew he just needed him alive long enough to help find Kristen.

Satisfied that he was still breathing, he was about to remove his hand when a strong grip grabbed him by the arm. Jayden screamed as the attacker tried to rip Sean from his seat. Confused by what was going on, his shoulder screamed in pain as it was pulled backward. He struggled to keep the truck on the road as he turned to see who had him. A man stared him dead in the eyes. He must have been behind the curtain in the backseat.

Why didn't I think to check the backseat?

The seatbelt held Sean in as the man tried to pull him from the driver's seat. The truck swerved back and forth on the road as the struggle went on. The seatbelt was now digging into Sean's neck. He felt his shoulder would dislocate any second. Frantically fumbling with the release button, he pushed it to gain relief. As the belt slid upward, he yelled to Jayden, "Hold onto something!" He slammed on the brake as hard as he could. Everyone in the cabin lurched forward. Jayden, who had moved behind the driver's seat, slammed into it hard. Marcus groaned in agony as the seat belt dug into his damaged body. Sean flung forward, the left side of his head and shoulder ramming into the steering wheel. The attacker flew into the front window with his head, causing the window to fracture.

The truck came to a hard and complete stop. Sean grabbed the man, opened the door, and jumped out, dragging the man to the pavement with him. They tumbled onto the ground in a heap. The man was on his feet before Sean and grabbed him by the leg. Sean reached for one of the weapons in his pocket, but as soon as he had it in his hand, he was flung across the road toward a ditch like a ragdoll. He skidded across the concrete, rolling to a stop. The phaser bounced into the grass somewhere nearby. He prepared for a hit by protecting his face with his hands as the attacker ran toward him.

"Ahhh!" yelled Jayden, jumping out of the truck. Sean turned in time to see Jayden running toward them with what looked like a wrench in his hand. The man stopped and turned his attention to Jayden.

"No, Jayden, run!" Sean yelled in desperation. Before the attacker could take a step, Sean locked his arms around the man's legs and brought him to the ground, immediately jumping on top of him and kneeing him in the lower back several times.

Jayden stopped advancing and stepped back. The man lay on the ground in screaming agony as Sean stood up.

"Get in the truck, now!" Sean exclaimed, fearful that he may not be able to protect the young boy. Hurt and bleeding, Sean jogged back to the truck. He immediately got the truck moving again, keeping an eye on the body contorting in pain lying on the road behind him.

"Sean," Marcus said in a laborious voice. "We have to go back. He knows everything we plan to do."

"What? How?" asked Sean, trying to concentrate while wiping blood from his forehead.

"They communicate when close to each other, remember? He knows because I couldn't keep him out of my brain. He knows, and if he lives, he will let them all know that we plan to stop them."

Sean's adrenaline was running high, but he could still think clearly. He knew what Marcus was implying he do. There was no other choice. Even if they tried to tie up the man and keep him away from everyone else, he was too strong.

Sean slowed the truck and looked in the side mirror. The man was still lying on the ground. He backed the truck up just a little, turning the wheel enough to block the view of the man in the mirror. He didn't want Jayden to be able to see what was about to happen.

"Stay here, Jayden," he commanded. "Do not get out." As he stepped out of the truck, he pulled the second phaser out of his pocket, readied it, and jogged toward the man. Everything in him was against what was about to happen. This was not something he ever thought he would have to do. He racked his brain for any other option, though he knew there was none. He approached the man who was still on the ground, helpless and in pain with a dark liquid running from his mouth. Sean stood there for a second, his hands shaking and tears building in his eyes. He raised his arm and took aim...and a second later, it was all over.

Sean returned to Jayden and Marcus waiting in the truck. He got into the seat and buckled up. Looking at Marcus, he gave him a small nod. No one spoke a word as they got back to driving.

Time seemed to travel slowly. Sean felt sick. He felt as though he could vomit and cry at the same time, but neither came. All the pains in his entire body were gone. He felt completely numb now. Everything had to be pushed down inside. There was a mission that had to be done, and it seemed that it was up to him to make it happen. For Jayden, for Kristen, for humanity.

They drove for over an hour before Sean realized that it was lunch time. He wasn't in the mood to eat anything, but Jayden must be hungry. There was a house by itself in the distance with a large white barn next to it. It was set back off the road, and if Sean could park between the house and barn, the truck wouldn't be easily seen from the main road.

"Let's make a little stop and get something to eat, huh?" Sean said, breaking the hour-long silence. He slowed the truck and turned. As they proceeded down the long driveway, there were wooden signs that let Sean know that this was an event venue. The property was one of the cleanest Sean had seen, and the landscaping was well taken care of. He almost felt bad driving on the grass to park the truck. The amount of room between the house and barn was perfect for the truck and trailer.

"I'm going to go check it out, and I'll be right back. Jayden, stay here with Marcus. Lock the door behind me." Sean stepped out and looked around. There was no sign of anyone nearby, but he readied the phaser anyway. The door to the house was unlocked, so he let himself in. He was in a room that was set up to be a lounge with TV's, couches, and even a small bar. He assumed it was for a bride or groom to get ready. Carefully checking the room, he went to the bar where there was a full-sized refrigerator. Opening it, he found it stocked with sodas, energy drinks, beer, and water. A charcuterie board with meats, cheeses, and crackers sat on the top shelf covered in plastic wrap. It didn't look too old and didn't seem too warm, but some condensation had collected on the wrap. He smelled the food.

Fancy and seems good enough. Should be fine.

With nothing to carry everything in, he shoved several water bottles in his pockets and brought the board back to the truck.

"Y'all hungry?"

Jayden shook his head. "No, but I'm a little thirsty."

Sean gave him some water and pulled the wrap off the board anyway.

"Thanks," Marcus said, shifting in his chair, "normally I'd finish something like that off all on my own, but I'm afraid I wouldn't keep it down more than a few seconds."

"I guess we better get back on the road then," Sean said, putting the board on the back seat and buckling up. His head and shoulder were throbbing from the attack earlier. It wasn't easy to back the semi out from between the houses, but after a few tries, Sean finally got it out and turned around toward the road. As they drove, Sean glanced back to check on Jayden. He was snacking on the board of food. At least he had something in his stomach now.

Only ten minutes down the road, they could see the excavation area in the distance. Sean pulled the truck over to the side of the road, and they watched for any activity. Just ahead, he could see that the pavement ended, and the road became a rocky, dirt road.

"Don't think we can just drive right in there and ask for that map, huh?" Sean said, trying to lighten the mood a bit.

"They'd know you weren't one of them as soon as they tried to communicate and couldn't read your mind," said Marcus. "I'm afraid I can't go with you, either. They'd read me in a second. You're going to have to sneak your way in there. The device will most likely be a computer or tablet of some sort."

"We'll have to wait for night then," Sean said, looking back at Jayden. Here he was, back in a situation in which he would have to leave Jayden behind again. He wasn't safe just sitting here in this large truck. And what if something happened to him and he couldn't make it back to Jayden? Who would take care of this eight-year-old boy? Marcus sure as hell wouldn't make it.

In the distance, he saw an abandoned shack slightly to the south near where the road turned from pavement to dirt. It was farther away from the site. The shack was in disrepair, but would be a lot less noticeable than the truck they were in.

"Here we go," he whispered to himself. "So Marcus, how far do you think they can read your mind from?" asked Sean.

"I don't know, maybe ten to fifteen feet or so," Marcus replied.

"Good," Sean said, getting the truck moving toward the shack. "You should be plenty far enough if I can hide y'all in that shack there. Jayden, if you have a jacket in your backpack, grab it. You can leave the backpack in here. See if you can find any blankets in the back seat to keep you two warm."

He parked the semi a good distance away from the little house. He didn't want the truck and trailer to draw attention to it. He got out and ran the distance to the door. He was prepared to break the already cracked window in the front, but the door was unlocked and just a little stuck. It didn't take much work to get it open. Peeking around the inside, it was obvious it hadn't been used for some time. The smell reminded him of an old attic. A dirty, used mattress standing up in the corner had seen better days. There was no sign of anyone or any animals in the small room. Sean laid the mattress down on the floor and ran back outside. Getting back to the truck, he opened Marcus's door.

"This is going to hurt, and it won't be a short trip, but we have to get you inside," Sean told him. Marcus nodded and tried to brace himself. It took several minutes to get him down out of the truck and all the way into the shack. The agony he was in seemed unbearable. Sean helped lay Marcus on the mattress. Jayden stood in the doorway holding several blankets from the truck.

Jayden didn't say anything but moved to Marcus, laying one of the blankets over him before going to Sean. "Sean, are we going to see Kristen again?" His lip quivered in the dim light as he spoke.

"Of course we are, buddy. I can feel it. She's okay, and we'll find her."

"But..." Jayden whispered, starting to cry, "what if we don't? What if she's—"

"Hey! You get those thoughts out of your head," Sean interrupted. "We're going to find her, and that's it. I know it's hard to be positive right now, but it's all we have control of. We have to keep going. Besides, you know how strong and badass your sister is. She's gotta be okay."

Jayden looked down at the floor. The tears dripped off his nose and fell to the ground. His statement acknowledged that he could guess Sean's next move. "I-I don't want you to go. Please don't leave me again." His sad eyes looked up at Sean.

"Hey, bud," Sean said, pulling the boy to him and holding him tight. "I'm going to stay right here with you until dark. Then I'll sneak over and grab something and come right back here. Simple and quick. And you're gonna be okay. You know why? Cause you're a badass too, that's why. Let me hear you say it."

Jayden shook his head and looked up at Sean with a small smile.

"Come on, you can say it. You won't be in trouble. Just say, 'I'm a badass!'"

"I'm a badass!" Jayden said with a full smile now, though tears still streamed from his eyes.

"Yeah you are!" Sean gave the boy a hug. "You're more of a badass than you know."

31

Angela

When Angela came to a barbed wire fence, she stopped and looked around. If she kept going straight toward the excavation site, she would end up right in the middle of all the action. Her best chance would be to get in through the barbed wire and make a giant arc to the right. Then she could come to the site from the opposite side. There were large trucks and heavy equipment lining that side. They would probably offer her some cover.

She looked up at the sun. She had no clue of the actual time as the car had no clock and the phone she held didn't show the time since it had no service. She suspected that it was getting closer to evening. The sun set between 6 and 7 pm this time of year. Maybe it was close to 4:30 or 5 pm, she thought.

Trying to squeeze through the barbed wire, she got her shoelace snagged. She fell to the ground as her shoe came off. Landing on her right wrist, she felt and heard a small pop. "Shit!" She retrieved her lost shoe and inspected it. The lace had torn partway through, but it would still hold. She wiped the dirt off her sock, put on the shoe, and dusted herself off. Moving her wrist in a circle, it felt sore, but beyond that, it seemed fine. She turned and started her loop around the area.

The large trucks cast huge shadows in the setting sun. Angela had completed the wide arc and waited behind a boulder in the field. The semi's were between her and the mining site. She wanted to wait until night to get any closer. She could feel her wrist throbbing now. Inspecting it further, she found swelling. Stiffness was setting in.

All this, and I mess up my wrist by tripping. No more mistakes, Angela. No more.

She felt worn out emotionally and physically but needed to stay awake. She sat on the earth behind the huge rock. Her eyes struggled to stay open. Her blinks became slower and slower. Against her better judgment, she closed her eyes.

32

Sean

Marcus had gone to sleep almost immediately. Sean would check on him here and there to make sure he was still alive. Neither Sean nor Jayden spoke much during the day and into the evening. Jayden stayed glued to Sean's side, even walking over to check on Marcus with him. After multiple long hours, it was finally time for Sean to go. The light in the shack was nearly all gone as the sun dipped in the sky.

"Jayden, I need you to stay here with Marcus," Sean said looking into his eyes. "But," he whispered, "if any trouble comes, I need you to run as fast as you can. Okay? Just keep running until you're safe. He won't be able to help you, and you won't be able to help him. You got it?"

"Okay," Jayden said, with a nervous and sad nod.

"Hey, I'll be back. I promise." Sean kneeled down and gave Jayden a tight hug. Standing up, he walked to the door, stopping just before exiting. "Hang in there, Marcus. We need you." He closed the door behind him and started his walk toward the excavation site. A small glimmer of light reflected off something in a patch of trees down the road. He looked again but didn't see anything.

The sun was now just behind some trees far away in the distance. Sean walked closer and squatted down in the ditch next to the dirt road. He would work his way north. There were large pieces of equipment like backhoes and bulldozers on the north side of the excavation area. The darkness of evening would soon give him plenty of cover.

Making it to the heavy equipment from the shack was fairly easy. The lights that lit the excavation area were pointing mostly inward to give light to those that seemed to be working. It was a perfectly dark night to be sneaking around. There were large heaps of earth that made up the area. Sean was still a good ways from the main area but would see the occasional head pop up as people were doing some type of work on top of the heaps.

His best course of action was to get as close as he could to see the whole situation. If he walked a little further north, he should be blocked from the view of everyone working. Cautiously aware that he would still be partially visible for a few moments, he jogged north while watching everyone he could see. While running in the dark, he stumbled over a large weed or bush of some kind. Not completely falling, he caught himself with his hands and quickly jogged forward. He couldn't see it in the low light, but he was sure there was a small cactus needle stuck in his left hand between his index finger and thumb. Ignoring it for now, he checked around, finding himself out of the line of sight of anyone.

Sean knew he had to be more cautious. He couldn't afford to get hurt when everyone was counting on him. He slowed to a brisk walk, keeping both an eye out for anyone and scanning for tripping hazards in the dark. As he neared one of the heaps of earth, he could hear noises from the other side. First, some sort of soft tone or beeping. Then, the sound of shovels digging in the rock and dirt. Some of the piles near Sean were close enough to just touch each other at the bottom, while others were so close that they touched at a point taller than him.

He found two mounds that were barely touching at the bottom. Supporting himself with one hand on a large rock from one of the mounds, he carefully leaned forward to see through the gap. Two men were digging, though for what he had no idea. They all focused on their work and were unaware that Sean was less than twenty feet from them. Some people did have small objects that looked like metal detectors, but he didn't see anything that resembled the tablet or computer that Marcus had told him about. He'd have to keep looking elsewhere. As Sean pushed himself upright and off the heap, the large rock he had his hand on shifted out of the pile and rolled down near his feet. The sound of it was loud enough to make Sean duck low in the shadows but not so loud as to be heard by the workers over the digging and beeping.

Standing up, he looked right and left, searching for what he thought would be the best direction to go. To his right, were piles of dirt and rock almost in a straight line that ended in a lit, open field. To his left, the mounds started a curve that arched around out of his sight into the darkness. Sean chose to go left. Staying in the dark felt like the way to go. He walked slowly and made his way from pile to pile, following the curve and checking at each conjunction for any sign of a tablet or station that would contain the map he was searching for.

The curve took him around the excavation site and back in the other direction. He could see large semis, trailers, and dump trucks at the end of the heaps on this side. He continued on, carefully moving toward the trucks. A very noticeable equipment sound was growing louder the closer he got to the trucks. Peeking in between some heaps, he could see the source—a conveyor belt in the middle transporting rocks toward a large cylindrical tank of some kind. It wasn't important to him, so he went on.

As he made his way behind the fourth to last heap, a rockslide came from the top toward him. He jumped back and looked up the pile. Standing near the top was a young man of maybe twenty with a device in his right hand. Sean froze, not knowing if the man could see him or if the dark concealed him enough. He didn't move, didn't breathe. It seemed as if the man was looking directly at Sean but not coming toward him. As he stood as still as possible, Sean noticed that the metal detector device in the man's hand was letting out the odd tone he had been hearing for a while now.

Sean squinted at the man on the pile. The man's eyes were transfixed on the device. It let out a couple of beeps, and the man stepped down, disappearing again down the heap of earth.

Sean took this as a chance to move and jogged forward past the next three heaps, stopping behind the last. He turned his head in time to see another young man now on top of the heap he had been at. The new man was digging with a shovel and tossing the rock and dirt back down toward where he had come.

Sure he couldn't be clearly seen from this distance, Sean then turned his attention toward the semis. There was a considerable distance between the last pile of earth and the semis and trailers. Glancing around toward the main excavation area, the lights were shining too brightly. He realized that there was next to no way he would be able to cross that field and get to the trucks without being seen. He looked off into the darkness much farther away from the excavation site. As much as he was anxious to get to the trucks now, it would probably be his best bet to make a huge trip out into the dark night out of view and come back up behind the trucks.

Sean had made up his mind to do it when he heard a large vehicle start up. It was a very huge excavator that had been parked in the middle of the area. He waited to see what it would do. A few moments later, it turned and started making its way toward the heap that Sean was behind. Trying not to panic, he continued to watch.

As it came closer to him, the excavator turned slightly, setting a course toward the trucks. He became excited. This could be his chance to make it to the trucks sooner! The heavy piece of equipment cast a large shadow on Sean's side of the excavation site. He crouched and waited for his chance to run beside the vehicle toward the truck area. Making one final look to see if anyone was watching, he took off in a full run as the machine went past the last heap. He managed to get beside it easily, but the ground was incredibly uneven. The tracks that propelled the excavator forward were nearly as tall as Sean. He worked hard to stay in the shadows as he dodged large rocks, brush, and dips. Sean could see the driver but was confident that it was too dark for the driver to see him. The driver's gaze also didn't move from his target. As the excavator moved across the field, it was moving away from the source of light. The shadow it cast slowly moved toward the front of the machine. Sean tried to keep up without getting completely in the eye shot of the driver and staying far enough away so as not to be crushed under the tracks.

Luckily, as the shadow was just about to be only in front of the moving equipment, Sean was close enough to make a quick left and get behind one of the trailers. He ducked down and watched the excavator continue to a dump truck that was currently dumping more earth. As the dump truck finished with its load and the back gate slammed shut, it drove off, away from the area. The excavator then scooped up more rock and dirt and went back to the first heap. Dropping it on the top of the pile, it then turned and came back for more.

33

A large slam of heavy machinery rang through the air. Angela's body jolted, and she sat up, realizing that she had fallen asleep. It was now pitch-black outside.

"Shit," she said under her breath, scanning the darkness for any movement. How could she have let herself fall asleep when she could be so close to getting her son? She turned and peeked over the boulder toward the main part of the excavation area. The trucks and trailers blocked most of her view, but she could still see movement going on. A dump truck was driving off into the night, and a large excavator was dumping more rock and dirt on the top of an already huge heap of rock. The excavator reminded her of a toy Michael used to play with as a child. He would call it a "digger truck". There were several tall lights positioned far away from where Angela was. They reminded her of lights on a baseball field. Even from this far away, huge swarms of bugs could be seen bouncing off and circling the lights.

She started making her way closer. Coming out from behind the boulder, she crept through the darkness toward the trucks. The trailers were tall enough for her to duck under without having to crawl. She went from one to another, staying crouched down, making her way toward the action. She was now close enough to see people walking around.

Sean's plan was to start checking the trucks for the tablet. With no building around, he assumed it would be contained in someplace out of the open. The trucks seemed like his only choice at the moment. He checked the first semi's cab. The door was unlocked, and he was able to slip in quickly. Once in, he scanned the cab for anything. Besides a foam cup and the smell of sweat, there wasn't anything in the cab. Before moving to the next truck, he wanted to check the trailer of the semi. He got out and went to the back. Slowly easing the latching mechanism for the back of the trailer open, he pulled the door up just a bit and looked inside. Unable to see anything in the darkness, he pulled it open more, just enough to slide in on his stomach. The door must have triggered a light to come on inside. It caught him off guard, but all seemed fine. It was a fairly bright light in the middle of the trailer, and it allowed him to see all the way to the front. The entire container was empty except for one pallet in the front corner. Not wanting to be seen, he slowly lowered the door and went to investigate the pallet.

It was a large wooden box, half full of shovels. He couldn't help feeling a little disheartened. But there were still at least eight more trucks to check out, and they couldn't all be carrying a single box of shovels. The light dimmed as he walked back to exit. It had to be on some sort of timer when the door was shut. He waited by the door for a second, trying to listen for anyone close by. Only the excavator could be heard. He bent down and opened the door just enough to peek outside. With the coast clear, he crawled out of the trailer and closed the door once again.

As Angela started for the last truck that was closest to the main area, she heard footsteps in the gravel to her right. She immediately ducked back under the trailer she had just emerged from and looked into the darkness. Her heart beat in her ears. She held her breath.

Angela squatted down to the dirt in order to get lower and more into the shadows of the trucks. As she put her right hand onto the ground to lower herself down, pain shot through her wrist and up her arm. She winced, unable to keep herself squatting. She fell onto her right side, striking her head on something protruding near the tire of the trailer. She wanted to let out a sound but stayed silent, not moving. She continued to stare into the night, searching for whatever or whomever made the noise in the gravel a moment ago.

Sean could swear he heard someone walking nearby; he ducked down to see. There was nothing but darkness and random beams of light shining here and there between the trucks. He stuck his head out to peer between the two trailers. Squinting in the darkness, he saw movement. It was gone in a second. He was pretty sure it was an animal crawling beneath one of the other trucks. He quickly jumped up on the back step of the trailer he was nearest and waited just in case.

There was a small thump from one of the trailers. He imagined it was probably the animal running into something underneath. He listened for a moment but heard nothing else. Staying on the back step, he grabbed the side handle of the trailer and leaned out enough to see. Nothing. Nothing but darkness. Since he was already at the back of this trailer, he decided to check this one next. Still wary, he opened it carefully. He found it completely empty. Stepping down, he went for the next one.

Angela thought she heard the faint sound of the trailer door of the semi she was under raise and lower, but she wasn't sure. The bump to her head coupled with the dose of adrenaline made it hard to hear amongst all the other noise of the area. After two full minutes of barely breathing and staring in the darkness, she was satisfied that there was no longer anything there.

Probably just my imagination or an animal.

She rolled onto her stomach and pushed herself up with her left arm. Wiping the dirt off her hand, she touched the spot on her head that still stung from the impact. Her hair around the spot was wet. Probably blood, but it couldn't be too bad as the blood seemed localized and not spreading into more of her hair. No time to worry about it now. She was too close. She wiped her hand off on her jeans and made sure the coast was clear to move in closer.

Getting to the last semi, she crawled on her stomach under the actual truck this time. It was tight and hard to crawl since she couldn't use her right hand to pull herself forward, but she managed. Getting her first close-up view of the area, she could see just about everything from her spot under the truck.

There were eleven huge mounds of rock and dirt making a sort of semicircle or 'U' shape with equipment in the middle. The opening of the semicircle was to her left as she faced it, putting her closest to the mound on the right. Since she faced the opening, she could see almost the entire area inside of it. There were three people at each mound. One had a device that appeared similar to a metal detector but much smaller. They would move the device back and forth, then the other two would dig with shovels. No one spoke a word, yet everyone seemed to know exactly what to do and where to dig.

The excavator that had awoken her was making trips back and forth, picking up more material from dump trucks and dumping it on the top of each mound in the semicircle. There were large carts with wheelbarrow sized metal containers near each mound. The workers that dug would dump the rock they shoveled into the containers.

The carts would periodically be pushed to a machine in the middle with a conveyor belt where the worker would dump the contents of the containers onto the belt. Angela squinted at the cart closest to her. She blinked her eyes several times. It looked like it was hovering inches off the ground.

Must have hit my head harder than I thought. What is going on?

She snapped back to reality as she heard a very low-pitched noise that penetrated deep into her head. The source seemed to be coming from a machine near the end of the conveyor. The conveyor that was dropping the dirt and rock into a large cylinder had stopped. The cylinder itself was making the noise. Angela could feel the vibration from far away.

It lasted for a few minutes before suddenly making an electric sound, and all was silent. A man near the cylinder walked to a small square door near the bottom and opened it. He then pulled out what looked like a bar of polished metal. It was about the size and length of a normal man's arm. Its surface was like a mirror, reflecting light all around. He closed the door, and the conveyor started once again. The man took the bar to a semi-trailer that was parked near the middle of the opening of the semicircle. He slid the bar into the back of the trailer. Angela watched as it disappeared from sight into the darkness.

She scanned the people working for any sign of her son. Her eyes stopped on a young man scanning the mound on the complete opposite side of the semicircle, the mound on the left of the opening. She started to shake with nerves as she squinted at the man. As his back turned completely to her, she let out a gasp. That was his shirt, she knew it! It was him!

I'm coming, Michael!

Crawling backward to get out from under the truck, she couldn't even feel her wrist pain anymore. She looked for a route toward the mound. She was so excited that she could hardly focus.

Come on, Angie. You're so close!

Facing the excavation site, she looked toward the mound closest to her, the one on the right side of the opening. It looked like at least a fifty-to-seventy-five-foot run through a well-lit open area to get behind it. Luckily everyone was working on the mounds on the inside of the semicircle, so if she could get to the backside of that first mound, she would be in the darkness and should be able to work her way around to the opposite side and to her son.

She crept to the back of the trailer and peered around it at the people working. They would see her for sure if she just took off running. If she tried to get farther away from the light, she would have to make a large arch, and it would take forever for her to get to her son. The grass was in patches, nearly one foot tall, and there were random small boulders and large rocks speckling the field. She might be able to get from one point to another if she went quickly and lay low anywhere she could.

She plotted her course meticulously. First, on the way to the closest mound, would be a large patch of tall grass that she would lie in. Then she would crawl through it to a group of rocks in a pile nearby. Then a short run and drop behind another pile of rocks. Then a large boulder before another crawl through some grass to the first mound. It had to work.

Taking one final look at the people working, she made a run toward the first patch of grass. It was taller than she thought, which made it easier to get down into and disappear from sight. She lay still for a moment and waited for any sign of movement. With no one noticing her, she looked toward the pile of rocks ahead and crawled on her stomach toward them. Her wrist was hurting again, but she pushed through the pain. Sharp rocks in the grass scraped her arms and stomach as she dragged herself forward.

The patch of grass thinned as she reached the edge. Now able to see the group of people, she checked for anyone looking her way and quickly crawled behind the rocks. She had to lie on her side and bring her knees toward her chest to be completely blocked from their line of sight. The next pile of rocks was larger but further away than it had previously appeared. Angela tried to stay low and rolled to her stomach. She peeked out enough to see the workers. From the angle she was now at, only a couple would be able to see her. Using her left arm, she quickly pushed herself up and ran for the next set of rocks. She slid behind them like a baseball player sliding in for a homerun. The slide caused a large amount of dirt to be thrown up from behind the rocks. The dust was highly visible in the night air as the light from the main area reflected off each particle floating away.

34

As Sean continued checking the semi's for the tablet that would contain the map, something caught his eye. At the opening of the U-shaped excavation site, on the opposite side back where he had started his journey, was a glowing blue light reflecting off an older man's face. Even at this distance, he could tell it was coming from a rectangular tablet that the man was standing in front of. It sat on a small metal podium.

His heart beat fast as he quickly started looking for a way to cross the field to get to the device. The dirt pile left by the dump truck was still large enough to hide behind, and on the other side of that was another semi and trailer with the back open. If he could get to that truck, it would still be a good distance to get to the tablet. But there was still the problem of a man standing near it.

A distraction! I need to make it big.

With a distraction, maybe all eyes would be away from both him and the device. He quickly snuck to the truck nearest his route across the field. Parked in front of it was a small forklift with a large propane tank. He couldn't think of anything he could use the forklift for since he had never driven one. So he got in the truck. He looked all around but didn't know what he was looking for. He couldn't just honk the horn because they would come straight to him. And it wasn't a big enough distraction anyway.

While searching the interior, he found a long sleeve shirt, some trash, and an unopened energy drink. Nothing he could use as a distraction. Then his hand ran into a lighter. Grabbing it, he smiled. He had a crazy idea that just might work.

Sean rolled the windows of the truck halfway down. He grabbed the shirt and hopped out of the truck. Walking to the fuel tank, he opened the cap and started trying to shove the sleeve of the shirt in the tank. After getting the entire sleeve in, he pulled it out. Diesel splashed out and onto his shoes. His hands were soaked in it. He ran back to the cab of the truck and started wringing it out all over the driver's seat. He then went back and repeated the process over and over, spreading the fuel over all the seats and surfaces. He lost count of how many times he went back and forth. The smell was intense, and he started to feel a bit sick. He had it all over his hands and shoes but had kept it mostly off the rest of himself.

Happy with the amount of diesel spread out, Sean snuck to the forklift and unhooked the tank of propane. Carrying it back to the truck, he put it in the passenger seat. He then pulled out the lighter. He laid the now completely wet shirt over the driver's seat and dangled the sleeve over the edge. The breeze was just enough to put a strain on the lighter. He used his body to try and block the wind while he used just his right hand to strike the lighter. After three strikes, the lighter lit, and he carefully held it near the sleeve of the draping shirt. The flame danced all around the shirt but wouldn't light.

The lighter began getting hot in his hand. "Come on, dammit!" he whispered in frustration. Just when he thought it was a bust, the sleeve caught fire. The fire slowly moved up the shirt toward the seat. Sean jumped down and ran to the front of the truck. The excavator was just leaving the pile left by the dump truck. Sean ran and ducked down behind the pile. He crawled on his stomach to the edge and looked around. Nobody was looking yet. He glanced back at the fire he had started. It was visible to him but not large yet. Smoke was starting to pour out of the windows he had opened.

He waited, not knowing if the fire would get large enough to see or if the propane tank would do anything either. It wasn't a movie, but he knew if enough pressure from the heat built up in the tank, it should blow. After several minutes, the flames started to grow. Sean was about fifty feet away as he watched. The flames got so large that they danced out of the windows. He could smell burnt rubber in the air, even over the diesel smell on his hands.

Giving the dust she'd stirred up time to dissipate, Angela again checked on the people working on the mounds. She squatted and took a deep breath, readying herself for the short run to the next boulder. A commotion started from the workers. She looked around, sure that someone had spotted her. Instead, she saw that one of the trucks back where she'd just come from was on fire. Most of the workers had stopped what they were doing and were running toward the flames. Whatever it was, it made a perfect distraction. She ran as fast as she could, bypassing the rest of her plan and heading straight for the first mound.

Sean's plan had worked. People stopped what they were doing, including the man near the device. They turned toward the fire and began to move toward it.

Now was his chance! Sean stood up and ran for the other side of the field, toward the left side of the opening of the site. Sean reached the tablet that lay on a stand. It was built much like a standard tablet except the symbols and words on the screen seemed to be on the very surface of the glass instead of behind it.

The trouble was that it was stuck to the stand it lay on. Sean couldn't see any clips. It was as though an incredibly strong magnet held it in place. He strained to remove it, with no luck. Unable to break it loose, he decided to drag the stand behind the closest mound of dirt. It took just a moment to finally get it behind the mound where he wouldn't be seen by anyone at the site.

Though Angela was not a runner, she did pride herself on staying fit. A combination of mostly unprocessed food, plenty of water, short daily workouts, and weekly yoga had kept her in pretty good shape. Right now, it was all paying off. She ran as fast as she could without tiring. She made the long trek around the outside of the semi-circle excavation site in record time. As she came near the mound that she had seen her son at, she stopped short, almost sliding in the rocks.

What am I going to do now? Stroll over and take him with me?

With too many people around, someone was bound to see her.

What if he's been turned into one of those 'zombies' too?

The thought shook her to the core, making her shudder. Just then, she saw movement near the mound at the end. She stood staring as the shadow of a man dragging a large object near the edge of the last pile of rocks.

As Sean made it behind the mound, he came face to face with a very young man. Just then, the propane tank in the flaming truck had finally reached a pressure that it couldn't handle. Sean never heard the explosion. He had no time to draw his weapon. The last thing he saw was the young man pointing one of the phasers at his chest—then nothing.

35

Angela

A young man stepped out from between the mounds and walked toward the approaching shadow. As the young man stepped into a beam of light, she recognized the shirt he was wearing. She ran toward the two people as the one dragging the object rounded the mound. Her son raised one of the handheld devices that she knew all too well. Her heart dropped as she slid to another stop, a million thoughts running through her exhausted brain. She fought to stay in control although she wanted to scream. The familiar sound that the device made was drowned out by an explosion on the other side of the excavation site. Watching her son, she could see the second man drop almost in slow motion. Shadows and light flickered all around as a ball of flame floated up from her left on the other side of the mounds and disappeared into the night. All sounds were partially muted in her ears. The echoes in the night, non-existent to her. The blast of light gave her a very clear view of the young man's face. A sick feeling of both relief and pain penetrated her heart. Relief from the fact that it was definitely not Michael who'd just shot the man, and pain from the fact that she hadn't found her son. This was just another young man of similar build wearing a shirt much like one her son owned.

Something came over her like never before. Maybe it was the memory of Bill's body hitting the concrete, or her neighbor Donald killed at his own home, or the loss of hope once again of not finding her son. But she snapped. She picked up a large rock in one hand and ran at the young man. He never had a chance to turn around. The rock struck him in the back of the head, and he went down like a ton of bricks. She quickly kicked the weapon he held into the darkness of the night. Turning her attention to the poor man that had been killed by the device, she bent down to get a look at him in what little light there was. To her surprise, he was breathing!

Angela took quick action and grabbed the man. She strained through the pain of her damaged wrist and managed to hook her elbows under his armpits. She lifted and successfully dragged the man more into the shadows, propping him up on a mound. Since the younger man had just shot this guy, she assumed he wasn't one of them.

Her rage subsiding, she began to think more clearly. She then went back to check on the young man she had struck with the rock. He lay unconscious but also breathing. Angela let out a sigh of relief, comforted that she had not just killed someone's child while in a rage. He lay at a spot where he may be seen from someone else at the right angle, so she gripped him under the arms and pulled him behind a mound as well, stopping to sit and think about what her next plan of action would be while she rested.

The object the second man had been dragging had fallen over when he went down. She went back and inspected it. Recognizing the tablet as having the same symbols as the computer at the hospital, she tried to remove it. It wouldn't budge. She didn't know how long she had.

Will one of these men awaken soon? Would someone currently preoccupied with the fire come to find this tablet?

Trying to hurry, she tapped the screen, but nothing happened. Then she held her finger to the screen for a second. Two blue circles popped up on the screen with symbols in them. The symbol on the right kind of looked familiar, but she couldn't be sure. Her shaking hand reached out and touched the symbol on the right. She held her finger to it. The circle turned green just as the one on the puck at the hospital had. The man who'd been shot with the device groaned. Angela immediately picked up another good-sized rock and jogged over to him.

She held it over her head, ready to strike him in the face. She thought he may be completely human, but she wasn't willing to bet her life on it. As the man grabbed his chest and blinked open his eyes, she raised the rock even higher. His wits returned to him, and he noticed her standing over him.

"Whoa!" he yelled, putting his hands up to protect his face.

Angela jumped back, still holding the rock at the ready in case he tried to attack her first. The man pushed himself up by sliding his back up the pile of rock and dirt behind him, never taking his eyes off Angela. He slowly put his hand behind his back like he was trying to pick up a rock of his own without her seeing.

"Are you human?" she blurted out aggressively. "I mean, are y-you know...human?"

The man stared at her for a moment, dropped his rock, and put his hands up to show he was not a threat.

"Yes, I'm human," he replied. "You had me scared. I thought you were one of them, and you were going to take me out."

Angela lowered the rock just a little, still keeping it ready. The man pushed himself off the mound. He let out a relieved sigh and rubbed his chest again. He suddenly looked around, appearing slightly panicked. Angela could tell what he was looking for. She pointed to the guy propped up on a mound nearby.

"He's over there...unconscious," she whispered, still unsure if anyone else was near.

He seemed hesitant to move, but slowly took a step forward to see if he could spot the man who'd just shot him.

Angela backed up even more, watching him intently.

"I don't blame you," he said, stepping back. "It's hard to trust anything right now. I feel like even my brain is lying to me with all this stuff going on. I'm hoping to wake up, and this will all have been a dream. I'm Sean by the way."

"Angela," she said, finally lowering the rock but not letting it go.

A noise nearby made them both crouch down and look around. When Angela realized there was no immediate danger, she spoke. "What are you doing here?"

Sean looked in the direction of the stand lying on the ground. "That thing has some sort of map for where people are and—" he paused. "It's stuck, and I can't get it off."

Angela looked at the tablet. She started to feel hopeful. Hopeful that someone might be able to help her find her son.

"I think I can get it off," she said, thinking of how she'd released the puck from the door back at the hospital. "Do you know how to read it?"

Sean shook his head. "No, but I have a friend nearby that I think can."

Angela ran back to the tablet, keeping her side to Sean so that she would see if he attacked. She held her finger to the screen again. The same two circles popped up, and she drew her finger in a circle just like the puck lock from the hospital. The tablet seemed to just let go of its hold to the stand. It nearly fell to the ground, but Angela caught it, dropping her rock in the process.

Sean looked on. He appeared to be impressed with Angela. Probably because she had subdued his attacker, been prepared to bash his head in if he wasn't *human*, and now had figured out how to release the tablet just like that.

"Thank you," he said. "We have a truck over there. Once we get to it, we can pick up my friends and go."

Angela peered in the direction Sean was pointing in. It was too dark to see any truck from here.

"Friends?" she asked, feeling more nervous. She still didn't trust this guy, and now *friends* were involved. "Who are your friends—"

She stopped mid-thought. A low but very distinct humming sound rumbled in the distance. The sound echoed off all the dirt and rock around them. They both looked to the sky to where the loudest sound seemed to be coming from.

"What the hell is that? Do you see anything?" asked Sean.

"No, nothing." She was wary but wasn't surprised that there was yet another thing to worry about. The sound grew louder, as if something in the distance was getting closer. She felt the thickness of impending doom in the air. "There!" yelled Angela, pointing toward a set of bright lights in the sky in the distance. "I don't think we should wait around to see what it is, though."

"Let's go!" Sean said, motioning her to follow him.

They crouched down and ran through the darkness away from the excavation site. Angela kept right behind Sean, allowing him to lead the way since she had no clue where she was going. The lights making the humming sound were nearly to the area, traveling at incredible speeds. The sound was almost deafening. It reverberated off everything around them, even shaking the ground they ran on. As they got to some heavy equipment, bulldozers and backhoes, the lights had reached the site. Angela and Sean ducked under the bucket of a backhoe and looked toward the lights.

Hovering just above the main excavation site were five crafts. The lights from the excavation site allowed them to see the aircraft as plain as day. They had the shape of eggs that were stretched. They hovered perfectly still, as if somehow locked into an exact position. Angela thought the crafts looked like a combination of metal and stone, with parts of them having an almost mirror-like sheen. It was hard at this distance to tell the real size, but they looked to maybe be the size of a pickup truck.

"What the hell are those?" she asked Sean, trying to be loud enough for him to hear her over the crafts.

"I think they're the alien's ships!" he yelled back.

She didn't have time to ask what he meant about aliens and how he knew this stuff. She just had to trust him for now and leave the questions for when they weren't being chased by mysterious flying vessels straight out of a Sci-Fi movie. They watched on as the crafts all formed a circle, hovering above the middle of the excavation site, rotating seemingly to face outward, though as far as Angela could tell, there were no windows or other indications to show where the *fronts* of the ships were. The earth-shaking sound lessened quickly, eventually becoming no more than a barely noticeable hum. The crafts then slowly started moving in all directions away from the site.

Sean pulled on Angela's arm to signal her to duck down lower in the shadows with him. One of the crafts was coming directly toward them. It moved slowly, as though it was scanning the ground for them. Sean pulled an object out of his pocket and fiddled with it. It was hard to tell in the darkness of the bucket of the backhoe they were under, but to Angela, it looked like one of the weapon devices.

"Damn, it's broken," he whispered, dropping it on the ground.

They froze as the flying craft went over top of them, not daring to let out even a loud breath. They lost sight of it for a moment as it flew now almost silently over the equipment in the area they hid.

Did it stop? Does it know we're here?

Her heart beat against her chest, and she had metallic taste on her tongue. She wondered if they should make a run for it. No. She remembered how fast those things had come in. There was no chance of outrunning it. With no way of seeing it, they just had to wait.

Sean tapped Angela and pointed to the craft, but she had already seen it as well. It was continuing past them, still at a slow pace.

"Got any plans?" she whispered.

"Working on it," he replied, looking around.

"Do you think they're looking for us?" Angela asked.

"Probably. They're moving slowly. Like they're scanning for something."

"Do you think it's this?" she asked, holding up the tablet.

"Doubtful. If they had some sort of tracker on it, they'd have found us when they flew over top." He pointed in the direction of a semi. One of the crafts was close to it now. "The truck is huge, and it'll probably draw too much attention to us. I think we're going to have to go on foot all the way to the shack. It's just down the road a bit, that way." He pointed into the darkness. "From there, we can try to get to the truck and go. Right around where the pavement ends, there's a broken-down shack that my—"

"That's kinda near where my car is," Angela blurted out. "I remember seeing it when I parked. We can take the car instead. It isn't very far." She hoped to convince him of her plan. A truck would be strong, but it also didn't make for an inconspicuous getaway vehicle.

"Great," he whispered. "The guy who can read that map and... a kid are in that shack ready to go."

Angela couldn't see his face well, but his voice sounded sad. Not sad about the kid, more like he wouldn't make it there.

"You, um, sound like you're not coming," she said nervously.

"I'm coming. And I know we just met, and this is a lot to ask, but if something goes wrong, would you please keep that kid safe for me?"

Angela suddenly understood the sadness in his voice. He didn't make it sound like it was his own child, but a child that he obviously cared about was in danger. She tried to reassure him as much as she could.

"Hey, we're going to make it. It'll end up okay," Angela said to Sean but having trouble believing it herself. "But if anything does happen...he'll be safe with me."

"Thank you," he replied, still with sadness in his voice. "Are you okay running?"

"Of course," Angela said with a tone that sounded like she had just accepted a challenge. They made one more look around. The lights of the crafts were just dots in the distance.

"Alright, on the count of three, we head straight for the road. One...two...three!"

They ducked out from under the backhoe and ran farther into the darkness of the night. Since they had been away from the bright lights of the excavation site, their eyes had adjusted somewhat. Visibility wasn't so low that they couldn't see each other, but dips and rocks were a different story. As they ran, Sean stayed in the lead, Angela on his heels keeping up with ease. A rock caught Sean's right foot and he tumbled to the ground, almost making Angela trip over him. He did a side roll as he hit and immediately was back to his feet running.

"Keep going!" he called to Angela, who had taken the lead.

They made it to the dirt road at about the same time and stopped, gasping for air. Not completely catching her breath, Angela was ready to start again.

"This way," Sean said, starting to run toward the shack.

"Wait!" Angela yelled back at him. "They're coming back." She pointed to the sky in the distance. The ships had stopped leaving the area and had circled back around. They now were flying in a spiral pattern, slowly closing in on the area. Angela looked around frantically.

"Quick, there!" she said, pointing to an old sheet of plywood lying in the ditch. The way it lay across the ditch left a small space between the ground and the board. It was probably used as a makeshift bridge to walk over when the ditch had water in it. They ran to the board and slightly pried it off the ground. A possum that was using it as shelter hissed and scurried off into the night. Less worried about animals than the crafts, they slid underneath. The ground was damp and smelled like the possum. It was a tight fit, and the weight of the board partially rested on their backs. There they waited, forced to have faith that they had not been seen and that the ships would pass them by unaware.

36

Sean

The position Sean was in when he crawled under the board left his chest pressed against the ground. He wasn't claustrophobic, but he struggled not to panic. With each breath, the board would rise slightly, then lower back down. He tried to breathe shallowly, hoping the board wouldn't draw attention, but if the tablet Angela held actually did have a tracker, it wouldn't matter much anyway.

From his position, he could see out into the night. The crafts would be passing over them soon, and he wanted to know when they were there. He refused to have it all end hiding under a sheet of plywood. Staring into the darkness, he watched as a craft came nearer and nearer. It was moving twice as fast as the last time one had flown over their heads.

Suddenly, it stopped close by. The speed in which it stopped actually scared him. There was no slow down or jerking. It was like it just got stuck in the sky. The light emanating from it intensified and changed into a spotlight that pointed down below it. Squinting, he could see what it was illuminating. The possum. It paused in the light before speeding up its fast-waddling crawl away. A small thud sound that reminded Sean of a loud blow dart gun cut through the air.

The possum bounced off the ground and lay on its side, spasming. He closed his eyes tight. If they were able to spot a possum walking, they might be able to see his eyes moving as he looked out from under the plywood. He felt like he was suffocating due to the long run across the field, the large sheet of wood on his back, and now the anxiety of this craft possibly finding and killing them. He tried to slow his breath even more. His head throbbed with each rapid heartbeat.

He slowly opened one eye just enough to see out. No light was visible, though the low hum of the craft was still evident.

It must not have seen us!

Angela nudged him with her foot. "Do you see anything?" she whispered.

"No," he whispered back. "I hear it, but I think it's past us. Stay here. I'm gonna take a look." Sean carefully dragged himself toward one of the open ends of the board. Once he got to the edge, he took a deep breath and stuck his head out to see. The craft that had just passed overhead was heading away. Dragging himself even further out, he looked for the next craft that should be approaching as they made their spiral in on the area. He let out a sigh of relief. "We should be in the clear. They look like they're all past us. I think we can make it to the shack."

They pulled themselves out from under the board, not bothering to wipe the dirt and filth off.

"This way," Sean called, jogging back to the dirt road and turning toward the shack. Angela followed, still watching the lights in the distance as she ran. Sean was looking for signs that anyone else had been near as they came up to the old building. He called out to Jayden in a hushed yell.

"Jayden. Jayden. It's me, Sean. You okay?" He waited for a reply. The door jiggled.

"The door's stuck," came the young boy's anxious voice from inside.

Sean felt a wave of relief go down his body. "Alright, stand back, man. I'll get it open." He grabbed the knob and gave the door a hit with his shoulder. It flexed but didn't open.

Angela spoke in a worried tone, "I think you better hurry. They're coming back."

Sean spun around to see. The crafts had made it back to the main excavation site and had started another spiral. This time they were circling outward away from the site. Hurriedly, he slammed his shoulder into the door again without it opening. He glanced at the flying ships once more and, leaning back, hit the door one more time with as much force as he could. It swung open, and he stumbled in with Angela right behind him. She quickly closed the door.

The shack was completely dark on the inside. Sean couldn't make out shapes in the room, but he felt the boy's arms wrap around his waist and squeeze.

"Told you I'd be back, bud," he said, standing in the middle of the room, Jayden not letting go. "I brought a new friend. Her name is Angela."

"Hi, Jayden. It's nice to meet you," Angela said in an out of breath but reassuring voice that only a mom could have in such an intense situation.

Sean was bracing himself for his next inquiry. He didn't even know if Marcus was still alive. With the number of experiments that had been done on him and as much pain as he had been in, he very well could be dead.

"Marcus?" he asked softly in the darkness. "Are you okay?" Sean listened for a reply as he felt his way toward the mattress. No reply.

"Here, take this," said Angela, handing him the phone from her pocket. "It doesn't have much battery left, so I turned it off."

The phone powered on just as he made it to Marcus. He bent down by the mattress and felt for him. His hand felt Marcus's leg first. He gave it a light grip and a small shake. "Marcus, are you okay?" Still no answer. A physical feeling of dread gripped Sean. It started at his shoulders, went up over his head, and down the rest of his body. The phone lit up, and Sean held it toward Marcus's face. He braced for the sight. Just then, the body moved slightly on its own.

"Uh," Marcus groaned, seemingly becoming conscious again. "I'm still alive if that's what you mean. I don't know about okay, though."

Sean sat down on the floor by the mattress. "Can you move at all?"

"Not fast, but I think so. I don't see any long walks on the beach anytime soon for me," joked Marcus, trying to use humor to lighten the tenseness in the air.

"We'll see about that. After we end all this, you'll be running marathons in no time," Sean joked back, though he agreed with Marcus. There was no way Marcus came out of this alive. Not in his shape and not with no one coming to help. He fumbled with the phone and found the flashlight setting. "Angela? Can you bring the tablet?" Sean said, feeling even more of an urgency while looking at Marcus's face. He could see Marcus's eyes looking more hazy, almost black. The veins in his neck cast their own shadows and sweat soaked his upper lip and face.

Angela was already beside him. She tapped his shoulder and handed him the tablet.

"Can't we do this outside or in the truck?" asked Marcus. "Anywhere there's at least a little more light?"

"We can't right now. Outside there's—" Sean paused, not wanting Jayden to feel any more unnecessary stress.

Angela stepped right in, immediately speaking in a bit of a louder whisper and stepping away. "So, Jayden. How old are you?" she asked, distracting the boy. She continued to talk to Jayden as Sean went on with Marcus.

"There are some ships circling outside. I think they're looking for us."

"So that's what those are," Marcus said, insinuating that he knew something was out there. "A little while ago, I heard them in my head. I get the feeling that I can't communicate with them but that they're blasting a message to me. Or to the drones, at least."

"What are they saying?" Sean asked, leaning in closer. His brain still hadn't really gotten wrapped around the ability to hear non-verbal speech, but he felt it was important to know what was going on.

"They're basically saying to continue working but if any humans are spotted to terminate them. I thought I might have been hallucinating at first, but now it makes more sense. The message just kept repeating itself and faded away. Like a faraway megaphone." He sat up by reaching out and grabbing Sean by the shoulder to pull himself upright. "Okay, so let's do this thing here, then."

Sean brought the tablet in front of Marcus's face. "Thank you, Marcus," he said, passing it to him. Sean waited as Marcus slowly started to work. He shifted where he could see what Marcus was doing on the screen.

"You can turn out that light. Unless you're trying to blind me," Marcus joked, holding a hand in front of his eyes.

Sean hadn't realized he'd been shining the phone's flashlight at Marcus the whole time. He quickly turned the flashlight off and put the phone away in his pocket.

"Funny," Marcus said. "I never was able to learn another language, even in high school. But now I somehow know exactly what these symbols stand for." As Marcus continued, more symbols appeared on the screen. He would tap them as if he could read them as well as English. Finally, what looked like a map popped up. It had symbols next to different shapes, but several things stood out to Sean.

First, there were land masses, rivers, and what looked like large roads on the map. And second, some tiny objects were moving. He recognized what those objects were. It must be the symbol for the ships flying outside. They seemed very far away now to Sean, if he understood the map at all.

Marcus stopped and pointed to the shape the ships circled around. "You are here," he said comically. Then he zoomed out on the map and pointed to a small shape far away. "This is the communications hub giving off the main signal. Go north. You need to get there and—" Marcus started into a coughing fit. He sounded like he was dying with every cough. Sean couldn't imagine how much pain he must be in. His fit subsided, and he tried to continue but had to stop for a few extra moments.

Angela came up and squatted beside Sean. "Is he okay?" she whispered.

"No," Sean replied. "They experimented on him a lot. His body didn't bond all the way with the alien stuff."

"Alien stuff?" she asked, sounding confused.

"I'll explain later." He leaned in to whisper in her ear. "I don't think he's going to last long." Turning back to Marcus, he put a hand on his shoulder and pulled the phone from his pocket. "Let me take a picture of that."

Angela suddenly seemed to feel the urgency of the situation with Marcus.

"Marcus?" she said in a kind, sympathetic voice. "Do you think you could find someone by name?"

"I...can," Marcus managed to say with a struggle. "If they've become a drone."

Any hope Angela might have had in hearing this was short-lived. The tablet started to flash. The entire screen lighting up and going black, again and again.

"What's going on?" Sean blurted out, a feeling of dread overtaking him.

"They're tracking it," Marcus replied. "Get rid of it...get out."

Sean grabbed the tablet from Marcus. "Jayden, Angela, you have to go now!" Sean said as he ran to the door and yanked it open. Taking a couple of steps, he threw the tablet like a boomerang as far as he could into the night and went back for the others. Angela and Jayden had just stepped outside.

"Where's your car?" he yelled in a panic.

"It's this way. Behind some trees."

Sean remembered the glimmering light he'd seen earlier in the trees. It must have been the light reflecting off the car. "Go! Take Jayden and get in. I'll meet you there."

Angela started moving, pulling Jayden by the hand. Sean grabbed her by the arm and stopped her. He handed her the phone and looked into her eyes. He spoke to her with a calm but authoritative tone.

"If I don't..." He paused, assuming she knew what he was implying. "Go! Okay?"

"Okay," she answered, giving him a look that let him know she would follow through with that promise if need be. She and Jayden flurried off into the night.

Sean was trying to come up with a plan as he ran back into the shack to get Marcus. "Marcus, Marcus. Get up," he said, dragging him painfully to his feet. "I know it hurts. I'm sorry, but we have to get you out of here! There's a car down the road by some trees," he explained while dragging the poor man to the door. As they emerged outside, Sean could hear the low tone of the crafts coming toward them.

"That way. Get to the car as quickly as—"

"Sean," Marcus interrupted.

"Just get there, and I'll get the truck and draw them—"

"Sean!" Marcus yelled with as much energy as he could. "I'm not going to make it. You and me both know it. But you can."

"No," Sean pleaded in desperation. "You're the only one who knows how to stop them."

"Sean. I can't help you anymore. I'm going to die. Let me help you."

Sean looked up. The lights were visible in the distance. He didn't know what to do. The rational side of his brain told him to leave with Angela and Jayden. He knew Marcus would slow them down and probably die soon anyway. It would be the only way they could make it and the only way they had a chance in stopping the aliens, finding Kristen, and protecting Jayden. His emotional side was screaming at him to find a way to save them all and take Marcus with them. Sean didn't know how to find Kristen or stop the aliens on his own. How could he navigate to the place he needed to go and somehow shut everything down? He turned and looked into Marcus's glassy eyes in the darkness of the night.

"I'm sorry," Sean said, his voice almost cracking. "Thank you for everything."

Marcus grabbed Sean by the shoulder and squeezed it tight.

"No, thank you for not letting me die on a table. I'll go on my own terms. Now, get outta here. It's up to you." He gave Sean a push, turned in the direction of the truck, and began hobbling down the dirt road, somehow finding the strength to walk on his own.

Sean didn't hesitate. He jogged toward the car, looking back to try and see Marcus, but he had already disappeared from view in the darkness. Sean approached the patch of trees and started looking for the car. He couldn't find it at first, finally catching a slight reflection of light off the windshield. He got in the passenger side. Jayden was in the back seat with Angela in the driver's.

"W-where's Marcus?" asked Jayden.

Sean didn't answer but looked at Angela's silhouette and spoke to her.

"Be ready to go."

"When?" she asked.

"I'm not sure. But he'll do something. And while they're paying attention to him, we need to get out."

The trio sat silent in the car, staring into the darkness. Sean could faintly hear whimpers from Jayden. He reached back and held the boy's hand. It was all he could do right now.

Three of the crafts had made it to the shack. They had it surrounded and were hovering so low it looked like they were resting on the ground. Two of the ships had their lights searching back and forth through the night, looking for any trace of the humans. Another had its light trained on what Sean assumed was the tablet. The last two ships were hanging over the main part of the excavation area.

Angela tapped Sean on the arm and pointed to the field next to the shack.

"Look," she whispered. "They're all here."

The workers from the excavation site had come to the area. One of them reached down and picked up the tablet. The craft then turned toward the shack like the other two. All three crafts moved into a line by the road and raised until they were two feet from the ground. Though the sound was muffled from inside the car, Angela, Sean, and Jayden all flinched as the crafts opened fire on the shack. Boards splintered and pieces flew from the building. In less than ten seconds, the entire building was destroyed and lay in shambles on the ground, dust filling the air illuminated by the lights from the ships.

"Sean," Angela said, "I think we're going to need to leave now. We're too close. They'll find us here any minute."

"Just wait a little longer," he pleaded. "He'll do something." He was trying to convince himself as well.

Come on, Marcus! I know you can do this. Make something happen!

The workers started searching the shack as another fifteen seconds ticked by.

"Sean," Angela begged.

"I know," he conceded. "Let's—"

Suddenly, the semi appeared on the other side of the three low-flying ships. With its lights off, they never had a chance to pull up. It plowed them over like large traffic cones. Swerving slightly, Marcus leveled the truck out and continued driving down the dirt road and past the trees that hid the car. The crafts lay on the ground. One partially in the road and the other two now in the ditch. Their lights dimmed and went dark.

"Now!" exclaimed Sean.

"Not yet," Angela quickly answered back. "Look!"

Sean searched the darkness until he spotted what Angela saw. The last two ships that had been over the site were now speeding toward the truck. The car shook as they flew past. Leaves and sticks from the trees slammed into the windshield as if thrown like rocks. As soon as the ships passed, Angela turned the key and started the car.

She kept the lights off and got them on the barely visible dirt road. They were heading north, the opposite way of where Marcus and the ships were going. Sean squinted in the dark, unsure how Angela was even staying on the road with no light. The right front bumper clipped what must have been one of the workers as they sped by the now destroyed shack. It made Sean flinch, but Angela didn't slow down. She accelerated, working hard to get them to safety.

Sean turned and looked back toward Marcus's truck. The crafts had caught up to it and must have started shooting. Sparks lit up the night around the truck and trailer. He continued to watch as the truck went off the road and rolled on its side, sparks still coming from it as it was pelted by the attackers.

"Thank you, Marcus," he whispered, tears gathering in the corners of his eyes. He turned back around to help Angela watch the dark road.

37

Lugal lay looking at the ceiling in a dark room. He watched the shadows emerge and leave as people walked past the blinds of the large window beside the couch he lay on. The leather couch squeaked and creaked as he shifted to try and find a more comfortable position. A soft knock at the door made him sit up. The door opened, and Arub stood in the doorway. He entered without turning the light on.

"I apologize for disturbing your repose," he said in his snake-like voice.

"No apologies needed, Arub." Lugal stood up and moved closer to Arub. "Humans need to rest for long periods of time. It is my curiosity, I think, that will allow me to better understand them."

"Very good," answered Arub, though he appeared slightly disgusted by the statement. "I desired to let you know the sentries have eliminated the threat to the excavation zone."

"Good," said Lugal, walking to the light switch and turning on the lights. "Are there any other issues that might damage or derail our systems?"

"There were several...hindrances in Australia. But they have been taken care of. There is no cause for concern."

"Are we still on track for our deadline?" asked Lugal.

"Yes, but many of the human's bodies are weaker than first presumed. We have had to replace many of the drones at the nuclear facilities throughout the system. However, there are more than enough to continue the process of shutting down the facilities."

"How regretful. Thank you, Arub. That is all I need for the moment. I am not feeling at my full level of health. I am going to receive my treatment. Please continue to oversee everything until I return."

"It is my duty," replied Arub with a bow.

38

Angela

Angela caught a glimpse of the bright red sunrise between some branches of a tree in the thick wooded area they were now in. The woods ran fairly parallel to the road, and as she walked, acorns and leaves cracked beneath her feet. She turned to look back in the direction they had left the car when it had run out of gas. Even with the added light of early morning, it was well beyond sight. Just a memory now. When the car stopped, they had eaten the fruit cups that Jess had given her. Now her mind was flipping the situation over and over in her head. Sean had given her as much information as he could while they were in the car. Everything he knew about the aliens and stopping them and how he and Jayden were looking for Kristen. She had told him about her son, Michael, as well.

Everything sounded crazy, but then again, the whole situation was crazy. Angela felt like she needed to help with the mission of stopping the signal. Though she still had no idea where her son was, this was her best bet of finding or saving him. And her desire as a mother to make sure this young boy, Jayden, was safe overpowered the hopelessness and helplessness she felt for her own child. She tried to keep a positive attitude on the outside, though inside, she was scared, broken, and panicked.

Time seemed to pass at a different speed lately. She didn't know if they had been walking for thirty minutes or two hours. It had to be around 7:30 am now, as that was when the sun usually rose here in October. She would normally be on her walk to work at this time.

She held onto Jayden's hand with her left as they walked, Sean a few steps ahead. Her right wrist was completely stiff and throbbing. She thought about the spot on her head where she had slammed it on the truck the night before. Feeling it carefully with her right hand, she felt a lump, and it was sore. The spot still felt wet. She pulled her hand back and tried to look at it in the limited light. She couldn't see anything, but there was a distinct oily smell. Like some sort of grease. She let out a relieved chuckle to herself. Her head wasn't cut. It was just some grease from the bottom of the truck. Jayden let go of her hand and caught up to Sean.

"Sean, I'm cold," he complained, his little body shivering.

"I know, man," replied Sean. "Let me warm you up for a minute." He stopped walking, crouched down, wrapped his arms around Jayden, and held him tight.

"The sun will be up soon, and it will warm up pretty fast," Angela said in a reassuring voice. She watched Sean holding Jayden, and it reminded her again of her son. How she desperately wanted to hold him and reassure him that everything was going to be okay. Right now she would settle with just seeing him or knowing that he was even still alive. Hope seemed almost completely lost now. It was hard to see any light at the end of the tunnel. Her eyes started to tear up as she felt an overwhelming wave of emotion go through her whole body. A lump in her throat choked her, causing a cough followed by a short, strained gasp for air. She knew it wasn't the best time, and she so wanted to hold it in, but her body wouldn't allow it any longer. Angela dropped to her hands and knees. Her intense sobs made almost no sound. Her body heaved with every breath in.

As Angela wept, a light hand touched her shoulder. She looked up through tear-soaked eyes just as Jayden wrapped his arms around her neck for a hug. She buried her face in his tiny shoulder and let it all out. The sounds that had been trapped within her now rang out through the trees in the early morning twilight. Jayden didn't say a word or let up on his hold. He allowed Angela to pull him into her arms and rock back and forth, holding him like he was her own child.

39

Sean

Sean couldn't even imagine how Angela felt. He assumed this was probably her first breakdown since everything started. Like him, she probably had been so engrossed in searching for her loved one that she hadn't stopped to ponder on the hopelessness of it all.

He missed Kristen. More than anything, he longed to just know if she was okay. But unlike Angela, the closest thing to a child he had was Jayden, who was safe. The anxiety and heartbreak she was going through as a mother was beyond his grasp.

This whole thing felt like a nightmare. Like a nightmare that you couldn't wake up from. A nightmare full of your worst fears. A nightmare that was real.

Sean stood and watched the pair, a small beam of light from the rising sun shining directly through the trees onto them. In the light, Sean could see that Jayden was crying too. He realized with everything that had been going on that he hadn't seen Jayden really break down either. The poor kid was now without the only family he had or even knew. Missing the woman that had raised him. He had essentially lost his mother.

Sean felt as if he could cry, but nothing came. No tears, no sounds, no anything. They all had been having to hold in so much emotion and keep moving forward. Maybe he couldn't let it out anymore. He tried reminding himself that if there was ever a time to release it, it was now. But still, nothing came. He felt broken and lost.

He had been helping others his whole life, always trying to take care of the needs of the people around him. The reason he had decided to become a lawyer in the first place was to help people. And now he didn't know if he could help anyone, including Jayden. The world was so messed up now. What could he really do to stop it?

"Sean, get down!" Angela exclaimed, snapping him back to reality.

Sean ducked down and looked in the direction she was staring in. A car was driving down the road in the distance behind them, heading the same way they were.

Angela motioned for Jayden to crawl over to Sean. Sean was sure that the car wouldn't be able to see them in the trees, especially in this light. Angela stayed low and made her way to them. They kept an eye on the car as it cruised by.

"Do you think it's *them*?" Jayden asked, wiping the tears from his cheeks.

Sean couldn't see who was in the car but could make out someone's arm sticking out of the passenger window. Their hand moved up and down, like it was riding a wave in the wind. Those taken over by the aliens usually seemed more deliberate in their actions.

"I don't think so," Sean said. "But I don't think we should let them know we're here. Just in case."

"Agreed," chimed in Angela, wiping her own tears away.

They continued to watch as the car slowly disappeared from view. Once they were sure it was gone, Sean picked Jayden up and swung him around for a piggyback ride. "Hopefully you'll be warmer up there. We should go."

As they walked through the woods, Sean and Angela spoke more of their lives before the takeover. The conversation was happy at times and saddening at others. The loss of what their lives had been was still fresh on their minds.

Finally, they hit the edge of the woods. Emerging out of the cover of the trees, they found themselves in a large, flat, open field. Jayden jumped off Sean's back and peered out at the land. The sun was now up, and they could see for miles across the vast open area. Being at just the start of autumn, the grass was still green and tall enough to make it up to Sean's knees. There were some more woods in the distance, and he could see what looked like the pitch of a roof peeking up from behind them.

Under different circumstances, this would make a great photo. All that is going on, and this beautiful landscape just sits here, alone. The world goes on, I guess, even if people don't.

"Should we go that way toward the house?" asked Angela, pointing toward the faraway trees.

"Yeah, I think I see some smoke over there," Sean said. "Someone's over there...or at least was."

Angela and Jayden began walking as Sean stared in the direction of the house. There was a small stream of white smoke barely visible from this distance. It dispersed as soon as it was higher than the trees. He stood in the sun and stretched. Holding Jayden on his back for so long had made him feel stiff. It had already started warming up outside, and he could tell that it was going to turn into a warm day. He looked at Angela and Jayden. They needed water, food, and possibly some clean clothes. Maybe that house would have something they could use. He could feel his own stomach grumbling, so he knew they had to be feeling the same way.

He turned his gaze toward the sky. He had never been a church-going man, and he didn't really believe in a single being or 'god' that controlled everything. But he did think there had to be something beyond.

"If there's anything or anyone out there, we could really use some help about now. I feel like I'm running out of ideas and options, and I just need to know what to do."

Jayden ran up to him and grabbed his arm. "Let's go, Sean. We have to keep moving." Jayden gave him a pull and ran to catch up with Angela.

Sean looked up to the sky again, this time speaking out loud in a whisper. "Just keep moving, huh? Alright. I can do that." He jogged a little to catch up with the pair as they strolled through the tall grass.

40

Angela

The group reached an old wooden fence that appeared to be at the edge of the property. Whoever lived on the property did a good job keeping it up since none of the fence was broken and there were several spots that had obviously been repaired with newer wood. Trees were blocking their view of the house, so someone would have to go get a good look.

Angela spoke up, not giving Sean a chance to volunteer. "I'm gonna go check it out," she said. "You two stay here." She started toward the fence, making it clear she would do this and there wouldn't be an argument. Beginning to climb the fence, she slipped and tried to catch herself with only her right hand. Intense pain shot up her arm, and she fell to the ground.

"Angela!" Sean exclaimed, running to her. "Are you okay?"

"I'll be fine. It's just my wrist. I-I think it's broken."

Sean helped her off the ground slowly, and she dusted herself off. Angela hated feeling like someone didn't think she could take care of things on her own. She knew she couldn't make her arm better. It definitely made her feel weak, like she would have to rely on someone else for help. She had lived most of her life on her own. She had raised her son on her own. She had even saved enough money to start her store without any help from anyone else. She liked handling things. Now Sean was looking at her like he pitied her for having a messed-up wrist, and she was struggling not to snap at him.

"I've got it," she said, taking a deep breath and trying not to sound angry. "I'll be fine."

"Are you sure? I can—"

"I said, I've got it. You stay with Jayden. I'll be right back."

Sean stepped back. The look on his face was that of acceptance and understanding, like he knew that trying to convince her to let him go instead was a losing battle.

"Okay, we'll wait right here," he said, trying to show with his tone and body language that he trusted her and knew she was capable.

Angela gave him a nod and looked down at Jayden who appeared worried. "I promise I'll be right back. And who knows, maybe I'll find something to eat."

She climbed the fence again, this time using only her left hand to help her over. She started through the woods and made her way toward the house. Sean and Jayden were barely out of eyesight when she caught a smell that gave her hope. The scent of smoked meat filled her nostrils. She immediately knew what the smoke they had seen was from, and it made her mouth water and stomach grumble. It also probably meant that there was an actual human nearby as she didn't think the drones would care about taking the time to make a delicious meal.

It didn't take long for her to catch a glimpse of the house as she made her way through the trees. It was a light blue two-story farm-house with a white wrap-around porch. Just like the fence around the property, it was well taken care of. It was set in a clearing that was completely surrounded by trees except the driveway that curved off into the woods. There was an old, small, white barn behind the house. It wasn't kept as nice but still looked in fair shape. The hint of smoke was coming from behind the barn. She stayed by the tree line and made her way carefully toward the back of the barn. Staying behind a large oak tree, she peeked out to look around. She could see a very large smoker on top of a flatbed trailer. Smoke rose slowly out of the chimney. Angela continued looking, trying to see if there was anyone around.

She was unsure on how to handle this. She could walk up to the house and knock on the front door. But how receptive would someone who lived set back in the woods be? Would they shoot first and ask questions later? It was too much of a gamble. She made her way back toward the house but stayed in the trees. The windows were all open along the side of the house. She decided to yell from the safety of the woods. If they were friendly, she could then walk up. If they weren't, the woods would give her some good cover to run.

"Hello?" she yelled at the house. "Is anyone there?" She waited.

About ten seconds passed when she saw movement from the window near the back of the house. She couldn't make out if it was a man or woman, but from the height of the figure, it was definitely an adult. The figure disappeared, and after a few moments, the front door opened slowly. A heavier set man with white hair stepped out and looked around with a rifle in his hand. Angela thought he was maybe in his late sixties or early seventies.

"Hello!" she called again. "My name is Angela. I'm not a threat. I'm just passing through."

"Come on out slowly!" the man yelled out, still scanning all around for Angela. "I don't want to hurt you."

She paused for a moment, debating in her head if it was a good choice to step out from behind cover. She almost didn't have a choice. They were in the middle of nowhere with no vehicle, no food, no shelter, and no idea exactly where they were going. She took the chance and stepped out. She took a couple slow steps with her hands up and stopped. The man saw her almost immediately and pointed the rifle in her direction.

"That's close enough," he yelled from his front porch. "What do you want?"

"I was wondering if I can get some directions and maybe some food, then I can get back on my way."

"Are you alone?"

She didn't want to give him too much information about them, but she also needed his help. Trust in strangers was becoming more of a necessity lately. "I left my two friends back beyond the woods," she yelled, her hands still raised.

The man looked around, seeming to ponder if he could trust Angela or not. She didn't blame him for being suspicious. How could you not be?

"Well you can put your hands down," he said, lowering his gun a bit. "But move slowly."

Angela lowered her arms and moved carefully toward the house. Careful not to make sudden movements. As she neared the man, she stopped at the bottom of the stairs to his porch.

"Thank you, sir. We're a bit lost and don't know how to get where we're going."

The man scanned the tree line again.

"How'd you know I was here?" he asked, still not looking at her.

"We saw some smoke and the top of your house from down the road."

"Dammit. I knew I shouldn't have used so much wood in the smoker," he blurted out, his demeanor changing. "Why don't you come on in and have a seat? The meat's not done yet, but I'll find you something to eat." He motioned for her to follow him and walked back inside.

Angela reluctantly followed him in, accidentally letting the screen door slam behind her.

"Don't worry about it, it happens. Have a seat and I'll find something for you."

Angela sat down on the couch in his living room. It was brand new and still had a tag hanging on one of the arm rests. The interior of the home was just as clean and taken care of as the outside. Looking around from her spot on the couch, she could see pictures of the man's family. She stood up to get a good look. The man looked happy in every photo with his wife and kids. There was a collage on the wall of three children as they grew and became adults. Angela always loved looking at photos of people through the years. Watching them grow and change with life. She got to the most recent-looking picture and stopped. It was that of just him and his children's families. His wife wasn't in it.

"It goes by so fast," he said entering the room and startling her.

"It certainly does, doesn't it? One moment you're holding them in your arms rocking them, the next they have a life of their own and…" Her voice cracked, and she turned her head so the man wouldn't see her eyes starting to water.

"But they'll always be your whole world," the man said, in a soothing voice. "I'm Jim, by the way." He turned on the light. When he noticed Angela was a bit surprised at him having electricity, he said, "My son had solar panels and batteries put in last year. Said he wanted to make the place '*green*'. I'm all for self-sufficiency anyway, so thought why not? Turned out to be pretty useful, eh?" He handed her a plastic water bottle, a bag of chips, and a jar with some kind of jerky in it.

"Thank you," she said, taking the food.

He turned to the pictures. "This is my family. Would you like to hear about them? I try not to be one of those old fools who ramble on, but I'm kind of a proud grandpa."

Angela nodded. She wanted to get back to Sean and Jayden, but she wanted to be courteous to this stranger who was feeding her as well. Jim commenced pointing out each person in the photographs, going through their names and telling her a little about each one as he did. Angela could see the pride and love he had for his family. He didn't stop smiling the whole time. When he made it to his wife's picture, he paused. His grin got even bigger.

"And this is the love of my life, Mary. She was our rock and our glue. We lost her several years ago... cancer. You've never met a better mother and woman. We were married for forty-eight wonderful years. She was my best friend. Still is. Not a day goes by I don't talk to her."

Angela sniffed back another tear. She could see the love he had in his eyes for his deceased wife.

"That sounds wonderful," she whispered. "You're a lucky man."

"Blessed beyond measure! But enough about me. Let's say we get those two friends of yours here, huh? We probably need to hurry in case the beasts are out."

41

Sean

Sean lay on the grass in the shade of some trees, looking up at the clouds as they moved in slow motion through the clear afternoon sky. It was pretty typical to see multiple contrails streaking through the blue, and near the city the pollution was much higher, so the slight haze was always muting the deep blue that was now visible. Jayden lay beside him asleep. Sean watched the rising and lowering of Jayden's chest as he breathed. Everything was so calm. A light breeze blew through the trees, creating a calm, rustling sound. No other sounds touched Sean's ears. No road noise, airplanes, or even birds.

Having nothing to do for the first time since this whole thing started gave him time to think. The whole world seemed damned, yet he felt that Kristen was somehow okay. She was one of the most independent, strongest, fiercest people he knew. She was a survivor, and if anyone would be okay, it was definitely her. But he had an almost zero percent chance of finding her right now. The only way he had even a micro-possibility to see her again was to successfully put an end to the control the aliens had on the people. This had to be his number one goal. If he failed, who knew what it would mean? For Kristen, for Jayden, or for humankind.

"Sean, I'm hungry." Jayden's sleepy voice ripped him out of his thoughts.

"Me too, buddy. Angela will be back soon, and I bet she found something to eat for us."

"She's been gone a long time. Do you think she's okay?" Jayden's face looked worried.

"I'm sure she's fine," Sean lied. She *had* been gone for quite a while, and he too was afraid something had happened to her. He didn't need Jayden worrying any more than he already was, so he decided that lying and just hoping for the best was the right thing to do in this situation.

"Is that her?" Jayden said, jumping up and starting to walk into the woods.

"Jayden!" Sean exclaimed, pulling him back and behind the closest tree. "You don't know what could be out there."

"I heard something. It's gotta be her! She came back."

Sean held Jayden and peeked out from behind the tree. He couldn't see anyone or anything. His eyes scanned back and forth, searching the trees and brush for any movement. He wanted it to be Angela as badly as Jayden did, but he had an uneasy feeling. He quickly glanced around for anything he could use as a weapon. His eyes stopped on an old, broken, wooden post maybe twenty feet away. It was probably left there from the last time the fence had been repaired.

"Stay here," he whispered to Jayden. "Do not move." Checking around one more time, he silently jogged to the broken post. Bending down to pick it up, he turned to head back toward Jayden. The hair on the back of his neck stood up. Almost halfway between him and Jayden, stood a large coyote. It was definitely bigger than any coyote Sean has ever seen, and it was staring directly at him. Its breaths were labored, as if it had just stopped running from a long chase. Its eyes were jet black, and its teeth were bared. The coyote opened its mouth and vomited a thick, black, tar-looking substance. Then immediately it looked back at Sean, growling with a deep, almost inaudible growl. The substance hung from its mouth like dripping strings of black molasses. Sean glanced at Jayden, who was frozen with fear. The look on his face was that of sheer panic.

"Don't move, Jayden," Sean said in as calm and soft of a voice as he could muster. "I don't think it knows you're there." He tightened his grip on the broken post in his hand, being careful not to make any sudden movements but readying it for the strike he knew would be necessary.

The coyote took a couple of slow steps toward Sean, making him less than a lunge away. Jayden let out the smallest of cries, almost a squeak, but just loud enough for Sean to hear. The coyote turned its head to look at Jayden.

"Hey!" Sean screamed in a panic, raising the post for a swing.

Time seemed to slow down. All Sean could see was Jayden and the coyote. Everything else disappeared. No trees, no ground, no wind. A savage anger arose from somewhere deep down inside of Sean. His blood boiled as his thoughts raced faster than time should allow. Nothing could happen to Jayden. Nothing would. He wouldn't allow it. This had to be it for the coyote. He would wrestle and kill this animal with his bare hands if he had to.

Almost leaping into the air, he lunged and swung at the animal that was now turning back toward him. The coyote reacted but not quickly enough. The post struck it on the left jaw and shattered. Splinters flew through the air. The coyote fell to the ground, but Sean didn't stop. He jumped on top of it and held it down. The post was no longer large enough to be used as a bat, so he used it more like a large rock. Holding it with both hands, he slammed it several times into the coyote's head. The splintered end was now sharp, so in his fury, he stabbed the coyote over and over again, grunting with every thrust. Sean's brain was devoid of any thoughts except Jayden's protection. A primal instinct had taken over. Safety of the young was all that mattered. There was a threat, and it would be eliminated.

"Sean!" came an adult voice from behind him, near where Jayden had been.

The voice snapped him out of his rage, and he turned his head to see Angela hugging Jayden. Her hand was keeping his face buried in her stomach to keep him from seeing the carnage. Sean looked down at what he had done. The coyote was obviously dead. It was almost indistinguishable as a coyote anymore. Black, tarry blood coated Sean's hands and the wretched corpse. Killing animals, even going hunting, was not something he liked to do, but he had completely lost control. And in front of Jayden too. Had he just scared Jayden? The last thing he wanted was for Jayden to see something like that. Everything flooded into his head at once. Kristen, Jayden, Marcus, Sarge, Stacey, the helpless drone-man he had stood over and killed, even the hopelessness he felt in trying to shut down the control over humans. All the feelings that he had been trying to let out earlier came out now like a volcano of uncontrollable emotion. He pushed himself off the dead animal and wept. With his hands soaked in the creature's tarry blood, he sat with the backs of his hands resting on the earth beside him, silently sobbing.

Angela kept Jayden's face toward her and bent down to speak to him.

"Let's go. Sean will catch up with us in a little bit." She turned and looked at Jim, who had walked with her to retrieve Sean and Jayden. He motioned for her to go back to the house. "Sean, this is

Jim. He's a friend," she called back so Sean would know that he was trustworthy. "Jayden and I will wait for you back at his place."

Jim stood holding his rifle and watching Angela and Jayden disappear through the trees before turning back to Sean. He slowly walked toward him and stood a few feet to his side.

"You don't know me, but I'm here to help," he said softly to Sean. "Do you mind if I sit?"

Sean glanced up at Jim and shook his head, his tears causing the sticky coyote blood on his face to ooze from his chin. Jim crouched down. His old joints made crackling noises as he lowered himself down to sit. He then lay the rifle carefully beside him on the ground and stared at the carcass of the coyote. Neither one of them said anything for a while. Sean tried to pull himself together the best he could. He wanted to get back to Jayden and hoped that Jayden wasn't scared of him now. He looked down at his shirt to find a spot with no blood. Jim must have known and handed him a dark blue bandana to wipe his face with.

"Thanks," Sean said in a cracked voice before clearing his throat and trying again. "Thanks."

"Don't mention it," replied Jim, now staring at Sean.

Sean turned and looked at Jim, getting his first good look at the older man. His eyes seemed to penetrate deep into Sean's. Though he was a stranger, it oddly made Sean more comfortable. There was something about Jim that put peace into his mind. Some kind of wise energy that made him feel safe. It was as if he was staring right into Sean's soul. Jim's face shifted almost to that of sympathy. No, it was more empathy than sympathy. Like he knew exactly how Sean felt. They stayed watching each other in silence. Finally, Jim took a deep breath to get ready to speak.

"Forgive me if I overstep, but I'm guessing what you're feeling right now isn't really just about this animal?"

Sean shook his head.

"Yeah, I didn't think so. I'm afraid I've seen that look before," he said with a sad tone in his voice. "It's been many years since I've seen it, but it's one that you can't mistake. It's in the eyes. The eyes of a man who will do whatever he has to protect those he cares about. The eyes of a man who has *had* to do things he thought he'd never have to ... and never wanted to."

Sean knew he would do whatever it took to protect Jayden. He would do whatever he had to find Kristen. His thoughts drifted back to the man he had killed in cold blood. It was something that his mind kept coming back to. Even though it was necessary, the guilt was heavy, and his chest physically hurt from it. Sean looked away quickly, suddenly feeling extremely uncomfortable. Could this old man sitting next to him really tell from Sean's eyes what he had done?

"I'm not asking what happened. I'm sure that whatever you did was done to help the three of you get to this point. It's probably one of the reasons you're still alive." He paused and took a breath. "Can I tell you a story? It's been over fifty years, but I was just a young man when I went off to Vietnam," he started without allowing Sean to answer. "It's not something I used to talk about. Lots of memories you try to forget. You think you're doing the right thing, but the pain and guilt you feel when you take another's life, or from surviving when others didn't, is almost too much to bare. And it is for some."

Sean glanced at Jim. He was looking off in the distance sadly, probably recollecting some painful, distant memory. He took another breath and started again.

"I kept trying to shove it down. To hide it. I think I thought that if I stomped the memories and guilt down low enough, I would eventually just not think of them anymore. Then one day, right after my second son was born, I got to the point where I was done. I couldn't hold it in any longer. I decided I was going to kill myself. I got one of my pistols, loaded it, got into my station wagon, and drove. I drove for a while. I wanted to go somewhere they'd never find me. Didn't want my family finding me like that, you know?"

Jim started tearing up as he kept going. Sean's eyes were stuck on him.

"I found the perfect spot. Somewhere way out where no one would ever find the car or me. I got ready to do it, but right before I did, I heard a small voice say, 'Daddy, why are you so sad?'" Jim chuckled and wiped away a tear. "I'll be damned if my oldest, who was maybe three at the time, didn't pop up out of the back seat of that car. The little stowaway. I squeezed him so tight. Sat there for who knows how long just holding him and crying. Of course, I drove him back. When we made it back home, his mama was freaking out. She'd been looking for him for a while. But instead of being mad at me, she just held us both. She could tell something was wrong. She was always good at that, you know? Later that night, after both kids were asleep, she cornered me. She was a stubborn woman. If she wanted something, she was going to get it, and all she wanted was to know what was wrong." He paused for a moment and smiled a half-smile.

"For the first time, I said it out loud. I told her everything. Every detail of the war I'd had running through my mind for years. How I felt helpless and alone. How I loved her and the kids but wanted to end it all. And that woman, God bless her, just sat there listening to every word. The terrible things that had happened, that I'd been a part of. She didn't judge me or make me feel ashamed. When I was done, she walked over to me, grabbed me by the shoulders, and looked deep into my eyes. Then she said, 'Jimmy, I have never met anyone as kind and loving as you. You've always tried to do what you think is right. There are times when we all have to do things that we feel we need to for those we love. Even if those things go against our nature. And I know you. You'll feel the guilt of some of those things for the rest of your life. But know this—you're a good man. You're a great father and a wonderful husband. And those things that happened back then don't change who you are and who you can continue to be. Be here now and keep moving forward.' From that time forward, she was my confidant. The guilt has never gone away, but when it hits me, I remember her words and push on. All these years later, and I still can hear them in my head."

Jim stood up and brushed himself off. Then he stuck out his hand to help Sean up. "Now you need to keep moving forward. For yourself and that kid."

Grabbing his hand, Sean came to his feet. "Sorry," Sean said, realizing that he had just gotten blood all over Jim's hand.

"No, big deal. I've had it on me before. You're not the only one to have had to kill these beasts. There's lots of them 'round here. Most of them seem to die on their own, but of course some don't."

"Thanks for the talk, too."

"Well, it helps to find someone who knows what it's like. Plus, I'm a pretty good judge of people, and I can tell just by looking at you that you're a good one." He looked down at Sean's clothes. "So, you want to go get washed up? It's hard to get that stuff off, but I have some soap that'd take the stripes off a zebra."

Sean nodded, and Jim led the way. They made their way through the woods in silence. The silence felt good to Sean. Though neither of them spoke, for the first time in a while, he didn't feel completely alone. Like someone was at least temporarily taking a burden off him. As they broke through the trees by Jim's house, Jim directed Sean back toward the barn.

"I have an outdoor shower in the back. It uses catchwater, so I wouldn't drink it if I were you, but it'll do the job. Head on back there, and I'll grab you some soap."

Sean walked to the back of the barn. The shower was a simple system. The catch water basin was overhead and connected to the shower head. A pull string valve controlled the flow of water. Jim rounded the corner and handed Sean a towel and a large bottle of orange pumice soap.

"I'll head back inside and grab you some clothes. I'll leave this thing here just in case any of those beasts show up," he said, pointing to a piece of lumber leaning on the barn. "I'd say take your time, but that tank is only half full. Haven't had a good rain in weeks."

"Thank you, Jim," Sean said. "I'm sure it'll be just fine."

Jim turned and went back toward the house. As Sean undressed and started to clean himself off, his thoughts hovered on Jayden. He felt tense, but it wasn't from the cold water. It was the anxiety over how this would affect his and Jayden's relationship. Jayden felt like a little brother. Someone Sean would look out for no matter the cost. He was family.

42

Angela

Inside the house, Angela was talking to Jayden about Sean. She was still trying to get to know them both better and wanted to distract Jayden from everything that had recently happened. Jayden was telling her a story from a time he, Sean, and Kristen had gone fishing.

"So they fell in the lake?" she asked.

"Not exactly," replied Jaden with a smirk on his face. "I kinda pushed them."

Angela started laughing. It was such an odd feeling to laugh. It felt like she hadn't laughed in forever, like it had become some vestigial expression. Though she couldn't stop the laughter, guilt of expressing joy while her son was still missing flowed in to sit along-side her emotions.

"Were they mad?" she asked.

"No," Jayden said, now laughing almost uncontrollably. "Sean's phone got wet and died, but they couldn't stop laughing." Jayden immediately stopped and looked down at his feet, his bottom lip starting to protrude. "That was before. When we were all to-gether...and happy."

Angela quickly slid over next to him on the couch and gave him a hug.

"I know. I know," she said in a calm, mothering voice. "You still have Sean, and he loves you. He's not going anywhere. I'm sure everything's gonna be okay." As it came out of her mouth, she realized that her last sentence felt like a lie. Everything didn't feel like it would be okay at all. It all felt so new but also like it had been going on forever. The world was messed up and would never go back to how it was before.

A knock on the screen door caught their attention. It was Sean. Angela waved him in. Sean entered wearing some of Jim's clothes. They were a bit baggy, and the out-of-date clothing made him look older than he actually was. He cleared his throat and awkwardly sat on an armchair next to the couch.

"Jayden...I—"

Jaden jumped up and ran to Sean. His short arms wrapped around Sean's neck as he crashed into him with his body, almost knocking the armchair over in the process. Sean squeezed him tightly, and they held each other. It made Angela feel warm inside. Love was hope, and that was love. They hadn't been apart long, but this reunion felt special. Sean made eye contact with Angela.

"He didn't see anything," she mouthed. She assumed Sean would be worried about that and wanted to reassure him that, to Jayden, it was like Sean had merely saved him from a monster. She had made sure of that when it happened. Wanting to give them some time alone, she stood up and walked into the kitchen where Jim was making some dinner. He stopped when she came in and pointed to the island counter. There were first aid supplies set up.

"I noticed that wrist of yours. Let me take care of it for you," he said, putting on some reading glasses. "I'm no doctor, but after raising three active children, I'm pretty good at bandaging things up."

She sat down at the kitchen table and looked at her hurt wrist. It seemed less swollen than earlier, but it had very small bruises on the underside. Jim worked delicately with her injury. Angela thought his bedside manner was better than any doctor she had ever had.

"Those two gonna be okay?" he asked.

"I think so. I'm just giving them some space right now."

"Good. They're lucky to have you. He's a man. Sure, a man will try and protect a child, but he never would have even thought about making sure a kid didn't see something like that. You saved more of that poor boy's innocence than you'll ever know."

Angela just nodded. She thought about her own son, Michael. She felt she had failed to protect more of his innocence, her mind going through all the what-ifs that could have kept him safe and with her. Jim finished wrapping her wrist and stood up.

"Supper is just about ready. I'm afraid I don't have a dinner table that is clean enough to eat on. After Mary passed away, it's just been me, so the table became more of a catch-all junk pile. I can bring the chairs into the kitchen if you're okay eating in here."

"That sounds just fine, but let me go grab them." She walked into the dining room and began bringing chairs into the kitchen, hooking them on her left elbow to avoid using her right arm.

"Dinner time, boys!" she yelled toward the living room. They came into the kitchen where Jim had laid out the spread. He had baked beans, corn, and brisket ready to be dished out. As they ate, they talked of their lives like this was a meal between good friends just catching up. Jim did most of the talking.

Once they were done eating, Jim turned to Jayden. "Do you like video games?"

Jayden looked surprised. "Yeah, I do!" he blurted out.

"There's a room just down the hall there that has some games in it. I'd be lying if I said it was just for my grandkids. I like a good game too. Go on ahead and have some fun."

Jaden jumped up and ran off to the room Jim had pointed out. "Whoa!" Jayden exclaimed from the room.

Jim laughed and leaned back in his chair.

"Thank you, Jim," Angela said, "for everything."

"Ah, it's no big deal. I had that meat smoking since yesterday. My Mary always said that if you got it, share it."

"Well, thank you, Jim," Sean chimed in. "You didn't have to do any of this, and we really appreciate it."

Angela glanced out the kitchen window. The sun would go down soon.

"I think it may be time for us to go soon. It's going to be dark—"

"Why don't you all stay the night? I have two couches and a guest bed with your names on them. Besides, you don't want to go out right now. You think that beast was bad in the day, you should see what they did to a couple of my goats. At night, they're worse, and there's plenty of 'em."

"That's really kind of you," Sean answered for them.

Angela intelligently knew that it was the best choice, but emotionally, she wanted to get moving as soon as possible. The longer it took, the further away her son felt. Reluctantly, she nodded in agreement.

"Great!" Jim said, standing up. "I'll get things all set up for you." He turned to Angela. "I have some of my wife's old things that I can bring out for you to wear. And I should have some old clothes for the little guy. Stuff my grandsons outgrew. Oh, and I have a working shower if you're needing it. The water's not hot, but it does get pretty warm." He was obviously excited to be able to help.

"Thank you," Angela said. She had to admit, a shower sounded pretty good about now.

43

Angela

"So you're telling me you think you can stop 'em?" Jim asked, trying not to be loud enough to wake Jayden sleeping in the living room. The three adults had been in the kitchen talking since the sun went down, and Sean had just unloaded everything he knew about the situation.

"We're gonna try," Angela sighed.

"Now I don't usually go around believing wild stories of aliens and such from people who wander on my property, but I gotta admit, it's the only thing that makes a lick of sense." He glanced around as if he were looking for something specific. "I have plenty of stuff to send you off with in the morning. I would love to go with you, but if my family's okay, this is where they'll go. They're all I got. Besides, an old man like me would just get in the way."

Angela hesitated to ask about a vehicle. Even with all his generosity, it seemed like a big request. "Do you, uh, happen to have a car we can use?"

He took a sip from the glass of whiskey he was holding.

"I'm afraid not. Wouldn't you believe that the day before all this started, the damn thing broke down. I think it's the starter. I got one ordered online, but I don't think it'll be coming anytime soon, if you know what I mean," he said with a wink. "I do know where you could find a vehicle pretty easily, though. It'll be a good walk, but there'll be plenty to choose from." He stopped and took another sip. "Take the road at the end of the driveway to the north. It goes all the way through town. After you get through the town, keep following it. The road will eventually run straight past a dealership out in the middle of nowhere. The owner and I go way back. I used to meet him up for coffee every Sunday morning. He doesn't keep the keys anywhere special. They're just hanging in his office. He does have the whole place locked up tight, though. Dogs are nothing to mess with, but I think you could find a way in. Probably easier to deal with those dogs than a car salesman anyway." He chuckled at his own joke.

Angela felt relieved and worried at the same time. The very real prospect of getting a vehicle that would run well was a load off her mind. Having a long walk to get there was disheartening, especially when there were more of those coyotes out. And on top of that, she and dogs didn't mix well. She didn't really have a reason to dislike dogs, she just didn't. She felt as though most dogs treated her like they knew she disliked them. Small dogs were more annoying than scary, but large dogs definitely gave her anxiety. But it looked like she didn't have much of a choice. The absolute only way to get her son back was to shut down that signal, and she needed a vehicle for that.

"That's good news," she said to him as he continued to sip his drink. She turned to Sean. "I think we should leave first thing in the morning. We need as much time as possible to get there and then to figure out how to get in."

"I think that's best," he said with a yawn. "That means we should try to get as much sleep as we can."

Standing up from the chairs around the kitchen island, they said their goodnights and went off to their separate spaces. Sean was in the living room on the recliner next to Jayden, who was asleep on the couch. Jim went to his own bed, and Angela had the guest bedroom.

She laid down and stared at the ceiling fan in the dark room. Her mind wouldn't switch off. Her son was out there, and she knew that shutting things down was her only chance to help him. If she thought she could do it alone, she would have been walking in the darkness with the coyotes in search of a vehicle. But she knew that she needed help. As much as she hated relying on someone else, Sean had the same goal, and it would take both of them to end the signal that held humans under control. She felt physically exhausted but mentally wired. With no clock, she had no idea how long she actually lay staring at the ceiling, tossing, and turning. She opened her eyes, not realizing that she had even fallen asleep until she rolled over and saw the light coming through the drapes.

Go time. She jumped up and started getting ready to leave. In the guest room, Jim had laid out some clothes the day before for the trio to go through and take. As a mom, Angela found it pretty easy to pinpoint the clothes she thought would fit Jayden and packed them in an old rolling suitcase that Jim had also given her. The back had some straps that made it wearable as a backpack. She packed some clothes for herself and Sean as well. They were a bit baggy on her, but at least they were clothes. The smell of freshly brewed coffee seeped down the hallway to the guest room. She found Jim sitting at the counter.

"Mornin'," he whispered with a nod. "I made some coffee. I don't have any creamer, but I pulled out some sugar if you want any."

"Thank you." She poured herself a cup and sat down next to him, grateful for the coffee. In three and a half days, what used to be a daily ritual had now become a luxury.

"The boys are asleep," he said. "I looked for my map for y'all but couldn't find it. I did put together some food for y'all to take. It's not much, but it should last you for a couple days." He paused and looked around to see if anyone else was coming into the kitchen, then he continued in a low, whispered voice. "Angela, I think you need to know something. Sean, he, uh, he seems like a good guy. I think he'll do whatever it takes to see this plan of yours through to the end, and I hope he does. But...he's going through something right now that's taking a toll on him. I've seen it with many of my friends and went through it myself. He may seem strong right now, but it's just a show. He sees that he has a duty, and he will probably try and fulfill that duty at all costs. I know you two just met, but he seems like a protector, right? Someone who will do whatever it takes to protect those he cares about?"

Angela nodded.

"Remember that even protectors can hit a wall and become hopeless." He looked around again like he was about to tell a secret. "I know this is going to sound bad. Now I'm not saying you have to... but just a suggestion. If he seems to be losing hope, um, using the kid he cares about or your son to motivate him to keep that sense of duty, may be the difference in him having a reason to push on... or give in."

"You mean... manipulate him?" Angela asked, though she knew the answer.

Jim shifted uncomfortably in his chair. "I mean give him a reminder by appealing to his drive to protect. Sean is a nice man, and I hope you don't have to. But in battle, you have to do things that make sure you win. Even if it means taking advantage of the kindness and character of others. Even if it means sacrificing everything. This is a battle you have to win. If it comes down to him sacrificing himself to win, you have to let him." There was an obvious shame in his eyes as he spoke, and he quickly looked out the window. The sound of the recliner clicking back into position let them know that Sean was now awake.

"Let's pray it never comes down to it," Angela whispered, "but I understand what you're saying." She knew he was right. They needed to win this battle, and they would have to do whatever it took. She just hoped it didn't mean manipulating or sacrificing anyone to do so.

Sean entered the kitchen rubbing his eyes.

"Good morning, sunshine," Jim said. "Coffee's in the pot if you want some."

"Thanks," he said after a long yawn. He turned and looked at Angela. "I'll wake up Jayden in a minute, and we can get moving."

Angela nodded and sipped her coffee, unable to make eye contact with Sean after the previous conversation about him. "I have some clothes packed for all of us," she told him. "I'm going to go sit outside and get some fresh air. Let me know when you're ready to leave." She stood up and walked to the front porch, bringing the bag of clothes she had packed with her and making sure not to let the screen door slam behind her. She really just needed some space to think. She stood out on the porch and stared out at the trees. Everything looked as peaceful as could be. A soft cool breeze blew the treetops back and forth. The tall grass looked like waves rippling across the property. The sun peeked out just above the tree line. How could so much suffering have happened everywhere yet peace like this seemed untouched?

The front door opened, and Jayden's voice broke the silence. "Hey, Angela! Are you ready to go?"

She turned and looked at the young boy. He was wearing a large backpack and a smile.

"I am," she said with a cheesy grin of her own. "You look ready."

"Yeah! Jim gave me this backpack and said I was in charge of carrying the food!"

"Well, I think that's a perfect job for you. Let me help you out there." She tightened the straps on the pack to make it easier for Jayden to carry. "There you go. Where's Sean?"

"Oh, they said they needed to have a little talk in there."

"Huh," Angela huffed, wondering in the back of her mind if their conversation was similar to her and Jim's this morning. A few seconds later, Jim and Sean emerged on the front porch as well. Jim carried a duffle bag, and Sean was carrying a large machete on his hip.

"Here, Sean," Jim said, handing the bag to him. "There's some first aid, flashlights, and other things I thought you might need in there."

"Thanks again, Jim, for everything," Sean said, shaking Jim's hand.

Jim just nodded. "Alright. I'm sad to see y'all go, but you have a job to do. I'm sure you'll be successful in your mission. After it's all over, come back and give me a visit. I'd like a chance to eat a meal with the people who saved the world."

"Yeah, we will!" Jayden blurted out.

"Thank you, Jim," Angela piped in, stepping up and giving Jim a large hug.

As they all said their goodbyes, Angela saw Jim mouth something to Sean. She wasn't sure, but it looked like, 'It's up to you.'

Picking up their stuff, the trio started the walk down the driveway that led through the trees and to the road. Jim stood on the porch and waved until they lost sight of him through the trees. Neither Angela nor Sean got many words in as they walked through the woods. Jayden's mouth, however, moved nonstop. Angela thought it was funny. Just by giving him a small job, like being in charge of the food, his entire mood and excitement level had changed. It reminded her of Michael when he was around Jayden's age. They had gone on a short hiking trip in the summer, and Michael had insisted on carrying the bag with food and water. He had been so proud and didn't complain about the heat even once.

When they finally reached the road, they still couldn't see any sign of a town nearby. They knew what direction the town was in, thanks to Jim, but the road from what they could see only went through open land and into another patch of trees in the distance. Angela's wrist was throbbing again in the wrap. She tried to keep her mind off it as they started down the long road toward the town. Luckily for them, the cool wind stayed steady. It was a pleasant temperature, even in the sun. October in Texas could be blistering hot one day and cold the next.

"Oh, do you want to know what time it is?" asked Jayden.

"How do you know what time it is?" Sean asked with a smirk.

"Jim gave me this watch, see?" He held up his wrist. There was an oversized silver watch dangling from his arm. "It doesn't take batteries. You wind it up every couple days like this." He got closer and showed them how he wound it up.

"That's super cool," Angela said, trying to sound excited for him. "So what time is it now?"

"It's..." He studied the watch, obviously struggling to read the time in analog. "It's 8:42."

"Wow!" said Angela. "In charge of the food and the time. Thank you, Jayden." Jayden's face beamed with pride as they walked. Angela looked over at Sean. The look on his face was definitely that of worry. She stared at him until his eyes met hers.

"You okay?" she mouthed, so Jayden wouldn't get concerned.

"I'm fine," he said, changing the look on his face and speaking in a normal voice. "As fine as we can be right now. How are you holding up?"

Truthfully, she was crushed inside. The little hope she had that her son was alive and okay was the only thing keeping her going. She had a feeling that Sean probably felt similar but wouldn't say it.

"Same here," she lied. She decided to change the subject. "So Jim said that it used to take him and his kids an hour and a half to walk to town. We have some walking to do, but we should be there well before lunch." Angela looked at Jayden who was walking a little in front of the group. He was bent over looking at something on the ground. "What'd you find, Jayden?"

"Just another dead bird," he called back.

"Well don't touch it," Sean remarked. "It could have diseases or something." They caught up to him and looked at the bird with him.

"Why do you think all the birds are dead, Sean?"

"I don't know, bud."

"My son did a research assignment last year on bird populations," Angela remarked. "He said that birds are sensitive to electromagnetic radiation and vibrations. Like cell towers and stuff. Maybe it has something to do with the Lightning Pillars being turned on. Or not, who knows?"

"That would sound about right," Sean huffed, hinting at the fact that the aliens were responsible for yet another disaster on Earth. "Let's keep moving, Jayden. We have a ways to go." They continued on their walk down the long stretch of road toward town.

44

. Sean

According to Jayden's constant updating on time, it was 10:22 am when they finally reached a point where the town was visible in the distance. The whole land was made up of open fields on either side of the road with patches of small, wooded areas dotting the landscape. The sun had grown more intense for the last half hour, so Sean was ready for some shade. He let out a long yawn and ran into Angela as she suddenly stopped and spoke.

"Is that the car that passed by us yesterday?" she asked, pointing to the ditch ahead on the right.

"I think it might be," Sean answered. "It doesn't look like anyone's in it, but let's be careful as we get closer." He kept an eye on the car for any movement as they walked. The car was upright in the ditch, and the passenger side door was open. "Stay here," he told them when they were about thirty feet away. He drew his machete and approached the car slowly, ready for anything.

The license plates were from Oklahoma, and there were stickers littering the back window, so many that it would be hard to see out from inside or in from the outside. Before he even reached the trunk, he could see blood smeared on the inside of the open door.

Handprints from someone obviously trying to get out. He glanced into the woods nearby for any evidence of where the person might have gone. He reached the side of the car and looked in. There were no people or bodies. Besides the blood and a small hole in the driver's door, there were no signs of a struggle or fight at all. The back seat was taken up by backpacks and boxes, and the keys dangled from the ignition.

"It's clear!" he yelled back to Angela and Jayden. "But stay there. I'm going to check and see if it will start." He got in the driver's seat. The entire car smelled of intense body odor. It was hard for him to take full breaths with the stench. Turning the key, he tried to start it, but nothing came on. The battery had to be so low that no lights even showed on the dashboard. Getting back out, he looked back at Angela and Jayden and shook his head. "Looks like we're walking a little more. Angela, can you help me check for supplies? Jayden, you stand by the trunk, bud." He wanted to be sure Jayden wouldn't see the bloody handprints on the door. Sean started checking the boxes in the back.

Angela came to the passenger side to do the same. "Oh, my god!" she gasped, seeing the bloody smears.

"I know," Sean whispered back so Jayden wouldn't get too interested and try to look. "They probably didn't make it. Let's just see if there's anything we can use and get out of here."

There were some food supplies in one box. Things like ramen noodles and cans of beans. He grabbed a couple and put them in his backpack. He looked in the next box and was caught off guard by its contents. It was filled to the top with marijuana products. Gummies, pre-rolled joints, and vaping cartridges were scattered like they had been aggressively thrown in the box. "Looks like they were ready to party, huh?" he said, holding some of it where Angela could see.

"Wow. Not what I'd grab in an alien takeover."

"Yeah, looks like they probably raided a dispensary."

Moving on, he opened the backpacks. They were filled with clothes, but there was nothing of use to them.

"Sean!" Jayden suddenly yelled from behind the car.

Sean rushed by his side to see what the matter was.

"What is it?"

"I saw someone in the trees!" Jayden continued. "I-I think it was a man. He had stuff all over his face."

"Where?" Sean asked, scanning the small patch of tree line beside the road.

"Over there!" Jayden said, pointing.

Sean pulled Jayden behind him in case anything jumped out from the woods. He drew the machete and held it by his side. Angela joined them.

"Are you sure it was someone?" she asked.

"I think. I mean, uh. Yeah, it was a man."

"Okay, just stay beside me. You're safe with us," Angela reassured him. She gave Sean a *'let's get out of here'* look.

He motioned for them to walk a little in front of him. He would've normally wanted to help the man, but without knowing the situation, he couldn't trust that the man wasn't a danger to their group.

Angela led them forward toward the town. She positioned herself between Jayden and the woods. Sean stayed close but made sure he was in a place to cut any attacker off before they reached the other two. He constantly scoured the trees for any signs of movement, his eyes as sharp as a hawk's. Even after they were well away from any trees and had only open fields around, he kept his guard up.

The rest of the walk into town took forever. Sean tried to relax the tension he was holding in all his muscles, finally feeling like he could release it for a few minutes as they had arrived into town.

The town didn't have much. There was a hardware store, two gas stations, a cafe, a volunteer fire station, and a tiny grocery store. Several trailers were set back off the road, and an old RV sat behind the cafe. They stopped in front of the first shop. All the businesses were visible from there, but there were no cars in the entire town.

"Well, should we check here first?" asked Angela, pointing at the hardware store. "Never know what we could find to use."

"Sounds good to me," Sean said, walking toward the shop.

There was a note taped to the front door. It read:

"Take what you need and leave the rest for others. We're in this together."

No one was in the store, and the front door was unlocked. People had obviously come in and grabbed things. There were a few tools and supplies on the ground, but for the most part, the shelves just seemed picked over, not messy. It was as though customers had shopped, and no one had restocked.

"Let's go around and see if there's anything we need," said Sean.

They split up and started looking for anything of use. Sean assumed that it would have been plundered for supplies when everything started, but by the looks of this store, it appeared that the shop owner was respected by the members of the town. He walked up and down the aisles, not finding anything they might need.

"I don't see anything," Angela called from the other side of the store.

"Me neither," he replied.

"What about this?" Jayden yelled from the counter with the cash register.

Sean turned to see him holding a small black tube. "What is it, bud?"

"It's a power bank. You know, for your phone."

"Smart guy," Angela said, making her way toward Jayden.

He stood taller, the pride showing on his face.

"Do you see a cord?" asked Sean, coming over too.

"Yeah, right here. Which kind do we need?"

Sean pulled out the phone. He handed it to Jayden so he could find the right one.

"Got it!" he said, sounding pleased with himself for once again being able to help. He handed the cord and bank to Sean who plugged it into the phone. They held their breath as they stared at the screen to see if it would start charging.

"Maybe it's dead," Angela suggested looking around for another power bank that might be lying around.

"Good job finding it anyway, man," Sean said to Jayden. He went to unplug the phone when Jayden stopped him.

"Patience, Sean. Just wait."

Sean looked at the screen to humor Jayden. Sure enough, a battery symbol appeared in the middle to show it was charging.

"What would we do without you, Jayden?"

Jayden just shrugged.

"I say we move on while it charges," suggested Angela.

Sean nodded, and they made their way out. The next store was the small grocery. It too had a sign that told people to take what they need. Sean was impressed with how this little town had banded together to take care of one another while everywhere else seemed to panic. It had obviously been picked over as well, definitely more so than the hardware store. There was plenty still there, but many shelves sat completely bare.

"It's just about lunch time," Angela said. "I'll find some food for us to eat. After that, we can get back on the road." She walked around trying to put together a meal for them.

Sean started searching for anything they could take with them. He found several baseball caps and picked them up. They weren't stylish by any means. They had a cheesy-looking purple panther embroidered on the front, probably the local school mascot. At least it would help keep the sun out of their eyes as they walked later. He checked the phone again to make sure it was still charging. He suddenly thought of a map. With no GPS, they would need a physical map to know where they were going.

"Hey, Jayden. Can you help me search for a map?" asked Sean.

Jayden looked at him, confused.

"Oh, that's right. You've probably never seen a paper map, have you?"

Jayden just shook his head.

"Okay, it will be a folded-up piece of paper or a large book about this size," he said, holding his hands apart to show Jayden the normal size of an atlas.

"I'll try," Jayden answered, still looking confused.

Sean shook his head and smiled. He walked down an aisle that didn't have much on the floor. It was mostly just random items that ranged from cold medicines to motor oil. A keychain caught his eye, so he took it. Further up, a Zippo lighter made him think of Kristen. They had once gone to a fair and rodeo together on a date. He had tried to win her a stuffed animal at one of the games but couldn't seem to win. Kristen took a turn and won on her first time. The prize she picked out for him had been a cheap Zippo-like lighter with the words 'Born to be wild' on the front. It was the first night they had said that they loved each other.

"I'll find you, Kristen," he said to himself. "We'll end this thing, and I promise I'll find you." He grabbed one of the lighters and filled it with some lighter fluid from the shelf next to it before putting it in his front pocket.

"Alright, guys!" Angela called from the front counter. "Lunch is served!"

He didn't know if it was just because he was so hungry, but Sean thought the spread looked delicious. There were apples, crackers, and pre-packaged cheese and beef sticks. "We also have the option of tuna or peanut butter sandwiches."

"I'll take a peanut butter, please," Jayden blurted out with cracker crumbs falling out of his mouth.

"Thank you, Angela," Sean said, picking up an apple.

They ate, using the counter as a table. When they had all finished, Sean pulled out the phone to see how much it had charged. The screen was black and no longer had the battery symbol.

"Hey, Jayden, it doesn't look like it's charging anymore."

"Let me see," said Jayden, taking the phone. "Oh, the power bank must have died too. But I bet the phone has a little charge now. I can turn it on and find—"

"No!" Sean exclaimed, snatching the phone from Jayden's hand. "Let's see if we can find a map first. Then at least we can mark where we're going on paper before the phone dies again."

"I didn't find any map book," Jayden said, licking peanut butter off the side of his hand.

"Did you happen to see any books or magazines?" Sean asked.

"Oh yeah, over there." He pointed to the front wall of the store.

Sean walked over and began searching. A very large United States Atlas lay flat on the bottom shelf. It was much too big and unwieldy to lean on the display wall with the other books and magazines. He picked it up and brought it back to the group.

"It's not going to be fun carrying this monster around, but at least we'll know where we're going."

"Do you need help with the map?" Angela asked.

"That would actually be great. Honestly, I've never been the best with maps."

"Don't worry. I am," she said confidently. "I grew up before GPS on phones and in cars. Plus, my mother and grandmother were terrible with navigation. As a teenager on road trips, it was up to me to be the navigator if we didn't want to be lost." She picked up a permanent marker from beside the cash register that must have been abandoned by a worker. "Jayden, can you take my bag and put as many of those apples in it as you can? You never know when we'll find fresh fruit again."

He struggled to pick up her heavy bag and walk over to the fruit.

She put the atlas on the counter and flipped to the map of Central Texas.

"Are you ready?" Sean asked, holding the phone in his hands. "We may not have long if the battery didn't charge much."

"Just a second. Let me figure out where we're at first." She scanned the map for a minute, pulled off the lid of the marker, and made a small circle on the map. "Ready!" she said with a deep breath.

Sean started powering up the phone. It came on and booted up. Notifications popped up about there being no service. He quickly closed them all and opened the photo gallery app.

"Okay! I have it. It has seven percent. Here." He handed the phone to Angela and watched over her shoulder.

"So I'm going to mark things down as much as I can." She went to work with the marker, zooming in and out on the photo to get a better look of where things were.

Sean didn't feel like he was helping, but Angela definitely looked like she knew exactly what she was doing. She mumbled to herself as she scribbled, drew lines, and circled areas of the map. She would draw on one page and then flip through the pages until she found the area she wanted.

"Not trying to hurry you, but it's down to 2%," Sean mentioned.

Angela didn't say anything. She kept marking things down and scanning the map and photo. She stopped, zoomed in, and pointed to a part of the map on the picture. "This is the spot he said we needed to go, right?"

"Yeah," Sean replied. "That's it." Just then the phone shut down. Sean hoped that she had finished. "Did you get it all?"

"Yeah, I got it all. It's just kind of weird. Of all places, why would they pick some little city in Kansas as their main base-fortress thing? I'm not judging the choice of some random alien race with endless technology. I just feel like there'd be better places to choose from."

"Kansas, huh?" Sean said, relieved that the phone had finished its job. "I can't say I've ever had a desire to visit Kansas, but I guess that's where we're headed."

Jayden came back with Angela's bag. He had a candy bar hanging out of his mouth. Sean stared at him with a smirk.

"What?" Jayden said smugly. "I grabbed some for you guys too."

"Well let's go find us a new car," Angela said, standing up.

They began gathering their bags. Sean picked up the atlas and held it in his hand since it was too large to put in his bag.

"Let me see that," said Angela, taking it from him. She flipped through it and ripped out several pages. "Here, we'll only take the ones we need." She folded up the pages and put them in her own bag.

"Let's go," said Sean, tightening up Jayden's backpack straps.

They left the store and got back on the street out of town. There wasn't much of a breeze, and the sun was quite bright. Sean felt sluggish, and from the look of the others, so did they. "You tired, too, Jayden?"

Jayden looked at Sean and pretended to close his eyes like he was going to sleep while walking.

"Yeah, me too, bud. I think it's because we had such a big, yummy meal. But hopefully it won't be too long before we find ourselves a car, and you can sleep as much as you want then."

They continued out of town and toward where Jim said the dealership was. The road was straight, so it was often hard to see how far they progressed. Still nervous about the man Jayden had seen earlier, Sean would look back toward the stores every once in a while. He never saw the man, but at least it gave him some perspective of how far they'd walked. The town was almost a spec in the distance now. But this time, he thought he saw movement coming from the town. It could just be the heat waves coming from the asphalt in the distance. He stopped and squinted to be sure.

"Shit!" he yelled. It was a vehicle, and it was moving in their direction.

45

Angela

The sudden feeling of dread had been a consistent and constant companion of Angela's over the last few days. Once again, it slammed back into her life as she heard Sean yell to get off the road and run for the closest trees. Without hesitation, she grabbed Jayden and pulled him with her, nearly dragging him off his feet. The previous days had conditioned her to react fast and not to second guess a situation. They were less than one hundred feet from a large, wooded area. It wasn't until they had made it to the tree line and ducked down that she even tried to figure out what was going on.

"What is it?" she asked, out of breath from being caught off guard and having to run with bags full of supplies. She could feel her heartbeat in the side of her neck.

Jayden was panting crouched beside her.

"It's a car," Sean said, trying to peek out from behind a tree. "Stay down, Jayden. It's coming this way."

Jayden dropped lower and leaned up against Angela for comfort, his little chest heaving with every breath.

"We'll be fine," she reassured him. "Just stay down, and they won't see us." She made eye contact with Sean so she could ask him a question without Jayden noticing. "Did they see us?" she mouthed.

"I don't know," he mouthed back, shrugging his shoulders. He started to peer out from behind the tree but quickly jerked his head back. He looked at Angela with worry in his eyes. "They've stopped. There's at least four of them. It looks like they're looking for something, but I think they're too far away for it to be us. Maybe…I don't know."

Angela tried to look but couldn't see anything from her spot squatting behind a downed tree trunk. "Should we run?" she asked.

"Maybe," he said, pointing in the direction they had been headed. "We'll run out of cover soon, so our best option is to head deeper into the woods away from the road."

Angela hated feeling like she didn't have enough information to make a good decision. She was just about to move to another place with a better view when Sean motioned for her to come to him.

"Jayden, you stay there," he said.

She crawled next to Sean to get a good look at the scene. There were four men standing near a large SUV well down the road. One of them was holding a device in the air and appeared to be scanning the trees.

"Do you think they're looking for us?" she whispered to Sean.

"I don't know. But we do have some time if we want to move."

"Okay, let's go." She went to move, but Sean stopped her and whispered so that Jayden couldn't hear him.

"If it looks like they're going to catch up to us, I need you to get Jayden out of here. I'll distract them and keep them busy as long as I can."

Angela looked him in the eyes for a few seconds before responding, Jim's prophetic words from earlier playing back in her head. She didn't want to accept the possibility, but finally nodded.

Don't make me do that. We need you. God, don't you let that happen.

"Okay, Jayden," Sean started, "we're going to move—" A scream rang through the trees, cutting him off mid-sentence.

The pitch and fear in the scream sent chills down Angela's spine. It was definitely human but similar to the sound of an animal being attacked by a predator. Like a pig being attacked. She and Sean immediately looked at the group. A man was being pulled from the ditch and carried toward the vehicle. Blood covered one of his arms and was smeared on his face. He kicked and screamed as one of the attackers aimed a weapon at his chest. The familiar sound it made reached their ears as the man went limp. They loaded him in the back of the SUV and started driving. As the vehicle neared where Angela and Sean were peeking out, it slowed down. They ducked back behind the tree and brush, almost lying down. They stayed as still as possible. Sean tapped Angela on the leg. Turning her head, she saw he had the machete in his hand.

"Get ready to run," he whispered. "When I say go, you go."

No! Don't do it. We can run together. We can make it. We have to.

No matter how much she didn't want to, she knew it was necessary. Someone would have to slow the attackers down enough for Jayden and herself to get away. They stayed still for a moment and listened. The sound of nearby leaves being stepped on alerted them that someone was close. Sean held up his fingers and counted. "3...2...1...go!" He jumped up with the machete raised above his head.

Angela didn't look back. She ran, picked up her bag, grabbed Jayden by the arm, and pulled him with her. He squealed in pain as her grip on his arm was strong, but she had no choice. Dragging him along, they barely made it ten steps when Sean's voice called out.

"Angela! Stop! It's okay! It's okay!"

She slowed down but didn't stop. Her brain was still in flee mode, and she couldn't think of anything that would make it okay to stay where they had been. She tried to get a glimpse of Sean through the trees but had no luck. She and Jayden were now at a brisk walk. Everything in her told her to keep going, but against her better judgment, she stopped.

"What do you mean?" she yelled, pushing Jayden into a squat behind a large bush with her.

"They're gone!" he yelled back.

"Are you sure?" It was hard for her to trust that they had just moved on after watching them pull that poor man from the ditch just a few moments ago. The sound of his screams was still fresh in her brain.

"I'm sure. They turned around and went back toward the town."

Angela stood up with Jayden, adjusted the backpack he wore, and they slowly crept back toward Sean. She held onto Jayden's pack to pull him if she needed. She kept scanning the area, half expecting someone to jump out at them.

"I heard someone near us. Didn't you?" she asked Sean as he came into view.

"Yeah," he said, waving them over and pointing toward something. He motioned for Jayden to stay quiet as he came alongside him.

Through the trees was a lone deer. The three of them stood staring at it as it stared right back at them, seemingly unsure if it should run or if it was safe.

"Whoa," Jayden whispered. "It's so close."

Angela admired the beauty of the moment but kept glancing up the road at the vehicle that was now just about back to the town. As she watched the deer, she had a thought. They had seen multiple animals. The possum, the crazed coyote, many dead birds, and now a deer. But it just occurred to her that she hadn't really seen any cows. With driving and walking so much, she should have at least seen a cow. In this part of Texas, you could usually see cattle grazing on land just off the side of the road near barbed wire fences.

"Well, I think we should get moving again, don't y'all?" asked Sean, interrupting her thought.

"Yeah, we need to get to that dealership and get a car," Angela said, shuffling the bag she carried to a different part of her shoulder.

"I'm tired of walking," Jayden whined. "My feet hurt."

"It's probably because you won't keep those shoes tied," Sean said, squatting down to help him tie his shoes.

Angela looked back toward the town behind them. She felt paranoid that the vehicle would come back at any moment. They would be out in the open when they started walking again. And this time, there would be no trees to hide in, just open fields on either side of the road. "We need to watch our back. We don't need another surprise sneaking up on us from behind."

Sean stood up after he finished tying Jayden's shoes. "That makes sense. You lead us, and I'll watch out for anything behind us."

They left the cover of the trees and started down the street once again. The road was long, and the combination of intense sun and all their silence made time seem to move slowly. Angela tried to keep her mind off her son and on the current task of getting to the dealership, but her thoughts kept wandering as she walked. An unhelpful 'what-if' would flood in and then be quickly replaced by the next. 'What if' she had told Michael not to go out? 'What if' she had woken up early before he left the house? 'What if' she had made him sleep in the room with her? 'What if' he had been treated like that man that had just been taken away? On and on it went. Finally unable to shut her mind up, she squeezed her hurt wrist. She didn't understand why she decided that was the best thing to do right now, but it worked. Pain shot up her hand and wrist and into her forearm, bringing her attention to her body and not on her son. It started throbbing again, and she realized that she must have noticeably winced from the pain because Jayden looked up to her and spoke.

"Does it still hurt, Miss Angela?"

"A little bit. But don't worry about me. I'm gonna be just fine," she said with a fake smile. "You just worry about those lines you're gonna get on your forehead from squinting so much."

"Oh," Sean said from behind. "I completely forgot. I grabbed these hats from the store back there. Figured they'd help us out in the sun." He pulled the three hats out of his bag and handed them each one.

"How do I look?" Angela asked Jayden, striking a pose. If she could distract Jayden, maybe it would keep both their minds from worrying.

"Great!" he replied, giving her a thumbs up.

"Good, cause at my age, wrinkles never go away," she joked.

They continued talking as they walked. Though her mind would constantly jump back to her son, the playful conversations they had helped to ease her anxiety and make time pass more smoothly. It wasn't hard to keep the discussions going. Sean was a lawyer, so he could converse and banter well. And all it took was asking Jayden questions about himself to keep him talking. Jayden was right in the middle of explaining one of his favorite video games when Angela stopped listening to look. She had spotted something in the distance. It was a large business sign with a huge American flag sticking out of the top.

"I think that's our destination," Angela blurted out with Jayden still in mid-sentence. She shifted her bag and hastened her steps.

Sean sped up too but continued to check behind them. Jayden had to speed up to a slow jog to keep up with Angela's stride. It took her a minute to realize that Jayden was having trouble staying with her. Her excitement of seeing the car dealership had put her in a one-track mind. She slowed her steps so that Jayden could return to a walk.

"I can't wait to sit down," Jayden said, breathing fast. "This backpack is so heavy."

"Just a bit longer, bud," said Sean, catching up beside them. "Let me take that bag for the rest of the walk." Sean grabbed the handle of the bag and Jayden slid both arms out at one time. "I'll take that, and you can take this." He pulled out a keychain. It was a flower hanging from a short chain."

"A sunflower! Kristen's favorite!" Jayden exclaimed.

"I know, bud. Let it remind you that we'll find her."

Angela watched Sean. He was already carrying the heaviest duffle bag. Watching him take on Jayden's load and give him hope made her feel both warm and worried. She could see everything that Jim had said about Sean. He was a kind, self-sacrificing man, and she just hoped she wouldn't have to take advantage of that to see the plan through.

46

Sean

It took ten more minutes of walking before they reached the dealership gates. Sean looked up at the tall road sign. The American flag on top whipped violently in the wind. It had seen better days. It was tattered and almost had a whole stripe in the middle that was missing.

The entire dealership was surrounded with a fence that was as tall as him. It was impossible to see through the fence as it had a black privacy screen from top to bottom. The only exception was the front gate. The gate was chain link and went only as high as his shoulders.

"Brunson's Auto," he read the sign out loud as he pulled on the fence to see if it was unlocked. "Do you think we should just jump the gate?"

"Jim said there were dogs here," replied Angela, then she pointed to a sign with the silhouette of a dog on it that read:

"Trespassers: you may make it in...but you won't make it out."

Angela shook her head. "I don't see any right now, but I don't know if jumping the gate would be the best if they're here." Her eyes darted back and forth. It was obvious that the thought of a dog being there scared her.

"You're probably right." Sean paused and thought for a second. He could see the front door of the dealership from here. The top half of the door was made of glass, so he was sure he could break it if he got to it. "Alright, I have an idea," he said, now in a whisper. "There's another gate over there on the side." He pointed to another gate on the right side of the lot. "If you and Jayden go over there and make a bunch of noise, the dogs, if they're even here, will pay attention to you. Then I can slip over and try to make it to the front door."

"What if they see you before you get there?" asked Angela.

"Well then hopefully I can outrun them," Sean said with a fake smirk.

"Wait," Jayden declared. He grabbed the backpack Sean had carried for him and dug through it.

"What are you looking for?" asked Angela.

"This!" he said, pulling out a large chunk of jerky.

Sean was confused for a second and then realized where Jayden's head was at and let out a chuckle. "What's that for?" Sean asked, giving him a chance to explain.

"So you can throw it if the dogs get too close," he answered. "It's not steak like in the movies, but it's close."

"I'm not sure if that actually wor—" Angela started to speak but quickly shut herself down, seemingly not wanting to hurt Jayden's feelings.

"Thanks, man!" Sean said, humoring the young boy. He was just trying to help as much as he could.

"I don't like this idea, but I can't think of another right now. Come on, Jayden," Angela nudged him to follow her. "I need your help making a lot of noise over there."

The pair walked over to the side gate as Sean prepared himself. He left his bag on the ground, thinking it would slow down his run toward the building. He would have to come back for it after they found a car. Sticking the jerky in his front pocket, he looked around for something to smash the window of the front door with. He'd have to be fast once he hit the glass since the dogs would definitely be alerted to him as soon as he hit it. Scanning all around, he saw a small metal trash can near the door.

That should do the job. I just hope it's not bolted to the ground.

He could see Angela and Jayden standing by the other gate. He made eye contact with Angela. She gave him a thumbs up to see if he was ready. He gave her one back and crouched down behind the privacy fence. He took a deep breath, preparing to climb the gate and make a run toward the door.

Angela and Jayden started jumping up and down while yelling. Sean kept one eye peeking around the fence. Sure enough, two dogs started barking and appeared from somewhere beside the building. Sean's anxiety suddenly vanished. There were just two Dachshunds. The younger one ran straight to the gate where Angela was, barking all the way. The older one had trouble walking and performed more of a waddle. Angela looked at Sean and threw up her arms with a smile, her anxiety also seemingly disappearing.

Sean made one final look around for any more animals, then climbed over the gate and jogged to the front door. The dogs didn't notice him at all. He pulled on the front door first to check if it was unlocked. Finding that it wasn't, he looked back at Angela and Jayden. The dogs had stopped barking and were now wagging their tails. Jayden had stuck his hand through the gate and was petting the dogs.

"Ferocious guard dogs," Sean laughed. He turned and picked up the small metal trash can. Lifting it up beside him, he slammed it into the window. It shattered on the first hit. The wiener dogs ran toward him, their high-pitched yips echoing off the walls of the building. He quickly but carefully stuck his hand through the window and twisted the lock. He turned to the dogs that had just made it to him. They stood a few feet away, barking but wagging their tails. Sean wasn't the biggest fan of dogs, but he knew how to react around them fairly well. He squatted down slowly and reached his hand out for them to smell. The young dog gave him a quick sniff and rolled over so he could pet its stomach. The older one stayed back and gave short, almost hoarse sounding barks, each with a little hop with its front feet. Sean stood up and waved to Angela and Jayden.

"I got it open. Come on in!" he yelled across the lot. Then he turned and opened the door. Both dogs ran in as if they were going to get fed.

Angela boosted Jayden up the gate they stood at and climbed over herself. Sean held the door until they caught up, and they all went inside.

"It stinks in here," Jayden commented, holding his nose.

"That's the smell of new cars," Sean pointed out. "Or at least used cars that have been cleaned to be like new." The building was larger than it appeared from outside. Unlike the typical showroom with large floor to ceiling windows and tons of natural light, this dealership's showroom had small windows throughout that let in just enough light to see the cars. It was probably normally lit by the large light fixtures that hung low above the vehicles. The cars inside were definitely the best at the dealership. They walked around the showroom, looking for a main office.

"That one looks so cool!" Jayden blurted out, running to a large, black, pickup truck that had been modified with a lift kit to an impractical height.

"Let's find the keys, and then we can see what cars will get us to where we're going," Angela said, scanning the room intently.

"Go check out some of these cars while we find the keys, bud," said Sean, wanting Jayden to have any bit of fun he could. "Just stay inside, okay?"

"Okay!" Jayden shouted as he struggled to reach the door latch to the truck.

Sean looked around and saw the dogs waiting by the door of an office.

"I'm thinking it's over there," he said, pointing it out to Angela.

She led the way to the door. The nameplate on the wall read, *"Matt Brunson."* Angela pushed on the door, and it swung right open.

"That was easy," she shrugged, entering the room.

Sean came in behind her. It was a large office with one of the biggest desks Sean had ever seen. There were two nice armchairs facing the front of the desk and a large swiveling office chair behind it. On one of the walls was a huge board with keys hung neatly all over it. Angela walked over to it and picked up some.

"Are we wanting a convertible or subcompact? Maybe a full-size sedan," she joked.

"Does it say what model they go to?" Sean asked.

Angela looked at the tag dangling from one of the sets of keys in her hand.

"No, not really. This one says it's a white 1500 truck, but another just says Gold with some numbers."

"I think we should find something with some decent gas mileage. Probably a newer model car."

"Got it," she said, putting some keys back and checking others. She went row by row as Sean kept sticking his head back out to check on Jayden. After a minute, Angela had finished and had several sets of keys in her hand. "Let's do it." She walked toward the door, Sean followed right behind.

"Jayden, man. Let's go get us a car!" Sean shouted across the showroom.

Jayden crawled out the back window of a smaller silver truck.

"Coming!"

Angela was the first one to the door. She was just about to pull it open when a ferocious bark came from the other side. She jumped back, frightened. It was not the bark of a small pup.

"What the hell?" she said, moving away from the door quickly.

Sean pushed on the door to hold it in place. He didn't want whatever was on the other side pushing its way through. Slowly, he peeked through the broken window. The head of a large German Shepherd almost came through the broken window, snapping and barking inches away from his face. The shock ran straight through Sean's body, starting in his neck and shooting all the way down to his toes. He recovered quickly and locked the door.

"Are you okay?" asked Angela.

"Yeah, but I think we've found the dog the sign warned about."

"There's two of them," Jayden said. He had moved to the side and was looking out a different window.

Angela and Sean joined him. Staring at the door were two huge German Shepherds. They both stood motionless as if they were perfect statues guarding the building.

"What are we going to do now?" asked Angela. "I don't think distracting these guys as we get into a car is going to work. Any plans?"

Sean sat down in a nearby chair and tried to think. These dogs were massive, fast, and, by the look and sound of them, aggressive. He wouldn't be able to beat them in a footrace, and if they got him, he didn't think he had a chance of winning in a fight. Even with a machete.

Jayden broke his thoughts.

"What about the jerky? If we give them food, maybe they'll like us," he suggested. "I saw a movie one time tha—"

"Jayden," Sean interrupted. He tried to sound calm and not annoyed. "This isn't like a movie. We are on those dogs' territory, and they will attack us if we go out there. They won't suddenly see us as friends because we give them food."

"But what if—"

"Jayden, stop! We need to think." Sean's annoyance was becoming very apparent in his voice. Days of low food, stress, and lack of sleep were taking its toll. It was like his brain wouldn't function as it normally did. He hated feeling like that. Like his mind was slipping away and unable to focus on the task at hand.

Angela stepped up to Jayden and put her hands on his shoulders to comfort him. She then looked at Sean and gave him a look that suggested he calm down.

Sean nodded his head. Though still annoyed, he didn't want Jayden to feel not listened to. "Sorry, bud. Can you give us a minute to think?"

"Why don't you go look at some more of these cool vehicles in here while Sean and I talk for a minute?" Angela suggested to Jayden.

Jayden's face looked a bit defeated, but he ran off obediently to check out more of the vehicles in the showroom. Angela sat in a chair across from Sean. Sean looked up at her and shrugged.

"I don't know what we're going to do. There's no way those dogs are going to let us stroll up and get into a car. And none of these vehicles in here are going to get more than fifteen miles a gallon. We can't take any of them and travel all the way to Kansas."

"I know," she said, sounding annoyed herself. "I do have a thought, but I don't think it's going to be easy."

"What is it? Any idea is better than anything I've got right now."

"Okay. So there are vehicles in here. The door over there is how they got them in." She pointed to a large sliding garage door. "If one of us can drive one of these vehicles out the door, we can get close to one of the ones we need. Then...maybe we can get that car back through the garage door and all load up. We can't all go while the dogs are out. There's no way all three of us plus our bags can make it from one car to the next."

Sean thought for a second. It did seem like the best option, but he wasn't sure about one part of it.

"I think I can get into one of those cars outside, but I feel like the dogs will try and come back inside if we reopen the garage door. How are you and Jayden going to get in without the dogs attacking?"

"Jayden and I can stay in another vehicle here. Then you can drive up next to it and we can climb out of our window into the new one's window." She looked around to see where Jayden was before continuing. "But if you get a chance to run those dogs over, it would make things a lot easier. Jayden will be with me, so he won't see anything that happens until we're ready to get in."

Sean couldn't help but agree. He presumed that these animals were pretty familiar with moving cars, so his chances of hitting them with a vehicle were slim, but he'd do whatever he needed to do to get a car for them.

"Okay," he said, taking a large breath. "Let's do it!"

47

Sean

"Jayden, keep all the other doors closed," Angela said. She had Jayden inside a full-size SUV that was parked close to the garage door. The front passenger door was open so she could run and jump inside quickly. She turned and met Sean at the silver truck he was getting into on the showroom floor.

"I'm ready," he said, closing the door and putting the key in the ignition.

Angela had placed a pile of keys in the center console next to him so he could find the best vehicle. His anxious brain was desperately searching for any alternative to the current plan with no avail. He wasn't nervous for himself but because there was a chance the dogs could get in the building with Angela and Jayden.

"As soon as I open the door, I'm going to jump into the vehicle with Jayden. You're on your own then," Angela said. "Good luck!"

He started the truck as Angela made her way to the garage door. Sean inched the truck close to the door. He gave Angela a thumbs up from inside the cab. She took a deep breath and gripped the chains that opened the door. Yanking downward, she ripped the door up as fast as she could. The tires of the truck made a short squeal as Sean hit the gas and pulled out of the building, narrowly missing the garage door with the roof of the truck. Once he was sure he was all the way out, he hit the brakes and stopped to get his bearings. Looking back, Angela was already in the SUV with Jayden. The doors were closed.

"Alright, Sean," he said to himself, "now let's go steal a car and try not to get attacked by two enormous beasts whose job it is to attack people stealing cars."

Both dogs came around the corner of the building and stopped to watch the truck, frozen like two intricate sculptures. Almost immediately upon the truck starting to move, the aggressive barking started. Sean hit the gas and lurched toward the animals. Just as he'd suspected, they were used to being around vehicles and moved to the side, staying as close to the side doors as possible. Sean rolled down the window several inches and slowly drove through the lot.

First, he went to the front gate and turned around. They needed the front gate open, and without the keys, he saw only one option. Since this wasn't the vehicle they would be driving toward Kansas and because it was sturdy, he shifted the car to reverse. Twisting around in his seat, he stared out the back window at the gate, hoping it wasn't as sturdy as it looked. Readying himself for impact, he mashed the accelerator and rammed the gate. The truck took a hefty jar from the hit, but the gate broke free and swung open. Now bent, it wedged itself in the grass, open enough to fit a vehicle out of the opening.

"Escape route, check," he said to himself. He watched the dogs for a moment, hoping they would try and escape themselves. They just stood, however, between him and the lot, watching intently.

He grabbed a set of keys from the pile in the console beside him. Flipping it over, the tag read: *PICKUP - DARK GRAY.*

Not a lot of information to go on. Thank you to whatever genius labeled the keys to this damn lot.

Pushing the lock button on the keys over and over, he listened for the beep of a horn. The German Shepherds continued to follow closely while barking.

It wasn't easy to hear over the dogs, but he eventually made out a faint horn nearby. "Nope," he said out loud as he saw it was a dark gray, almost black single cab truck. A truck wouldn't give them the mileage they needed to make it to their destination. "Next." He threw those keys on the floorboard out of the way and reached for the next pair. The tag on them read: *SUB – WHITE 6492*. This time, the vehicle was easy to find. In the next row up from where he was driving, its lights flashed as he pressed the lock button. It was a smallish white car with four doors. It looked brand new and was oriented directly between two other white cars. He pulled the truck around and looked for the easiest way to get to it without blocking it in.

His best course would be to put the passenger side door of the truck near the car and park as close as he could. The dogs seemed to stay on the driver's side. They probably were used to people exiting and entering that side. From that position, the front driver's side door of the car would be the fastest to enter. He watched the dogs. They moved closer and closer to the driver's side, just as he'd suspected. He unlocked the car, turned off the truck, and moved himself to the passenger seat. The adrenaline hitting his bloodstream made his heartbeat in his ears. The thumps partially muted the sounds around him, making each bark seem far away.

Checking for the animals one more time, he slowly opened the truck door. The beasts stayed on the driver's side. His body prepared to move, and he jumped out. Instantly, the dogs were alerted and started to run around the truck. Sean grabbed the handle of the car door and yanked it open. The barking turned to attacking snarls that Sean could feel reverberating in his neck. Leaping into the driver's seat, he pulled the door hard. It bounced slightly open as it slammed onto one of the dog's snouts. A loud yelp of pain filled the small space of the car. Sean's hand still on the door, he jerked it closed. The second dog reared onto the side of the car next to his face, looking through the window and snapping. Its fangs and mouth oozed with saliva and foam. He flinched from the sudden jolt but immediately felt the release of being in the safety of the car.

Sean had only taken several steps, but he was breathing like he just finished a two-mile run. He peeked out for the other dog. It pawed at its face, blood dripping from its mouth and nose. Even in the current situation they were all facing, Sean couldn't help but feel sorry for the animal. It was trying to do exactly what it was supposed to—stop him from stealing a car.

He shook off the guilt and sat up straight in the seat. It was time to try and get back to the building. The car started easily. He looked down at the glowing instrument panel.

Yes! A full gas tank!

The fuel economy on the instrument panel read that it got an average of thirty-four miles per gallon, and it had only been driven seven thousand miles. "Thank you, universe!" Sean shouted aloud, his hands moving to the top of his head in relief.

One of the dogs slammed into the driver's side window, snarling and showing all its teeth. Sean jumped a little but didn't pay much mind to it. Putting the car in drive, he slowly pulled out of the spot, being careful to not hit the truck he had just vacated.

As soon as he was past the truck, he made his way back to the garage door side of the building. The animals followed close by, staying far enough away to not be run over but close enough to leap and grab anyone who tried to get in or out of the vehicle.

Sean gave a short honk with the horn to let Angela know he was coming. He carefully pulled into the showroom and got as close as he could to the SUV Angela and Jayden were in. He positioned the backseat window on the driver's side next to the SUV's passenger front window, putting the vehicles too close for the dogs to come in between. The difference in vehicle height would make it awkward but not impossible for Jayden and Angela to slide down into the car. When he started to lower the window, the car shook as one of the dogs jumped onto the hood and then the roof of the car.

"Shit!" he yelled, quickly rolling the window back up.

The dog with the injured face had moved to the front of the car and stood growling near the hood. Sean cracked his window open just enough to yell out. Angela cracked hers too.

"Angela! This isn't going to work. Any ideas?"

Angela had a frightened look on her face, and just shook her head. Sean could see Jayden was saying something to Angela. With the clicking and scratching of the dog's nails on the roof of the car, he couldn't hear what they were talking about, but Angela's expression changed to somewhat hopeful, and she nodded to him. Sean watched as Jayden dug around in his bag again. He pulled out something small and dark brown and then flung it through the slightly open window toward the dog on the roof. Sean recognized what it was immediately. Jerky. The sound of scrambling let Sean know that the dog was immediately going for the jerky.

Another piece of jerky came flying out, this time landing on the hood of the car. Both dogs went to the meat this time. The one with an injured face got to it first. It sniffed the food and chomped down on it. In less than one second, it was down the animal's throat and gone. The second dog was now sniffing the mouth of its friend, trying to figure out if his companion had missed any. It then stuck its nose to the hood in search of any more.

It worked! Holy shit, it worked!

Until now, it hadn't even crossed his mind of how hungry the animals must have been without their owner nearby to feed them.

"Angela!" he yelled. "Get ready to come over. Throw some out of the other side so they go over there."

Angela rolled the driver's side window of the SUV part way down and let out a whistle. Both dogs ran to her partially open window and waited. She tossed out a couple pieces and watched as they quickly devoured them.

"Okay, we're ready!" she yelled back to Sean.

He rolled the back window down and prepared to help Angela and Jayden in. Jayden began sliding the bags into the back seat of the car as Angela kept the dogs distracted with food on the other side of the vehicle.

"Now you come, Jayden," Sean said. He helped pull Jayden through and into the back seat. "Your turn, Angela!"

She took the pieces of jerky she had left and ripped them into a bunch of small pieces. Then she threw them as far as she could away from her vehicle, scattering them across the showroom floor. As the dogs ran to find all the jerky, she climbed over and shimmied through the window and into the car, her hips only getting stuck for a second.

"Jayden!" Sean blurted out after they had the windows up and a moment to stop. "Your plan worked! Remind me to always listen to your ideas in the future, bud. You saved the day! Sorry I doubted your idea."

"I told you," Jayden beamed.

"It truly was great," Angela commented while breathing heavily. "Not to sound pushy, but can we talk about it some more when we're on the road?"

Sean put the car in reverse and backed out of the building. He set out toward the wrecked gate while Angela climbed into the front passenger seat. The dogs were no longer barking but still followed the car closely.

"Jayden, do you have any more of that jerky?"

"Yeah," he replied, holding up a piece in the rear-view mirror for Sean to see.

"Alright, I'm going to pull up next to the bag I left out here. You throw out a piece as far as you can so I can grab it." Sean lowered Jayden's window halfway down causing the dogs to start jumping in anticipation of food.

The car rolled to the gate, and Sean positioned his door next to the bag. Jayden chunked the food out of the window, and Sean quickly grabbed the bag. As they drove away, Jayden watched the dogs chase after them down the street in a dead sprint until finally they disappeared from view.

48

Angela

From a young age, Angela loved reading maps. As a teen, she would highlight what route they were going to take on their trips. Then she would sit in the passenger seat giving directions to the driver. This skill came in handy now that GPS didn't exist. She would tell Sean where to turn and how far until they needed to turn again. She poured over the unfolded maps in her lap, carefully plotting the best and most direct roads to take. They had been driving for several hours now, and the sun was just starting to drop behind some of the buildings in the distance as they approached Fort Worth.

She yawned and rubbed her eyes. The now limited light left them strained and tired since she'd been studying the map so hard. Sean caught the contagious reflex and returned his own yawn.

"Exhausted?" he asked, mid-yawn. "I'm feeling it too. Maybe we should stop up here and find someplace to sleep."

Angela was worn out physically and emotionally, but her drive to end this and find Michael made her want to keep going. Even if she could take over and drive just a few more miles, she was that much closer to putting an end to this whole thing.

"I can dri—" She yawned again before finishing. "I can drive."

"I want to keep going too, but it's almost dark, and we'll be easily seen if we keep driving with our lights on. I think starting tomorrow feeling clear and rested will help us make better decisions." He motioned to the back seat with his head.

Angela peered back and saw Jayden's sleeping body. His head lay across one of the bags, his mouth partially open. A glimmer of drool sparkled on the corner of his lips. She hated to admit it, but she knew Sean was right. With the constant bombardment of situations every day, a clear head would be best, and they were already sticking out like a sore thumb in the evening light.

"You're right. There's gotta be somewhere in this city to sleep. Maybe a hotel or something."

"Perfect. Let's keep our eyes out for one. I'm sure anywhere will work, but a hotel would probably be best."

They continued to drive as the sun completely set. The city looked so abnormal without streetlights. Everywhere was so dark. Traffic lights, businesses, parking lots; it was creepy and disconcerting. The towering highways and tall buildings shut out so much light, both Angela and Sean had to sit forward and scour the buildings in search of a hotel.

Finally, Angela spotted one. "Over there! To the left."

They pulled up to the large five-story hotel. The parking lot had some scattered cars, so they weren't worried about their's drawing attention.

"Jim put some flashlights in my bag," Sean told her.

Angela had to move Jayden to reach the bag and pull one out. "Y'all stay here, and I'll go check-in," she said with an exhausted smile.

The front door wouldn't open when she got to it. It was an automatic door, and with no power, she wasn't sure what to do.

Shattering the glass might draw attention to anyone who passed in the night. She first tried getting her fingers in between the two sliding doors and separating them. They wiggled but didn't move apart from each other. Using her flashlight to scan the door and frame, she could make out words from a large sticker on the other side at the top. The words were backwards since they faced inside, and getting her light just right so there wasn't a huge glare wasn't easy. The sticker read: IN EMERGENCY – PUSH DOORS.

"It can't be that easy," she said to herself. But as soon as she was able to get her fingers between the doors again, she gave one a hard pull, and it popped open, swinging out toward her. It scared her for a second, as she thought she had pulled it off the track, and it might fall, but it stayed upright.

The lobby was even more unnerving than the darkened streets. It was open to the second floor with giant chandeliers hung throughout. There didn't appear to be any bedrooms on the first floor, so she found the stairs and made her way to the second floor. Trying to ignore how scary the hallway was, she came to the first room, Room 244, and stopped at the door. She checked to make sure she wasn't lucky enough for it to be unlocked. No such luck. Like out of a detective movie, she stepped back and kicked the door next to the doorknob. The stomp made a loud thud but didn't budge. She tried it several more times. Inspecting it with her flashlight, she could tell that nothing was happening.

Unsure of what to do, Angela began walking the hallway in search of ideas. She found an abandoned housekeeping cart in front of one of the doors around a corner.

Maybe one of the rooms nearby is propped open from the cleaners.

Again, no luck. She checked the cart for anything that might help her. Dirty towels, trash bags, cleaning supplies; all things she couldn't use. Then she had an idea. There was a short dust broom hanging on the edge of the cart. If she used the stick of the broom, she might be able to break a hole in the drywall next to a door. Then she could poke her arm through and unlock the door from the inside.

Angela carried the broom back toward the first door she had tried to get in.

If someone comes upstairs, they'll be able to see a mess on the floor right away. I gotta pick a different door. Somewhere further down the hall.

She picked a room away from direct eyesight of someone who might come from the stairwell. Room 229. She set the flashlight on the floor so she could see the door. Being careful not to hurt herself, she used the broom stick like a spear and repeatedly struck the drywall next to the doorknob. After several jabs, damage was appearing. Once she had broken a large enough hole to get her arm into, she felt around. She pulled fluffy, yellow fiberglass insulation from the wall so she could reach the internal wall of the room. Taking a short break, she wiped the sweat from her face. It wasn't very warm in the hallway, but with no air movement and her constant exertion, she had worked up some perspiration. Positioning the broomstick in the hole, she got to work breaking a hole into the room. Finally, after a few more strikes, the wall gave way enough for her whole arm to reach through. She felt for the lock and twisted. The sound of the door unlocking gave her a huge feeling of relief. She opened the door and stepped over the drywall debris from the wall.

The room was a large studio-type with a king size bed, a couch, and desk. Angela inspected the room. It had definitely been cleaned since someone last stayed in it. The bed was made, the pillows sat nicely on the bed, and fresh towels were rolled up on the shelf in the bathroom. With her brain so task focused over the last few days, she hadn't given much thought about cleanliness. She'd taken a quick shower at Jim's house the night before, but seeing the fresh towels made the toil of the day become evident in her nostrils. She was normally a very clean person with impeccable hygiene, but besides a few moments here and there when she caught a whiff of herself, it hadn't really crossed her mind until now.

The door had a silver latch on the inside that could be flipped to securely stop the door from opening. She opened the door and flipped the latch so the door wouldn't close all the way. Leaving the room, she made her way back outside to retrieve Jayden and Sean. The night breeze outside felt so much better than the stuffy air she experienced in the hallway.

"Your room is ready, sir. I hope you enjoy your stay," she said jokingly. "It's Room 229. The stairs are on the right."

"Thank you, ma'am," he joked back. "I'm sure it will be more than acceptable." He opened the back door gently and carefully lifted Jayden out.

Jayden never opened his eyes. He wrapped his arms around Sean's neck and latched on like a koala. Sean used a separate flashlight to find his way in, as Angela carried all the bags and locked the car. Once they were all inside the hotel, she pulled the front door closed so they didn't draw any attention to the building. Making their way up to the room, Sean laid Jayden on the bed. He crawled and snuggled himself under the blanket and went straight back to sleep.

"I'm going to go check for more toiletries and things," Angela whispered. "I don't know about you, but I smell like a teenage boy and my teeth feel disgusting."

"Same here," Sean whispered back. "I'll stay right here with Jayden. Be careful."

Angela went back downstairs. She noticed the door to the room with an indoor swimming pool was propped open with a rug. It smelled heavily of chlorine but looked sparklingly clear in the light of the flashlight.

Oh, how I need a bath! This'll work just fine.

Leaving, she found a small room near the front desk with snacks and spare essentials to purchase. She loaded up on razors, toothbrushes, toothpaste paste, and water bottles. She thought how odd it was that you don't appreciate the little things until you no longer have them.

She walked around a little longer, seeing if there was anything else of value. Walking past the workout facilities, she shined the light in and stopped. Her health was important to her, and in the past, she always used the gyms at hotels.

"A different life," she whispered like she was at a funeral trying to show reverence. "A different life," she repeated, beginning to fully comprehend that her old life was over. There was no going back. Old habits, old securities, it was all gone. Even completing their upcoming mission wasn't ever going to put things back to the way they were. "Come on, Angela. Hold it together."

Making it back to the room with the boys, she laid the supplies on the couch. "Here we go," she whispered so as not to wake Jayden.

"Nice, thanks."

"There's a pool downstairs that we can bathe in. If you want to go first, I can wait with him until you get back."

"No, you go first. I'll wait here, and we can switch when you're back."

She nodded and started collecting what she needed, including soap, shampoo, and two towels from the bathroom. Right before she left the room, Sean stopped her.

"Angela, I just want you to know how much we... I appreciate everything you've done for us. We wouldn't have gotten this far without you. Thank you."

"You too," she said awkwardly. She didn't know what else to say. She could tell he really meant it, but when people complimented or thanked her, it made her very uncomfortable. It always had. To break the tension, she smiled and shined the light in his eyes playfully.

He let out a quiet chuckle and put up his hands to block the light as she walked out the door.

Angela pulled the pool door closed behind her to be safe even though she didn't expect any company. She didn't think anyone would have a reason to single out the one hotel in all of Fort Worth that they happened to be in, but the possibility still existed. She sat her things on the edge of the pool and placed the flashlight to shine across its length, lighting up much of the water. She looked around, more out of reflex than anything else, and got undressed.

Angela slowly unwrapped her bandaged wrist and placed the wrap by her clothes. Her wrist was stiff, swollen, and purple. She had very little range of motion and hoped that the water would give her some relief from the annoying, constant pain it was in. Slipping slowly into the water felt so satisfying. It wasn't too hot or cold, and though the room smelled of chlorine, the water really didn't. She could feel the scratches and wounds she'd gotten on her body over the last several days.

She didn't want to make Sean wait for a long time, but the weightless feeling as she drifted from one side to the other was beyond calming. Skinny dipping wasn't her thing, but based on how the water felt on her body, she could see why people like it. When she got to the opposite side, she dove under, kicked off the wall, and glided all the way back to where she left her things so she could start cleaning off. Her hair was so greasy that it took three rounds of shampoo to feel normal. Standing on a step, she quickly scrubbed her body with some soap and rinsed off.

When she had finished bathing, she got out, wrapped herself up in a towel, and began to shave. No one was going to be looking at her legs or armpits anytime soon. Shaving right now was only for comfort. Only for some sense of normalcy. "Ah," she breathed. It felt so good to be clean. After getting dressed in the clean pair of clothes she brought down with her, she went back to the room. Sean was asleep sitting up in a chair, so she gently woke him. He jolted awake and looked around as though he didn't know where he was for a second.

"Hey, Sean, your turn. I propped the pool door open. It's down the hallway from the lobby."

He nodded, stood up slowly, and yawned. Stumbling toward the door, he grabbed the pile of clothes and things he had set out for himself and disappeared out into the hall.

Sean had readied the couch, which had a pull-out bed. He would no doubt offer to sleep on the pull out as it was less comfortable than the bed, but she was fine using it. And if she was asleep when he got back, he wouldn't wake her up and try to be a martyr. Using a bottle of water to brush her teeth in the sink, she stared at her reflection in the mirror for a minute while thinking. Tomorrow afternoon, they could possibly be at their destination in Kansas.

"Whatever it takes," she whispered to her reflection. "Tomorrow this ends."

49

Sean

"I can't get to you!" yelled Sean frantically. He got down on one knee to look through a space between the mess of black wires that made a wall between him and Jayden.

Jayden looked panicked and alone on the other side. "I think someone's coming! Help, Sean, please!"

"I'll look for a way around. Stay there, Jayden!" He backed up and looked for any way to get to Jayden. His mind spun as he glanced back and forth. The structure Jayden was in was completely made of wire that attached to the ground and ran as far up as Sean could see. It seemingly reached left and right forever. This was the only part he could work with. He stuck his arm as far as he could into the wires, pushing them aside and feeling for the boy. His chest and shoulders were too large to fit through the tight cables. "Try and reach for me, Jayden! Find my hand!" He pushed even further into the wires. They dug into his body and tightened like a boa constrictor squeezing its prey. He paid no attention to the pain. Losing Jayden was not an option. He pushed until the top half of his body was entangled in the wires.

"Help, Sean! They've got me," the scared boy's voice rang out.

Pushing as hard as he could through the corded nightmare, he was able to see Jayden through a gap. Two men had him and were carrying him away. He kicked and shrieked as he disappeared from view.

"No! No! Jayden!" Sean screamed as the wall of wires closed in around his body, completely devouring him.

"Sean, Sean. It's okay!" Angela's voice jolted him awake.

"Where's Jayden?" he frantically asked, sitting up in the bed panting.

Gentle morning light beamed in through a slit in the hotel curtains.

"He's fine. He woke up early, so I got him to bathe in the hot tub. It was cold, but it didn't seem to bother him any. He's going to the restroom right now. Then we're going to go eat some pre-packaged muffins for breakfast. A true breakfast of champions."

Sean rubbed sweat from his face and tried to steady his breathing. It had just been a dream. Jayden was safe. Relieved, he flopped back on the wet pillow.

"Nightmare?"

"Yeah. A bad one."

"I had one too. Though waking up and realizing all that's happened feels like I'm stuck in another one."

"Yeah, me too. Well, thanks for helping Jayden. Does he seem okay today?"

"He woke up a little sad about his sister, but we talked, and I think he's feeling better. He at least seemed better playing in the water this morning."

"Well thank you for that, too."

"No problem. Oh, I found a French press while searching the lobby. It won't be warm, but I'm trying to make some coffee right now if you want some. The bags are packed and by the front door in the lobby. When you're ready, we'll see you downstairs."

As Jayden came out of the bathroom, Angela led him out of the room to give Sean some time and space to get ready. Before he disappeared out the door, he spun around and called back to Sean.

"I stunk it up, Sean! You're welcome!"

"Ew, Jayden," Angela said, playfully looking disgusted and closing the room door.

At least he still has his sense of humor. Hold onto it, bud. Don't lose it.

Sean looked around, instinctively trying to see what time it was on the hotel alarm clock. Remembering that there was no power, he pushed himself to his feet and stretched. He walked to the window and opened the curtains. The light made him squint. The sun was out, but not above the buildings yet. It had to be early, maybe 7:30 or 8 am.

After getting dressed, he made his way down to the lobby.

"Hey, Sean! There's plenty of chocolate muffins if you want any!" Jayden said excitedly upon seeing him. "I've had two already."

"Have you, now?" He glanced at Angela who shrugged her shoulders and handed him a paper cup with coffee in it.

"It's not the best. A little watery and grainy, but it's better than nothing."

He took the cup with a nod. "Thanks. Are y'all ready to get back on the road?"

"Yep!" Jayden said, jumping up. "Oh, wait—" He ran down the hall and around the corner. A moment later, he returned holding several packages of muffins in his hands. "Now I'm ready."

Cautiously, they left the hotel. Sean had an uneasy feeling. Not for himself but for Jayden. He didn't know if it was just from the dream, but he couldn't seem to shake it. He loaded all their bags in the trunk, and they piled in the car. Sean was in the driver's seat so Angela could navigate. Jayden took the back seat. The streets were much easier to traverse in the daylight. The tall buildings looked peaceful in the clear air. As they left the city, fluffy clouds littered the deep blue skies.

They still had half a tank, but Angela pointed out a subdivision for possible gas. She explained to Sean what Bill had taught her about siphoning gas. Vehicles lined the streets and driveways. Everything was tranquil, almost pleasant. Sean could imagine that everyone was still in their homes. Children and families enjoying a quiet morning together instead of being gone. But they were gone. Everyone was gone.

"Let's check that one!" Angela yelled excitedly. She was pointing to a covered car in a driveway.

By its shape, Sean was sure he knew what kind of car it was. They pulled up to it and got out. He removed the cover and gazed at the car. It was a black El Camino, though he didn't know what year. As a teen, he had always wanted one.

"Here's a hose," Angela yelled, walking around to the side of the house. She came back dragging a long, gray water hose.

Sean remembered seeing a large knife in the bag that Jim had given him. He quickly found it and brought it back to the hose and began to cut off a piece to use.

While Sean sawed on the hose, Angela backed their car beside the older car so the gas tanks would be right next to each other. It took both of them and several minutes to get the gas flowing. While Angela held the hose in place as the gas transferred to their car, Sean cut another section of hose to put in the trunk in case they needed it for later. Once they had gotten as much gas as they could, they loaded back up.

"Almost a full tank," Sean commented, pulling out on the street and heading back toward the main highway.

The smell of gasoline on their hands lingered in the car. They drove for a while with the windows down to relieve them of the odor. The air was cool and crisp, a perfect October morning. Sean watched Jayden's face in the mirror. His eyes squinted in the wind, his hand bobbing up and down out the window as though he was just out for an autumn Sunday drive.

As they exited the city, some Lightning Pillars were visible in the distance. The towers were few and far between and usually set back away from roadways. These happened to be closer to the road than others they'd seen. As they passed, both he and Angela stared at them.

"Do you think if we could destroy those towers, it would stop the signal?" Angela asked.

"I thought of that too, but they overlap, and the main communication hub sends signals to all of them. So messing these up wouldn't do anything. I am worried about how we're going to destroy the main one, though. We have no idea how it works, how large it is, or anything else really. I know the Lightning Towers are supposed to be strong."

"I know, I know," said Angela. "I've heard all the news about how they can survive winds, rains, and extreme temperatures. But I also heard that hurricanes and tornadoes could damage them. I wonder if it's because projectiles could hit them. Maybe hitting it hard enough could break it. Who knows?"

Sean didn't know how they were supposed to stop the communication hub, but whatever he had to do, he would do it. He'd find a way. He tried to push it out of his head for now and get focused back on the road. It was the only thing he had control of at the moment.

The car sped along the highway, the lonely machine piercing the still sound of its environment. More empty highways with scattered abandoned cars here and there. Two hours passed as they drove. Small conversations broke bouts of silence but never lasted long.

Sean leaned forward in his seat to stretch his lower back because he'd been sitting for so long. They'd crossed into Oklahoma nearly an hour ago, and according to the car's clock, it was 11:19 am.

"I can drive if you want," said Angela. "Give you a break."

"Naw, I'll be okay. Just needed to stretch."

Jayden's head popped up between the front seats. "Sean, I need to go to the bathroom."

"You're in luck! A sign just said there's a rest stop up here," commented Angela. "They might have open bathrooms. Since it's getting close to lunch time, we can eat and move our bodies for a minute."

Sean nodded and looked for the stop. Pulling into the lot, there were two pickup trucks and a beat-up car parked outside a small building with lots of glass windows. It made the uneasy feeling Sean had been having even more intense. He parked a few spaces away and watched the other vehicles for movement.

"I have a weird feeling," he whispered to Angela, trying to not let Jayden hear. "Y'all stay here and leave the car running. I'll go check it out and come back to let you know if it's safe."

Angela nodded. She was watching the cars too. "Wait—take this." She pulled out and handed Sean the knife he had used to cut the hose with.

Sean thought the machete would have been better, but it was in the trunk with the suitcases and other bags. Stepping out, he walked slowly to the first vehicle, the beat-up car, and looked in. There was nobody in the front or back. He moved then to the first truck, his eyes jumping back and forth between the vehicles and building. He saw movement in the corner of his eye that made him jump. He let out a relieved breath as he realized it was just a bunny hopping near the bushes of the building. The young rabbit didn't seem very threatened by Sean, only curious and wary.

Sean made it to the side of the first truck. It was a newer pickup with a raised suspension. It was so high that Sean had to stand on the step bars to see in. Squinting through the tinted glass, he could tell there was no one in it either.

The second truck sat in the spot closest to the entrance. He walked up to it and could tell quickly that it, too, was empty. More reassured, he walked to the front door of the building. He could see through the glass. It was a large lobby-like room with maps and other pamphlets. The only other doors in the lobby were the doors to the two restrooms inside and an emergency exit that led out the back. His comfort level continued to increase as he pulled on the front door and it opened. Thankful it wasn't locked, he held up a finger to Angela so he could let her know he needed one more minute.

Out of sight of the car and potentially inside a building with someone else, he held the knife tightly in his right hand, moving the handle in his sweaty hand to get a better grip. The stench of public restrooms filled his nostrils. The windows of the building were not great at keeping out the sun, so it felt a little like a sauna. The women's restroom was the door on the left, the men's on the right. He tried to quietly and slowly open the women's door. The loud creak it made was enough to let anyone who may be there know that he was too. He stopped and listened, not moving the door another inch. The only noise was the faint sound of his own breathing. While holding the door, he noticed there was a kick down door stop, so he stepped on it, locking the door open and in place. He checked each stall to find the women's was empty. He treated the men's the same way, finding it empty as well. Satisfied that all was clear, he returned to the car to let the others know.

"It's all good. Just a warning, though, it smells like a port-a-potty in there."

"Come on, Jayden. I have to go too," Angela said, stepping out and stretching her arms. "But Sean, I'm driving next, so you get the navigation seat for a while."

He smiled and nodded, conceding to her will. A little break from driving would be good anyway. Angela and Jayden went into the building, and Sean sat in the passenger seat of the car. He put the knife in the center console, close at hand but out of the way. Since he still had a bad feeling, he got out and sat on the hood. He could see the road, the parking lot, and the front door from where he sat. He watched intently, aware of everything around him. The day had started nice and cool but was now heating up with the sun. After sitting for a few minutes, he got up from the warm hood and reached his hands to the ground to stretch his back and legs. As he stood back up, he saw it.

Entering the lot was a full-size SUV. He had made eye contact with the driver as soon as he saw it, so he didn't have time to duck or use the car for cover. His first reflex was to run toward the building and get to Jayden and Angela. But that would alert the people in the vehicle that he wasn't alone. No. If these were drones, he had to slow the attackers down and be loud enough to let Angela know something was wrong. That was the only way they even had a chance to escape. He reached in the car and grabbed the knife. Turning toward the incoming vehicle, he ran to the middle of the parking lot. There, Angela should be able to see him easily, but it would make the people driving up look across the lot toward him instead of directly at the windows of the building Jayden and Angela were in.

The vehicle stopped, and three people stepped out. He could see into their eyes from the distance he was at and instantly realized his fear was correct. There was a small possibility that he could win this fight, but he didn't care what happened to him if he didn't. He had to try and give Jayden and Angela a fighting chance. It was up to him. He held the knife in front of his body, ready to fight. As he started toward the three drones, all the sounds around him seemed to dull. Time didn't slow, but his brain was processing things faster than it ever had. Could he fight off three extra strong humans, or was this the end? Again, it didn't matter. Jayden would be safe with Angela. Slowing the drones down was the goal.

He let out the loudest yell his facilities could muster, hoping it was enough to alert Angela inside. They didn't move toward him, but one of the men raised their arm toward Sean, a phaser in his hand. The millisecond the arm went up, Sean knew he would never make it close enough to even get a strike in, but he was committed. Screaming like a warrior charging into battle and running with a speed he'd never had before, he raised the knife for a desperate swing. A swing that would never happen.

50

Angela

Angela had come out of the restroom and was looking at some posters on the wall of the rest stop while waiting for Jayden. She suspected that it would take at least three to four hours to reach the spot they were looking for in Kansas.

In four hours, we could be putting an end to this mess. We just need to—

She saw a small flash of light outside, like light reflecting off a car door closing. She didn't think much of it, Sean was probably moving around in the car, but just to be on the safe side, she walked to the windows that stretched across the entire lobby of the building. She saw Sean run into the center of the parking lot with the knife firmly in hand. A metallic taste hit her tongue as fear shot through her body. There could only be one reason. Someone was there.

"Jayden!" she shrieked, her eyes scanning and finding the SUV. Jayden burst out of the men's room, a look of horror on his own face from Angela's scream. She grabbed him by the arm and pulled him across the lobby. Trying not to draw attention, she pushed the emergency exit open gently. Sean's yell perforated the air like a mama bear trying to scare off something going for her cubs. It only lasted a few seconds, and Angela could guess why. Pushing Jayden out the door first, she started to close it quietly behind them, getting one last look through the front window toward Sean. She saw the heads of three men looking down at the ground. She couldn't spot what they were looking at, but in her heart, she knew.

Behind the rest stop building was another parking lot. From the long lines of the pavement, it was apparent that it was set up for semi or RV parking. Past the lot was nothing but open fields. Dead, yellow grass stretched out for acres. The only thing that would work as cover was the dumpster. It sat visible through an open gate, surrounded by three concrete walls. If they wedged in behind it, they would basically be invisible.

Angela dragged the now crying Jayden with her, and they squeezed in between the concrete walls and the back of the dumpster. The smell of rotting garbage in the hot sun penetrated every inch of space around them, making it hard to breathe fully. She looked at Jayden and motioned for him to stay quiet. His sad, poor little face gazed up at her, tears sliding down the side of his nose and cheeks.

"What about Sean?" he whimpered.

She wrapped her arms around him and squeezed him as tightly as she could. What could she tell him? Sean could be dead, lying in the parking lot by himself. Or he could be just unconscious like before. There was no way of knowing right now. Now they just needed to stay quiet, still, and pray that no one thought to look behind the dumpster.

Jayden was quiet, but she could feel him sobbing. His little body heaved and shook in her arms.

What sounded like a vehicle door shutting echoed off the concrete walls of their enclosure. Angela couldn't trust that they were leaving. She stayed put, listening intently for even the slightest hint of movement. She was spot on, as just a moment later, the sound of approaching footsteps reached her ears. Squeezing Jayden even tighter, she fixed her eyes on the only entrance where someone could squeeze by and see them. She also readied herself to jump up and fight if the face of a human, or anything else for that matter, poked around the corner. The emergency exit door of the building creaked open and then closed. Two different sets of footsteps were now close. Jayden had his eyes open and watched the gap. Angela could feel her pulse throughout her body, the solid thumps of her heart anything but rhythmic.

The steps were nearly in unison, sounding almost like one person. The sound grew closer and closer. The march suddenly stopped, and the gate that blocked in the dumpster started to move on its track. Neither of them dared breathe. Jayden's small frame quivered in fear. They stayed there crouched behind garbage with no other plan. Then, just a few seconds later, the sound of the steps returned and slowly faded away as quickly as they had come. They waited there for an eon before they heard the SUV doors close again.

"Stay here," Angela whispered sternly to Jayden. "I'm going to go check on things."

She knew that if Sean was alive, the only way they stood a chance in getting him back was to follow the SUV. But to do that, she'd have to know which way they were going. She started to stand up, but Jayden's grip didn't release from her arm. She shot him a glance. He was in no shape to be alone—she knew that. The despairing look on his face physically hurt her. Here was a boy who had lost everyone he ever knew or cared about. She couldn't leave him alone, even for his safety.

"Okay, you can come with me, but stay quiet and be ready to run."

He nodded and clutched her arm even more as they stood up and wiggled their way out from behind the dumpster, finally getting a taste of the fresh air. She walked slowly and rounded the corner of the building. Using a tree growing near the front of the building as cover, she squatted behind its large trunk, towing Jayden behind. She peeked around at the vehicle that was now pulling out of the lot and going north, the same direction she, Jayden, and Sean had been traveling. There was no sign of Sean in the parking lot.

"Hurry! Get in the car!" she cried, pushing Jayden in its direction.

They got in and started after the other vehicle. Not wanting to be directly behind it as they would easily be seen, she drove over the grassy median to the other side of the highway and used the lanes meant to be driving south. They could probably still be seen, but at least it wouldn't be as easy. She tried to just keep them in her sights, a small dot on the horizon.

Jayden didn't say a word. He sat in the back seat, watching out the front windshield at the vehicle they followed, his eyes as wide open as they could go, though the tears had stopped flowing. A thirty-minute eternity passed by as they tailed the SUV. It suddenly pulled off the road into a parking lot. Angela instinctively stopped, unsure if they had been seen and the vehicle was turning around to come after them. Angela and Jayden were on the edge of their seats, staring at the vehicle in the distance. When it was apparent that they weren't turning around, she inched forward for a better look. The parking lot they had pulled into belonged to a bar.

The doors of the SUV were open, and it didn't appear that anyone was in any of the seats. She scanned the area, looking for movement.

Maybe they're in the bar looking for more people to capture. If they took Sean, he has to be alive... Hopefully.

Suddenly, a middle-aged lady jumped out the side door of the SUV and stumbled on the ground. She looked pale and sickly. Pulling herself to her feet, she began to hobble down the highway away from the bar and in the direction the vehicle had driven from. She was followed by a man. Based on the way he moved, he appeared to be healthy and uninjured. Angela recognized him almost instantly. It was Sean.

"Seatbelt on!" Angela almost screamed to Jayden. She stomped her foot on the gas pedal. The tires screeched, and the car lurched across the grass median.

Sean must have seen them as he slightly adjusted the direction of his run toward the oncoming car. He caught up to the woman, slowing down to help her the best he could.

Angela was now almost to them when a mist of blood exploded from the woman's shoulder, and she fell to the ground. It was as though something had gone through her arm mid-step. Sean stumbled and turned, trying to help her to her feet. The woman rolled around, holding her shoulder in pain.

Looking toward the bar, Angela saw a man running at Sean and the injured woman. He was holding up his arm with one of the weapon devices in his hand. Sean roughly pulled the lady to her feet and began to move again toward the car, holding her up with the back of his neck under her good arm. Angela didn't slow down. She knew the man would make it to Sean before he and the woman could get into the vehicle. His focus seemed to be only on the escapees... not the car speeding his way.

"Close your eyes!" she screamed at Jayden.

A second later, the car smashed into the man, dead center. Blood the color of merlot sprayed across the hood and windshield as his head and upper body slammed into the hood. His lower body crumbled and went down, completely yanking him beneath the car. The gruesome sound of his body being run over reverberated through the vehicle. Stopping the car, she didn't dare look in the rear-view mirror. She didn't have to. There was no way that man was alive.

Sean came running to the passenger side and jerked the rear door open.

"Move over, Jayden!" he yelled, trying to help the lady in. Slamming the door, he started to step in but quickly jumped back out.

"Wait!"

Wait? What? Get in the fucking car, Sean!

He ran toward the back of the car and returned a few seconds later with something in his hand. Angela took off before he even closed the door. They flew past the SUV as the two other men stepped out of the bar and proceeded to run to their vehicle.

"They're following us!" Sean exclaimed, watching out the back window.

Angela watched the vehicle coming up fast in the rear-view mirror. She hit the gas even harder, but their pursuers continued to gain on them.

"What do we do?" she yelled to Sean.

"I-I think I have an idea. Just keep going. When they get closer, I'll try and stop them."

Angela had no clue what he had in mind, but he had been proven trustworthy time and time again. She kept her foot to the floor and drove straight, gripping the steering wheel so tightly that she felt it may snap off.

Sean rolled down the window and fiddled with something in his hand. Angela glanced down to see he was holding one of the weapons. The lighted symbol on it turned to red, and he reached his arm out the window.

A moment later, an intense vibration pulsed through the air, followed by part of the road behind them exploding. Pieces of asphalt rained down beside the SUV, but they kept speeding along. A few seconds later, another vibration and another rain of asphalt. This time the debris smashed into the windshield of the opposing vehicle.

Sean shot the weapon one more time. This time the explosion came from the SUV itself, just shy of the middle of the grill. The vehicle swerved back and forth before cutting sideways into the grassy median. It immediately began to roll. It bounced, flipped, and rolled several times, coming to rest on its side. Smoke and dust rushed in to block the carnage from Angela's view.

Sean rolled up the window and brought his attention to the woman in the back seat. He turned around and got on his knees in the front seat.

"Kim, stay with us. You're gonna be okay."

Kim appeared to be conscious but in shock. She was holding her arm and shaking. Sweat dripped down her neck and face. Jayden looked panicked in the seat behind Angela.

"Jayden, hand me that small hand towel on the floor." Taking the towel, he moved Kim's hand out of the way and looked at the wound. "Okay, Kim, you're not bleeding, but there is a good-sized wound. I'm going to put this towel over it and hold it in place."

She didn't answer.

Sean placed the towel over her injury and held it there.

"How you doing, Kim? Are you in a lot of pain?"

Again, she didn't reply.

"Okay, I'm going to tie this on. Just try to relax and sit back."

He tied the hand towel around her arm and buckled her in the seatbelt. She mumbled something and seemed to be coming out of her shock. Within a few minutes, Sean had made sure she was comfortable and sat back in his seat facing the front.

"Are you okay, Sean?" Jayden asked quietly. "Your nose is bleeding."

Sean looked in the visor mirror and wiped the blood off his face with the sleeve of his t-shirt. "I'll be fine, man. Just a little nosebleed."

No one spoke again for several minutes. Sean had reached back and was holding Jayden's hand. In the quiet, Angela had time to replay the experience in her head. She knew it wasn't helpful, but she kept thinking of the man she'd just killed. Running him over was necessary, but she wished it hadn't been. He was under the control of someone else. He didn't deserve that.

No, whatever it takes. If that man had to die so we could end this for everyone else, so be it.

No more rationale was needed. It wouldn't serve her now. Sean finally broke the silence. He glanced back at Jayden. "Are you okay, buddy?"

Jayden nodded and sat back in his seat. Sean looked at Angela. It seemed like he could tell that she was struggling.

She tried to change her facial expression and sit up taller so he wouldn't bother her about how she felt.

He leaned closer to her and whispered, "Thank you. You did what you had to. Otherwise I wouldn't be here. If it's any consolation, I appreciate it more than you could even know."

Jayden reached up, put his hand on her right arm, and squeezed as if he just wanted to give her a small hug from the back seat. She didn't say anything, but it did make her feel a little better. This was her support team, and it was a good one. A young child who'd lost so much, and a man she'd just met. She somehow felt like she'd always known them both. Like there wasn't a time before them. Then she thought of Michael. Her newfound confidence reminded her that up until now, she'd done what was necessary, and she would continue to do so.

51

"They appear to be coming this way. They are too close," Arub argued. "Destroy them."

"I have it under control," Lugal said, walking to the large display of the map. "We cannot be sure that they even know of the Primary —or where it is." To keep Arub from speaking again, he quickly turned his attention to the woman at the computer. "How many humans are there?"

"The drones have reported three adults and one child," the woman replied.

"A young vessel is with them?" asked Lugal. "Interesting."

Arub rose from his chair, slowly hobbled toward him, and leaned on a desk. The rate of his labored breaths had increased. "They must be stopped," he hissed in frustration.

"I told you, I have it under control," returned Lugal, equally frustrated. "Call for more drones to be sent here as guards," he said, turning his attention to the woman. "If they are traveling here, they cannot be allowed to enter."

"Send sentries. Have them neutralize all humans they find," barked Arub.

"I do not desire to neutralize the humans, especially if they have a vessel with them. It is better to add more fortification here. I see no need to use resources to stop three humans. If they are indeed coming here to the Primary, then, if possible, I will speak with them.

I would like to know what they know. And if they attack, they will be neutralized. Remember, you are here to assist me, Arub. Know your place."

"Speak with them?" breathed Arub, his teeth bared in anger. "Lugal, to be a strong leader, you must suppress any threat before it becomes a problem. If you cannot, I will."

"That sounds like a threat," Lugal countered, raising his voice, his fists beginning to clench. "I am beginning to believe that you and I do not share the same motives. Decimating everyone is not why we are here. Do not test me, Arub. I am in charge. The council chose me. Remove yourself. Now."

Arub stood staring for a moment. His breaths echoing through the room. Like a teenager conceding to their parents, he turned to walk out of the room. Stopping at the door, he addressed Lugal one more time.

"I believe the council has chosen the wrong candidate to lead. We shall see what they have to say on this matter."

Lugal took a deep breath. He unclenched his fists and turned to see Arub had already made his exit. "Request a conference for me with the council as soon as possible," he said to the woman.

Outside in the hallway, Arub stopped a man walking by.

"Contact the Minor and arrange a Conveyor to be sent here. Then initiate the immediate transfer of all pods containing vessels. They are to be taken to the nearest repositories. And," he grabbed the man and pulled him closer, "do not allow Lugal to know it is being done."

The man turned and walked back down the hallway where he had come from, leaving Arub alone in the hall with a small, sneering grin on his face.

52

Angela

"Crap!"

"What is it?" Sean asked.

"The temperature warning light just came on," Angela replied. "We need to stop."

Sean sighed and leaned back in his seat. "Hood's pretty smashed in. Bet the radiator took some damage. Pull over, and I'll check it out."

"I need to look at the map again anyway. We should be near one of our last turns."

"I'm hungry again," Jayden said, trying not to interrupt the conversation.

"I'll grab us all something to eat while we're stopped," Angela said as she pulled over to the shoulder and angled the car. She wanted it to look like some of the abandoned cars that they passed every so often. They had to blend in; there was no way she was going to let anyone catch them again.

Sean got out to check the radiator. Kim was asleep again. She had woken up and talked to them several times over the last three hours, but she was badly hurt and seemed really sick. When the aliens had first initiated the drone-making signal, her health had gone downhill fast. To Angela, the symptoms seemed like someone who had a severe infection. She had vomiting, dizziness, fever, and now a massive wound in her shoulder from a weapon's blast.

Kim was a 46-year-old teacher. She said she had taught several different grades, but after a recent divorce, she'd just moved cities to become a 4th grade teacher. Though she couldn't have any of her own, she said she really loved kids. Even while injured, she was easily able to connect with Jayden in a way that helped him feel comfortable.

Angela grabbed the map to check it but watched as Sean struggled with the hood for a moment. It was bent in the middle where the man's body had slammed down on it.

"It's stuck. Can you pull on the release while I try and get it open?"

She held the release, and after fiddling with it for a while longer, he was finally able to get it open. She got out to move to the passenger side and take over the final navigation. It felt like a cold front was coming in. The cool wind blew in short gusts, tossing her hair into her face and causing a chill to go through her body.

At least if the car won't work, it's not miserably hot.

Getting in the car, she took a look at the map. They were almost there. One more turn and maybe thirty more minutes of driving and that was it. Nothing would stop her now. If she had to walk the rest of the way, she would do whatever it took. Sean flopped in the driver's seat.

"Well, it looks like we'll be here for a while. There must be a leak in the radiator or hose. I can't see it, but I can sure smell it. We still have some coolant, but I don't know how much. Once it cools down a bit, we can throw some of our water in the radiator. That should get us a little farther at least. How are we on gas?"

"We're getting close to empty, but we can make it... I think."

"How much longer do you think until we get to where we're going?"

"I'm thinking thirty minutes or less," she said, surprising herself with the hint of excitement in her voice.

"I guess since we're gonna be here for a little while, I'll get the bag with food and get us all a snack."

"Oh, I totally forgot—"

"Don't worry about it, Angela. Let me take care of this. You just sit back and relax for a bit. You've been doing it all. Let me help."

They each had a snack and sat resting in the car. The blasts of wind frequently shook the car. Sean offered to keep watch for any approaching vehicles so they could get some sleep, but Angela was too anxious. They were so close.

"So any ideas of how we're going to shut down this signal thing when we get there?" she whispered, glancing back at Jayden to make sure she hadn't woken him.

"No, but we'll do what we have to. If I have to bring a whole tower to the ground, I will. All I know is that Marcus said that the signal goes to all the Lightning Pillars. So if we stop the signal at this main communication hub, it'll stop everywhere...or at least should. I bet it looks similar to the normal pillars."

"Do you think there'll be guards or something? Maybe like those flying ships that attacked us earlier?"

"Dunno. I assume there may be some sort of security. I'm hoping it's like some of the other places. They haven't been super impossible to sneak around in, but we won't know until we get there."

"I guess so." It had been in the back of Angela's mind for a while now. What if Marcus hadn't known what he was talking about? Was there even a way to shut down the signal? Was there even a signal at all? She was pretty sure there was. She remembered that box in the hospital. It looked like it put out some sort of vibration that seemed to shut down the control that people were under. The lady had woken up almost immediately when the box was pointed at her. Then she remembered that the lady had started to scream. Had she been in pain, or was it just some side effect of her coming out of the control she was under that caused her to freak out?

Maybe this whole plan was crazy, and maybe she only believed it just because she needed hope to latch on to. Or maybe, hopefully, Marcus had been right, and they would soon be able to shut everything down.

She looked back at Kim who was asleep. "What about her? Do you think she's going to make it? I mean, it doesn't look good for her."

Sean glanced back at her too. "I know. I couldn't leave her. I hope that it's just the signal that's making her sick. When we shut it down, hopefully she'll get better, but...who knows."

The minutes dragged on forever as they sat in the car. Sean was under the hood again; it had cooled down enough to add some water. Jayden and Kim were awake. Jayden was excitedly telling her about everything that they'd gone through since it all had begun. Sean suddenly let the hood slam shut and ran to the door, intense worry on his face.

"Get down! Get down!" he yelled. He laid down his seat as far as he could, making sure Jayden had enough room to duck down. "There's a vehicle coming this way."

Angela quickly laid her seat back too while Kim leaned over toward Jayden across the back seat. The car shouldn't look suspicious, and due to the angle it was parked at, no one driving by quickly would be able to see any of them lying down.

They stayed there listening for an approaching automobile. Sure enough, they heard it getting closer and closer. Angela held Jayden's hand as the vehicle sounded like it was almost to them. He squeezed it tightly. The car shook from the pressure wave of air as it passed them. They waited until the sound was almost gone to peek up. It was a semi speeding north, the same direction they were all heading.

"That was close," Sean sighed. "I'm so tired of hiding."

"Then let's go put an end to it, huh? Is the car ready to drive?" asked Angela.

"As ready as it can be," he replied. He started the car. The engine light was on. Speaking to the car, he said, "You can make it. Just get us there."

As they drove, Angela noticed her heart rate wasn't returning to normal. Neither was her breathing. She focused hard to slow her breath to a normal pace but couldn't seem to do so. It was as though she couldn't take in a full inhale. Instead of slowing, it increased. She had never felt like this before. Dizziness set in as her breathing went completely out of control. She could feel her heartbeat in almost every part of her body. It was like a hummingbird flapping its wings. Her arms felt weak, like they were too heavy to lift and move around. Her face went numb starting at her chin and spreading.

"Angela!" Sean's muffled voice hit her ears. "Angela, focus on me."

She could barely tell the car had stopped. Her body dipped forward and then a hand pushed her back in the seat. Her vision darkened. Sean released her seatbelt and leaned in front of her so that she could see him.

"Angela, I think you're having a panic attack. Look at me and breathe with me. You're gonna be okay. Here we go. In...out...in...out...in—"

She focused as hard as she could to match Sean's breathing. After what seemed like forever, her vision slowly returned to normal. She still felt dizzy and weak, but everything else started to feel under her control again, though the tops of her cheeks still felt numb.

"I'm sorry," she said, embarrassed and confused. "I don't know what happened. I've never had a panic attack. I just...I ju—"

"It's okay," Sean interrupted. His tone was calm and soothing. "It's not something you can just decide not to happen. You've been through a lot, and well, you're human. I mean, you are human...right?" he joked.

Angela smiled and nodded. "We'll see," she joked back.

Jayden and Kim sat silently in the backseat with concerned looks on their faces.

"It's gonna be okay," Sean continued. "We're almost there. These aliens are no match for you. They don't know what it's like to go up against a mom."

"Thanks," she said, still embarrassed.

Sean nodded and got the car moving again. Several minutes later, Angela felt almost completely back to normal. Besides her head throbbing, it was like nothing had happened. She looked back at Jayden. His eyes were glistening, like he was on the edge of bursting in tears. Without a word, he lurched forward and wrapped his arms around Angela's neck.

"I'm okay," she said, trying to reassure him and herself at the same time. "I'm okay."

53

Sean

"We made it on fumes and a prayer, but we're here. Welcome to Belle Plaine, Kansas," Sean said. They went over a bumpy railroad crossing as the mid-afternoon sun shifted behind some clouds. "Are you sure the symbol on the map led here? It's the middle of nowhere."

"I'm pretty sure. Everything on their map lines up with here. But it *is* weird. It's so small. Why would they pick this area to send a signal out of?" asked Angela.

"Maybe it's easier to keep it undercover in a small town," Kim suggested. "I mean, they had to have everything ready ahead of time, right? Too many people in a big city would ask questions if you were building something weird."

That made sense to Sean. He had to deal with politics semi-frequently as an attorney. A small town like this probably welcomed any chance of growth and revenue.

They passed the city limit sign and pulled down a back road. It was a quaint little town. Older-looking houses on small plots of land. Not like any of the crammed subdivisions he was used to. It reminded him a little of his hometown except with more houses.

They stopped near a body of water and got out. Sean and Angela needed to talk and come up with a plan. A plan that wouldn't involve Jayden being put in any danger.

"Hey, bud, why don't you go check out that little bridge there. I need to talk to Angela and Kim really fast. Just don't fall in the water."

Jayden seemed hesitant but obliged. He walked off toward the little white bridge, leaving the adults to talk.

"What's the plan?" Angela blurted out as soon as Jayden was far enough away to not hear.

"So," replied Sean, "I can't leave Jayden by himself, and I won't let him come with us. It's too dangerous." He looked at Kim who seemed to be feeling a little better. "You're in no shape to come with us either. I know it's a big ask, but could you stay with Jayden and keep him safe until we get back?"

Kim looked at him for a moment before answering. "I'll stay with him. And I'll take care of him like my own child."

"Thank you. I think we should find a place for you two to stay. Then Angela and I can go out and search for wherever this signal is coming from."

Sean felt a water droplet hit him on the back of the hand. He glanced up at the clouds. More drops fell on his face. A cold, light sprinkle began to come down.

"How about there?" Angela suggested, pointing to a house near the water. It was a large house and looked well taken care of. The entire exterior looked to have been recently painted. "We can get in before it starts raining."

Fetching Jayden, they walked to the house and went to the front door. Sean didn't expect the front door would be unlocked, but as soon as he turned the knob, it opened right up. He and Angela left the group and walked through the house first, checking for anyone that could be home. Finding no one, they called in Kim and Jayden. Everyone went into the kitchen except Sean. He went straight to the master bedroom of the house. While checking the rooms, he'd seen the butt of a rifle behind some clothes hanging in the master closet. A rifle wasn't exactly inconspicuous, but it was a weapon, and they would probably need one for the mission they were about to go on. Pulling the clothes back to get a good look at the weapon, he found that it was a shotgun. It was already loaded with several shells. But beside it, he saw something even better. Sitting on a short shelf were two cases for pistols. Latches kept them closed, and neither of them had locks. He pulled the top case out and opened it. There were several loaded clips but no gun. He had better luck with the second case. A pistol lay on top of a charcoal-colored piece of foam. He carefully picked it up and inspected it. It was a .40cal S&W semi-automatic handgun. It was loaded and held eleven rounds in the clip. He put the pistol in his waistband, picked up the shotgun, and joined the others in the kitchen.

Kim and Jayden were sitting down around a kitchen island enjoying some food that Angela had found in the pantry. Sean walked up to Kim, holding up the shotgun

"Do you know how to use this?" he asked.

Kim shook her head. "I don't like guns, but if you show me... I'll learn."

Sean took out the shells and gave her a quick tutorial on how to use the weapon. When he had finished, he reloaded the gun and gave it to Kim, who looked exhausted and worried.

"I'm going to put this where little hands won't get to it." She found a spot on top of the refrigerator and sat down again, looking as though she could pass out.

Should I leave Jayden with her? What if she doesn't make it? What if I don't come—

Angela got Sean's attention and signaled for him to meet her in the attached dining room while Jayden ate at the counter.

"You're going to have to talk to Jayden. I'm pretty sure he knows you want him to stay here. He's being a bit clingy with me. See?" She pointed behind him.

Sean turned just in time to see Jayden's head disappear into the other room. "Yeah, I'll talk to him when he's done eating."

"Be understanding but firm. It's not easy for you, but it's probably ten times worse for him."

Sean nodded. He appreciated Angela's wisdom on the matter, though he had no idea of what to say.

They joined the others in the kitchen. Jayden was sitting back, holding his stomach. He had obviously scarfed down his meal.

"Sean, do you want some tuna? Angela made it. It's really good," Jayden said.

"No thanks, bud. I'm not really hungry right now. And tuna? I thought you hated tuna."

"Just the way you make it. She makes it better." Jayden smiled, a drip of mayonnaise stuck to his chin.

"I'll have to get the recipe then."

Angela gave Sean a 'go talk to him' look.

"Jayden, can we talk for a second in the living room?"

"Sure," he said, jumping off the bar stool.

Once they were sitting on the couch together, Sean nervously started the conversation.

"So, bud, you know that Angela and I are going to go stop this signal, right?"

Jayden's eyes suddenly looked worried. He shifted positions nervously.

"It's going to be dangerous," Sean continued. "Probably really dangerous. I—uh—don't think it would be best for you to come along."

"But I—" Tears immediately welled in Jayden's eyes.

"I know, man. You are a helpful, strong, super smart young man. But I can't put you in that much danger."

Jayden's bottom lip was sticking out and quivering. Tears ran down his nose and cheeks. "Don't...leave me," he managed to whimper.

Sean grabbed and squeezed him tight to his chest. "I'll be back, bud. But I have to do this."

"Why? Just stay here with me."

Sean tried not to cry. A lump was building in his throat. Swallowing it back, he continued. "Do you know what duty is?"

Jayden didn't answer.

"Think of it like this, bud. What if there was something only you could do, and it would help the whole world? And no one else could or even knew how to do it. That would be something that you needed to do, right? For everyone?"

Jayden still didn't reply. His face stayed buried in Sean's chest.

"That's what this is, bud. Angela and I are the only ones who can put an end to this. No one else in the whole wide world can."

"I don't care!" Jayden half yelled, half screamed. "I just want you to stay! Please stay Sean!"

They sat for a minute holding each other and not speaking. Sean didn't know what to say. He could only imagine what Jayden was going through. If Sean was being honest with himself, he didn't want to leave Jayden either. They could just stay in this house forever. The thought of leaving him was tearing him up inside. There may never be a reunion if things went bad. Before Sean could come up with anything to say, Jayden spoke quietly.

"Promise to come back?"

Sean was shocked at Jayden's sudden acceptance and maturity. Without even thinking, he immediately answered, "I will, man."

"Trust?"

Sean took a breath. He didn't know if he would be able to fulfill a promise like that. He hated lying to Jayden, but he desperately needed him to be okay. "Trust," he breathed out, his body having a visceral response to the statement. "But you have a duty, too, while I'm gone. I need you to help Kim. She's sick and hurt and can't do a lot. She needs you. Can you do that?"

Jayden didn't answer. His arms were wrapped around Sean, hugging him as tightly as he could. The lump in Sean's throat was too much to hold back anymore, and he couldn't hold back the tears. The two sat on the couch holding each other and silently crying for several minutes. Finally, Sean looked down at Jayden's face, wiping the tears dripping down his chin. They didn't say anything. They stared at each other for a moment and nodded before returning to the kitchen. Angela had a look of sympathy when they walked in. Jayden walked to her and gave her a hug too.

"You ready?" Sean asked Angela, wiping away any remaining tears from his face.

She nodded and walked outside. The rain had stopped, but a stormy breeze scattered her hair as she undid her ponytail and re-tied it. Sean gave Jayden one last hug. The lump in his throat returned even larger than before. Turning, Sean joined Angela outside, and they started back toward the car. Jayden ran outside and stopped on the front porch.

"I love you, Sean!" he cried.

"I love you too, bud!" Sean croaked back, sniffing back tears.

"Trust...remember!"

Sean gave him a thumbs up as he walked away, unable to form words. It was silent all the way back to the car. Sean was second guessing his decision to leave. Was he doing the right thing? What if he both failed his mission and left Jayden? Jayden would be without anyone he loved or who loved him. Plus, would Kim even survive? Would Jayden be completely alone? Sean loved Kristen deeply, more than he had ever loved another human in his whole life, but she might not even be alive anymore. He was risking abandoning Jayden, the only other human he truly loved, on a plan he didn't completely have and didn't know would even work.

As soon as Sean sat down in the driver's seat of the car, he broke down again. Angela placed her hand on his shoulder and didn't speak, letting him get this out so he could have a clear head.

When Sean sat upright and took a deep breath, Angela spoke. "I know this is hard. Jayden is safer this way and... we have to do this. Not just for the ones we love, like Jayden, Kristen, and Michael, but for everyone."

He looked at her. The look on her face showed how determined she was to go through with this. He felt a little selfish for even wondering if he should stay. He wasn't the only one struggling. Angela had lost her son, Kristen may still be out there, and essentially all of humanity was trapped.

Damn the cost. This has to end, today.

He nodded and tried to start the car. It turned over a couple times before finally cranking up. "The car's having some trouble, and I don't know how much gas we have. But at least it's not a big city if we break down."

They started the drive into town. Sean wasn't focused on the scenery or even the pleasant temperature outside. His focus had narrowed. It was only on finding and stopping the signal, then getting back to Jayden.

The downtown area of the town looked like a tribute to older days. There was construction on the main buildings to update them, but they seemed to keep their charm. The street was wide and inviting, like it could be on the cover of a magazine. Several cars were still parked in front of the businesses that lined the road.

"What are we looking for?" Angela asked as the car coasted slowly down the street.

"I'm not sure. Hopefully we'll know it when we see it."

He looked up at the sun peeking out behind a storm cloud. Glancing at the car's clock, it was a little after 4 pm. Time didn't seem to matter much anymore, though. There was just daylight and darkness. Days blended together in an amorphous blob.

"Why don't we get out and walk?" Sean suggested. "That way if we need the car, it may at least still have some gas. We're past 'E' as it is."

They pulled over and left the car in front of a building that was for lease. The breeze kept cool air on their backs, but the tension and anxiety overpowered any pleasantries they may have felt from the weather.

Angela stopped when they neared the end of the main strip less than a minute into walking. "Do you feel that?" she asked.

Sean nodded. He had felt it since they got out of the car, and it seemed to be getting stronger. A low vibration that pierced deep into his head. It wasn't intense, but it was constant.

"We have to be getting close," he said, scanning the area around them.

"Which way do you think from here?" she asked, a strange combination of desperation and annoyance in her voice.

"Dunno. What do you think? Maybe keep following the street? I don't see any towers, but there are some taller buildings that way."

Angela continued walking, her steps determined and quick. Sean didn't take her annoyance personally. She was allowed to feel overwhelmed. They really had no idea what they were looking for. He followed close behind almost in a power walk. She suddenly stopped.

"Sean, look!"

He stepped up to her and peered in the direction of her stare. Ahead was a modern set of buildings. They were all two stories tall with large, windowed fronts. The second story of each had windows that looked out to the street. Construction on them must have been completed very recently. A few stray construction dumpsters lingered nearby. Several stickers from the manufacturers still clung to windows that had been installed. There was one that stood out, though. It had no windows they could see and just a single door in the front. The gray, stucco building sat a few feet further back from the road than those on either side of it. Just above the door was a sign with a wireless network symbol and words that read, "Primary Connections Communication Co."

Subtle, aliens. Very subtle.

The biggest detail that caught their interest was the object on top that could barely be seen from the ground. From where Sean stood, he could see just the top of it. It was a microsized version of the Lightning Pillars. Its dark black exterior and obelisk shape was unmistakable.

"That has to be it," Angela whispered, like someone was listening close by. "But why is it so small? The other towers are so large and always in threes."

"I don't know why it's so small, but it has to be powerful. I can feel it vibrating my whole body." A semi parked down the street caught Sean's eye. He wasn't sure, but it looked awfully similar to the one that had passed them while they were broken down on the side of the road. Had it been full of supplies...or people? He didn't care to find out.

"Let's go around back and see if there's another way in," Sean suggested. "I doubt we can just bust through the front door and politely ask them to turn it off."

There were long, skinny alleys between all the new buildings. He couldn't remember ever seeing an alley this narrow. A typical truck would probably scrape the buildings on both sides if it tried to drive down the alleys. Second-story fire escapes on either side cast large shadows on the ground. As they proceeded down one of the alleys, the vibration grew more powerful, reverberating off the walls. It penetrated so deep within Sean that he began to feel sick to his stomach. On the edge of vomiting, he quickened his pace. Emerging onto an odd-looking street gave instant relief.

54

Angela

Angela bent down and touched the street. It was the smoothest material she had ever felt—dark gray and hard like concrete yet almost rubbery. As a quick sprinkle began to hit the street, the droplets absorbed into the material, sucking through it like a sponge leaving the street completely dry. The street stretched left to right behind the buildings, like it was a street the businesses would use for loading or unloading from their back doors. Angela followed the road to the right with her eyes. It led directly past their target, the Primary Connections Communication building.

She and Sean surveyed back and forth as they made their way toward the back of the building. The vibration wasn't as prevalent here at the bottom of the building as it had been in the alley, but the low buzz of its presence could still be felt in her bones. Angela suddenly stepped back and pushed Sean behind the adjacent building.

"Guards," she whispered. The rear of the building had large double doors and a single window on the second story overlooking the entire area. A lone guard stood stationary, almost statue-like. They had found the building, the source of the signal, and now Angela had a plan. "I think we need to get to the roof. That signal has to be coming from that small Lightning Pillar up there. We have to destroy it."

"Yeah," Sean whispered back. "I think I know just how to get up there. Follow me." He turned around and started back from where they came.

Angela followed him, hoping they weren't going back down one of those sickening alleys. When they were well out of sight and earshot of the guard, Sean divulged his own plan.

"The building right next to the hub is really close. If we can get to the top of the building, I think we can lay something across the alley and go from roof to roof." He pointed to the large dumpsters nearby. "There is a lot of scrap wood left over from when they built these buildings. I bet we can find something long and sturdy enough to reach across the alley."

She looked down an alley. It was probably narrow enough for the plan to work. Keeping an eye out for anyone walking around, they inspected the dumpsters. It didn't take long for them to find something long enough to work. Lying next to one of the dumpsters, was a pile of unused wood. In it was a set of two boards that were nailed together to make it several inches thick. Sean said he guessed they were at least twelve inches wide and had probably been nailed together to be used as a strong beam or support. They were wet from the rain but definitely long and stable enough for their plan to work. Sean was able to pick them up by himself, but it was so heavy and awkward that Angela's help made it much easier to carry, even with her one arm.

Angela had no desire to go back down an alley and feel the intense vibration that bounced off the walls. Maybe the back door would work. "Put it down right here, and I'll go check this door." She carefully jogged to the back door of the building that was next to the communication hub. She tried to turn the knob of the metal door. It didn't budge. Giving it a couple more tries and failing, she returned to Sean. "No luck. We're going to have to go back down an alley to get to the front of the building."

Without a word, Sean bent down and started picking up the wood. The determination flared in his eyes even more than she had seen before, and for some reason, it made her sad. She didn't know why the feeling hit her. They were both doing what was necessary to accomplish their mission, but his eyes just seemed somehow troubled and determined at the same time. She didn't want to, nor did she have time to process her sadness. They had a job to do, and it needed done now. She helped with the boards, and they started back down an alley toward the front of the building.

While proceeding down the alley, the sickening vibration was just as bad as before. Pure willpower and a mostly empty stomach were the only things keeping Angela from throwing up. As they came to the edge of the front of the building, Angela poked her head out for a look. The streets were still empty of people and movement. They carried the wood to the front door and looked in through the windows that made up the entire front of the space. Angela could see all the way to the back of the building. The inside wasn't complete. It was mostly a large open room. Beams and insulation were still visible, and a set of metal stairs were installed on the back wall, leading to a second story. Being careful to look around for anyone else, she pulled on the front door. To her surprise, it opened up. "It's open. Let's go," she whispered to Sean.

He nodded and bent down to pick up the boards. Angela held the door open with one foot and tried to pick up the other side of the boards. Sean suddenly dropped his side of the wood, causing it to make a solid *thump* on the ground.

"Get inside!" he said, running to Angela and pushing her through the doorway with him. "Hide!"

She said nothing. Without hesitation, Angela followed him, and they ducked behind a tall pile of drywall stacked on the floor. She felt like Sean was one of the most competent men she'd ever been around, and her trust in him had grown to the point that she didn't second guess his intentions or decisions.

"What is it?" asked Angela after they had been hiding for a minute. She assumed there was somebody they were hiding from but wanted to know what Sean knew.

"There are a lot of people walking up the street. I don't think they saw us." Sean slowly peeked around the side of the pile. "Shit!" he said, ducking back behind it. "They're standing out in front right now."

Angela checked too. There was a man and woman standing just outside the windows, looking toward the street. Just like the guard behind the building, they weren't moving. She racked her brain on what to do. The board was still outside, and now multiple drones were in their way. Being so close to their objective made her feel desperate, almost reckless.

"Do you think we can take them?" Angela asked.

He looked at her as though she was crazy. "No. There were a lot more than just those two walking around out there."

They were both sitting now, attempting to find a solution to the mess they were in. It was hard for Angela to focus. She looked out across the empty room. The back door gave her an idea. If she could create a distraction, far enough away, then Sean could get the board and bring it in.

"Sean!" she whispered, excited about her plan. "The car isn't that far away. If I go out the back door, I can probably get to it. Then I can drive past and distract everyone out there. When they chase after me, you can get the board and bring it inside."

"What about you?" he asked, his voice very concerned that she wouldn't be okay. "What if they catch you?"

"I'm sure I'll be fine. Don't worry. We have to stop this thing! You just get those boards and go shut down the signal." She could tell that he didn't like the idea much, but she needed him to go along with it. Jim's words about motivating Sean to do what he needed once again rang in her head. "We have to finish this, Sean. No matter what. For Jayden, Kristen, Michael, and everyone. You have to see it through."

"Okay, but take this." He tried to give her the phaser from his pocket.

"I don't know how to use that thing. You keep it."

"Well how about this," he said, pulling out the pistol.

"That I can use," she said, taking it. She snuck to the back door, watching the people by the windows the whole time. She turned to Sean one more time, whispering loudly, "No matter what happens, put an end to this, okay? End it!" She didn't wait for him to say anything. She turned and left out the door.

Once outside, she scanned the area as she made her way behind the buildings in the direction they had left the car. It was still sprinkling, but barely. When she thought she was far enough away from the newer buildings, she headed back toward the main street. The vibration from the signal was much less intense at this distance. It was barely a dull buzz in her ears.

Angela got to the corner of a building and looked out. There were ten to fifteen people standing either in the middle of the streets or by buildings. However, none were close to her or the car. Even with drones being much faster than normal humans, if she ran, there was no way anyone could catch her.

Her shoe felt loose, so she bent down and tied it as tight as she could without snapping the almost completely ripped shoestring.

She didn't want another reason to slip on the already wet ground. She held the keys in her hand and took one final breath to build her confidence.

The initial part of the run was great; she never even looked to see if anyone saw her. The last few steps to the car were the problem. Her shoestring that she had just pulled to its limit, gave up the ghost. She stumbled completely out of her shoe and slammed into the side of the car, using her arms to catch her fall. The pain in her wrist shot down her arm. The keys which had been in that hand fell to the damp ground with her. There wasn't enough adrenaline in the world to stop the pain she felt. Sounds of agony emitted from her throat behind closed lips. Picking up the keys and opening the door, she realized her right hand wouldn't move. She fell into the car, clumsily and quickly pulling her legs in. She used her left hand to awkwardly put the keys in the ignition. She glanced up as she did. All the drones from the street were now running in her direction.

"Come on, dammit!" she screamed, finally able to turn the key. The engine didn't initially start up. Panicking, she pumped the gas pedal and tried again. The sound of the engine starting gave her little relief. The car was facing the oncoming drones. The tires squealed as she used her left hand to put it in drive and flip a tight U-turn. She didn't want her followers to give up, but she didn't want them to catch her either. Making sure not to go too fast, she watched in her rear-view mirror as they gained on her. One of them was almost to the car. She pushed the gas down harder and could see her chaser raising his arm, holding one of the infamous weapons. She felt a shockwave of energy strike the car, and the engine completely died. All power was lost. The car slowed significantly. Without power steering, her left arm alone wasn't enough to allow her to avoid a collision. A parked vehicle stopped her abruptly. The airbag didn't deploy, and without a seatbelt, she slammed into the steering wheel.

Her left elbow and forearm slowed her down, but she lost consciousness almost immediately as the side of her head rammed the dashboard just above the radio.

When Angela awoke, she didn't know where she was. She was seated, and her right wrist was in very little pain. She moved it. It had full range of motion and felt just a bit sore. The biggest pain was her splitting headache. The room moved as if she had been spinning around in circles.

"Glad to see you are conscious," said a strange voice from beside her.

She scanned the lowly lit room for who had spoken. The room was open with just the armchair she sat in, a black couch on the opposite wall, and a small wooden end table beside it. A strange, pale-looking man in a dark suit sat on the couch. He was completely devoid of hair, and though she had trouble focusing straight, she swore she could see every vein under his skin.

"Who are you?" she managed to get out. "Where am I?"

"My name is Lugal, and you are at the Primary."

"The what?" she asked, rubbing her eyes and realizing that she wasn't restrained at all. As she pushed her feet into the floor and tried to stand, she registered that she was also wearing shoes. They were new shoes at that. White and black high top Nike's. Not exactly her style, but they fit well. The vertigo overwhelmed her, and she fell back into the chair.

"Please be careful with your body. It has been in quite an accident, and while we have repaired it, you will need to take care as your cells continue to aid in the healing process," Lugal said, standing up. "You are in the Primary. Our headquarters, if you will. I am sure you are befuddled as to why I have brought you here."

Angela didn't speak, so Lugal continued.

"I am what you would call... a hybrid. A melding together of your human DNA with another, more advanced race."

A hybrid? Advanced race? Where—

Angela suddenly realized exactly where she was. She was in the very building she'd been trying to get to for the last few days. She was too out of it to stand and fight, so she needed to stall until she felt better. Her brain still cloudy, she tried to come up with anything to keep him talking. The only thing she could think of was that it was odd that he spoke. Sean had told her that the aliens communicated nonverbally.

"How come you can talk?" Angela asked, stalling for time.

"Ah, human curiosity. Let me explain. The link that allows drones to communicate was manufactured specifically for human genetics. As I only share partial DNA with humans, I do not have that link. I am much like you at the moment in the fact that I, too, need to speak with sound to transmit ideas. My own curiosity in you and your companions is why I had you brought here. I will answer your questions, and you will answer mine. Let me start by stating a fact that I perceive you are unaware of. I have been sent here to help your kind."

55

Sean

Sean peered out of one of the second story windows of the building he was in. He'd seen Angela's wreck as he grabbed the board to pull it inside. He'd had to fight hard not to help her. Her last words to him resounded in his head. "No matter what." He had a duty now that hurt more than anything to do. Before, he felt that even if he got hurt, Angela could make it back to Jayden. Now, he needed to do his best to survive and make it back. The only other hope was that Kim would start to feel better when the signal was destroyed so she could care for Jayden.

I'm sorry, Jayden. I'll do my best to keep that promise. But at least you'll be safer when this is all over. At least you'll have a chance.

He swallowed back another lump forming in his throat, went to the second story emergency exit, and stepped outside to the fire escape. The heavy wood that he would use to cross to the other building was already leaning on the wall and poking just above the roof line. He'd eaten very little food lately, and it had taken him quite a lot of energy to get the board to that point.

Sean glanced across at the target building again. There were no stairs or fire escapes on that building, so he would have to make it to the roof to get across. A metal ladder was mounted on the wall and led up to the roof from the fire escape he stood on. It was no longer sprinkling, but a steady mist soaked everything it touched. He shook out his exhausted arms and body.

"You can do this," he whispered to himself. "You have to."

Sean watched the ground for drones as he climbed the ladder. He was the last hope. No backup was coming, no assistance on his mission. He couldn't afford to be caught now. He reached the roof and stepped up. Leaning over, he gripped the heavy board sticking up and strained to pull it up. Like a weightlifter barely getting the lift, he managed to get it to the roof, his fatigued muscles aching. The powerful vibrations coming from the roof of the communication building sunk in deep as he sat down next to the board.

He went to the edge and looked across at the other roof and all around. No one was on the roof; the obelisk stood alone. Like a special effect in a movie, its vibration made visual waves in the air and mist around it. He couldn't see the front street from where he was, but he could see the back street.

Movement from behind the communication building made him duck down. He crawled to the back of the roof to get a better look. There was a craft parked just outside on the odd-looking road that ran behind the buildings. It was large, ovalish, and long, about the size of two semis with trailers side by side. Those same small, black capsules that Marcus had called vessel pods back when they'd first met, were being taken from the building and loaded onto the craft by people. Sean watched as they finished loading them. A hooded person slowly hobbled out and started to board the craft as well. The person stopped halfway up the ramp and handed something small and black to a man wearing a white t-shirt. It was impossible to tell from this distance, but Sean was fairly sure it was a phaser. The hooded person then turned and went into the craft. It made no noise as it lifted into the air, hovered for a moment, and then slowly flew off to the west.

He was slightly curious as to what could be in those pods, but right now, it didn't matter. He was so close to shutting down the signal. It was literally less than fifty feet from where he stood. Returning to the boards, he checked the alley below for anyone that may see him and started trying to stretch the wood over.

"Whoa," he grunted, pulling it back to him. The boards were too heavy to reach across without them tipping forward and falling off the side of the roof. He just couldn't hold his end enough to get the boards across the distance; his arms were too fatigued, and everything was too wet. Standing the boards up and dropping it over the gap between buildings didn't seem like the answer either. The impact would make a loud noise and definitely alert anyone close by of where he was at.

He stepped back to think, looking around the roof for ideas. There was nothing up here but a bucket of roof sealant and random trash that the construction crew must have left behind. He searched through the wet trash, hoping a rope or chain just happened to be in the pile. If he could find something to hold up the opposite side of the boards, he could push them across without letting them fall. A chunk of wooden 2x4 about the size of a baseball bat sat at the bottom of the trash. It would give him a good weapon to smash into the obelisk once he got onto the building. While he was just about to give up on the idea of a rope, the pink paracord bracelet on his wrist caught his eye.

"Jayden, you life saver," he said out loud. He sat down and started to take apart the piece of jewelry. His fingers were too large to get some of the loops loose, but an old screw from the pile helped him eventually unfasten the cord. He stretched it out over the length of the boards. It didn't lay flat since it had been wound so tight into a bracelet, but just as Jayden had said, it was probably nineteen feet. He carefully tied a solid knot around the far end of the board and made a loop for his wrist at the other end so he could hold onto it without slipping.

It was easy at first. He kept the thin cord taut as he slid the boards closer to the other building. The farther the boards went, the heavier it got. The thin, wet string was much harder to hold on to, and it began to stop circulation in his hand. He slowed his movements and eased it forward. The pain of the string cutting into his wrist was almost unbearable.

"Come on," he grunted through clenched teeth. The boards touched the other side but sat just below the ledge of the roof, pushed against the side wall of the building. He strained to lift it, but the angle he was at made it almost impossible to pull up on the string. Placing one foot against his side of the boards so they didn't slide back to him, he wrapped the rope around his other hand. It immediately began squeezing him to the point he thought it would damage that hand as well. He steadied himself and gave it a hard yank up, pushing the boards with his foot. It moved upward and barely sat on the ledge. He quickly pushed it until it sat equally on his side and the other. After some obscenities, he pulled the rope off his hand and wrist. Deep impressions lined his wrist and hands. He shook and rubbed them to get the blood moving again and make sure he still had full function of all his digits.

Taking a deep breath, he went into go mode. He grabbed the 2x4 and made his first step off the roof and onto the boards. He squatted down and sat on the boards to get better balance. With the 2x4 in one hand and the other on the boards, he scooted across. It flexed as he moved further toward the middle. The combination of the mist and vibration made movement harder. He struggled to stay balanced with each move. Reaching just past the mid-point, he looked down and almost dropped the 2x4. Below him, walking down the alley, was a young man.

Sean froze and watched the man. He was pretty sure that he hadn't been seen but didn't want to chance moving and draw attention. He could pull out the phaser, but even if he got a shot out, the signal was making it hard to focus his eyes on anything. With it being evening and the mist blocking out all shadows, the only way he'd be found is if the man looked up. He passed directly under Sean and kept going. Sean watched him disappear down the alley and around the back of the communication building.

Sean's head was throbbing now, and the cool air made him shiver, though he could also feel himself sweating. He continued slowly and carefully across the boards. The vibration intensified with every inch forward. As he made it to the other side, he placed the 2x4 down and stepped firmly onto the solid ground of the roof.

The vibration felt like it surrounded him now, wrapping him in a stiffening blanket of nausea. He could feel the signal in his feet and see it in the air. It was so pervasive that he struggled to move. Vomit curled up in his throat. He fell to his knees and threw up what little he had in his stomach. Looking up at the evil black contraption, he grabbed the 2x4 and gripped it tight in his hand.

"This ends now," he breathed.

56

Angela

"What do you mean, help our kind? By taking control of humans and forcing them to do whatever you want?" Angela yelled. Her mind was becoming less cloudy, and her vision was slowly returning to normal. "By killing countless people?" She glanced around and noticed two things—a weird machine with tubes hanging down by the armchair, and her gun sitting on the small end table beside the couch Lugal sat on.

"I do not expect you to understand, so please, allow me to explain it to you," Lugal responded calmly. "Your race, humans, are on the cusp of destroying everything on this planet. You wage war upon your own kind, killing for land and power. Pollution on this planet is like nothing we have ever seen before. Your dense populations have added to the problem as well. With the number of humans inhabiting this planet in pockets, disease will continue to increase and become even more deadly. *We* are the cure. We are here to save you from yourselves."

Angela didn't trust anything he was saying, but she pushed for more, trying to distract him long enough to see if she could get to the gun. "So how does you killing so many people and not allowing them to live their lives save us?" she asked, standing and steadying herself.

"We have technologies that you cannot even fathom." He pointed to her wrist that had previously been broken. "Technologies that accelerate the mending of the body. Systems that will help heal this planet and set it back on its path. We have given humans a way to overcome and eradicate every disease. We understood that some human DNA would not bond well with the link we have administered. Their deaths are regrettable and unfortunate. But as our race has learned, we must do what will offer the greatest good in the end. It is all for the continuation of your species and all life on this planet." He paused for a moment and looked deep into Angela's eyes, as if he was searching for something. "Now I will ask a question of you. Based on our information, you have traveled a great distance to come here. What is your motivation for making such a journey? Why did you not just stay where you were?"

The question caught Angela off guard. Why did he care about her motivations? How did the aliens know that they had traveled all the way from Texas to here in Kansas? Did they also know why they had come to that building? Did they know that Sean was trying to get onto the roof and destroy the signal? She wanted that gun even more. She would answer his question to keep him distracted but try not to let him know what they planned to do. "Love...I guess. Love for our families and love for our people." The honest answer surprised her as it left her mouth. She inched closer to him as she spoke. She didn't know why she was being this honest, but it worked on him.

He stared at her with a confused look on his face. "Love? I have studied this... feeling, though I do not completely understand it. It is something I must continue to study within humans when we release them. Why did you come—"

"Release them?" Angela asked, now completely invested in whatever came out of his mouth next.

"Yes, we will release control of all the humans soon. We were unable to persuade humans to change of their own free will, so we only took control to use them to create the technologies that will end all dangerous pollution and war. Once everything is ready, we will allow them to live their lives in peace. I have been chosen to lead you in this time of transition. To instill laws that govern you until you learn to govern yourselves. We are giving you a world of peace and comfort like none of your kind has ever known."

Angela still had her doubts about what he was saying, but looking into his gray eyes, she thought he was telling the truth. But if they were there to help, how could they justify so many people dying? And what about the violence the drones seemed to have toward normal people, or the ships that ruthlessly shot up the shack they'd been in?

"Okay, say I believe you. Couldn't you have met with our governments and persuaded them to do this? There had to be another way. So many people have died." She continued to move in closer, getting the weapon was still her main goal. She dared not glance at it, but kept it within her peripheral vision.

"We have been here for many of your generations and have tried numerous times to persuade your leaders. But we have been met with hostility and aggression. Wars have continued, and the destruction of all the species of this planet moves closer. You are almost at a point of no return. Your governments have shown that power is more important than the lives of its peoples."

No matter the reason, Angela saw it as heartless to knowingly do something that would harm so many. Even if it was for the so-called good of all. That was the whole mindset behind so many wars to begin with. She kept eye contact with him and moved even closer.

"No, if you cared about helping us, you would let everyone go now. I'm sure we could get people to listen."

"I am afraid that you do not comprehend the inevitable outcome if we did not step in. And we are not at a point to let everyone go. To do so now would bring a more swift destruction upon this planet."

Angela's heart sank. "What do you mean by a more swift destruction?" she asked quickly, a knot forming in her throat as a wave of intense anxiety washed over her while thinking of Sean.

"The technology we have used to gain access to your race is extremely complicated. We are still in the stages of constructing the means to break the link permanently. To shut down the link now would spell—"

A man in a white t-shirt burst through the door, made eye contact with Angela, and then turned and looked at Lugal. Lugal's expression was that of utter confusion. He obviously had no idea why this man had come so forcefully into the room. He turned his body completely toward Lugal, raised his arm, and shot him with one of the black weapons.

Though the vertigo was still affecting her, Angela darted to the gun. She aimed it toward the man and squeezed the trigger three times. His body dropped to the ground in the middle of the room. He was dead; dark blood flowed from under his body and soaked his white shirt. She stared at him for a moment, trying to comprehend what had just happened. Her attention was immediately back to Lugal. He was seated on the floor, his back against the front of the couch. She couldn't tell if he was alive, but she saw a ring of red blood staining his white, collared shirt. The large ring was around a small burn hole in his shirt just below his collar bone.

He slowly opened his eyes. The confused look now mixed with a twisted face of pain. Angela couldn't help but have some pity for him. She didn't care if he died, but he was in pain. And now she had to know what would happen if Sean was successful in stopping the signal.

"Stay with me," she said, squatting down in front of him. "I need you to tell me. What will happen if the signal is stopped and the link is broken?"

Lugal squirmed with pain before answering. "Stopping it now would bring much more death. Many humans will not survive the broken link."

"So they'll just die?" she asked frantically.

"Yes, but what is worse is your primitive nuclear power plants. They—" he tried to adjust himself into a better position but couldn't find one. "We have started the process of shutting them down, but it is not complete yet. Without our help, they will melt down and release an amount of radiation upon this world that will end much life."

Dizziness from shock overtook Angela, and she fell back on her butt. Her mind raced. Had Sean made it to the roof? She had to stop him. She started to ask Lugal how to get to the roof, but he was gone. His lifeless body slumped sideways to the floor.

Angela gripped the gun, jumped to her feet, and ran to the door. Ripping it open, she stumbled into a hallway filled with doors. The hallway seemed endless, and her vertigo made it hard to walk straight. She didn't even know what floor she was on, but she had to make it to the roof before Sean could stop the signal.

Sean's body was struggling, but his mind was set. He was going to break this signal and free everyone. With as much willpower as he could muster, he placed his feet underneath himself and pushed himself to stand. Dragging the 2x4 behind, he wrestled with each step toward the small, black obelisk. It was about twice his height and twice his width. His skull felt like it was pulsating in size. For a moment, he thought he faintly heard several gunshots. But with each step, the sound of the machine engulfed him further and further.

Drawing the phaser from his pocket, he readied it and aimed. No shot ever came. It was as though the signal was disrupting the device, rendering it useless. He reached the mini Lightning Pillar. The jet-black surface of the small structure had the same texture as the roadway behind the building. The mist around the object visually vibrated in odd patterns but never touched the surface. Ripples and spirals buzzed through the air. He gripped the 2x4 in both hands. The weight of the board would normally have felt quite light to him, but right now, it felt as though he was trying to lift an anvil. He grunted and strained to get the board to his shoulder. His vision was so blurry now that all he could see was a fuzzy black shape. He let out a loud yell as he swung the first blow to the object. The signal glitched, the ripples in the air slowing then ramping back. He readied the 2x4 and swung again. The vibration seemed to sputter then return to normal, like a lawnmower running over grass that was too high. He prepared for another swing but fell. His body struggled not to shut down.

The muffled sound of a yell behind him made him jerk. There was someone on the roof with him! He didn't turn to see who it was. He wouldn't stop. It was now or never. He stood up and readied himself for another swing.

Angela could feel and see Sean was close to stopping the signal as she burst onto the roof. He stood beside the small obelisk, a club in hand. She yelled at him to stop, but the sound of her voice was drowned out by the vibration of the signal. Her vision blurred from the power it produced. Her dizziness increased. Angela knew she would never make it in time to stop him. The moment she had wished would never come was here. She felt instrumental in motivating Sean to get to this point, but she never dreamed that if he died, it would be by her hand. She lifted her gun with tears in her eyes, pointed it at the outline of Sean, screamed, and squeezed the trigger.

The bullet struck him somewhere in the left hip. He stumbled and fought to regain his footing but didn't go down. Instead, he made a last ditch effort and swung one more time. Angela couldn't even hear her own screams as they left her mouth. The signal grew more intense this time.

For Sean, the power that came from the small Lightning Pillar penetrated so deeply that everything started to go dark; his vision closed in like an old TV turning off. Then it all stopped. There was no more vibration. No more sounds. No more signal. His vision started to return as he forced himself to not pass out. He looked at the obelisk to be sure it had stopped. He had done it! It was finally over.

He collapsed to the ground in pain, unable to hold himself up any longer. Suddenly remembering the intruder on the roof with him, he scanned the area. Angela was kneeling on the ground sobbing.

Thank God! She must have stopped whoever attacked me!

The feeling of comfort was almost immediately crushed by the expression on her face. She didn't appear to be crying out of relief like he initially thought. But why? This was what they wanted.

She must just feel completely overwhelmed that it's finally over. We saved everyone.

"We did it, Angela," he said, trying to stand but stumbling back down. "We shut it do—"

A powerful scream came from inside the building. Like an animal being attacked by a predator, it was the sound of someone in brutal agony. Several more screams came from in front of the building at street level. Angela ran to the edge and looked out. Multiple people were in the fetal position on the asphalt. More gathered around them in efforts to help.

"What's going on?" Sean asked, an unexplainable sense of panic and remorse creeping into his chest.

Angela looked at him with tears soaking her face and spoke, "We've killed us all."

Arub watched as a human man lay convulsing on the ground near the ship. He looked out across the long, black courtyard he now stood in. A man was approaching, his demeanor that of a soldier itching to go to battle. Several gray humanoid creatures followed behind him, marching in unison.

"Lugal was a failure," Arub said in discontent. "The council decided he needed to be removed from his station. They have chosen you, Usha, to take his place. They believe your proposal with this planet will succeed where his failed.

"I will get started right away, my teacher," Usha said with a small bow.

"Do not underestimate the humans, Usha. Their efforts to hinder our progress must be crushed."

Usha nodded and boarded the craft with his company. "I will not mishandle this mission," he said as the door closed.

Arub returned his attention to the human man on the ground. The man looked up at him with terror and pain in his eyes. "Weak," said Arub as he pointed a weapon at the man. "Weak, pathetic creatures."

A suppressed sound resonated across the courtyard. Another life extinguished.

Acknowledgements

Writing a novel can seem like a daunting experience. From a basic idea scribbled in a notebook, to a polished story full of people with real personalities, it has been a fun ride.

The idea started out from a dream (or nightmare) I had in 2019. The dream stuck with me even after I was fully awake. After telling my wife, Heather, the dream, she said, "I think that would make a great book." To which I probably replied something along the lines of, "Yeah it would," though I had no aspirations of making it a reality. But she pushed on with things like, "So when are you going to write that book?" and, "If you don't write it, the idea's just going to go to someone else."

It wasn't until December of 2020 that I began to put "fingers to keyboard" for the novel. With the support of my wife and my three kids, I worked on it here and there. Sometimes an hour a day, sometimes not at all for several weeks. But their support and belief in my ability to generate my ideas into reality kept bringing me back to the computer.

And so I finally finished it, or so I thought. I started back at the beginning and began to edit it, spending days on chapters to get them right. I had my mother, Donnalu Evans (an aspiring author herself) and Heather read them as I finished. My mother enjoyed the book and gave me some insight from another author's perspective. Heather tore my book a new one... in a good way. She became my content editor, helping patch holes that my brain hadn't filled (since the story was already filled in my head).

After patching the holes, I had my teen daughters read the book. They said they couldn't put it down. I don't know if there is a better compliment from two teenage girls. It gave me the confidence boost to push on and start the second book of the series (the premise had come to me when I was just three chapters into this one). My younger son would even peek over my shoulder while I wrote asking me what happened next or what something meant.

Heather then content edited the whole story once again, adding ideas of her own that were beyond good. It is very safe to say that if it hadn't been for the support and insight of my wife and kids, this novel would have never been written. Thank you family for believing in me... and listening to my sometimes ridiculous ideas.

~Bryan Evans

BRYAN EVANS

is the author of *The Cure*, his debut young adult novel. Growing up in Southeast Texas, he's coached martial arts for over 23 years, specializing in character development. When he isn't writing or teaching athletes how to kick someone to the head, he's involved in his favorite pastime: hanging out with his beautiful wife and 3 children.